BEGIN AGAIN

Also by Helly Acton

The Shelf
The Couple

BEGIN AGAIN

A NOVEL

HELLY ACTON

AVON

An Imprint of HarperCollinsPublishers

BEGIN AGAIN. Copyright © 2023 by Helly Acton Ltd. All rights reserved. Printed in the United States of America. No part of this book may be used or reproduced in any manner whatsoever without written permission except in the case of brief quotations embodied in critical articles and reviews. For information, address HarperCollins Publishers, 195 Broadway, New York, NY 10007.

HarperCollins books may be purchased for educational, business, or sales promotional use. For information, please email the Special Markets Department at SPsales@harpercollins.com.

Originally published in the United Kingdom in 2023 by Zaffre.

FIRST U.S. EDITION

Library of Congress Cataloging-in-Publication Data has been applied for.

ISBN 978-0-06-334534-8

23 24 25 26 27 LBC 6 5 4 3 2

For twenty-nine-year-old me, who began again
on January 8, 2013

BEGIN
AGAIN

BEGIN
AGAIN

PART ONE

Frankie FALAFALLS on kebab, MEATS untimely DEATH

One

Had Frankie McKenzie known she was going to die in a puddle of kebab sauce in precisely one hour and thirty-two minutes, she wouldn't have worn her favorite white chiffon top. The pearl bead detailing running along her neckline was far too delicate for such an inelegant death. Nor would she have chosen to spend her last precious moment—and birthday—on a date with a stranger who's taking a painfully long time to pick a wine. Can you die of boredom? At this rate, death by old age seems more likely. Little does Frankie know, it's definitely more likely than the one that's fast approaching.

One hour, thirty-one minutes left to live.

Frankie runs a bloodred fingernail along a crack in the blue mosaic tile on the edge of the table. She almost went for a bold red lip too, but decided the smudge risk was too high, and opted for a nude gloss instead. It feels sticky on her lips as she presses them together, making sure she doesn't catch a

1

curly blond strand and racking her brain about what to say next.

They've been seated uncomfortably close to the pianist, who has a handlebar mustache and a black beret balancing backward on his head. As he warbles a slow rendition of Ed Sheeran's "Perfect," a speck of spit shoots from his shivering lips and splats on the floor somewhere in front of Frankie. The hovering waitress closes her eyes, sucks her pen and sways in time to the music.

Frankie twitches her foot nervously under the table. A sharp pain from a bubbling blister presses on her right Achilles, heel like a red-hot poker and she quietly gasps. Using her other foot, she slides the new pleather boot off and feels a cool wave of relief. These boots have been killing her since 8 a.m.

Every morning without fail, on her way out, Frankie waters the flowerpots she bought for her mansion block when she first moved in and picks up *The Times* for Mr. Graham, the elderly resident at Number 1. Today, it took her twice as long to hobble around the hallway. She was on her way upstairs to change her shoes when Mr. Graham caught her at his door with a long story about a strange dream he'd had and she was already running late for work. She had to grin and bear it.

Much like this date.

Frankie scans the room, seeking a distraction from the pain, and turns her head to the exposed brick wall above their table. A flashing pink neon sign orders her to *Feel The Love*.

It's statements like these that make singles like her feel like stone-cold failures. Frankie does not *feel the love*. She hasn't felt it for years. Feeling the love isn't something you can force. There are 7.8 billion people on this planet, how are you meant to filter through them to find The One Because The One doesn't exist. She's convinced that anyone who claims to have found The One has simply settled for *some*one. Frankie is looking for a plus one. Guaranteed company for the gigs, galleries, park walks and pub lunches. A plus one to share big nights out and lazy days in.

She used to have a plus three, but her friends aren't as reliable as they used to be. They're too busy parenting, buying properties or being loved-up homebodies. They can't be at every party or on a plane to somewhere hot and cheap with Frankie and a few bottles of duty-free. She doesn't resent her friends for making grown-up choices, of course. They're happy and she's happy for them. But when they fell in love—with their babies, their homes and their partner—she fell short of her serial sidekicks.

"Sorry!" Oli says, sucking in air through his dazzling teeth.

"Don't worry, no rush!" Frankie smiles. "I'm just enjoying my front-row seat to Ted Shooran over here."

Oli glances at the pianist, grimaces behind his hand and then grins.

Apart from wasting some of Frankie's precious last minutes to perform a simple task like choosing a wine from a list of just five, there's nothing wrong with Oli Sarpong.

Yet.

But Frankie is only ten minutes into this first date. She has plenty of time to assemble a grazing board of his flaws by the time this actual grazing board between them is down to its last fig. The waitress plonked the charcuterie in front of them the second they sat down, telling them it was on the house with a fleeting smile that vanished the moment she swiveled on her heels. Frankie, forever the cynic, is certain it was sent back by another table. Oli, with his air of sweet innocence, looked chuffed.

"You go first, Frankie," Oli says, catching her glance briefly with kind, pistachio-colored eyes. Frankie's pleasantly surprised he's remembered her name. Her last date called her Abbie for half the night until she plucked up the courage after her third wine to correct him. Despite the correction, he'd continued.

"Pint of the pale ale, please," Frankie says swiftly, looking up at the waitress. She's returned and is tapping her notepad impatiently. Frankie looks back at Oli to see his response.

"Pinot Noir for me, please," Oli says, smiling at the waitress as he hands the wine list back.

Frankie always starts a first date with a pint. She doesn't particularly like it. But ordering a pint is a test. A fast way to figure out if she's on a date with a sexist pig. The tiniest tremor of an eyebrow and it's game over.

But Oli Sarpong didn't flinch.

Nor does Oli flinch after the waitress puts their drinks on the table and Frankie abruptly announces that she's been single for six years, not that he'd asked. She braces herself for the cookie-cutter response: eyes like dinner plates, then a quick glimpse up and down as he hunts for hairy palms, a tail thrashing under her shirt, or a Nickelback neck tattoo.

4

But instead, Oli lifts his glass and loudly proclaims, "Here's to never settling for just anyone!"

Well, that was refreshing.

Frankie suspects that Oli doesn't flinch at much. He's calm. Very calm. Too calm? His sweet innocence could be an act, Frankie thinks, catching a glimpse of silky skin between the buttons of his starched white shirt. Then she wonders if Oli would even flinch if she grabbed the Camembert wheel from the center of the grazing board and crammed the whole thing into her mouth like a piece of wedding cake.

She'd missed lunch today. She does every Thursday. It's deadline day for "To Be Frankie," her horribly "candid" celebrity gossip column at *The Leak*, a tabloid that claims to expose the truth when all they do is twist it.

Today was tricky. Frankie couldn't crack a headline about pop star ANNA, who was being outrageously normal by eating lunch at a London café, which happened to be in her ex's neighborhood. But *ANNA eats a three-bean salad and sips water* wouldn't smash those click targets. So, Frankie opted for, *Caught RED-HANDED! ANNA BEGS for ex's attention in SCARLET nail polish.*

Frankie's been at *The Leak* for thirteen years. Ten years longer than she wanted, but she's nestled in now. Her column is like a big bum dent on a cozy old sofa. Creating a bum dent on a new sofa would take too long, and change isn't her strength. Change takes effort, and Frankie's been scoring an F in that subject for most of her life. So far, it's been a long, safe cruise in the left lane, letting others overtake her. But she's fine with that. Live fast, die young? Not for her. Live slow, die old is her life motto. Little does she know.

One hour, twenty-two minutes left to live.

Frankie sips her pint and nods at something Oli's explaining about his job, or childhood, or day. She isn't really listening. She's too distracted by her hunger pangs and it's not like this date will go anywhere. Frankie will find a way to fuck it up. Driving men away is what she's best at these days.

Frankie stares at the bowl of cashew nuts in front of Oli and reaches across the board.

Oh, for crying out loud.

The tassels on her white sleeve have dipped into the tomato chutney and now she's dragging a trail of red goo across the Camembert. Frankie slowly retracts her arm with a single nut pinched between her fingertips, pops it in her mouth and crunches down.

Bloody hell.

Frankie quietly gags. Who serves pickled garlic at a restaurant called Date Night? Frankie hates this place. She hates its name, its food, its waitress, its try-hard decor and she particularly hates the pianist, whose spine-tingling attempt at the top notes of Dolly Parton's "I Will Always Love You" is now making her hairs stand on end.

Mostly, Frankie hates herself for feeling this way. Why can't she be more positive for once?

Luckily, Oli is too busy examining the surface of his wine to notice her discomfort. He sighs as he concludes his story. A story that will forever remain a mystery to her.

"Reeeally?" Frankie says, hoping her generic answer doesn't reveal that she hasn't been listening for the last few minutes. She's been staring at the couple sitting by the window at the table behind him. Their food is untouched and their faces are two inches apart. Young, glossy, and glowing with infatuation under the fairy lights. Frankie tries to recall the last time her face was two inches away from a man's.

Tom doesn't count.

Frankie met Tom a few days after breaking up with her uni sweetheart, Toby. He's her neighbor and her naughtiest friend, and the proud new owner of a spare key to her small one-bedroom flat. Last Saturday, he snuck in at 8 a.m., and woke her bolt upright by singing "Good Morning!" from *Singing in the Rain* at the top of his voice as he threw her bedroom curtains wide open and tap-danced across the hardwood floor around her bed.

Frankie sighs, as the couple kiss.

"Oh, bloody hell!" Oli blurts out.

Frankie darts her eyes back to see him scrunching up his nose. She quickly grabs a handful of her blond waves and presses them to her mouth. Has she finally succeeded in making him flinch, with a hit of garlic fumes straight to his nostrils? Oli swallows dramatically, picks up the bowl of pickled garlic and sniffs the contents. "Who thought pickled garlic was a good idea for a bar called Date Night? I thought they were cashews!" He laughs, shaking his head.

Frankie allows a smile to creep onto her face. Perhaps this plus one candidate could be a proper contender for once.

"Although, an interesting fact," Oli adds, rotating the bowl to examine it. "Pickled garlic doesn't actually make your breath smell. The acid in the vinegar neutralizes it, and breaks down the cloves so they become odorless water-soluble compounds."

In her mind, Frankie flashes forward forty years. The pair of them are in a sitting room watching *Who Want to Be a Millionaire*, while Oli ponders loudly and at length over how much tea the average Brit consumes in their lifetime. A clock ticks in the background. Frankie screams.

OOLONG time coming? KILLER wife POISONS husband's BREW!

"Oh God, that wasn't interesting at all, was it?" Oli says, sighing, and putting the bowl down and shrugging sweetly. "I'm sorry, it's been a while since I've done this. And by this," he says, waving his hand in the air between them, "I mean having a close conversation with another human being instead of the robots I Zoom with. Chicken would find it fascinating, of course. She finds most things I do fascinating, particularly if they involve food."

Frankie frowns at him and tilts her head.

"My rescue poodle, Chicken," he says, taking his phone from his pocket and showing her the wallpaper. It's a picture of Chicken wearing a pink bow on her fluffy head.

"She's adorable." Frankie smiles, because she guesses it's rude not to say that when someone shows you a picture of their dog or baby. To be fair, Chicken is bloody cute and if Frankie thought she would get a second date, she would insist on Chicken joining them next time.

"Oh, and doesn't she know it!" Oli laughs, putting his phone away in his pocket. "I would've brought her, but I didn't want her to steal the show."

They reach for the olives at the same time, their hands almost colliding. At the last second, Frankie diverts her fingers to the bowl of cornichons, pretending it was her target all along.

Pickles and garlic. If that's not a recipe for a high-five goodbye from afar at the end of a date, what is?

"Do you know what's really weird?" Frankie says, to fill a brief silence that's threatening to turn awkward. "I have a rescue chicken called Poodle."

Oli stops chewing, in shock.

"Not really." Frankie smiles. A nervous rash creeps up her neck and her inner demons loudly demand to know why she's such a dickhead.

Oli bursts out laughing, making Frankie jump in her chair.

"You're hilarious!" Oli exclaims, chuckling into his knuckle.

Frankie can't decide if he's being honest or patronizing.

"I'm really gullible, you could have carried on with that one," he says, sipping his wine.

"But then I would have to go through with it," Frankie responds, tucking her hair behind her ear. "I would have to rescue a chicken and call it Poodle. Then Poodle would need friends, so I'd probably end up with a rabbit called Pig. And then a pig called Horse. I mean, it would snowball, wouldn't it? And I'm not sure my landlord would be comfortable with a petting zoo in his flat."

"Great side hustle, though! Charge a fiver at the door?" Oli

9

says, tapping his finger against his temple, which Frankie notices has a few flecks of gray that give him an air of sophistication. "I know a six-year-old girl who'd be first in line!"

"You have a daughter?" Frankie says, with a high voice and a dropped heart, as she rotates a greasy olive between her thumb and her index finger. It's a habit she's had since she was a child. Alice, her lifelong mate and the love-life meddler who set them up, didn't tell Frankie that Oli had a kid. Frankie doesn't *mind* kids. There's just nothing she can relate to less than being a parent. She doesn't get kids, and they don't get her. The first and last time she babysat Alice's two-year-old daughter, Ellie, was a disaster. Frankie figured a nature documentary would be educational, but now Ellie can't look at a tiger without bursting into tears.

"Oh no, I'm talking about my niece, Remi," Oli responds. "Sorry, that was misleading!"

"You could have pulled a Will and Marcus on me." Frankie smiles.

Oli looks at her, confused.

"*About a Boy*?" Frankie clarifies. Explaining a joke is the worst.

"Ah, yes, great film!" Oli replies.

Rubbish joke when you have to spell it out.

Frankie studies Oli's face as he starts to talk about his niece animatedly.

He is handsome. In a clean, sweet, Reggie Yates way. And healthy too. The whites of his eyes are properly white, unlike Frankie's, which are permanently yellow and bloodshot from sleepless nights staring at social media and reading budget arti- cles about hoarders, hilarious house renovations or D-list child actors who've aged badly, until she falls asleep with her phone on her chest. Oli probably goes to the gym every morning, drinks eight glasses of water a day, has a clean food diet and read—and understand—*The Economist* before switching his light off at a sensible 10 p.m.

Oli Sarpong seems perfectly normal. He works in IT project management, he cooks, and he probably has a regular family. Frankie is none of the above. She's a tabloid journalist, who survives on a diet of beige carbs and white wine. And her fam- ily is . . . quirky. Her mum's catchphrase—"We put the 'fun' in dysfunctional!"—doesn't make it funny, no matter how often she says it.

In the unlikely event that Oli gets the plus-one job, which comes with very few perks, he's going to have to manage some pretty unmanageable team members.

"Another?" Oli says, noticing Frankie's empty glass, lifting his hand up to gesture at the waitress.

"Yeah, great, I'll have . . . I'll just have the house white," Frankie responds.

"I'm going to choose something different," Oli says, picking the menu up.

Nooooo.

Then Oli looks up, does a surprisingly sexy wink, and says, "Just kidding. I think the waitress would stab me in the eye with her pen. And to be honest, I'm enjoying my view!" He smiles.

Frankie smiles, feeling her cheeks burn. She isn't used to a date being this direct. Is this actually going well?

"One house white and one Pinot Noir, please," she says, looking up at the waitress to avoid any lingering eye contact.

"So, Frankie, tell me about your family," Oli says.

Well, it was nice while it lasted.

"OK," Frankie begins, inhaling a mouthful of wine as soon as the waitress deposits it on the table. "My deafeningly loud mother was the lead singer in a failed ska band and now lives in a hippie commune in Goa. My painfully mute father is a retired doctor, and has basically moved onto his carrot allotment in Surrey. His second wife is obsessed with her three Chihuahuas, who she insists on calling my stepsiblings. My thirty-two-year-old brother lives in their garage. He's an artist. His medium is black-and-white photography with red acrylic. And his latest subject is his on-and-off girlfriend, Jade. So, his art looks like the work of an obsessed stalker from an episode of *Midsomer Murders*."

Oli hasn't blinked for thirty seconds.

"Yeah, it's a lot, isn't it?" Frankie laughs and rolls her eyes, dying inside. "We're more like the McKrazies than the McKenzies. We put the "fun" in 'dysfunctional'!"

Oli laughs at this, to her relief.

Thanks, Mum.

"I don't have a tail thrashing under my shirt or anything, promise!" Frankie jokes.

"But you definitely have webbed feet, right?" Oli replies.

Frankie laughs. Admittedly, she's had worse reactions.

"I'm an excellent swimmer," Frankie retorts.

"Well, your family sounds way more interesting than mine," Oli responds. "I don't think my parents have left Southend since getting here from Ghana in the sixties. I think the furthest they've been is Sheppey."

"Ghana? That's interesting," Frankie says genuinely. "Have you been?"

"A couple of times when I was a kid. I'd like to go again, though. Explore my ancestral roots." He smiles. "I'd like to go for my fortieth next year."

"OK, great. I mean, I'll have to check my diary but I'm pretty sure I'm free," Frankie replies, swept up in the moment, wanting to make Oli laugh again.

But he doesn't.

He smiles weakly, and the table goes horribly quiet.

Say something. Anything, quickly.

"It's my birthday," she blurts out to move on.

She really didn't want to tell him this. First, he might think she's desperate for spending her birthday on a date instead of with friends. Second, she dreads the attention.

Oli looks at her in shock.

"Yup. The big three-six!"

"You should have said something earlier!" Oli exclaims.

"Why?" Frankie laughs. "I'm not a birthday person. You know how some people have a birthday month? I have a birthday minute. When I wake up on my birthday, I spend sixty

13

seconds thinking about how little I've done with my life so far. Sixty seconds. Depressing, right?"

"Maybe you're just a speed-thinker." Oli smiles.

"More like an overthinker!" Frankie jokes, wishing she hadn't revealed that about herself.

In just two minutes, Frankie has word vomited all over him about her family, invited herself on holiday with him next year, and confessed she's a complete Debbie Downer who's achieved the bare minimum in life.

"Aren't we all overthinkers?" Oli chuckles. "Come on, a journalist at *The Leak* with her name on a column must have accomplished a lot in her short life!"

"Hmmm," Frankie responds, taking a large sip.

Why stop now?

"Single for six years. Job coasting for ten. All my friends own places, and all I own is a Pinterest board of property porn. I can't afford to buy in the city, but I don't want to live in the suburbs. I can't decide if I want kids or just feel like I *should* want them. I only have three proper friends, whereas every other woman seems to have a 'girl squad' they're constantly hanging out with."

Oh my god STOP.

Frankie ignores her inner voice, reminding her to follow the rule she finds hardest on first dates. Talking about herself positively.

"And recently, I've been seriously considering living in a van because I stumbled across #vanlife on TikTok and figured it's basically the same size as my flat. At least in a van I'd get to enjoy a different view every day. My current view is of the back of a boarded-up Burger King."

"Any good graffiti at least?" Oli asks.

"Oh yes, I'm greeted by a ten-foot-long penis every morning, which is probably worth an absolute fortune," she replies quickly, making him snort.

"You're still talking about graffiti, right?" Oli asks, with one eyebrow raised.

She laughs. Really laughs, which takes her by surprise.

"No, sorry, I thought we'd moved on to my prized dildo collection? I'll show it to you later, if you like?" she replies, and attempts her own sexy wink. But her lashes stick with the clumpy year-old mascara she still uses and now it just looks like she has something in her eye. She shouldn't have continued the joke. She should just stab herself in the tongue with her knife so she can't reveal anything more. This date is spiraling fast. The problem isn't him, it's her. It always is.

Frankie notices Oli shift in his seat, drains her wine and gestures to the waitress.

"Another one?" She tests him.

Frankie knows she's sealed her fate. A few moments ago, she thought this had potential. But good dates don't start with a miserable outburst, followed by a crass joke about massive dildos. There's no point in pretending to be someone she isn't. And there's no point in them pretending this will lead to anything. It's been the same script for years. They'll have a weak cheek kiss goodbye. Frankie will ask which way Oli is going and then rush off in the opposite direction, even if it's the wrong way and she has to walk around the block until she's sure that he's gone. They'll exchange pleasant thank you texts the next day, and then after that—silence.

What Frankie doesn't know is that tonight, the script has been rewritten and the clock is ticking.

One hour and one minute left to live.

Two

Frankie didn't want to go on this date in the first place. Alice had been trying to set them up for months and finally forced her, when she found out Frankie had deleted her dating apps and hadn't been on a date in five months.

She was taking a break after the last one, which ended up with Frankie pretending to be her date's sister, so she could help him get the hot waitress's number.

"Alice, can you honestly see me with a guy who works in IT?" Frankie had responded.

"Stop making feeble excuses. Besides, what's wrong with IT? Justin works in IT!" Alice cried.

"Yeah, I know, the clue was when you said Oli works with Justin. There's nothing wrong with IT, it's just not very me, is it?"

"Frankiekins, you always do this!" Alice cried.

"What?"

"Make excuses so you don't have to put yourself out there. I mean, what are you looking for, someone who has a rival column called 'To Be Frank?'"

Despite the growing distance between them, Frankie and Alice are still close. But with Alice's daily #mumlife posts, Frankie is constantly reminded of their separation. In their twenties, Alice chose the suburbs, marriage and children. Frankie chose the city, single life and men-children.

Frankie eventually agreed with Alice's probably empty promise of a spa weekend together if it went horribly wrong. Besides, if Frankie wasn't out on this date, she'd probably just be at home watching budget true crime documentaries about serial killers, while stalking old friends from school on Instagram. She isn't going to find a plus one that way, is she?

"Are you all right, birthday girl?" Oli asks. "You're frowning . . . quite hard."

He hasn't agreed to another drink, which means it's a no.

"Sorry." She smiles, straightening her eyebrows and sitting up. "I've got this blister and it's killing me. I'm just going to run to the bathroom to try and sort it out. Well . . . limp."

"Of course," he says, staring a little too hard at her.

Frankie limps around the corner toward the bathroom, hoping Oli hasn't noticed she has her jacket and bag. She shoves open the door and slams it shut behind her, throwing her jacket and bag onto the bathroom counter and inspecting the stain on her sleeve. It's ruined, and all for a date with a nice, albeit slightly nerdy guy who's probably wondering what he did in a past life to deserve being here. She shouldn't have

18

ordered that third drink. She only did it to avoid a lull in the conversation.

Frankie looks in the mirror and blows a curl off her forehead with a heavy puff, and spots a delicate piece of graffiti scribbled at the bottom in eyeliner:

I am not what happened to me, I am what I choose to become—Jung

Frankie leans forward and bites down hard on her lip when she feels it start to tremble. When did she become this insecure? She fumbles in her bag for her phone and scrolls to the "Manchester" group on WhatsApp. It's a legacy name from a weekend the friends planned years ago that got canceled because Priya was closing on her flat, Alice's kids were sick again, and Tom decided he couldn't afford it.

Frankie finds it impossible to make choices on her own. It's exhausting weighing up options and predicting outcomes alone. And the way Frankie's life has gone so far, she doesn't trust herself to make the right one.

> **Frankie:** News from the loo. I fucked up with a joke about dildos, a weird wink and now I'm in hiding. Can I leave without saying goodbye, before I humiliate myself further?

Priya starts typing immediately.

> **Priya:** Dildos? LOL. And YEAH.
> It's your birthday, babes. Take charge.
> If you aren't happy, get the hell out of
> there. YOLO.

Of course Priya would say that. Frankie's fellow Leaker is the queen of strong, fast decisions and putting her needs first. A loud and proud single serial dater, Priya believes that her time is a precious commodity and she won't let anyone less than adequate steal it from her. She's worked hard to create her life, and she refuses to feel controlled by guilt or obligation.

> **Tom:** Don't be such a winker!
> Think you owe him a goodbye, at
> least. Get another wine down you.
> It is your birthday, after all. Drink
> more, talk less.

It's a classic response from Tom, whose eye is always on the prize. The prize in most cases being a free drink.

> **Alice:** FRANKIE NO! Quit sabotaging
> yourself and get back out there! You're
> looking for someone to love your
> weirdness. Stop hiding it in the loo!

There she goes again with "sabotage."

Alice is always telling Frankie she's a self-saboteur who goes out of her way to fuck up dates in the first five minutes. Sure, it's true, but it still simmers a low-key rage in Frankie each time she does it.

What frustrates Frankie the most is that Alice has never properly dated anyone. Excluding a couple of stolen Smirnoff Ices behind the cinema with Tyler in Year 12, the first and last date Alice went on was with Justin at uni and they've been together ever since. Alice can't claim to understand what dating is like in your thirties. How can she pass judgment? It would be like Frankie trying to advise her on parenting. Laughable. Alice got lucky. Or did she? Sure, she found her forever person early, but what about all those life experiences she missed out on? She's only ever had sex with one person. She has no dating stories, no exes and their new girlfriends to stalk, no idea what it's like to play chicken with who sends the first text, no experience of the agony of analyzing said message and the torture of crafting a cool girl reply. She found Justin before some of the most formative years of her life began. She never met anyone to show her new bands, exotic places, strange foods. No chances to learn from different adventures. It was just more of the same, year in and year out.

The unspoken truth is that Alice resents Frankie for splitting up with her uni boyfriend. *Her* Justin. Toby. In the past, she's playfully hinted that Frankie spoiled the "awesome foursome" thing they had going on, ruined the rest of their Ibiza trip and made birthday parties incredibly awkward from that day on.

Frankie puts her phone away, her jacket on and slips her bag onto her slumping shoulder. This is exactly why she quit dating five months ago. It's all too stressful. Too superficial. She could choose to sit back down and continue this charade for another thirty minutes, cringing slowly in the wake of her emotional outpour. Or she could reclaim her time, return to the coziness of her sofa and pretend like tonight never happened. Finding a plus one can wait. She should just stick to what she's comfortable with, like stopping at Kebab Palace on the way home. Oli would get over it. He's a catch for someone else. Frankie is doing him a favor by not wasting the rest of his evening. He'll be relieved for dodging the Frankie bullet, she's sure.

She lowers her head as she slinks her way through the maze of couples toward the exit, wincing with each step from the blister, which has reached a spontaneous combustion level of pain. Spotting her waitress lurking at the bar, she hands her a twenty quid note. Frankie might be rude, but she's not tight.

"Can you tell him that I'm sorry, but I'm feeling sick?" Frankie says to the waitress.

The waitress raises her eyebrows judgmentally.

Fair enough, Frankie thinks.

"Look, I know I'm awful, OK?" Frankie sighs. "But believe me, that's why I'm leaving. I'm giving him an hour of his life back. It's the decent thing to do."

*

"Oh, Frankie Pants, you aren't a loser," Tom assures her on the other end of the phone.

"I'm limping down Clapham High Street alone with a sleeve soaked in chutney. On my birthday. If that doesn't scream 'loser,' I'm not sure what does," Frankie moans.

"Why don't you go and stand by a puddle and wait for a passing car to soak you? You know, to really sell this whole sad case story," Tom suggests. "Anyway, why are you limping? Foot in mouth syndrome?"

"More like a blister the size of my fist," Frankie whines.

"Wow, that is big. We don't call you Frankie 'Ham Hands' McKenzie behind your back for nothing."

"Tom!"

"I'm kidding. They're like cute mini pork pies."

"I knew I shouldn't have worn these new boots. I deserve this blister. I shouldn't have ditched him. I'm a bad person."

"The worst. But look, it's done now. You can't go back, so just move on. Treading slowly and carefully," Tom replies. "Or just get a cab like a normal person."

"I can't get a cab, I'm a ten-minute walk from the flat, they'll think I'm taking the piss. Besides, I have a very important stop to make on my way home."

"Kebab Palace?"

"I mean, where else would I be on my birthday at 10 p.m.?" Frankie sighs, stepping over a dropped kebab on the pavement outside the shop and squinting into the bright white lights of the kebab shop. "Do you think I should text him to apologize? Or explain?" she asks.

"What's there to explain? I'm pretty sure he's got the message by now," Tom says.

"I don't know, maybe I could lie and say I was sick in the sink or something. Wouldn't that make him feel better?" Frankie suggests, thinking of Oli sitting alone in the restaurant and feeling a surge of guilt.

"Texting him would just open up a dialogue, which is probably the last thing you want to do."

"Hey, Emir, can I get my usual, please?" Frankie asks the man behind the counter.

"First name terms with the kebab man? Cute! What's *he* doing later?" Tom asks.

"Extra chili sauce, Frankie?" Emir responds, smiling.

"Oooooh, yes, please, Emir, I'd love to wrap my lips around some of your extra-hot meat tonight, wink," Tom groans in Frankie's right ear.

She whips her phone to her face to check it isn't on speaker, before nodding at Emir and whispering to Tom, "What can I say? They're family here. If my last ever meal was a chicken shish from Kebab Palace, I'd die a happy woman."

"OK, now it's official. You are a loser." Tom laughs. "Anyway, I've got to go. Joel's throwing eye daggers at me from across the sofa, with *Vegangsters* on pause."

"Give him a smooch from me," Frankie says.

"No! I'm scared he might bite," Tom whispers. "Are we still on for post-birthday breakfast in bed?"

"Not before seven." Frankie laughs.

"Hugs and kisses, Ham Hands!" Tom sings.

"Pork Pie!" she shouts, but he's gone.

"You want a pork pie?" Emir asks her from across the counter, looking confused.

"No, no, just the kebab," Frankie replies, blushing.

She moves her phone from her ear to the pay machine Emir is holding up, waves it and throws it back in her bag. Her oversized bag is always far too heavy, laden with her laptop, multiple chargers, makeup, three hairbrushes, five notebooks, and two half-empty bottles of week-old peach iced tea.

"'Night, Emir," she says, picking up the warm kebab and holding it to her chest with the love and care she would a newborn baby.

"See you soon, Frankie!" Emir replies, waving a cloth in the air.

She lifts her right heel out of her boot, squashes it down on the pleather and takes a few pain-free steps. Feeling too ravenous to wait, she unravels the kebab wrap as she hobbles toward the door, the smell of onions and coriander making her mouth water. With both hands, she crams the hot bread into her mouth and tears off a large chunk. The kind of bite she'd normally reserve for behind closed doors. But let's face it, who's watching her? She closes her eyes as she savors that first mouthful, stepping out of the door and onto the pavement outside. With the kebab blocking the view of her path, her left foot catches on the step and she stumbles, so hard that her bag slips off her shoulder and lands with a thud at her elbow. Her balance lost, Frankie sways violently as she tries desperately to find her footing, losing her boot in the scramble. Her left heel lands hard on something slimy and her leg skids at speed across the concrete pavement. She tries to scream but inhales a huge chicken chunk into her lungs, before spraying her kebab into the clear night air. The weight of her body and her bag pull her backward, fast, her arms flailing behind her as she tries in vain to recover.

But it's too late.

Frankie stares wide-eyed in horror as her hands let go of the kebab and the contents explode above her. Her head hits the concrete with a thunderous crack, followed by deafening silence.

She rolls her head back up to face the sky and sees Emir towering over her. His bald head is glowing.

"Frankie?" he shouts with a voice so deep and slow that it sounds like he's talking through treacle.

Through the slits of her half-open eyelids, she watches the stars above expand until the entire sky turns a dazzling white.

"Emir?" she whispers.

"Frankie, can you hear me? What day is it?" he shouts.

"It's my birthday."

Three

Frankie snaps her eyes open and gasps into the white space above her, gagging for as much oxygen as her lungs can pack without popping. She drapes her right arm over her eyes, shielding them from the glare.

"Can someone dim the lights, please?" she croaks into the emptiness. When she's met by silence, she removes her arm and lifts herself onto her elbows, squinting into the brilliance and blinking frantically to focus her sight.

"Hello?" she cries, reaching for the back of her head to feel for bumps, blood, bruising or bandages. Nothing. Her entire head is numb. Praise be for hospital-grade painkillers, she thinks, leaning forward and looking around, the vast emptiness giving her sudden vertigo.

"Hello?" Frankie cries out, the panic brewing as she begins to thrash her arms out in front of her to feel something, anything, that her hands can connect with. But her clawing fingers grasp thin air and all she hears is her echoing wail, which reverberates a few times before fading away.

"Emir?" she calls, squinting into the distance. A small black dot has appeared in her view, like a peppercorn in snow. It's getting bigger, and for a second, she's comforted that her vision is returning.

But the dot isn't growing at all. It's Frankie who's flying toward it like a bullet train with broken brakes, tearing toward a tunnel. The speed rush whistles in her ears, silencing her scream as she folds her arms around her face and buries her head into her knees, bracing for impact.

The noise abruptly stops.

There's no crash. No bang. No screeching of metal as it scrapes and twists against rock. All Frankie hears is her own heavy panting, her shoulders trembling and her fists clenched as she lifts her head gingerly to see what's ahead.

The tunnel isn't a tunnel at all. It's a screen. And on it are her parents. A piece of text flashes up briefly.

August 2005

Her parents are sitting on opposite sides of their old floral sofa, looking straight at her.

"Mum? Dad?" Current Frankie whispers.

Neither responds.

"What the fuck are you doing, Jet?" cries a familiar, shrill voice.

Frankie scrambles back and gasps.

It's her.

It's Frankie. She's eighteen years old again on the screen, sitting on the armchair on the other side of their old living room in her gold velour tracksuit, from her J-Lo phase. The same one that's still sitting in bin bags at the back of her cupboard, eighteen years later. Huddled on the floor next to her is her brother, Jet, leaning over a sketching pad with a stick of charcoal in his left hand. He looks fourteen again.

"Language, Frankie," her dad mutters.

"Oh, Eric, let her express herself!" her mum snaps, twirling and pulling at her bright pink hair with her finger—a different ring adorning each one.

Like the Ghost of Christmas Past, Frankie hovers, watching the scene unfold. It's one she's played repeatedly in her head, but it's never been this vivid. This dream is wild.

"What?" Jet replies, without looking up at Screen Frankie. "This is like the biggest thing that's *ever* happened to me. I want to capture the moment," he says, biting his lower lip and curling over his A4 artist's pad. "Smithy thinks I could submit it for my coursework and get some pity points," he murmurs.

"How does Smithy know already?" Frankie's dad says, looking surprised.

"All my mates do," Jet responds, holding up his old Nokia.

"I'm proud of you for sharing your feelings, baby boy," her mum says, blowing him a kiss through her signature scarlet lipstick.

"Why don't we all just pose for one last family photo?" Screen Frankie says, standing up and sitting immediately back down again. At that moment, she felt so unsteady. Were they

29

going to sell the house? Where was she supposed to go during the holidays? She'd been feeling sick with nerves about starting uni the next day, and this didn't help.

"Maybe I'll get it framed and hang it above my new dorm bed," Screen Frankie continues. "Every night, before going to sleep, I can be reminded of the precious moment my parents decided to announce their divorce. On the night before I leave for uni. Such warm memories. Really, a moment to treasure."

"A photo wouldn't capture how we feel," Jet replies nonchalantly, scrubbing at the paper. "Besides, why must we only take photos of happy memories? Real life isn't a bed of roses, Frankie. We need sorrow to help us savor joy. But I guess you wouldn't understand that, because, you know, you're an emotional vacuum."

"Oh, shut up, you pretentious twat," Screen Frankie barks. "Maybe you should spend more time reading the room, instead of the daily quotes section on the Yahoo! homepage and passing them off as your own."

"That's it, let it all out," Jet replies. "The angrier you are, the more interesting my sketch will be."

"Frankie, let Jet process this in his own way," her mum says calmly, taking a sip of green tea from the "Keep Om and Camel On' mug she recently bought, having discovered yoga in the community center down the road.

"Frankie, you're an adult now," her dad adds. "You can handle this. Besides, is it really that much of a surprise? Look at us both. We're like chalk and cheese."

"Like carrots and cava," her mum nods, making her dad chuckle.

Frankie darts her eyes between them. The truth is, she did always wonder what they have in common. Her dad, whose happy place is solitary silence on a deck chair in his vegetable patch, drinking tepid milky tea from an old camping flask. Her mum, whose happy place is on a stage at a sticky speakeasy in Soho.

"We'll always be friends," her mum says. "We just want different things from the one life we have. And now that you're adults, you don't need us to be together as much as you did. We raised you as a team. And now that you're grown-ups, our job as that team is done."

"Jet's only fourteen!"

"But he's very wise for his years," her mum responds.

"Always has been," her dad murmurs in agreement.

"I am." Jet nods sagely.

"I'm just about to start uni, why couldn't you have just waited a little bit before making me feel even more unsettled than I already am? GOD!" Screen Frankie cries.

Frankie winces at her reaction. Should she have been kinder? More understanding? If either of her parents had shown any kind of upset, she might have been. But they seemed frustratingly fine about it. Had their entire relationship been a lie her whole life?

Jet lifts his sketch up to reveal nothing but smudged black squiggles.

"Magnificent, darling! Raw emotion just roaring from the page," Frankie's mum exclaims.

"Yes, interesting, I like all those . . . squiggles," her dad adds.

Screen Frankie grabs Jet's picture, rips it in two and storms out of the sitting room.

Frankie left for uni at six o'clock the next morning. They hugged limply goodbye and she didn't speak to any of them for months. She wasn't angry about the divorce. Upon reflection, it was inevitable. But she was angry about how they'd handled it, expecting her to nod, shrug and carry on playing *Snake* on her phone. Since Frankie could remember, her parents told her she was "old enough" to do things. By six, she was making her own breakfast. By ten, she was doing her own laundry. They drilled independence into her, insisting that the most important life lesson of all was how to cope on your own. But all Frankie craved was their attention and care.

Her trip down that miserable memory lane is interrupted by a rapid movement in front of her and she's back in the room. If this even is a room. On the screen in front of her, the footage slides to the left, and is replaced by another scene she knows well.

August 2008

A familiar trombone melody fills the air. "A Message to You, Rudy," by The Specials. Her mum's favorite. She'd play it at full volume and on repeat on the school run in her battered old pea-green Vauxhall Astra, making Frankie long to be swallowed by a sinkhole.

Frankie sees her twenty-one-year-old self curled up on

the corner of her mum's corduroy sofa at her studio flat in Streatham. She's pulling at the tassels on the pink velvet cushion, her eyes fixed on the ashtray full of suspicious-looking Rizla butts. The wall above her is cluttered with framed gig posters for Ska-let Fever, her mum's ska band.

Her mum enters with a chipped mug of tea and a slice of Mr Kipling Battenberg cake on a paper towel.

"How long are you going for?" Screen Frankie asks, picking at the cake and squishing the marzipan into oblivion between her thumb and her forefinger.

"Oh, my love, I'm not really sure. Anoo said it would take a couple of months to build the commune, but I have my doubts. It's Goa! They take things easy over there. And that's the whole appeal. I'm so tired of the rat race. I'm looking forward to going slow for once."

"Yes, your commute to the corner store for Rizlas and cava must be really stressful," Screen Frankie replies archly, putting the picked-at cake on the coffee table.

"Why must you hurt my feelings, Frankie?" her mum says, with an almost comical look of anguish across her face.

Seeing her mum's injured expression triggers a flash of guilt in Frankie. Now that she's older, wiser and maybe a bit kinder, she wonders if she was too harsh on her at the time.

"Because you've hurt my feelings by telling me you're moving indefinitely to Goa!" Screen Frankie cries.

" 'An eye for an eye will leave the whole world blind,' " her mum responds. "Gandhi."

"Whatever, Mum! I've only just come back from uni and

now you're moving away. Forgive me for having abandonment issues."

"I'm not abandoning you, love," her mum replies. "I'd never abandon you."

"What, like the time you abandoned me at the Pyramid Stage at Glastonbury?" Screen Frankie comments, leaning back.

"I was giving you the freedom to roam, explore, discover things for yourself!"

"You crowd-surfed away from me during "Brown Eyed Girl" and I had to find my own way back to our tent in the pouring rain. I was eight years old, Mum."

"Well, aren't you glad we did you the favor of teaching you how to look after yourself?" her mum says.

"Surprise, surprise, you've missed the point entirely." Screen Frankie rolls her eyes.

"You seem very tense, Frankie. Why don't you come with me? It'll be a tonic for a broken heart."

"My heart isn't broken, Mum. *I* split up with Toby, not the other way around."

"Our hearts are blank canvases when we're born, Frankie. And everyone we meet in life leaves an indelible mark. Toby's made his mark on your heart and now it's time to accept what's happened and move on with the rest of your life."

"I might have initiated the breakup but it doesn't make it any easier." Screen Frankie frowns.

"It'll be easier with a change of scene." Her mum pushes the point. "It would do you some good to get out of the rat race too. You work so hard."

"I've only just got to London! And I'm working part-time in a pub. I haven't even started the rat race. Maybe I'll like it when I do. Beats being a snail in the suburbs."

"I don't think the suburbs would suit you either. You're like me, an explorer."

"I'm not like you, Mum! I just want an ordinary life. I want to have a normal job, meet new people, hang out in clubs, go to parties, and . . . scoff down a kebab while I stagger home. Like everyone else my age. Besides, I can't afford to travel right now. I have student loans, phone bills. I need money."

"OK, darling, whatever makes you happy, I support you and all of your decisions. Always have, always will. You have my full approval."

Frankie watches her screen self, staring at the back of her mum's head as she clears the table. She remembers exactly what she was thinking at that moment. She didn't want her mum's approval. She wanted to feel like her mum cared. She wished her mum would turn around, take her in her arms and tell her she was going to stay. That she'd be here for whenever Frankie needed her. Whenever she messed up at work. Whenever she needed a Sunday-night spag bol. Was she selfish for wishing that?

The footage slides left and Frankie's heart starts thumping.

August 2010

It's Toby. The minute after he asked Frankie to marry him. The same minute Frankie said no.

35

Four

Toby's face is frozen in shock, dramatically framed by the fiery sunset above Torre des Savinar in Ibiza. The sun is sinking, along with their future together. Toby still has the ring poised, an emerald-cut diamond that belonged to his grandmother, Agnes. A woman with an angel face and a demon tongue, who would hiss at Frankie whenever Toby was out of earshot. When Frankie offered to cook the roast potatoes for Toby's twenty-first birthday, Agnes snapped that Toby only liked hers. And from that day onward, Agnes only ever put one roast potato on Frankie's plate at Sunday lunches. Agnes despised Frankie, and the feeling was mutual. Why would Toby use her ring? It was all wrong.

This time, Toby is the one who storms off the screen.

But, ever the nice guy, he didn't leave her behind. He waited quietly in the rental car at the bottom of the hill, and they drove back to the villa in silence.

The footage slides again.

36

August 2012

Alice and a twenty-five-year-old Frankie are at a bar in central London. The pub they would always go to for Friday drinks. Alice arrives at the table, and Frankie pours her a glass of their usual rosé and lifts her glass. Frankie takes a glug, but Alice just plays with her stem.

"Are you feeling sick or something?" Frankie asks.

"Not yet," Alice responds with a shy smile, fumbling in her bag.

Whatever she finds, she slides across the table furtively. Screen Frankie freezes when she sees what's underneath Alice's hand.

"I'm pregnant!" Alice cries.

Frankie studies her face on the screen. She remembers the negative thoughts sprinting through her mind, and not wanting to answer immediately in case one of them accidentally escaped.

Best mate makes FETAL ERROR and DESTROYS FRIENDSHIP!

At three seconds of silence, her time to panic was up.

"What? Wow! Alice! That's . . . huge!" Young Frankie shrieks, jumping out of her chair and rushing around the table to hug her, whooping on the outside and weeping on the inside.

Frankie remembers squeezing Alice hard. Squeezing her goodbye. Squeezing *them* goodbye. Their nights like this goodbye. Their hungover mornings goodbye. Their long post-work debrief calls goodbye. Of course, she couldn't let Alice know this felt like a wrecking-ball-sized blow. She had to push aside her feelings of mourning, loss, rejection and failure to the far side of her brain for now and focus only on her genuine excitement and delight for her best friend. The little person inside Alice was now number one. Alice would no longer be available whenever Frankie needed her. Alice's plus one meant Frankie was now minus one and she never had felt more alone.

"I can't believe I'm going to be an auntie!" Frankie smiles.

"Eek! Me neither!" Alice grins and squeezes her shoulders up around her neck.

"I also can't believe you put this on the table. That's gross."

The footage slides.

August 2017

It's Tom and Joel's nineties-themed wedding. Specifically, their first dance to Savage Garden's "Truly, Madly, Deeply." Old Frankie watches her thirty-year-old self scan the table.

Opposite her are Alice, Justin and their two toddlers, Ellie and Matthew, who are wriggling and wrestling on their laps. They had spent the entire day refusing to stay put at the kids' table, making it impossible for Frankie to have an adult conversation with Alice that lasted more than a minute before being interrupted with a wee, a poo or a scream. On her left is Priya, whose back is turned to Frankie as she drunkenly fondles the beard hair of her man of the month. A fireman she found outside Tooting fire station two weeks ago, who's the size of a house and as talkative as one too. On the right of Frankie is an empty chair, which is now being used as a handbag station. It was meant for Callum, the last official boyfriend she had, but he was called away on a work trip at the last minute. Again.

Young Frankie downs the dregs of her wine and reaches for the bottle in front of her. Of course she was happy for Tom and Joel, they're a perfect match. Joel was the epitome of lovely, and it's not like Tom ditched her the moment they met. The opposite, in fact. They always included her in their plans. While she appreciated it, she couldn't help but feel like a spare wheel. And as they boarded the boat to the next stage of life, Frankie felt left on the dock again.

The footage slides yet again, and Today Frankie starts to wonder how many more reminders of her regrets she'll have to endure in this nightmare.

August 2022

This time, they're on two single chairs in Priya's new two-bed in Bracknell, drinking a bottle of Prosecco Frankie bought to celebrate out of plastic cups. A year ago. Old Frankie watches herself walking around and wondering how Priya managed to save a deposit, when all Frankie seems to have saved at the end of the month is a single-serve tin of tuna and a packet of French onion soup mix. Last month, she gave her cupboard leftovers to the food bank at the end of the road, as she tries to do every month, and was so embarrassed by her offering that she shopped for more en route.

Unlike Frankie, Priya makes sensible choices with money. Adult choices. She budgets carefully. She invests wisely. She always takes a train, never a cab. She makes all her lunches for the week on a Sunday. Frankie spends her salary on lunchtime Pret A Manger feasts, three £4 coffees a day, and a gym membership that she hasn't used in eight months. She once bought some Bitcoin after seeing an article about it on Buzzfeed, then sold it as soon as she saw it dropping. She lost £160 in approximately five seconds and promptly deleted the app from her phone.

Priya has made smart choices and built a safety net. Frankie doesn't have a safety net. All she has is the contents of her flat. If she sold them, they wouldn't even cover her rent.

The footage slides left again.

August 2023

It's the dead of night and Frankie is alone in bed, her face lit up blue by her phone screen as she swipes through pictures of Toby's holiday to Corfu this summer. His wife looks kind. His two kids, adorable. Alice says she's lovely too, which annoys Frankie. Freya is a music teacher at the school where he teaches geography. Freya runs marathons. Freya cooks elaborate layered semi-naked cakes. They got married at twenty-five and had two kids by thirty. Exactly like Alice and Justin. Exactly what Frankie didn't want.

Frankie has to wake up from this night terror. This might be the worst one yet. A movie of the lowest points of her life. If this even is a night terror. Is this a coma? Do comas trigger hallucinations from hell?

Frankie's night terrors started when she turned thirty. She has about one a week, usually on a Friday after a few wines.

She once saw an old woman at the foot of her bed, trying to saw off her toes with a bread knife. She tends to wake up if they're too horrifying, but she can't seem to shake herself out of this one.

The lights suddenly switch on and Frankie finds herself on the floor of a lift with a mirrored back wall. She slowly stands up and staggers toward her reflection. She was half expecting to see evidence of the sacrificial kebab in her hair. A piece of onion or tomato smudged into her temple. But her hair looks perfect. Better than she remembers it ever looking. She slides up the sleeve of her leather jacket and frowns. There's no chutney stain. She leans forward to examine her makeup. Recently, Frankie's been unkind to her reflection, her late nights increasingly evidenced by saggy eye bags, gray cheeks and psoriasis on her hairline. But in this nightmare, Frankie looks like she's had fourteen hours of sleep, five pints of water and an hour in the sun.

Suddenly, the lift pings and Frankie spins around.

"Welcome to The Station, Frankie."

PART TWO

Woman in KILLER boots DERAILS at train station from HELL

Five

Frankie hears the hum of the hellscape before she sees it.

Framed by the open lift doors, a horde of densely packed, panicked commuters rushes across a train station foyer, zigzagging in different directions. They look like sardines desperately trying to escape a net, staring up at the ceiling and walls and bumping into each other as they do.

Frankie, trembling, inches herself away from the chaos until she hits the lift's back wall. An old woman with a wooden walking stick and a floral folded shopping trolley shuffles in front of her view, pauses, and rotates her head toward the lift. Frankie whimpers, her eyes darting around the lift for a door close button. None. The old woman angles herself toward the lift and begins to move inside. Frankie, predicting the walking stick is a machete and the trolley a body bag, squeezes past her and into the mob without making eye contact. She crab-walks for a few steps against the wall outside, her head dashing left

45

and right and her breathing shallow as her chest clamps tight. This is the kind of nightmare that wakes her up sobbing.

The windowless foyer is floor-to-ceiling Carrara marble, just like the kitchen counter in Callum's Mayfair townhouse. It must be a metaphor. Frankie isn't surprised her ex has made a guest appearance tonight—not a day goes by where she doesn't have a fleeting thought about what he's doing or who he's doing. He isn't ghosting her. He's haunting her. She half expects the crowd to part and for Callum to come swaggering toward her with someone new on his arm. Perhaps it'll be someone she knows, like Priya. Frankie wouldn't put it past her own mind to be that cruel to her.

When Frankie spots a group of stationary shell-shocked commuters gawping at the wall to her left, she gains the courage to take a few steps forward and peer back over her shoulder. On the wall is a flashing board. It isn't a list of station departures, it's a list of names. Hundreds of names arranged alphabetically and next to each one is a room number.

"Move, woman!" barks a voice close behind her. She spins around to see a burly middle-aged man in a boiler suit craning his thick neck toward the board. "Find your name, find your room, then step aside! We aren't getting any younger, are we?"

"Or older, apparently," adds a woman with a shock of curly white hair standing next to them, smirking. She's wearing a black Sex Pistols T-shirt, sequined silver skirt and red Doc Martens. She reminds Frankie of her mum.

"Sorry," Frankie whispers, her cheeks ablaze as she steps to one side, colliding seconds later with a person in a ski suit and helmet who bulldozes her out of their way with their skis slung over one shoulder. Why does everyone else seem to know where they're going except her? Maybe it's a metaphor for her life.

"You all right, darlin'?" the woman asks in a soft Essex voice, her eyes fixed on the board. "See here," she says, inching closer and pointing at the board. "You have to search for your name. Then next to your name will be a room number. That's where you have to go."

"Thank you," Frankie replies softly.

"It's a bit of a nightmare at first, I get it." The woman smiles.

"I just want to know when the nightmare will end," Frankie replies, wondering what the time is and how tired she'll be when she wakes up.

It's Friday tomorrow and Frankie can't be late to work again. She's been late every day for the past two weeks, for no reason other than she's in no rush to get to her desk. She feels like a factory worker most days, with her mechanical commute. Watering the flowerpots. Dropping Mr. Graham's paper off. Walking head down to the Tube, grabbing a quick coffee in her KeepCup from the van outside Clapham Common. A robotic wave to Jolly Janine at reception, who never seems to have an off day. A heavy slump onto her desk chair, emails open, scrolling through the latest celebrity sightings sent in from the public. Most of them are dubious. Last week a man claimed he saw Princess Anne knocking back Slippery Nipples at Bonga Bonga in Battersea before joining a conga line. When she asked for photographic proof, he sent her a grainy picture of a woman who was certainly not Princess Anne, unless Princess Anne had aged backward by twenty years, got blond hair extensions and a boob job.

"'Ere, lemme 'elp you. What's your name?" the woman asks, grabbing Frankie's arm.

"Frankie McKenzie," Frankie replies, suspicious about why the curly-haired woman is being so kind. This is a night terror, after all. She'll probably draw a dagger out of her hat before lurching at her jugular. But the woman doesn't. She scans the board calmly, humming chirpily as she does.

"Nice to meet you, Frankie. My name's Winnie. Gotcha!" she exclaims eventually. "You're in Room 2, 171, swee'art. An' it's green!"

"What does green mean?" Frankie asks.

"Green means they're ready for you, love. That way," she says, pointing toward the far left corner of the foyer.

"Thank you," Frankie says, taking a deep breath when she sees the swell behind her.

"Go round the room. It'll take longer, but it's better than battlin' your way through the pack."

Frankie flashes a small but appreciative smile.

"Cheer up, pet!" the woman shouts after her. "It ain't often you get a second chance like this!"

Frankie turns to ask her what she means, but the woman is swallowed by the herd before she can.

Frankie moves slowly around the room, one hesitant step at a time. When the cacophony of shouting becomes more than she can bear, she covers her ears with her hands and speeds up until she's running like the rest of them, her boots clacking against the marble. After what feels like a lifetime, Frankie reaches the corridor on the other side of the room and slows down again. It's lined with frosted-glass doors, the room numbers embossed on a brass plaque outside.

Two-thousand one hundred and sixty-eight, sixty-nine, seventy, seventy. . . . her distressed inner voice reads. She slows down to a walk, catching her breath, and bends over to rest her hands on her knees . . . *one.*

When Frankie stands up straight, she notices a handsome man her age waiting outside the room next door, watching her. His chiseled face is pale and he's rattling his hands in the pockets of his skinny jeans anxiously.

"What the actual fuck, right?" He laughs nervously, shaking his head. American. Texas, Frankie thinks. She's always had a thing for cowboy types, not that she's ever met one in real life. Perhaps this nightmare is about to take a very pleasant fantasy turn with this dreamboat.

Frankie, racking her mind for a response, is interrupted by a Tannoy speaker emitting from the plaque: *Frankie McKenzie. Please enter.*

"I guess we'll soon find out," Frankie says, placing her hand on the cool frosted glass.

*

A tall woman with a blunt black bob and a thick fringe is standing behind a glass desk, clutching a clipboard to her chest.

She's wearing a white suit, oversized red glasses and is tapping a pen gently against her chin with her right hand.

"Hello, Frankie, welcome to The Station. Please, take a seat," she says, using the pen to point to an office chair in front of the desk and lowering herself onto her chair. "I'm Mabel. I'll be your guide here, helping you reach the next stage of your journey."

Frankie remains tight-lipped as she approaches the desk, sits slowly and scours the room, searching for clues on what her imagination will hurl at her next. This nightmare is so vivid, she should remember to write it down when she wakes up. It could be her meal ticket out of *The Leak*. A futuristic horror film about a woman getting lost in a parallel universe. A dystopian romcom where she's trapped in a reality show against her will. Maybe the cowboy next door is the love interest. Frankie's mind wanders momentarily into the story, imagining how it could unfold.

Behind Mabel's chair is a lift. Taking up most of the wall on her right is an enormous screen. And on one side of the desk is a large computer monitor, which is making Mabel's face glow blue. In the reflection of Mabel's glasses, Frankie sees a scrolling list. Frankie leans forward a few inches and squints.

"Confused?" Mabel asks abruptly, making Frankie jump back in her seat. "Understandable. Don't worry, everything will be clearer in a few minutes," Mabel says, clicking her computer mouse a few times. "Busy out there today, huh?" She doesn't wait for Frankie to respond before she continues. "Oh, and before I forget, happy birthday, Frankie." Mabel smiles.

Frankie rolls her eyes.

"Unhappy birthday?" Mabel says, removing her fingers from the mouse and resting her chin on her hands.

"Well, I don't see any cake and balloons, do you?" Frankie says.

"Do you want cake? I can get you cake if you'd like some," Mabel answers. "Carrot's your favorite, right?"

Frankie shakes her head then frowns. "Wait, how did you know—?"

But Mabel interrupts. "You don't do birthdays, do you, Frankie? You'd rather they pass under the radar, isn't that right?" Mabel asks, as she starts scrolling again. "What do you call them again? Birthday minutes. Sixty seconds thinking about what you've done in your—"

Frankie squeezes her eyes tight and lets out an almighty scream, so loud that it scares even her. She has *got* to wake up. After five seconds, she clamps her mouth shut and pops open her eyes.

Mabel's hands are paused over the keyboard, her eyes wide open behind her lenses. "Jeez. Scream louder, why don't you? I don't think that Hell heard you."

"I am in Hell!" Frankie shouts.

"Believe me, you'd know if you were in Hell." Mabel sniggers. "They certainly don't offer cake down there. Or herbal tea. How about a cup of herbal tea? Calm those nerves?"

"I don't need cake, I don't need herbal tea, I need to wake the fuck up," Frankie says, burying her head in her knees.

"Oh, Frankie. You can't wake up when you aren't asleep!" Mabel says.

"But I am asleep."

"Believe me, you're not."

"I am and this is a literal nightmare. I'm a celebrity colum-nist, get me out of here."

"No, Frankie, you're dead."

Six

Frankie's cause of death was a subdural hematoma, which quickly formed from hitting her head hard on the steps of Kebab Palace, Mabel explains matter-of-factly. Her wonky boot slipped on a dropped kebab, she didn't regain her balance, and she fell so heavily and so fast that it took only five minutes.

"It was painless. And you were pronounced dead at the scene by a paramedic called Eric," Mabel concludes. "Eric the paramedic! Sounds like the star of a TV show." She chuckles.

"Oh, SHISH! Woman's a GONER slipping on a DONER," Frankie responds, barely audible, her eyes staring blankly ahead.

"I'm sorry?" Mabel asks.

"That's my death headline," Frankie murmurs.

She's been at *The Leak* for so long that she's started to think in clickbait headlines. She antagonizes her friends by headlining their recent news, no matter how mundane. Last Friday, Tom texted her to tell her he couldn't come over for a drink.

Frankie texted back:

> Woman SPURNED vows DECADE
> of SILENT treatment.

He responded with "THANK GOD" and then a kiss face a few minutes later.

"Well, I'm sure they'll be a little kinder if they report it," Mabel replies.

"Oh, believe me, they won't be kinder," Frankie says, leaning back in her chair and crossing her legs, the white leather squeaking.

Frankie pinches the skin on her left palm for ten seconds until it's too painful to bear. She is not dead. Maybe she's in hospital with some kind of concussion or coma. Maybe she's on some super drug that makes her nightmares extra far-fetched.

She gasps in a deep breath, traps it in her lungs, and then slaps her own cheek, wincing at the sting.

"Ouch! Don't do that!" Mabel says firmly. "I know this is all very hard to take in, but it's not a nightmare. It's not a concussion. It's not a coma. You really are dead. All you're achieving by trying in vain to wake yourself up is delaying the inevitable start of the next stage of your journey. And—" Mabel leans forward to examine Frankie's cheek "—giving yourself a nasty mark."

"Listen, Mabel," Frankie pushes her chair closer to the glass desk and uncrosses her legs, "I know when I'm having a nightmare. I've been having them for years. I've seen sweet old women sawing off my toes in the night. I've been chased down a stairwell by an angry priest with buttons for eyes and pins for teeth. I've been trapped in a lift with an army of tarantulas. I've been in plane crashes, boat sinkings; I've been buried alive and I've been woken up by Boris Johnson bending over at the bottom of my bed in a lacy thong. I've seen it all and more. But congratulations to my brain, because this is its darkest one yet. If I can't wake myself up, I'll just have to wait this one out. It can't last that much longer, that's the only good thing about sleeping so little."

"I know," Mabel says. "And it's not healthy. No wonder you have nightmares. Your mind is far too full of thoughts."

"Have you been watching me or something?" Frankie asks.

"Yes, I have. I've been watching you your whole life," Mabel replies.

"OK, tell me something that no one else knows about me."

"On Monday, you ordered enough Wagamama's for three," Mabel says quickly. "You ate ten pork gyozas, a bowl of popcorn shrimp, a ramen, a katsu curry, teriyaki salmon and rice, and two banoffee puddings. Then, when Tom told you he was coming over, you hid the evidence by wrapping the leftover containers in cling film so it didn't smell and throwing it all in a co-op bag, which you then put in Flat Fourteen's bin. Following that, you sprayed your flat with Febreze and lit a patchouli candle."

"Well, in my defense, I didn't want Tom to know. I didn't want him to worry about me again," Frankie responds.

"There's no shame in being hungry," Mabel comments.

55

"I know." Frankie sighs. "But he'd probably think I'd been drinking alone again or something."

"Had you?"

"Yes," Frankie mutters.

Tom had told her the night before that he was worried about her. That he didn't think that she was happy. That she wasn't keeping in touch with her family as much and that she needed to call her mum more. That she needed to forgive her parents and take a healing trip to Goa. That he worried she was more unhappy in her job than she let on. That she kept crying when she was drunk, instead of laughing until she cried like she used to. That she'd started drinking a bottle of wine alone several nights a week. That she should talk to someone about it, professionally.

He had touched a raw nerve. He was right. She wasn't happy. She had a lot of things weighing her down and the wine seemed to be the only thing that lifted her up, even if it was a temporary fix to forget and feel better. She found it hard to be light-hearted about much at the moment. But she didn't want his pity. There's nothing more offensive than someone feeling sorry for you. Had he been talking to the others about it behind her back? She imagined his conversations with Joel over supper. *"Poor Frankie!"* *"What are we going to do about Frankie?"* *"What will Frankie do with her life?"* Then Joel would mutter some joke about *"Frankie says relax'* and then they'd snigger into their Sunday roast. That's unfair. Frankie knows Tom would never snigger about her. He's a good friend. Her very best one, since Alice's friendship had faded into the suburban shadows. But Frankie's inner demons paint dark false pictures sometimes.

"This is absurd," Frankie responds eventually. "Of course you know everything about me! I created you."

"Um, no, you didn't," Mabel replies. "But you aren't the first person to take a lot of convincing."

"So, if this is all real, which it isn't, but if it is, even though it's not . . ." Frankie pauses, gathering her rambling thoughts. "Where am I? I mean, where's my actual body?"

"St George's, Tooting," Mabel answers.

"Am I alone?" Frankie asks, a lump unexpectedly forming in her throat.

"Your brother and your dad are with you," Mabel says, a softness spreading across her previously hard business face. "Are you sure I can't get you some of that herbal tea?"

"You sound like my mum," Frankie replies. "What next, a gong bath?"

Frankie pictures the phone call, the landline ringing in Dad and Lesley's hall. He'd make a beeline for his carrot patch and she'd make a beef bourguignon, half of which would go to the stepsiblings. Cooking was her auto response to any news, good or bad. Jet would draw a self-portrait using charcoal and tears, or crushed Oreos and jam because he'd recently ventured into the medium of food as a symbol of society's wastefulness, despite Frankie pointing out that he was wasting food by doing that. Her mum would perform some wacky ceremony involving fire, beads and feathers on the beach with a bunch of chanting naked strangers.

"They're devastated, Frankie," Mabel says, as if she's reading her thoughts. "Dad and Jet haven't left your side. Your mum is on the next flight. Your family loves you more than you realize," she adds. "Even if you feel they never cared. They did care, in their own way."

Frankie's lump grows so sharp that it starts to pierce her throat.

"Tell me why you've been so unhappy, Frankie," Mabel says.

Frankie blinks a few times, before resting a wide-eyed gaze on a light reflecting on the glass of Mabel's desk. Has she been *that* unhappy? Admittedly, on most days, she could feel a simmering anxiety in the pit of her stomach, but isn't that just being human? Isn't it normal to overthink things, question your life and compare it to everyone else's?

Her inner monologue had been particularly vocal for the last few years, but it wasn't all bad. Frankie had friends, a job, a roof over her head. Some people have none of those. Some people are struggling to survive, relying on the food banks Frankie donates to. The only visitor Mr. Graham ever has is her. Maybe she's being a spoiled brat to feel so dissatisfied. There are plenty of mornings when she wakes up feeling energized, positive and able to push her anxiety so far down inside her that she can't feel it anymore.

"What's the point? I'm dead, aren't I?" Frankie sniffs.

"What have you got to lose by letting it all out?" Mabel responds.

Frankie takes a deep breath, her lip trembling as she tries to calm down. If she can't shake herself from this nightmare, perhaps she should use this as an opportunity to reflect. A chance to think about what is really going wrong for her. To get to the bottom of these recurring dark dreams. A wake-up call, for when she eventually does wake up.

Seven

Frankie leans back on the chair and lowers her head to inspect her nails. Anything to avoid eye contact. She's never been comfortable in a spotlight, and Mabel's dark-brown eyes are like two blazing torches burning a hole in her forehead.

"I'm just not sure what I actually want from my life," Frankie starts, after a heavy pause. "Recently, I've been finding it hard to decide what I want to do next, so I've been delaying. Scared to commit to any direction. I don't mind being single, but I feel like I *should* mind being single. I feel surrounded by people and messages offering to help me find someone. Friends setting me up, a constant stream of dating app ads on my feeds. But would being in a relationship really make me any happier? Is being single the root cause of this sense of life dissatisfaction? I don't think it is. Or at least, I refuse to think it is. Sure, I can feel a bit lonely at times, especially now my friends have moved on with other people or to other places. Kids, partners, suburbs. Sometimes I think that having someone share my life

60

would make me *un*happier. I'd feel tied down and under sur-
veillance and I'm used to having my bed and my flat to myself.
I've wasted years of my life on shitty dates with shithead men.
Do I want to waste any more? I'd rather find and fixate on a
minor flaw that gives me the excuse I feel I need to be on my
own. Or convince myself that they won't like me, so what's the
point of making any effort? But I'd hate to put my unhappiness
down to being single. It has *got* to be more than that."

"Have you ever thought about taking up the violin?" Mabel
asks.

"What?"

"You know, like a really small one." Mabel smiles and pretends to play a tiny violin.

"Bit harsh," Frankie says.

"I'm sorry, that was mean. I have a tendency to make inap-
propriate jokes."

Frankie can relate.

"Please, carry on," Mabel says.

"My living conditions aren't exactly ideal," Frankie continues. "I rent a small flat that feels like a downgrade from
my university dorm. The heating works only half the time,
and there's a suspicious-looking patch on my bedroom ceiling
which I'm pretty sure is black mold that is slowly killing me
in my sleep. Yet, I don't want to give it up because it's close to
the Tube, in Zone Two, and I'm only ever a few minutes away
from anything I need. And it's where I met Tom. I can't bear
the thought of leaving our memories behind, just for a bit more
space. Plus, it's cheap for where it is. Although, I still have

this gnawing feeling that I'm only one paycheck away from living under a bridge. The stress of it has given me a permanent stomach knot, so I basically always feel nauseous. I could do a Priya and move further out for a bit more floor space and clean walls, but I don't want to. I'd be too far away from the office, miles away from the bars I love and from the shops I can't afford. I just can't imagine living anywhere else. If I moved to the suburbs, I think I'd feel even more isolated. Surrounded by young families I have nothing in common with."

"You wanted to explore the world when you were younger. What changed?" Mabel asks.

Frankie recalls the stash of volunteering leaflets hidden from Toby in her bottom drawer. A few weeks after her uni finals, she'd attended a fair about teaching English as a foreign language abroad. She had suggested it to Toby, given he had his heart set on being a teacher, but he'd dismissed the idea instantly. His Postgraduate Certificate in Education place was already confirmed and he didn't want to delay it any longer. Toby had always been sure of exactly what he wanted to do. He was fast to decide, certain of his decisions and confident of his path. No questioning the direction, no wondering about the sights he'd see if he wandered along a different route.

"Reality hit. The student loans stacked up. At the time I just felt like I couldn't afford to," Frankie says, remembering Toby convincing her of it. "I needed money. I thought I could just delay it for a bit until I was more comfortable, but then the cost of living in London meant I couldn't save, and the dream just . . . fizzled out. When I hit thirty, I thought I was too old to go volunteering with gap-year kids, so I parked it. Permanently."

"The only thing you're too old for," Mabel says, "is taking a joyride in a supermarket trolley."

"What?" Frankie asks, and then remembers a recent night out with Tom that ended up with them playing supermarket sweep at the Tesco Superstore on Cromwell Road. "That was one time! We'd had shots."

Mabel raises her eyebrows. "What about your work?" she asks.

"I'm more passionate about taking my bins out than I am about my job." Frankie sighs. "But I'm too scared to leave it because I've been there too long. I don't want to begin again, at the bottom. So I guess right now I'm comfortably uncomfortable. I've come to accept that I'm never going to achieve anything huge with my life. I used to imagine becoming the next Moira Stuart, but the thought of the pressure made me panic, so I eventually parked that idea too."

"Parked right next to the travel dreams," Mabel comments, twirling a pen around her finger, then using it to push up her glasses. "Ever talk to anyone about it?"

"Like who? And no. What's the point? These are my problems, no one else's. The last thing I would ever want is to be a whining burden. I have to figure it out on my own. My parents taught me that. I made my decisions, it wasn't luck of the draw. Bad losers blame luck. I *choose* to be single. I *choose* to stay in the city. I *choose* to spend, not scrimp. I *choose* to coast at *The Leak*. I don't know if I'd be any happier if I chose differently.

It's not like I sit around pining for marriage, a mortgage, kids or an exciting job. Everyone else seems to be headed there on autopilot, but being on my own in my little flat sounds a lot less tiring. A lot less responsibility. Maybe I just want to stay sixteen or something, I don't know."

Frankie shrugs, then squeezes her thumb and her index finger together until they feel like they're going to burst.

"Was life better for you when you were sixteen?" Mabel asks.

Of course it was. Frankie didn't have to worry about date nights, the black mold on her bedroom ceiling, utility bills, overdrafts and click targets. Best of all there was no social media to serve her a daily reminder of her so-called failure to become a fully-fledged adult.

"Why am I the only one of my friends," Frankie continues, "to think that being an adult is quite shit? It's all work, no play, and bills to pay. Why is everyone in such a rush to get there? Growing up feels like giving up if you ask me. My friend Alice had her first child when she was twenty-five. Overnight she aged ten years. It's like she chose to skip a decade of her life. We could have had a really fun decade too. Why didn't she wait a bit? Did she not like the life we had? Was I not enough for her? And look at Priya. Why would she move to Bracknell, *just* so she could get on the property market? Why is being on the property ladder so important to everyone? Sure, I'd love to have the security of owning a place, but not at any cost. Not if I had to sacrifice my whole lifestyle. Her flat is just . . . it's fucking miles away! Now she has to leave an hour early every time we go out so she can get the last train home. Which means I have to go home early too. It's annoying."

"Don't you like going home?" Mabel asks.

"I didn't mean that. I meant because we have to cut the night short. When I get home I feel like I've been robbed of fun," Frankie replies.

The truth is, recently Frankie hasn't loved going home. Being alone with her spinning thoughts and social media "friends" for company. Most of the time, her mind strays into dangerous territory, where she questions her entire being. Is she one of life's failures? Is she one of life's forgotten? Is her time running out to secure what society says should make her happy: the home, the husband, the kids? Is she one of life's arseholes for the rotten column she writes?

"If it's been your choices that have led you to this life, why not make some different ones?" Mabel asks.

"Because how do I know those choices would be right? How do I know that they wouldn't make life worse? I could choose to be with someone who I end up hating. I could choose to save up for a house, only to find myself alone in the middle of nowhere. Or I could choose to switch jobs only to find myself with a boss who starts every email with "As per my last email . . ." or something equally hateful."

"Let's circle back," Mabel suggests.

"Going forward," Frankie adds.

"Happy Friday!" Mabel continues.

"Happy FriYAY!"

They both grimace.

"So your life is like quicksand?" Mabel gets back to the point.

"How so?"

"You feel stuck, but you're scared that if you move you'll sink deeper."

"Guess so," Frankie agrees. "I've never been good at change."

"Most choices mean change. And it sounds like making choices is your biggest challenge. Maybe the key is not to over-think the consequences. Stop fixating on the outcome. Accept the universal truth that it's pointless trying to plan the future." Mabel shrugs.

"Well, hey—" Frankie shrugs "—on the plus side, I don't have to worry about the future anymore. You know, now that I'm *dead*."

"I'm afraid that's where you're wrong," Mabel says.

"I *knew* I wasn't dead!" Frankie says, sitting up.

"Sorry, that was misleading. You are dead. Well, sort of."

"Gee, that's super helpful, thanks," Frankie replies.

"You're dead, but you're not done. You haven't reached the end of your journey. You're actually at the start. Because, Frankie, you've been given a second chance to begin again."

Eight

Frankie's parents sold the family house six months after they divorced, without giving her any notice. Her dad downsized to a small house around the corner from an allotment. Her mum, who didn't want to be tied down by "the man," meaning the bank, the government, any authority, rented a studio flat in Streatham opposite a bar with a regular open mic night. That stung. How were Frankie and Jet ever supposed to stay with her, somewhere so small? Her parents asked Frankie to choose where she wanted her base to be. She told them she'd find her own base. It felt like they were asking her to choose who she loved more, and she was so bitter at that time, she wasn't sure she loved either of them. It was the first major decision in a long line of ones she refused to make.

Frankie sold the contents of her childhood bedroom on Gumtree. Everything but Potato, her prized kangaroo plushie. That Christmas, she spent the holiday with Toby's family in Godalming. Every evening, they'd curl up in front of the fire at his parents' converted barn with two ancient Yorkies on their laps, Bangers and Mash, while the family took it in turns to make tea every hour. Frankie felt more at home there than anywhere.

Frankie and Toby had only been dating for three months, but their relationship hit fast-forward on the day they first met in the campus laundry. It was a classic meet-cute, a mix-up with the washing where Frankie accidentally added her load to his. The following evening, Toby knocked on her bedroom door to ask if she had any laundry to be done. A few beers, a bowl of Balti mix, and a two-hour debate on the best way to fold shirts later, and Frankie was all in. Frankie used to find Toby's shirt folding cute. The way he slowly smoothed each side, folded in the arms in slow motion, shifted the seams to align perfectly. Four years later, she couldn't bear to watch it.

"What do you mean, to begin again?" Frankie asks Mabel.

"Begin the rest of your life." She smiles.

"So, I am going back!" Frankie exhales in relief.

"To life as you knew it? No," Mabel replies. "Here at The Station, we assess all the people who've died before they were supposed to. Old, young, sick, healthy. People who took a wrong turn, got lost, and died before she was ready for them up *there*." Mabel nods her head toward the ceiling.

"Who's she?" Frankie asks.

"The Big Dog. Not an official name, of course."

"And what's up there?"

"The Final Destination."

"What's the final—" Frankie begins.

"Stop. That's nothing you need to know about now," Mabel says quickly, shutting Frankie up. "It's our job as guides to assess the choices people like you have made. Choices that cut their life short. Then we pop them back into the living world to see if different choices will keep them on the right path. Some cases are simple. Earlier today I assessed a thrill-seeker who ignored the storm signs and filmed himself jumping off a jetty screaming "YOLO, bitches!' "

"You only live once?" Frankie comments. "Little did he know, right?"

"Right." Mabel nods. "He was spun around in the water like a coin in a dryer and then crash, bang, he was spat out into The Station. All I had to do was question why he had a death wish and convince him to be careful with his choices next time."

"I mean, I slipped on a kebab. Why don't you just tell me to watch my step and send me on my way?" Frankie shrugs.

"I could do. But Jetty Jumper was happy with his life choices, apart from that final one. The difference is that you don't seem to be happy with any of your life choices. In fact, you don't seem to be making any life choices at all. And *that*, Frankie, is no kind of life to go back to. That's not really living. A wise woman once said, 'Life isn't about filling time, it's about fulfilling it.' "

Frankie lifts her eyebrows, remembering her last conversation with Toby.

"You've convinced yourself that if you'd chosen differently, you'd be happier."

"Well, maybe I'm right?"

"That's exactly why you're here. To find out."

"Why does it feel like I was wiser back then?" she asks rhetorically.

"You weren't wiser, you just had the courage of youth. The more you live, the more mistakes you make, the more knocks you get on your confidence."

"But doesn't everyone make decisions based on past experiences?"

"But you aren't making *any* decisions. You're too scared to make any choices to change your life for the better, because you're scared of the consequences. You're frittering away your precious time on the *what-ifs,* knowing you're unhappy and doing nothing about it. I can't let you continue like that."

"Lucky me." Frankie scoffs.

"Yes, lucky you! Frankie, you've been given the chance to find out what your life would look like if you'd made different choices. Every one of your *what-ifs* is going to be answered. Would your life be better if you'd done this? Would you be happier if you'd gone there? Etcetera . . ." Mabel pauses and smiles. "Then, you can choose to return to *whichever life you think will make you happiest.*"

Mabel picks up the remote control, points it at the screen on the wall and clicks to reveal a timeline.

"You've had five life crossroads. Turning points where you had to make major life choices."

"Is that what you treated me to on my way here?" Frankie asks.

Mabel looks at her, puzzled.

"The film I saw before I ended up on the lift floor?" Frankie clarifies.

"Ah, no. Those weren't crossroads. Those were just flash-backs of your life's most poignant moments."

"Well, thanks for the warm welcome," Frankie says sarcastically.

"Pleasure," Mabel says.

"So what happens now?" Frankie asks.

"What happens now is that I'm going to send you back to five different lives. Each one will show you how your life would have turned out if you'd made a different decision at these crossroads. You have twenty-four hours to live each life and find out if you'd be happier if you'd made a different choice."

A deafening siren suddenly sounds in the air above them. Frankie shrieks and the enormous screen starts flashing a red message saying "CODE 33."

"Fucking hell," Mabel says, standing up.

"What's happening?" Frankie shouts over the siren, alarmed.

"I'll be back," Mabel says when the siren finally stops. She purses her lips and places the remote gently back on her desk. Then she stands up calmly, excuses herself and dashes out of the office, leaving Frankie alone with her reflection in the lift door.

Nine

Frankie's mind is strolling into the freak-out zone, as is often the case when she finds herself alone and without a phone to distract her.

"This is insane," She sighs, shaking her head.

She stands up and stares at her reflection. "Wake up. Wake up. WAKE UP!" she shouts.

Nothing.

"OK, so maybe I can't wake up because I'm in a coma," she carries on talking to herself, pacing the room. "Maybe this coma is the best thing that's ever happened to me? Maybe I'll be like Reese Witherspoon. I'll haunt Mark Ruffalo and we'll end up together. That would be nice. Or perhaps I'll wake up with a positive new perspective on life. I could wake up and take up cycling, train for the marathon, do volunteer work or quit *The Leak* and go traveling?"

Frankie pictures herself walking along a Mexican beach at sunset. Or she could visit her mum and see what's so great about living in Goa with a bunch of barefoot drifters. Or she could stay put, download a dating app and open her heart up to someone.

If this is a coma, perhaps she'll wake up speaking fluent Italian and be one of the miracle stories she's read about in the tabloids. She'll move to Tuscany and teach English to local kids. They'll call to her from their windows on her morning walk through the piazza. She'll write a column about her life and call it . . . "To Be Frankie Sinatra."

Frankie shakes her head to return to the room. She isn't going to wake up by just walking back and forth and imagining ridiculous worlds. She rushes toward the door, grabs the heavy metal handle. It doesn't move. She's locked in. She pulls, pushes and hammers on the glass with her palm.

"Let me out!" she screams.

When no one responds, she marches over to Mabel's desk, picks up a phone and dials 999.

"This number does not exist. Please try again."

Frankie hangs up and dials Alice's number. She's had the same one since university.

"This number does not exist. Please try again."

"For fuck's sake!" Frankie shouts, dialing zero.

"You've reached The Station. How can I redirect you?" a man replies.

"Hello?" Frankie shouts. "Yes, hi, my name is Frankie McKenzie, I'm in Room 2171. I want to leave, but the door is locked."

There's a pause on the other end of the line.

"One moment, please," the man replies calmly, before Frankie hears the office door clink. "Room 2171 is now open. You're free to go."

"Really?" Frankie replies, surprised by how easy that was.

"Everything's a choice here, Frankie. Can I help you with anything else?" he says.

"No . . . thanks," Frankie says, frowning and placing the phone back.

*

Back in the foyer, Frankie stands to one side of the room searching for the safest route through the throng to the lift she arrived in. If the lift brought her here, perhaps it could take her back. She takes a deep breath, a first step, and immediately comes within an inch of colliding with a woman wearing a lab coat and goggles.

"Sorry!" Frankie cries, stepping forward again, before spotting the back of someone familiar.

Winnie—the wild curly-haired woman from earlier—is standing still in the middle of the crowd, staring straight ahead. When Frankie taps her on the shoulder, she jumps and spins around.

"Sorry, swee'art, I was miles away!" She laughs, then coughs. "Hey! Frankie! What's wrong? Still can't find your room?"

"No, I found my room," Frankie says, "I just . . . I just didn't want to stay there."

Winnie tilts her head and smiles, her eyes creasing. "I know how you feel. Come on, darlin', you look like you could do with a chat. And I could do with a coffee."

"There's coffee here?" Frankie says, stunned.

"Well, they call it coffee. I call it lukewarm sick." Winnie chuckles, coughing again, as she takes Frankie's arm in hers and directs her toward a corridor behind them.

"Actually, I was trying to get back to the lift," Frankie says. "See if I could go home."

"Oh, love," Winnie says, putting her hand on Frankie's arm. "That doesn't work. Believe me I've tried. And I've watched others try too. That lift won't budge."

The coffee shop is bare and empty, in stark contrast to the messy hustle and bustle outside. With cold white plastic chairs and tables, it looks like it belongs in a hospital and doesn't offer Frankie much comfort at all. Frankie stares at the deadpan waiter, also in white, as he puts their two coffees down on the table between them, and wanders silently off like a ghost.

"How long have you been here?" Frankie asks.

"Oh I dunno, time means nothing in The Station," Winnie says, pouring a third packet of brown sugar into her cup. "They don't seem to care how long you're here for. The fact is you can't leave until you've made your choice."

"Is that why you're still here? You can't decide?" Frankie asks.

Winnie takes a sip and grimaces, her brow furrowing. "Exactly. Forward or backward. I can't seem to decide. But I know I can't bear this shit-show much longer, these crowds are startin' to do my 'ead in. And that's from someone who goes to Glastonbury every year!"

"Forward or backward? What do you mean?" Frankie asks.

"Go forward to The Final Destination or backward to life as it was before," Winnie replies. "Isn't that what they offered you?"

"No." Frankie shakes her head. "They offered me a choice of different lives to go back to."

"Whatcha mean?" Winnie says, pushing the coffee away.

"They said I could go back and see what my life would look like if I'd made different decisions along the way. See if I'd be happier."

"That's amazing, swee'art, lucky you!" Winnie cries.

"Am I? I'm still stuck here," Frankie says, glancing out of the window and into the foyer. "In this nightmare."

"Oh, it's no nightmare, darlin'. That's what I thought when I first got here. This is real, as hard as it is to believe."

"Oh yeah?" Frankie says, smiling. "And how do I know you're not part of it? Like . . . an imaginary friend."

Winnie laughs. "True, I can't prove anything, I suppose. Tell you what, even if this is a nightmare, just go along with it. Even if it's all in your 'ead, aren't you just a bit curious? My biggest piece of advice is . . . don't get stuck here for weeks like me. If I had your options, I'd be laughing and dancing all the way down."

"Sometimes it's easier to have fewer options," Frankie replies.

"I'm not so sure about that," Winnie replies. "I'm not racing

76

to go back to my old life. I was forced into retirement from the library job I loved. My brother's in a care home for the terminally ill. And a doctor told me recently that my liver can't take any more booze. I do have my mates though. They'll miss me. But I was tired, Frankie. I've lived a full life. Perhaps it is time to hang up my disco boots and stride into the exciting unknown." She nods upward.

"Do you mind me asking how it happened? How did you . . . get here?" Frankie says cautiously.

"I was hit by the 453 bus on the Old Kent Road. Totally my fault. Poor bus driver will be scarred for life. I was distracted, I had my earphones in and I was searching for my favorite song. Wasn't looking where I was going, stepped onto the road and boom. Still, at least the last thing I heard was Annie Lennox singing 'Sweet Dreams.'"

"I'm so sorry," Frankie says, shifting in her seat. Death isn't a conversation she's used to or comfortable with.

"What for? Not the worst way to go, if you ask me. I could have accidentally pressed 'Sweet Caroline' and that would have been a real shitter!"

Frankie laughs, loosening up a little.

"So, do you know anything about The Final Destination? What's up there?" Frankie asks quietly, leaning forward.

"Haven't a clue!" Winnie shrugs. "That's what makes it so bloody hard to decide. But I've always loved adventure. So I can either choose to go back to what I know, or choose to see what's up there. I don't want to stay here forever, that's for sure. And neither should you. Don't waste your time trying to decide, weighing up the pros and cons. Be brave. Dive in headfirst and deal with the consequences later. Standing still . . . well, it gets you nowhere, doesn't it?"

Frankie turns her head toward the foyer. Winnie is right. Even if The Station isn't real, she has nothing to lose by playing the game. If she succeeds in waking herself up now, she's in exactly the same position as she was before, questioning everything she's ever done. She might as well go along for the ride to see if she can stumble on some answers.

"Thank you," Frankie says, pushing her cup to one side.

"What for, love?" Winnie replies.

"For helping me make my first decision," Frankie replies.

"Well, good luck, swee'art. Here's hoping we don't bump into each other again." She smiles.

*

Frankie knocks on the glass door of Room 2,171. The buzzer sounds and the Enter light turns green. Breathing in, Frankie pushes the door forward.

"Fancy seeing you here," Mabel says, staring at the screen.

"I suppose you knew I'd come back, didn't you?" Frankie asks.

"How many times do I have to tell you, I know everything!" Mabel smiles.

"OK, so what am I thinking right now?" Frankie says, taking a seat.

"You're ready to visit your crossroads?"

78

"Are you going to tell me what they are?" Frankie asks, shifting.

"You haven't guessed them already?" Mabel turns to her.

Frankie racks her brain trying to imagine what they could be. Doesn't she face a million crossroads every day? When she's having a tough time at work, she imagines missing her Tube stop intentionally and heading straight to the airport to catch a spontaneous flight somewhere. Anywhere. But she'd never really have the guts to do it. When she was online dating, her auto response was to click "no." Were those rejects all crossroads? Would her life really be different—better—if she'd clicked yes on a date with Barnaby, forty-three, from Clapton-on-Sea?

"Let me help you," Mabel says, clicking her mouse to reveal a numbered list on the screen above. Frankie squints her eyes.

1. The One-Way Flight
2. The Marriage Proposal
3. The Fortune
4. The Fame
5. The *What-If*

"Mean much to you?" Mabel asks, raising one eyebrow.

"Nothing," Frankie replies.

"Well, I won't give too much away. Don't want you to *do a Frankie* before you even get there," Mabel responds.

"What's that supposed to mean?"

"Overthink it." Mabel turns to her.

"As long as I don't end up in prison," Frankie responds.

Mabel stares at her as she sucks air through her teeth.

"Oh my god, do I end up in prison?" Frankie shrieks.

"Just kidding," Mabel says, breaking into a smile. "Although I suppose I can't control what you do when you're down there."

"Maybe I'll rob a bank," Frankie muses.

"Sounds like a sensible use of the twenty-four hours you have in each life," Mabel replies, as she stands up and gestures at Frankie to join her at the lift.

Frankie doesn't take her eyes off the screen as she slowly approaches, wondering where The One-Way Flight will take her.

"*Adios!*" Mabel shouts as she gently shoves Frankie into the lift and waves enthusiastically through the closing doors.

In the darkness, Frankie feels the lift start to lower, slowly at first, but speeding up until the whoosh of the fall roars in her ears.

PART THREE

Woman takes JUAN WAY FLIGHT, lives her BEST BIKINI life

Ten

After free-falling for a few minutes, the lift gradually slows to a gentle stop. The whoosh in her ears comes and goes in steady, rhythmic waves and Frankie feels her body swaying from side to side. On each sway to the right, the darkness alights with an orange orb, which glows behind her eyelids and warms her cheeks. Frankie opens her eyes and is quickly stunned by a fiercely hot sun, peering out from behind the fronds of a giant palm tree towering over her and the hammock she's sleeping on.

She quickly lifts her head and looks around, instantly losing her balance. The hammock swings uncontrollably until it tosses Frankie out onto her towel below. She scrambles up to a standing position and dusts herself off, spotting two towels next to her feet. She twists her head to read "I HEART MEXICO" on both, before scraping salty hair away from her eyes and noticing absentmindedly how much longer it is. She lifts her gaze and gasps with delight at the view. Frankie curls her toes into the silky hot sand beneath them and stares out toward the dazzling turquoise sea. She's landed in paradise.

"Decision made, Mabel!" she whispers excitedly, lifting her hand to her forehead to shade her eyes from the glare, and staring down the length of the pristine tropical beach. A few bathers are scattered in the shallows, but otherwise she's alone. Isn't she? Something lightweight falls at her feet. She glances down to see a lanyard with a plastic card attached, and picks it up for a closer look.

Frankie McKenzie, TEFL, San Miguel School of International Studies

She's in San Miguel, Mexico.

She's an English teacher.

She took the one-way flight she chose to miss all those years ago.

Frankie drops the card, turns toward the sea and sprints across the sand, running into the waves and plunging into the water. When she comes up for air, she screams with joy at the top of her lungs, diving under the surface and rising again to savor the feeling of the cool water running over her hot skin, to taste the freedom of that salty water on her grinning lips. Giggling at her outburst, she waves across the water at an older bather nearby who's laughing with her. The stranger ties his white hair in a short ponytail at the nape of his neck before brushing the water across his tanned leathery arms. He looks like he's spent a long time here.

"I'm sorry!" she shouts. "I'm just so happy I'm here!"

"Si, señora!" The old man smiles, as he gives her a thumbs-up.

Frankie laughs, lifting her face toward the sun and closing her eyes while she makes a mental note to treasure this perfect moment of pure joy. Winnie was right about being lucky. She opens her eyes, lowers herself into the water and raises her legs up in front of her, allowing the soft waves to bob her along as she studies the line of palm trees across the beach. On the right of them is a rustic café with plastic tables placed unevenly across the sand and a drum barrel bellowing out barbecue smoke. A sign for pineapple margaritas and spicy fish tacos makes Frankie's mouth instantly water. She leans forward and starts swimming toward the shoreline, hoping the straw bag she spies lying under her hammock has some cash—and some answers to the questions that are starting to pop up in her head.

Like where the hell does she live?

Frankie feels breathless as she turns the bag upside down, emptying the entire contents onto the towels. A car key, two phones, two wallets and a set of house keys with no address. She picks up her ancient pink faux leather wallet, with its familiar frayed edges. It was a gift from her mum for her eighteenth birthday, and despite the wear, Frankie's never wanted another. Seeing it still here with her in this life, she feels comforted by its familiarity.

She picks up the car key and sighs. What's she meant to do, try the key in every car along the beach? Maybe the car's GPS will show her the last place she visited, and she feels momentarily pleased with herself for her Poirot moment. Frankie slowly picks up the second wallet and looks around. She must be here with someone, she thinks, as she opens it slowly and carefully, her brow creasing further with each card she slides out from the fabric slots. Finally, she finds a Mexican driving license, belonging to a "Raphael Romero."

Frankie throws the keys and wallets back in the straw bag and picks up the towel to dry herself off, the sand scratching her sun-kissed skin. As she shakes herself forcefully with the towel, she notices a man rising up from the sea in a pair of white Speedos. The man pauses on the sand to wring out his shiny black hair, waving his head from side to side and spraying water all around him. Frankie hides a smile as she watches him, glancing around to see if she can see any cameras. Surely this is a shampoo commercial. His golden-tanned physique is comically muscular, his jawline could slice through a steak and his eyes are so sultry as he stares . . . hold on. He's staring directly at her. Frankie looks behind her, then from left to right. He grins as he walks across the sand toward her, revealing a set of brilliant white teeth behind deep dimples.

Frankie wraps the towel quickly around her, and throws her hair to one side, smiling shyly at him as he closes in on her, then yelping as he silently wraps his strong arms around her waist and lifts her in the air. Her towel drops onto the sand at their feet, as he leans his neck to one side and kisses her passionately on the lips, his eyes shut tightly. Unlike Frankie's eyes, which are wide open in shock.

"Merry birthday, *mi amor*," he whispers in a heavenly Spanish accent, pulling back.

He plops her down onto the sand and reaches into the bag.

"OK," Frankie whispers, staring at this perfect specimen in front of her, finding it hard to believe he is with her and wondering how long he has been.

"We should go," he says, putting the phone back in the bag. "It's quarter past four."

Twenty-three hours, forty-five minutes left to live.

Raphael walks across to the hammock, where he picks up a set of clothes. He hands her a beach dress, and stretches his big arms up into the air. The smooth skin on his chest glows brown in the sun, the muscles underneath flexing as he does.

"OK," Frankie repeats, throwing the dress on and picking up the bag and towels, wondering where they're going and why the time is so relevant.

"I'll bring the motorbike closer," he says.

"OK." Frankie smiles.

And he has a motorbike too.

"OK, OK, OK." Raphael chuckles. "You're my English teacher, Ms McKenzie, you need to teach me more words than . . . *OK*!"

"O—sorry. Yep. Absolutely," she replies, flinching at "Ms. McKenzie."

"I think we're probably at a stage where you can call me Frankie," she replies.

Raphael reaches into his shorts pocket and pulls out a pair of thick-framed glasses.

"Ahhbsohlootly." He mimics her English accent, chuckling, as he slides them up his nose.

In that second, it takes all her willpower not to lunge at him and kiss him all over his face, he's so bloody hot.

As she watches him walk away, his calf muscles clenching with each stride in the sand, she hears a phone ping. She reaches into the bag, pulls out what she presumes is her phone and stares at the message, confused. A message from her mum is rare.

> **Mum:** I'm worried about you darling
> Are you all right?
> xxx

Am I all right? Frankie thinks. *I'm more than all right. I'm bloody brilliant.* As she types a message back to that effect, she pauses to wonder at the meaning of her mum's text. Her mum hardly ever texts her. And why is her mum worried? Has something happened here?

A revving engine breaks her concentration. When she looks up, Raphael is waving at her from a motorbike. Frankie smiles, as she walks across the sand to her knight on shining leather. She hesitates briefly before getting on. She's never been on a motorbike before. What's she meant to do? She lifts her legs and shuffles herself onto the back. First, she puts her arms by her sides. Then around his back.

"Are you going to hold on?" he shouts.

"Yes, sorry!" she says, wrapping her arms quickly around his rock-solid waist and hugging him tightly as they speed down the length of the beach. She closes her eyes. Out of fear, at first. Then keeps them closed out of pure pleasure, feeling the fading sun beating down on her bronzed arms and lapping up the warm air that's rushing through her hair. This sure as hell beats the sticky air from a Northern Line window in a heat wave.

Frankie McKenzie can't remember the last time she felt joy like this.

Eleven

The dusty streets of San Miguel are framed by a rainbow of colonial buildings. Their lime, yellow, magenta and sky-blue facades have been faded by the sun and sandpapered by the wind, but they still look full of life. The smell of sticky, sizzling barbecue and chili makes Frankie feel even hotter, and around every corner a radio blasts dance music. The white pavements are chalky with unruly grass reaching through the cracks and underneath the well-worn wheels of vintage cars haphazardly parked wherever they can fit. Frankie feels like she's entered a time machine, and in a way she has. It's exactly how she dreamed it would be when she applied for a teaching placement here in her early-twenties.

Frankie didn't tell her friends or family that she was planning to go. She wanted to see if she got the job first before making any major life decisions. She was just a few weeks into her role at *The Leak*, and had even thrown a party to celebrate. How could she tell everyone that she'd decided to pack it in and go traveling? Her mum would say *I told you so!* because she'd been trying to convince Frankie that she needed time out of London. Her friends would think she was having a breakdown. Alice would think she was running away from the breakup with Toby. In a truth she could never admit, she was probably running away from Alice's new grown-up life. A life where Frankie would gradually mean less.

The reason she applied in the first place was because she'd had another tough day at work, followed by a rough commute home to Clapham. Drenched from a downpour, stuck in a tunnel on a delayed Northern Line and with her nose under the breath of a boozed-up banker type, her eyes landed on a Tube advert for teaching in Mexico. The beach on the ad looked like heaven. She etched the web address into her memory and applied as soon as she got home.

Frankie received the acceptance letter in April. On the same day, she booked her flight for that July. It was the most spontaneous thing she'd ever done. The flight was only three months away. She'd need to give two months' notice at the flat, a month's notice at *The Leak* and she'd need to tell her friends soon. Tom had been talking about a trip to Berlin in October, and had been pressing Frankie for confirmation.

A few weeks after she booked her flight, the mood in London changed. The summer arrived, and Frankie had a few article wins at work which led to talk of her having her own column and a pay rise. It was a huge opportunity, and she'd be crazy to turn it down, especially with her lingering student debt.

When the Mexican school sent her a reminder letter to confirm, she was having breakfast with Tom.

"What's happened, what's wrong?" he said, seeing the confusion spreading across her face.

Frankie looked up from the letter and spluttered, "No, nothing. My credit card bill, eek!"

"Ugh, nightmare, babes," he replied, sliding some bacon onto her plate from the frying pan. "You OK to cover it? I mean, I'm hardly rolling in it, but I have a little extra this month. I can help out with the trip too?"

Frankie looked up at him and smiled softly, feeling a surge of affection. Who would be her Tom in San Miguel? Why was she even doing this? What was she running away from? She downed her Bloody Mary and ripped up the letter into tiny pieces before marching over to the kitchen and pouring it into the bin like confetti. The first thing she did at home was cancel her flight.

Frankie and Raphael pull up outside a shabby chic café called Hora de los Huevos, nestled underneath a small block of apartments. A group of young people sit barefoot, relaxed and laughing along a bench out front.

"*Hola*, Frankie!" one cries out. Frankie waves back, as she climbs off the back of Raphael's motorbike.

"Home, sweet home," Raphael comments, switching the engine off.

"Will you come up for a sec?" Frankie asks Raphael, aware that she has no idea what apartment she lives in.

"*Sí*," Raphael replies, taking her bags and nodding at the group at the café.

Frankie follows him up the white staircase, spotting a few geckos scuttling into wall cracks. They pass through an open metal door gate and Raphael stops at the first door on the left. Frankie takes the keys, glances at the lock and makes her best guess as to which one works. As she rattles the keys around, the door springs open and Frankie's greeted by a large sitting room bathed in light from the balcony window. She drops her bags and turns to Raphael, who's leaning against the doorframe and playing with his keys in one hand.

"I see you later, *mi amor*," he says, leaning down to kiss her gently on the cheek.

As he walks away, she calls out after him. "What time?"

He turns, smiles and shrugs. "Ten, eleven, perhaps?"

She nods.

A booty call. Typical.

"Ask Sophie, she's the one who made the booking." He smiles, taps the doorframe and gives her a wave as he disappears around the corner.

"I would if I knew who the fuck she is," Frankie mutters, looking around the apartment.

"What?" he says, suddenly reappearing.

"I will!" She plasters on a smile and waves goodbye.

"Bye, bye!" he shouts.

Frankie slides open the balcony door, slips off her flip-flops and slowly walks across the cool tiles. She rests her elbows on the low wall and takes in another deep breath of the intoxicating hot air you only get on holiday, listening to the sound of Spanish chatter and clucking chickens underneath her. They're silenced by Raphael's motorbike, which roars into life. Frankie leans over to watch him weave his way down the road and around the street corner, quickly swerving to miss a miniature goat jumping up and down on the curb.

Inside, Frankie explores her new home. Compared to Clapham, it's a castle. The ceilings of the apartment are high and airy, the tiles are terra-cotta and cool. Flowerpots line the balcony, which reminds her of the foyer and Mr. Graham back home. She picks up a watering can that's sitting on the balcony table and tips it across them.

That Frankie loves taking care of flowers has always surprised her. She could barely muster the effort to feed and water herself properly, as evidenced by the contents in her kitchen cupboard.

The old wooden cabinets creak when Frankie opens them, and show dismal offerings. A box of something that resembles sugary kids' cereal, a packet of rice and a dusty can of butter beans. Frankie wouldn't be surprised if the café downstairs caters for her every meal.

On the fridge door, there is a collection of magnets from different places in Mexico she must have visited. A Mayan ruin in Tulum, El Castillo pyramid in Chichén Itzá, the Copper Canyon railway. Frankie sighs as she strokes them, disappointed that the memory of these visits is lost on her. If she chooses this life, she'll just have to explore again to see them all for the first time in her mind. At the bottom of the fridge is a photo. She grins when she sees it. It's a photo of her and Tom, next to scuba-diving gear. Frankie takes off the magnet and turns the photo over: "Scuba in Cabo Pulmo, November 2012."

She's glad to see her old habit of photo labeling hasn't died. She got it from her dad. His favorite toy was a label-maker from the early nineties, which he still uses today. The first thing he labeled was the maker itself.

Tom must have visited her just months after she arrived.

Flapping the photo in her hand, keeping it close to her, she wanders back into the sitting room and over to a desk in the corner. She eyes the wooden ceiling fan above, which looks like it could fall and decapitate her if she dares to turn it on. Taking a rickety seat, she puts the photo beside her and opens a laptop that looks so old, she'd be surprised if it switches on. But, amazingly, it does switch on, and when Frankie enters the same password she's had since she was sixteen . . . it works. She leans back on the chair and waits, as the egg timer on the screen flips up and down. In her pocket, her phone pings.

> **Mum:** Free for a chat?

Just as Frankie hits reply, the laptop lights up and her inbox appears on-screen. She places her phone on the desk, and scrolls through the messages. Two stand out.

From: Alice Woods
To: Frankie McKenzie
Subject: Happy birthday for tomorrow!
What are you going to be doing? Having margaritas

poured for you by a naked Raph before a skinny dip in the
sea? God, I'm jealous. The only thing pouring here is the rain
and the tears. Matt has decided he hates wearing pants and
has thrown every pair he has into the loo. CAN WE PLEASE
SWAP LIVES?

Frankie smiles. She's spent so long hungering for the security of Alice's life that it feels wickedly good to wear the envi-
able-life shoes for once.

From: Tom Curry
To: Frankie McKenzie
Subject: CALL ME
FRANKIEPOOS! How's everything going? Hope you've
managed to sort the bank stuff out? Call me tomorrow for
your annual birthday sing-song x

Bank stuff? What does that mean? And how's she supposed
to find out?
"Mabel?" Frankie calls out. "Any chance of a clue down
here?"
Frankie looks around the desk and attempts to pull out the
drawer. It sticks. She yanks it hard and the entire drawer flies
open and out, crashing onto the floor. From out of the top, some
letters spill onto the tiles. They look official. And ominous. Red
stamps all over the envelopes. Overdue phone bills. Overdue
credit card payments. Worst of all, a final warning from the
apartment landlord to pay her rent.

Frankie's heart starts to pound in her chest.

What TEQUILED her? BROKE blond found DEAD in MEXICO. MALNUTRITION suspected.

She might be a bit skint back home, but she's never been this irresponsible with money. Like her dad always taught her, she checks her bank balance every morning, pays her bills the very same day, and she's never once been late with her rent, even if it meant surviving on ramen for a couple of days. She's got to log in to her bank account to see what's going on. She's had the same bank and PIN for years, so it shouldn't be hard.

Just as she clicks *log in,* there's a loud bang on the door. Frankie closes her laptop, stuffs the letters into the drawer and shoves it under her desk with her foot. She doesn't want anyone to see her living like this, it's humiliating. Maybe that's why her mum is so desperate to get hold of her. She knows about the debts.

Frankie opens the door and jumps back when she's greeted by a giant bouquet of silver helium balloons in her face.

"FOO FOO!" a voice shrieks from behind.

Like a cat sticking its head through a cat flap, a sunny face with big brown eyes greets her with a huge grin under hot-pink lips.

"Special delivery for the birthday girl!" the stranger sings in an Irish accent, before barging through the door, releasing the balloons to the ceiling above and grabbing Frankie in her arms for an enormous bear hug.

Frankie smiles broadly, her cheeks squished against the

stranger's. She hasn't a clue who this is, but she's happy to see a friendly face.

"Bloody hell, it's boiling in here!" the irishwoman cries, reaching to switch the fan on.

"No, wait!" Frankie cries, but it's too late.

Both of them scream and fall to the floor as the balloons start exploding like shotguns above them. When the last balloon goes, they stare at each other in shock and terror, before the woman's face creases into hysterical laughter.

"Jesus, when will I stop being such a massive eejit?" the Irishwoman says, standing up and dusting herself off. "My name should be Doh!phie not Sophie!" She laughs.

So this is Sophie. And just like it was with Tom, this is love at first sight.

Twelve

Frankie and Sophie have been watching the sun set on the balcony for an hour, sipping on strawberry and basil margaritas that Sophie brought from her home. Frankie assessed Sophie lived close when she mentioned that she needed to pop home for extra basil and took all of thirty seconds to do so. As it turns out, Sophie's home is on the third floor.

Frankie has also managed to quietly calculate Sophie's age by suggesting they take it in turns to play songs from their birth year. Much to Frankie's horror, Sophie has never heard of The Bangles. And when Sophie played "Hot in Herre' by Nelly, Frankie winced. She's only twenty-one. Frankie knows it's from 2002, because Alice would drive her mad with it on repeat in the summer after they received their General Certificates of Secondary Education.

Frankie watches Sophie singing along to "Papa Don't Preach" as she tops up her glass. The Kelly Osbourne version, which is the only one she knows. That didn't exactly make Frankie feel any younger.

Despite the fifteen-year age gap, the pair have a lot in common; it appears that they teach at the same school, they both studied journalism, their parents are divorced and they have brothers who wind them up with every word that comes out of their mouths.

What they don't have in common is their energy levels.

Frankie, who's never had to play catch-up with any of her friends, is finding it hard to keep up with Sophie. Ironically, Sophie's drinking like it's *her* last day on Earth. She's also spent the evening bouncing among the kitchen, loo and balcony like a spring lamb in stilettos. Just watching her is exhausting, Frankie thinks, as she curls her feet up onto the chair and picks at the salt around her glass like a quiet house cat.

Sophie is wild but hilarious. With her bright eyes and bouncy brown waves, infectious laugh and appetite for adventure, she makes Frankie feel excited about this life choice. And, as she talks to Frankie at speed about the weekend getaway she's planned for them around the Yucatán Peninsula, Frankie decides to put her financial woes to one side and enjoy what she has right now. A fun friend on her doorstep, a super-hot boyfriend, her own apartment by the beach of her dreams and a life that feels like one long holiday.

Back in London, she'd rack her brains every Wednesday wondering how to spend her weekend, and trying to make plans to look forward to. Alice would invite her along to soft play with the kids, but Frankie had been burned by that one too many times. She didn't want to waste an hour-long trip out to Surrey, only to turn around thirty minutes later because Ellie or Matt stubbed their toe, fell off a climbing frame or lost their tooth on a piece of fudge.

Priya always wanted to go somewhere dressy, which Frankie didn't feel like, or couldn't afford, half the time.

Tom was her reliable weekend buddy. But recently, he and Joel had been on a saving mission to buy their first house together and "fun" meant staying in to eat takeaway and watch talent shows on TV. The idea of him leaving Clapham was difficult for Frankie to hear, but she knew the way things were couldn't last forever.

Frankie loved her friends, of course, but she'd felt increasingly isolated from them for some time. Maybe being in Mexico, in a strange way, had meant they spent less time together but more quality time when they did. In a "you don't know what you've got till it's gone" type of way.

Of course, there was the occasional weekend when their stars would collide and they'd plan a weekend break in the countryside. Although the last time that happened was about two years ago, and Alice had to leave early because Justin texted her an SOS telling her that he couldn't cope with the kids by himself. When Alice had suggested to the other three that Justin bring the kids to join them, she'd received a unanimous "NO!" Alice sulked for the night and left early on Sunday morning.

Being in Mexico makes Frankie feel like she's doing something extraordinary with her life. It makes her feel special, fearless, in control of her destiny. Alice has the kids. Priya has the flat. Tom has the husband. She has adventure. She wonders if her mum felt the same when she landed in Goa.

When Sophie reappears from the kitchen, she's carrying a plate with two tiny cupcakes holding miniature candles on each.

"It's not even my birthday yet! You really shouldn't have made such an effort!" Frankie laughs, as Sophie starts to warble "Happy Birthday." She plonks the plate down in front of Frankie and gestures for Frankie to blow out the cupcakes, with her phone posed for a photo. Frankie blows out the candles and does a ta-dah gesture.

"Gorgeous!" Sophie shouts.

Frankie removes the cupcake paper delicately, remembering the chocolate cake her mum used to make for her every year. Her mum, who was not a good cook, always put such an effort into it. Frankie never had the heart to tell her that it tasted awful.

"My mum used to make me a birthday cake every year, you know," Frankie comments, twisting the cupcake around in her hand. "It was *terrible*, but she would always stay up late the night before, to make sure I could have a slice for breakfast. She'd sink half a bottle of wine while she made it, which meant there was always something slightly off. One year, I'm sure she got the salt and sugar amounts mixed up. But I always devoured it, and told her it was delicious, knowing how delighted she was to have done it for me."

"Ah, I can't wait to meet your mam," Sophie says. "She sounds like such a rock star."

"She is." Frankie smiles. "Well, I think she really wanted to be a rock star but it didn't quite work out for her. Marriage, kids, all that got in the way."

"Well, it isn't too late," Sophie says. "Cher's like a hundred years old and she's still a foxy fucking legend. You're lucky you're friends with your mam. My mam is very much a parent, if you know what I mean. I can't tell her half the stuff I do out here. Makes it hard to get advice, ya know?"

The comment surprises Frankie. She hasn't felt close to her mum in years. And she'd always complained that her mum was too much of a friend, and not enough of a parent. She'd also struggled to forgive her for choosing a life in Goa over a life near her family.

On second thought, wasn't Frankie doing the same here?

"Do you want kids, Sophie?" Frankie asks. "Knowing that you'd have to give all this up?"

Sophie takes a bite of the cupcake and hums.

"Yeah, I think I do," she says. "Maybe in my thirties. Besides, I'm not sure I could be here forever. You've done well to be here for as long as you have. What is it, like, ten years?"

"Sounds about right." Frankie nods. The thought of being here for that long makes her stomach cramp. It's an awfully long time to be so far away from the people you know and love.

"At least your friends have come over to see you," Sophie says. "Unlike mine. They're crap. I've been here for almost two years and no one has even mentioned a trip. It seems like you have a lot of people who love you, Foo."

Frankie feels her eyes well up, when she thinks about how far away they all are.

103

"But I guess you have people who love you here too. Raph, the students. *Me*, obvs. I think it's criminal what the school is doing to you, you know," Sophie comments. "You're by far the best teacher they have. And the most popular with the students."

Frankie's ears prick up. "What do you mean?"

"Cutting so many of your classes! How do they expect you to live earning a fraction of the salary you're used to? There's no way that app they've built can do what you do. Texting is not the same as talking. I'm surprised you haven't handed in your notice by now. I'd be fuming. Have you found any posts on the mainland?"

Suddenly the money problems make sense. It isn't because Frankie has been reckless.

"I haven't looked yet," Frankie replies. "I will, though."

Or maybe I'll look for posts back in London.

"Did you speak to Raph about it yet?"

"No, not really," Frankie responds.

"He needs to know, Foo. You guys have been together for almost six months, it must be getting pretty serious by now. He's besotted with you. And I think that feeling's mutual, isn't it?"

Raphael is a beautiful stranger. How is Frankie supposed to know how she feels when she's spent no more than an hour with him?

"Yeah, he's all right, I guess." Frankie smiles.

"Jesus, tough crowd! If I had someone like Raph, I wouldn't let them out of my sight. He might be the nicest person I've ever met. He runs a children's charity, for Chrissake. He picks you up and drops you off on a Harley-Davidson every day. He cooks for you, like *all* the time. And he looks like James Bond. Or maybe a James Bond villain. I'm not sure, which is sexier?"

"Villains for sure," Frankie comments.

"You know what's sexy? TEQUILA!" Sophie says, jumping up from her seat.

Frankie groans. "Shouldn't we start thinking about leaving?"

Sophie pops her head back out the balcony door, blowing her hair out of her eyes.

"Are ye joking?" She laughs. "It's eight o'clock, Grandma! I only booked The Coz for ten!"

Bloody hell.

Frankie isn't sure she has another two minutes in her, let alone two hours. But when in Mexico, she thinks, as she sits up and shakes her head, trying to muster up some Sophie-level energy and scrolling through her playlists to find a song that'll get her in the mood for the long night ahead.

Sophie pours their second tequilas into the shot glasses, spilling half on the table. Frankie downs her glass quickly and throws her arms in the air when "Tragedy" comes on.

"What the hell is this shite?" Sophie giggles.

Frankie sighs, slamming the shot glass on the table. "Firstly, how dare you. Secondly, you have so much to learn."

Thirteen

The bar is a short walk from the apartment. Or, in Frankie and Sophie's case, a short stagger. It's 10 p.m. but the air is still warm, and the streets are buzzing with partygoers heading out for the evening. Outside The Coz, a barbecue spews meaty smoke across the revelers, and trays of mescal crowd-surf through the air above. Frankie's head spins as she follows Sophie through the huddle, down an alley full of smokers at the side of the bar and into a small beer garden out at the back, which is lit up with crisscrossing fairy lights. A crowd of strangers collectively shout various greetings at the sight of them, and Sophie prances over to the group, kissing them one by one. Raphael, who's been standing at the side, opens his arms to Frankie and kisses her on the temple as he squeezes her tight.

"For you," he says, reaching toward the table and returning his arm with a mojito in his grip.

"Thanks." Frankie smiles, craning her neck up from under

his armpit and squinting at his neck through her tequila haze. His skin is so smooth and caramelly that Frankie feels an urge to lick it. Instead, she sips her mojito, wincing when the heavy rum hits her lips.

"Hey, is there soda water in here?" she mutters to Raphael, twisting her glass around her nose.

"I doubt it, we're in Mexico!" He chuckles.

"*Hola*, Ms Frankie!" cries another voice, as someone grabs her from the side and kisses her cheek. Sweet perfume hits Frankie's nostrils as the arms spin her around and she's face-to-face with a woman with short green hair and piercings in each nostril. The kind of woman Frankie imagined her mother wanted to be when she was young.

"Hiii!" Frankie replies with a broad smile, pretending she knows exactly who she is.

"Happy birthday! I got you something, it's very small," Green Hair explains, handing over a tiny parcel which she's wrapped beautifully with a miniature ribbon.

"Ah, thank you!" Frankie cries, handing Raphael her mojito so she can unwrap the box.

Inside is a tiny silver heart-shaped locket. Frankie glances up at Green Hair, and moves forward to hug her, jumping back again when Green Hair shouts, "You've got to open it!"

Frankie struggles to pinch the clasp, but she eventually pops it open and her mouth drops again. It's an old photo of her mum.

"You've helped me so much with my lessons here, I just wanted to give you something back in return."

"It's beautiful," Frankie replies, looking closer at the photo. "Where did you get this from?"

"I hope you don't mind, but I DM'd your mum on Facebook." Green Hair smiles. "She sent me the picture. She said she is thirty-six in this photo. And then she said she is proud of you for living your dreams in Mexico, but she misses you very much."

"Thank you," Frankie whispers, on the brink of bursting into tears in front of everyone.

She swallows and clicks the locket shut, gesturing at Green Hair to help her put it on and holding it tightly to her chest when she turns around. Grabbing her mojito from Raph, she takes a large swig to extinguish the fiery lump in her throat.

Five mojitos down and many incoherent conversations later and the beer garden has morphed into a dance floor. Talking is near impossible with the human-sized speakers overhead pumping out house music, and the only form of communication possible is a "woo-hoo" and a finger point.

Frankie, who's starting to tire of Raphael's touch, shakes her hand out of his and squeezes away from him through the crowd. She hasn't had a second without him clasping on to some part of her body since they arrived at the bar. Raphael might be hot and sweet, but his care and attention are creeping dangerously into claustrophobic territory. Whenever she turns around, he has a fresh drink in his hand for her. Whenever she takes a break from dancing, he follows behind like she has treats in her pocket and he's a well-trained puppy. Frankie's starting to worry that he'll hand her a stash of toilet paper from under the bathroom door if she goes to the loo.

"Where are you going?" Raphael shouts after her, reaching for her waist as she creeps away.

"Just the bathroom!" she cries back, swerving from his hand.

"I come with," he says, starting to follow her.

"No, it's fine, I'll just be two minutes!" Frankie shouts, rolling her eyes when she turns around.

She hasn't seen Sophie since three drinks ago. Sophie might not be a familiar face, but she's the most familiar face Frankie has here.

"Sophie?" Frankie shouts in the queue for the ladies' bathroom, which is fifteen-women deep.

When there's no response, Frankie leans against the tiles and looks around her. Everyone here is at least ten years younger than her. Most of them seem at least ten drinks more sober too. But maybe that's how it is when you're twenty. Perhaps it's finally time for Frankie to accept that her thirty-six-year-old body can't handle this level of booze like it used to. A wave of nausea suddenly hits her stomach hard. She runs ahead of the queue and bangs on the door in a panic.

"Please, hurry, I'm going to be sick!" she cries, over the protesting murmurs from the women in front. When the door doesn't open, Frankie dashes along the cubicles to the bin at the other end, throws her head in and projectile vomits her entire insides. In a way, she feels relieved that she's purged the poison inside her. She lifts her head to one side slowly when she feels a tap on her shoulder. Wiping her sticky hair away from her chin, she comes face-to-face with an angel holding a tissue. A literal angel, in fancy dress wings.

"Thank you," Frankie says, coughing. "I'm so embarrassed, I haven't done that since I was at uni!"

"*Que?*" says the angel softly, her immaculate eyebrows creasing.

"*Gracias,*" Frankie says, wiping her mouth and glancing at the queue behind her. To Frankie's relief, they're all glued to their phones.

The angel smiles sweetly and wraps her arm around Frankie's shoulder. Then she lifts her phone up and takes a selfie, with Frankie in the background.

"No problem, Ms Frankie. See you at class on Monday."

Well, that's not ideal.

"Foo?" a familiar voice chirps.

Sophie appears from one of the cubicles, followed by a tall topless man in a cowboy hat who slinks past the queue and out of the bathroom to jeers from the crowd.

Sophie turns to them with both hands on her hips. "Oh, pipe down, the lot o' ya, like ye haven't done that before. What are yas, nuns?"

Frankie stares at Sophie as she casually reapplies her makeup in the mirror, smacking her hot-pink lips together like nothing happened.

"Who was that?" Frankie asks, half laughing, half grossed out.

"Fuck knows," Sophie replies with a nonchalant shrug. "We didn't say a word to each other. Just how I like it! Wait, what happened, you look like death. You OK?"

"Yeah, fine," Frankie fibs. "Just feeling a bit sick. And Raph is doing my head in a bit. He's always right *there*. I mean, he's got a nice face but it's not the only face I want to see all the time."

"I hear ya, girl. He does it every time we're out, I know. Come, let's go out the front and get some tacos in you and have a break from his face," Sophie suggests, grabbing Frankie's hand and pulling her past the glowering queue.

Frankie's heart sinks when she sees Raph waiting outside the loos. He's holding a bottle of water and looking worried.

"Ah, jeez, that's sweet of you, Raph," Sophie says, chuckling as she catches Frankie's eye.

"Are you OK, Frankie?" he says, opening the water for her.

"I'm fine, thanks, Raph," Frankie says, taking the water and having a big glug. Why can't she appreciate this gesture more? Back in London, she craved having someone look after her like this. Like Toby used to too. Now it feels like history—and her feeling—are repeating themselves.

"Raph, I need some girly chat with our Foo Foo here," Sophie shouts at him over the music. "We'll see you in a bit!"

"But we'll still go to the beach to watch the sunrise on your birthday, yes?" Raph asks, looking concerned.

"Yeah, yeah, 'course, we won't be a minute," Sophie shouts over her shoulder.

Frankie turns back to Raph as Sophie marches ahead holding her hand. He takes off his glasses and cleans them on his shirt, waving at her with a disappointed smile as he disappears behind the crowd. For a moment, Frankie wants to run back and tell him it's OK. But more than that, she wants to get out of this bar—maybe this whole place—entirely.

It isn't just Raph who's too much. This night is too much. As Frankie sinks her teeth into a beef taco that's dripping in melted cheese, she feels grateful to have Sophie by her side to guide her here. But is this really how they spend their nights out? Frankie panics at the thought of doing this again any time soon.

"Magic!" Sophie smiles, as she dabs at her mouth with a paper napkin. "Works like a charm every time, doesn't it?"

Frankie nods, as she swallows her last mouthful and wipes her fingers with a napkin.

"Did I just make you uncomfortable in the bathroom over there, Foo?" Sophie asks her.

Frankie, surprised by how direct Sophie is, stutters an inaudible answer.

"Oh, I'm sorry, I did, didn't I?" Sophie replies. "I guess I was just feeling a bit lonely. You know you have Raph, Anna has Stefan. I just felt like I needed someone for once. Even if it was just for five minutes." She giggles. "You looked a bit shocked!"

"Well, to be fair I'd just spewed my insides into a bin. And you never have to explain yourself to me, Sophie." Frankie shrugs, shoving her napkin into her pocket. "There's no judgment here. Besides, you should never let anyone tell you how you should be. Just be you. My mum used to say that to me all the time."

"Are you going to call her back?" Sophie says.

Frankie looks at her, confused.

"I saw you dodging her calls yesterday," Sophie comments.

"Only because you were there," Frankie replies, guessing Sophie was there.

"As long as you're really OK, though," Sophie presses her. "You know you can tell me anything, right? We've been besties here for almost a year, I'd do anything for you."

What Sophie doesn't know is that Frankie has known her for all of ten—drunken—hours.

"I know," Frankie replies quietly. "I'm just not feeling that well. Maybe my age is catching up to me."

"Frankie McKenzie, don't you dare ever say that. You're only thirty-six, for Christ's sake! It's not your age that's catching up to you, it's those tequilas. It's my fault. I made us go too hard too soon." Sophie laughs.

A familiar face appears from behind Sophie's shoulder. Raph is holding Frankie's bag up and being followed by the group from the back garden.

"Hey." Frankie smiles, taking her bag.

"We're going to the beach now, yes?" Raph says, reaching for her hand.

"Would you hate me if I went home?" Frankie asks, squishing her face.

"Everything OK?" Raph says, stroking her shoulder.

"I'm just feeling a little woozy, that's all," Frankie says.

"What is this 'woozy?'" Raph asks, confused.

Frankie imitates being sick.

"I'll come with you, make sure you're OK," Raph says, his face concerned.

"I think I just need to go straight to bed," Frankie says. "You go with Sophie. I think she might need a babysitter."

They turn to Sophie, who's flinging taco crumbs onto the pavement and cooing at a passing chicken.

Raph turns back to her, softly kisses her cheek, and runs his fingers through her hair.

"But I wanted to wake up with you on your birthday."

"I know, I'm sorry. I just think she needs you more," Frankie says, turning to Sophie.

"Call me if you need anything, OK?" Raph replies.

Frankie glances at her phone. It's almost 4 a.m.

Twelve hours left.

*

Back in the apartment, Frankie sips a tea and slinks down into the sofa, relishing the relative peace and quiet. Outside, a few barking dogs break the silence, and a motorbike gang roars past. There's so much she should love about it here. The sun, the ocean, the colors, the streets chock-full of life. Maybe she just needs to make some life adjustments. She doesn't need to be with Raphael, for a start. She could take on some private pupils to make up for the cash shortage. She could even move to a different part of the country to start afresh. Just as Mabel reminded her, there are no rules about changing her life once she's here.

Frankie opens up her social media and scrolls down the feed. Everyone in London seems to be moaning about a two-week-long rain deluge, Tube delays and news that the average price of coffee in the city has just surpassed £4. Does she really want to return to that?

Frankie closes the feed of doom down and clicks on her messages to reply to her mum. She's never felt like she needed her mum more. Through tears, she scrolls up through their old messages, her brow furrowing as they reveal the truth about her life here. Feelings that it appears she's had for weeks.

> **Frankie:** I'm so lonely here

> **Frankie:** Everyone here is a traveler

> **Frankie:** They're all half my age

> **Frankie:** I miss London

> **Frankie:** I miss you and Dad

> **Frankie:** Maybe even Jet (at a push)

> **Frankie:** I don't know what I'm doing with my life

> **Frankie:** I have no money to get home

∗

Frankie's startled awake by the urgent repeating chime of a doorbell. She sits up on the sofa, her phone falling from her lap and clattering on the tiles. She grabs her pounding head and groans, the smell of stale tequila filling the air. The doorbell chimes several times again.

"OK, OK!" she croaks.

This hangover makes her want to fast-forward this life to the end. She slowly stands up and stumbles toward the door, glancing at her reflection in the mirror.

"Jesus," she whispers, when she sees her blotchy, bloated face in the reflection, as she swings open the front door.

When she sees who's standing on her doorstep, she screams.

Her mum drops her suitcases to the floor, grabs Frankie in both arms and holds her close to her chest. Frankie clutches her waist like she'll never let go and sobs uncontrollably, spilling hot tears onto her mum's gold-sequined cardigan.

"Happy birthday, my darling," her mum whispers.

Fourteen

THURSDAY, AUGUST 31, 2023

Astrid emerges from her shower in a purple polka-dot maxi skirt and the pair of fluffy bear slippers she's been wearing since Frankie was a child. For as long as Frankie can remember, the slippers have had holes worn in at the front, which her feet stick out of, making the bears look like they have wiggly toe teeth. It would always amuse her mum to paint her toenails red, pretend it was blood and chase her and Jet screaming up to bed.

"I can't believe you still have those slippers!" Frankie laughs.

"Why wouldn't I?" Astrid cries, wiggling her toes and growling. It used to make Frankie shriek with delight. "I'm not going to toss out perfectly good slippers. Did you know that the fast fashion industry emits more carbon than international air travel and shipping combined? It's criminal what they're doing to this planet, Frankie."

"OK, Mum," Frankie says, trying to steer away from a conversation about climate change that will take up precious time.

"It's very important to know these things," Astrid replies. "I was never brilliant at teaching you about school stuff, but I've always thought I taught you how to be a decent human being."

And she did. Although, there are many times when Frankie hasn't felt like such a decent human being. Mostly when Frankie was being a brat about her mum wearing her bear slippers to drop her off, or her hair like Bjork to school functions.

The pair of them go out onto the balcony. After listening to her phone ping repeatedly with texts from Raph and Sophie, and someone called Anna, Frankie had responded to tell them the good news of her mum's arrival and then switched her phone off. She was grateful that they cared about her, but she was glad for the break from them.

"God, it's stunning, isn't it?" her mum says, blowing steam into the cool dawn air. "I can see why you've spent so long here. I could easily live here, it's so peaceful."

"Not always." Frankie smiles.

"Oh, good," Astrid says. "Truthfully, I was getting worried that it's a little *too* quiet. It's always comforting to hear a little life outside your four walls. That's why I bought my chickens back in Palolem. I mean, I know it's meant to be a *silent* yoga retreat, but the silence was so deafening after a few weeks I almost went mad! Now I have the chickens to chat to every morning, while the rest of them are sleeping so they don't hear me breaking the rules. And you, at night, of course. I love our long chats, Frankie. It's what I look forward to most when I wake up every day."

When her mum announced that she was moving to Goa,

Frankie was shocked. When Astrid explained it was a silent yoga retreat, she was floored. The family didn't expect her to last more than five minutes without squealing with joy about a tasty chai tea, or screaming blue murder at a speeding car.

"Me too, Mum," Frankie says, feeling ashamed that she didn't do this in London and sad that she can't remember the long chats now. Her mum tried to call her for weeks, and she would always have an excuse. She was going out, she had a headache, she had a deadline. Why did she have such a problem speaking with her mum back then? Why doesn't she have this problem now?

"I think what I love most about our chats is learning how alike we are. Two peas in a pod."

Frankie nods. She never saw it until now. But here she is, living a life of adventure on her own in a far-flung land.

"I always thought Jet was the apple of your eye," Frankie replies with a teasing smile.

"You know I love you and your brother equally. Truth is, your brother is much more like your darling dad. Sure he has my creative passions, but he isn't out traveling the world and daring to do different things. He's a homebody. Loves his routine. And that's absolutely fine. That's what makes him happy."

"What makes you happy, Mum?"

"Having something to look forward to every day, I suppose." Astrid ponders. "It can be the smallest thing. Like lying on my bed first thing in the morning, staring up at the ceiling and soaking up the simple joy of being alone."

Frankie thinks back to her London life and tries to think

of the small things she looks forward to every day. Her first sip of coffee in the morning. Her lunchtime text marathons with Tom. Her morning ritual of watering the flowerpots in the hallway.

"My daily calls with you," Astrid continues. "Even though I have to hide in the bushes by the lagoon to have them. Speaking of which, shall we go for a walk? My lungs feel like a pair of charcoal sacks, full of that awful airplane air. What they put in those air-conditioning units doesn't bear thinking about, you know . . ."

Frankie smiles as she sits on the sofa and leans back into the cushions, watching her mum throw her arms up in the air to emphasize each point she shouts. Her voice fades as Frankie closes her eyes to listen to the soothing jingle of her mum's jewelery, a sense of peace washing over her as she does. Why did she convince herself that her mum abandoned her without care all those years ago? All her mum has ever done is cared about her. Frankie's breathing gets heavier and heavier until her mum's voice fades into silence.

*

When Frankie opens her eyes, she hears a familiar song coming from the kitchen and a huge smile stretches across her face as she listens to her mum singing along to the lyrics.

Frankie wanders into the kitchen and watches her mum swaying to the music as she unpacks at least ten bags of groceries into the empty cupboards above the gas stove.

Frankie looks at the clock on the wall.

Two hours left.

"Mum, stop!" Frankie cries.

"Frankie!" her mum cries back, clutching her necklace. "My heart!"

"I can't believe I fell asleep," Frankie says, feeling warm tears start to well.

She could kick herself for wasting her hours. All she wants to do now is walk along a beach with her mum. Just the two of them. Talking and making up for so much lost time.

"Calm down, love, we've got all the time in the world!" Astrid says, taking the silver glitter flip-flops that Frankie's passing to her.

"That's exactly what we don't have, Mum," Frankie says.

*

Stingray Beach is teeming with cyclists, runners and snorkel groups, who weave between Frankie and her mum as they stroll arm in arm along the promenade, listening to the lapping waves kiss the concrete.

"I really *could* live here," Astrid comments, pausing to look toward the horizon. "A change of scene would be nice. How about it, darling?"

"I'm not sure I'll be here for much longer," Frankie replies, tugging at her mum's arm to get her to sit on a blue weather-beaten bench.

"Is this the part where you finally tell me what's been going on with you?" Astrid says, sitting down with a satisfied sigh. "I've flown all this way to find out, Frankie, it's only fair. Do you regret coming here? I've always worried that moving here was just a flight response to your big breakup with Toby. You were only twenty-three, you'd been through a lot. A new city, a marriage proposal, your first proper job. Were you running away from it all?"

"I don't think I regret it," Frankie replies, with zero confidence. "I guess it was a pretty big year. But money seems to be my main stress right now."

"Why have you suddenly got money problems? You aren't exactly thrifty, but you've never been in debt. If you tell me you've got into some kind of cartel situation here, I'm going to be absolutely livid, and you know me, Frankie, it takes a lot to make me livid."

"Yes, Mum. That's exactly it. I owe a kingpin millions and I need to go on the run. How much cocaine do you think your suitcase can hold? Five, ten kilograms?" Frankie eyes her mum up and down.

"I don't think so!" Astrid laughs.

"If you loved me, you would, Mum," Frankie replies.

"I'd do anything for my daughter, but I won't do that," Astrid replies.

They both erupt into giggles.

"In seriousness, the school has cut some of the lessons I teach. Apparently they've got this new app that they want their students to use. I guess it kind of makes me a bit redundant."

"Big tech." Astrid shakes her head. "Destroying lives, paying no taxes, racing to Mars. I hope they get there, and stay there."

"Yeah, I'm not sure that the San Miguel School of International Studies in Cozumel is exactly SpaceX," Frankie comments. "Besides, it's not just money that's the problem, Mum. It's me. I'm just feeling really lost at the moment. I don't know what to do with my life. Where to live. Who to live with. I'm thirty-six years old and I feel like I don't have an awful lot to show for it."

"What! What are you talking about, Frankie, you have all this to show for it," she says, gesturing around the beach. "It takes real guts to come and live in a place like this. I like to think you got those guts from me. The closest your dad has ever got to an adventure is a trip to IKEA in Wembley."

"Why did you choose to marry Dad? Why did you settle down, have kids, when you could have pursued music and travel?" Frankie asks.

"I thought you knew this?" Astrid asks.

"Knew what?" Frankie replies.

"I fell pregnant with you a few weeks after our first date," Astrid comments.

"Oh yes, I was your happy accident." Frankie laughs.

"Crumpets, for a moment there I thought I'd kept you in the dark all these years. Look, you really were a happy accident. You and Jet are the best things I've ever done. I know I've had my fair share of adventures, but the journey to becoming a mum was by far my biggest. The joy I get from music doesn't even begin to compare to the joy I felt when I first held you in my arms."

"But you didn't have to stay with Dad," Frankie replies. "Didn't he drive you crazy?"

"Oh, he drove me up the wall! But he's a good person. I learned to swallow my irritation at the little things. Like when he'd hand me a plate every time I took a biscuit out of the cupboard."

Toby used to hand Frankie a pair of kitchen scissors when she plucked a single grape from the bowl. She remembers the red mist descending each time.

"But together we made a good team," Astrid continues. "I brought creativity to the table. He brought convention."

"And carrots," Frankie adds.

"And bloody carrots, yes. Look, I always wanted to live abroad, and that longing didn't disappear when I had kids. So, I put my dreams on pause until you two were old enough to cope with us heading off in different directions."

"And Dad was OK with that? Did he know that you were planning to take off?" Frankie asks.

"I told him all the time. Although, I'm not sure he was listening," Astrid replied. "But our break was very amicable. I think he was looking forward to having a bit of peace after nineteen years of me prancing around the house!"

"You're lucky. Most breakups aren't like that, are they?" Frankie asks rhetorically.

"You know, I think it worked because we were always honest and open with what we both wanted. Your dad wanted a calm, quiet life. To follow the rules and tow the line. Which is perfectly fine, because that's what made him happy and I supported that. But I didn't want that for myself. I wouldn't let anyone tell me who I should be, how I should live, what I should be doing with my life. In a way, I feel lucky that my life has had two chapters. The first, my family. The second, myself. If you're feeling lost, Frankie, the only place you should be searching for what you want is your heart. No decision has to be final, either. Hell, your life could have ten chapters if that's what you want."

"But I just feel like everyone else knows exactly what they want from life, and they're going out and grabbing it. Everyone's changing. Everyone's growing up. And here I am, stuck behind, pretending I'm still sixteen years old," Frankie replies.

"How can you say you're stuck? You're stuck when you have a mortgage, or a job you can't afford to quit. And if I was stuck anywhere, I'd want this to be it. Frankie, you never regret the money you spend on travel. Experiences are more enriching than money. I'd bet my life on the fact that your friends in London see your paradise photos and wish they could break free from the shackles of their ordinary lives."

"Not so sure about that." Frankie laughs, although she suspects there's some truth in it.

"You should feel really proud of yourself, Frankie. I know I'm proud of you. I hate that we live so far from each other, but I love that you're proving to everyone that there is more to life than living chained to a desk in Canary Wharf."

"Well, with this whole money thing, I'm not sure I can lead this life much longer," Frankie comments.

"What about Goa?" Astrid asks. "You've been here a long time now. Maybe it's time to explore a new corner of the world. I know a TEFL teacher a few beaches down. I could introduce you?"

"Don't you think it's about time I go back to London, and . . . settle down or something? Think about having a family myself?" Frankie asks.

"Is that what you want?" Astrid asks.

"I don't really know," Frankie replies.

"There's your answer. If you don't know, the time isn't right for you. For god's sake, Frankie, you're only thirty-six. You've got plenty of time to figure the rest of your life out. Besides, what's stopping you from settling down in Goa? You'll love it there. Sunshine, beaches, naked yoga every morning . . ."

"No, Mum, not that," Frankie says, trying to stop her.

"It's very liberating, Frankie. It might help you release some of this stress that's built up."

"I know what might release some of my stress," Frankie replies, glancing at her mum.

Her mum leans forward and whispers, "Do you know a guy?"

"Mum! I'm not talking about weed," Frankie hisses back, looking around. "I'm talking about food. Let's go get some lunch."

"Oh, all right then." Astrid sighs.

Outside Hora de los Huevos, the pair of them examine the chalkboard menu.

"I'll have the egg and cheese burrito," Astrid says. "God, it's been a long time since I tasted real cheese. Magdu uses this nutritional yeast substitute for cheese. It's . . . well, truth be told, it's disgusting. But I wouldn't dare admit that to the commune. I love living there, but sometimes I just want a cheap ham and cheese sandwich on white bread."

Frankie glances at her phone. It's 3:56 p.m. She inhales a big breath, takes her mother in her arms and squeezes her tightly. It isn't goodbye forever, of course. But being here together, she feels closer to her mum than ever before. Whatever life she ends up choosing, she'll never let the distance grow between them again.

"One egg and cheese burrito coming up," Frankie calls back, as she wanders into the café.

She turns to look at her mum through the café door. Astrid has already struck up a conversation with an old local outside, heaven knows about what. Frankie smiles as she watches her purple hair blowing freely in the breeze, and her polka-dot skirt floating around her legs against the backdrop of the colored buildings. Astrid looks up, beams at her and waves. As Frankie waves back, the colors start to fade until there's nothing but white light around her.

Fifteen

"So, trouble in paradise, eh?" Mabel says, when Frankie emerges from the lift.

"More like not enough time in paradise," Frankie replies, wiping her eyes as she takes her seat.

"Time for what?"

"Traveling around, seeing the sights, getting to know Raph better?" Frankie replies.

"Do you know that he funded and founded a free primary school in his family's rural village?" Mabel comments. "And he also makes a mean plate of enchiladas mexicanas. Usually in nothing but an apron. And those sexy specs."

"You're probably going to tell me that he donated a kidney to a three-legged dog or something," Frankie comments.

"Two-legged cat, actually," Mabel murmurs, before turning to Frankie. "You did make a choice while you were down there, you know. You chose to go home, instead of going to the beach with him."

"Well, I'm glad I did, otherwise I would have missed that time with my mum," Frankie replies.

"That's true." Mabel shrugs.

"I wasn't really focused on romance while I was there. I was more focused on the fact that I followed my wanderlust, only to find myself more lost than I felt back in London. And even more skint."

"Come on, Frankie. It wasn't all bad, was it?" Mabel asks. "I mean, didn't you feel free?"

Frankie thinks back to the wind rushing through her hair on the back of Raph's motorbike. Wandering the streets of San Miguel in flip-flops with dust in her toes, dodging runaway chickens and random goats. She did feel free. And her paradise troubles could be solved. She didn't have to hang out at heaving student bars. She didn't have to stay in that job. She didn't have to stay in Mexico at all; she had the freedom to travel anywhere else, just like her mum suggested. No one was stopping her.

"You're right, it was pretty liberating. Great, actually. Maybe even a bit of a life-changer. Or . . . death-changer?" Frankie replies.

Mabel looks at her quizzically.

"The best bit was seeing Mum. Definitely." Frankie explains, "I was only with her for a few hours but I haven't felt so close to her in years. I'm not sure I knew we could be that close anymore. Maybe the distance between us has drawn us together, in a weird way. I've spent so long feeling angry with her for moving to Goa. And I've harbored all this resentment, where it didn't really belong. Because the truth is, I don't resent her. Not at all. I now completely understand why she had to do what she did. And I feel proud of her for doing it. She isn't a bad mother. She's a badass. It's inspiring, actually."

"Can you see yourself following in her footsteps?" Mabel asks.

Frankie nods. She really can.

Then again, what about the longing she felt for her friends at home? They could come visit, and it seems like they did. But the longer she spends away, the more likely it is that they'll drift apart. The common habits, habitats and hobbies that brought them together would eventually fade. Their lives would be so different; how could they relate to each other? Could their friendships really survive it? Frankie would like to think they could. But there's no guarantee. By coming to Mexico so soon after moving to London, she's missed out on years of experiences with them. She thinks of all the memories she made with Tom in her twenties and thirties. Her stomach cramps.

"Back in London," Frankie continues, "it felt like I was the one getting left behind. But getting that one-way flight, it felt like I was the one leaving them behind. In London, I felt like life was happening to me. In Mexico, it felt like I was the one who was making my life happen."

"Maybe Mexico is where you're meant to be," Mabel suggests.

"Maybe it is," Frankie replies.

"Maybe you need to visit your other crossroads before you make that decision," Mabel says, turning to the screen.

The Marriage Proposal

Frankie takes a deep breath.

"Shall we have a cheeky replay of the proposal?" Mabel asks.

"Do you enjoy tormenting me?" Frankie replies.

"I really do," Mabel says, pointing the clicker at the screen.

Sixteen

The screen behind Mabel erupts into that same brilliant pink sunset in the sky above Torre des Savinar that Frankie's replayed in her head so many times. Frankie and Toby are standing arm in arm in a scene straight out of the end of a romantic movie. They're babies. Just twenty-three years old.

"Hard to tell where the sunset starts and you begin," Mabel says, tilting her head.

"Everyone burns on the first day," Frankie replies defensively. "I once ran a pictorial of celebrities with sunburn."

"How lovely," Mabel remarks.

"Ouch! Ten Stars with Sunburn, to Tickle You Pink!" Frankie says.

"What?" Mabel asks.

"That was the headline," Frankie responds.

"Wow," Mabel says.

Frankie sighs when she sees the prized boho belt that she wore to death, along with the matching cowboy boots and frayed denim skirt. She still pines for that belt. The day they left Ibiza, headed back to London, she felt so panicked by the proposal that she packed in a rush and left it behind. Alice found Frankie's fixation on leaving the belt behind particularly irksome.

"You've just broken up with the love of your life and all you can think about is that bloody belt!" she hissed in Frankie's ear on the plane, having swapped seats with Toby.

"Have I ever said that he's the love of my life? I'm only twenty-three, Al, I've got plenty of life left to find love," Frankie replied. "That belt, on the other hand, was one of a kind. I'll never find another like it."

It wasn't just a belt. It was her identity. Her independence. She liked it because Toby *didn't* like it and she wore it to show him she was her own person. By the time Ibiza came, Frankie was feeling trapped and suffocated by the relationship. She couldn't do anything or go anywhere in the city without him tagging along. And when she said she wanted to go alone, he'd look at her, concerned, and say, "Are you OK?" Like it was *her* with the problem. Why didn't he ever crave space? *That* was weird. He was always there, even when he wasn't there. No one ever asked her, *"What are you doing this weekend?"* it was always, *"What are you and Toby doing this weekend?"* It was never, *"How are you, Frankie?"* it was always, *"How are you and Toby, Frankie?"* Why was she never enough?

Frankie, a master in hiding her emotions, sometimes even from herself, struggled to contain her irritation toward the end. As it started to seep through her pores, she began pouncing on every little thing he did. It got petty, like when she would purposely drop his folded pile of shirts and put the milk bottle back in the fridge with just a millimeter left. Then it got childish, like when she'd purposely mess up what he'd just tidied within minutes. He'd find his magazine stacks spread across the coffee table. Coffee mugs next to coasters, instead of on them. Loose pens without lids in drawers, the loo paper ripped asymmetrically, and the hand towels scrunched up. Pathetic of her, really. On reflection, she isn't proud of herself.

The scene on the screen in front of them suggests a couple madly in love. The reality is that Frankie didn't want to be there at all. She was annoyed that the boys had tagged along in the first place. It was meant to be a girls' trip, but Alice had suggested the boys come too so they could get a bigger place. She was also annoyed with Toby for dragging her away from the villa on the first night. Everyone knows that the first night of the holiday is the best one. You make empty promises on the plane that you'll take it easy to enjoy the first morning. But the excitement of being on holiday kicks in the moment the front door bursts open. Just one celebratory welcome drink. Then another, and another, until the night descends into dancing, debauchery and demolishing the week's entire booze supply. Not this time. This time, Toby insisted they go and watch the sunset that first night, just the two of them.

"I don't think I can watch this again. It was painful enough in real life," Frankie says to Mabel.

Toby's face glows as he turns toward Frankie. He was handsome. Is still handsome, judging by the wedding photos

Frankie's seen online. With his wavy sandy-brown hair, dark eyes, olive skin and dimples, he could have passed for an Ibizan local. In Mabel's office, Frankie scrunches her face and lowers her head.

"Can I take a picture of you against the sunset?" she hears Toby ask.

Frankie, who hates having her picture taken, groans.

"Oh my god, Toby! No! I'm a total beetroot! Weren't you listening to me in the car? Being seen by strangers with a burn like this is mortifying enough, why would I want it immortalized on camera? Wait until tomorrow and I might consider it," she says, laughing, but irritated that he'd suggested it when he knows how she feels about the camera and that they have this conversation every time.

"You always look amazing, Franks." He smiles.

"No . . . I look like Percy Pig if she got trapped in a sunbed," Frankie says.

Frankie was not a good girlfriend, especially at the end. She was horrible. Maybe she is horrible. Maybe she didn't—or doesn't—deserve a love like his.

"Please, Franks," Toby insists. "It'll take two seconds. Just . . . stay right there." He smiles, as he takes a few steps away from her, turns around, drops to his knees and lifts up both his hands. In one hand is a disposable camera, and in the other, a black velvet ring box opened to reveal an emerald-cut diamond ring.

"Oh my god," Frankie whispers, throwing her hands up to her wide-open mouth.

Toby is grinning, completely unaware of what was running through her mind at the time.

Save me.

"Frankie McKenzie, will you marry me?" he says, grinning.

Frankie lifts up her head, looks him dead in the eye and shouts, "No way!"

"Yes way!" Toby shouts back, misunderstanding her. "This is really happening, Franks!"

He clicks the camera, and Frankie jerks her hands up to hide her face.

"Stop, Toby. That's not what I meant," she says, quieter this time.

"What?" he asks, his smile frozen on his face.

Softly, she says, "I'm sorry, Toby, I'm saying no. I don't want to marry you," shaking her head.

"What?" Toby repeats, the grin fading.

"Toby! We can't get married, we're only twenty-three!" Frankie cries.

Toby stands up, puts the camera in his pocket and walks slowly toward her, the ring box still open and aimed at her like a loaded gun.

"Franks, there aren't any rules about when you can get married," Toby says, laughing. "Look, I know we're young and this is a little unexpected. I just figured that we're going to get married one day, so why do we need to wait? You're my forever person for me, Franks. You're . . . beautiful."

Then Toby takes his phone out of his pocket, flips it open and James Blunt's "You're Beautiful" starts to play.

Back in Mabel's office, Frankie finally looks up.

"I was furious with him," she says quietly.

"I'd be too," Mabel comments. "James Blunt? Come on, Toby."

"I felt like he'd taken control of my entire future and suddenly I didn't have a say about it. I didn't see that ring as a symbol of love, I saw it as a symbol of loss. Freedom, my time, my space. Me. Plus, I was fuming that he proposed on the first day and spoiled the rest of a holiday he wasn't even supposed to be on."

"He didn't think you would say no," Mabel remarks.

"I know that. Bit presumptuous of him, right? What also bothered me was that my rejection made me look cold and heartless. But if he'd really been listening to me in the months leading up to this moment, he'd have known not to pull a stunt like this. He knew I was still feeling sensitive about my parents' divorce, even though it had been five years. And I'd told him repeatedly that over-the-top romantic gestures make me feel really uncomfortable. I'd rather he'd asked me with a Post-it note and a Haribo ring. Although, I still would have said no."

"Did you tell him how upset you were about your parents' divorce?"

"No."

"You like to keep everything bottled up, don't you?" Mabel comments.

"Not wine," Frankie replies unhelpfully.

The two of them turn back to the screen, when they hear shouting.

"Are you serious, Frankie?" Toby yells.

"You're stifling me, Toby. I feel like I've lost control of my life, and I'm only at the very beginning of it! What about traveling? We haven't even seen half of London yet, and we've been here for two years! I haven't even been to the Columbia Road Flower Market!"

"We can go on holiday! We can go to the Columbia Road Flower Market! But what about going to Surrey with Alice and Justin? I thought that's what you wanted? Just last week we were all talking about how we were going to move to Kingston, get houses next door to each other, share the school run with our kids, have a treehouse built over the fence so our kids could have some kind of *Dawson's Creek* romance. I thought you wanted *Dawson's Creek*, Frankie?"

"Maybe I want *Sex and the City*," Frankie replies. "Or . . . *Around The World In 80 Days*, I don't know. Anyway, that was at 3 a.m. after a round of flaming sambucas. It wasn't serious, we were talking bollocks. Toby, we have *so* much to enjoy before settling down. And a holiday isn't the same as traveling. Don't you want to see the world? Why do you want to settle down when you've barely lived? We have the rest of our lives for Kingston, kids, catchment areas. We could do anything. We could go and pick grapes in France. Or herd cattle in Australia. Or . . . or . . . or hitchhike along Route 66 and stay in murdery motels along the way."

His face contorts.

"I don't want to stay in a murdery motel, Frankie. And I don't want to wait years. I'm ready now. I've been teaching in

London for two years, and to be honest, that's enough for me. I'm ready to leave and move on with my life. Step up to the next stage."

"Well, I'm not." Frankie sighs.

"When will you be?" Toby asks.

"I dunno. Ten years, maybe?"

"How are we going to fill ten years?" Toby asks, looking dumbfounded.

"*Fill* ten years?" Frankie laughs. "Toby, life shouldn't be about filling time, it should be about fulfilling time! It's about embracing as many crazy experiences as we can. It's meant to be spontaneous, exciting, an adventure! Do you really want to look back on it when you're seventy and realize you've only read a few pages of this great big novel?"

In that moment, it dawned on Frankie how different they were. And how the dreams they once had together had drifted apart. She was raring to try everything life offers a twenty-three-year-old. To tough it out in a big city, to rough it in South America. The plans she had for the next few years were utterly different from his. Perhaps she hadn't been vocal enough in telling him that.

"If we get married, settle in the suburbs and have kids at twenty-five, then how is that experiencing life?" Frankie asks.

"Isn't creating life like the biggest life experience you could ever have?" Toby retorted.

Frankie's face contorts as she replies, "Sure, when you've experienced everything else!"

"I don't want to be an old dad," he says.

"Well, I don't want to be a young mum," she replies.

Frankie watches herself on-screen, as she turns to face the sunset. She remembers realizing this wasn't a marriage proposal, it was a breakup.

Toby puts the ring box back in his pocket, turns and walks off-screen and Frankie's shoulders drop an inch as the tension leaves her body.

Years later, she would lie alone in bed, having never gone to Australia or along Route 66. She'd be haunted by this exact moment and continually question whether she'd made the worst mistake of her life.

Frankie doesn't need Mabel's screen to remember what happened next. The rest of the Ibiza holiday was a disaster. The second they stepped through the villa's front door, Alice and Justin popped a bottle of champagne and exploded poppers all over them. When Alice saw Frankie's stony face through the paper ribbons, she realized it hadn't gone to plan and immediately ushered Justin to start clearing up. Toby marched straight to the bedroom and didn't reappear for the rest of the night. For five days, Toby wouldn't look Frankie in the eye. He sat in silence at mealtimes. He relocated into the sitting room. He moped around the villa moving from lounge to lounger on repeat all day.

Alice was a bit taken aback by Frankie's response, but incredibly supportive nonetheless. She did wonder whether Frankie could have said yes for the sake of the holiday to save them all from the misery and awkwardness. But she also forced Justin to share a room with Toby so she could be with Frankie. And after a skinful one night, she gave Toby a mouthful for not seeing it from Frankie's point of view. For not understanding how difficult the subject of marriage was for someone whose parents had gone through a divorce.

"So, the big question. What do you think would have happened if you'd said yes?" Mabel asks.

"I guess we'd have hugged. Gone back to the villa. And had a lovely holiday. And I'd still have my favorite belt," Frankie replies.

"Wow, again with the belt. The last time anyone wore a belt like that was 2007," Mabel says.

"It would be vintage!" Frankie shrugs.

"You've really got to stop clinging on to the past," Mabel responds. "Besides, you know I meant beyond that. What if you'd said yes? How would your life have turned out?"

"We'd probably be in Kingston with two kids. Safe, secure. I wouldn't be lonely, that's for sure. We'd go on happy family holidays to Center Parcs and we'd have a roast every Sunday with the extended family. Living that Disney dream."

"Shall we find out what life would have been like if you'd said yes?" Mabel asks, standing up and nodding toward the lift behind her.

Frankie groans.

"Come on, aren't you a bit curious?"

"Try terrified," Frankie says, standing up slowly.

"You'll be fine," Mabel says, pressing the button.

The door slides open and Frankie steps into the lift, her fingers trembling as she clasps them together and takes a deep breath.

PART FOUR

Meet the UNI SWEETHEARTS with a marriage MADE IN HEAVEN

Seventeen

Frankie opens her eyes to the sound of gentle birdsong and the smell of fresh linen fabric conditioner from the squishy pillow beneath her. As she blinks herself awake, wondering what heaven or hell lies ahead in her new life, she notices a black-and-white picture in a silver frame on the bedside table next to her. She rubs her eyes, stretches out her arm and takes the frame from the table to bring it closer. It's a photo of her and Toby on their wedding day.

Frankie's wearing a long vintage dress with a lace sleeve overlay and her hair pinned in a low bun at the back and a few curls framing her face. In her hands, she's clutching a small, tightly wound bouquet of roses. The scene is simple, calm and conventional. The opposite of her parents' wedding photo, taken at Dreamland in Margate. Her mum wore a pink ball gown paired with gold biker boots, a fake ruby–encrusted

145

crown from a fancy dress shop and a blue feather boa bouquet. Frankie sits up on the pillows and brings the picture to within an inch of her nose, squinting for a closer examination of her face. She wonders what was going through her mind at the time. To her surprise, she looks like the picture of pure joy. She's mid-giggle with her head leaning on Toby's shoulder. He's grinning so broadly that his cheeks look like apples. His eyes are locked on her smile and his arm tightly wound around her waist. She wonders what the joke was.

The sunlight from the window catches something on her left hand. She gasps quietly and drops the picture frame onto the plain white bedcover. The bloody diamond ring. Next to it, a plain gold band. Holding her left hand with her right, Frankie twists and turns her fingers in the way that new brides do. She extends her arm to examine it from afar, tilting her head left to right as she does. It isn't that bad, she guesses. If it hadn't belonged to Agnes she'd probably love it. She's surprised that she never asked Toby to swap it. Old Frankie would have. Maybe Young Frankie wasn't as bold back then.

The silver frame is engraved *July 27, 2011.* They've been married for twelve years. Frankie's mind races with thoughts of what else has happened in the last decade. Do they have kids? She sits up and looks around the bedroom for more framed photos, but there are none. She's relieved. Being forced into a mum role would require acting beyond her ability. What holidays have they been on? Where do they live? Wherever she is doesn't sound like London. No howling sirens, no clanking tubes, no whirring buses. She glances toward the windows and sees an oak tree outside, its leaves swaying in a breeze. Her best guess is Surrey. Probably Kingston. Where else would they be? Although the tiny prospect that she could be in an entirely different country sends a bolt of excitement through her. She turns to the side table again to find a charging phone, but there isn't one there.

Frankie shivers and shoves her hands back under the duvet covers, rubbing them energetically together to warm up. It's summer, but there's a chilly air in the room. It brings back memories of waking up with foggy breath and feeling instantly irritated with Toby. Toby was always on his high horse about having the central heating switched on, even in the dead of winter. As if there were something admirable about weathering the cold. When Frankie reached for the central heating switch, he'd get her a jumper, she'd give him the middle finger, and then use the middle finger to flick it on. When she was asleep, Toby would creep down into the kitchen, turn the heating off and tell her the next morning that humans sleep better in cold air. That Scandinavian parents put their babies out to nap in the snow because it makes them sleep longer and deeper. Every time, Frankie's response was that she was neither Scandinavian nor a baby, but that he was very welcome to sleep outside if he wanted to. He thought she was joking.

Frankie scans the bedroom and smiles when she sees the wallpaper. It's dark navy, with a city skyline etched in white running along the bottom. Battersea Power Station, Westminster, the London Eye, St. Paul's. She follows the sketch upward to the ceiling, where the navy continues and is interrupted by tiny yellow speckles for stars. London at night. The true love of her life.

On the wall to Frankie's left is a familiar portrait, which her mum painted when she was sixteen. Her head is thrown back in laughter, the square jaw she's always been self-conscious of on show. She's wearing a black velvet choker with a diamanté cross pendant and she has silver glitter butterfly clips arranged in two neat rows at her temples. Her mum used one of Frankie's favorite photographs of her and Alice, taken on the night of their GCSE dance. She accidentally over-plucked Alice's left eyebrow while they were getting ready, and to win her forgiveness, Frankie over-plucked hers. She took it too far again and left herself with one slightly raised eyebrow, which never fully grew back. "It makes you look really judgmental." Alice had giggled, as her shoulders shook and she struggled to get the words out. "Well, I guess it really suits me, then," Frankie sighed back, smiling and raising the eyebrow even higher, causing Alice to collapse in a fit of laughter on the bed.

Frankie lifts her hand and runs her fingers along said brow, smiling as she remembers how carefree she felt in that moment. The biggest decision she had to make was hair up or down. Frankie misses laughing without abandon with Alice like that

A reversing truck beeping outside disrupts her daydream.

Frankie climbs out of bed quietly and squishes her toes into the super-soft deep-pile carpet. She'd release a ridiculously loud "ahhh" if she wasn't afraid that Toby might hear her, wherever he is. Frankie isn't ready to face him yet. She looks down at the carpet, spots the tie-dye T-shirt she's wearing, and feels comforted. When she was fourteen, her mum had a stall for the summer at Spitalfields Market called "Art and Soul"

148

where punters could pay £5 for a tie-dye T-shirt or a live song. Frankie was roped in to help flog the T-shirts, as her mum performed regardless of being paid. The stall didn't take off, which meant the family got tie-dye T-shirts in their Christmas stockings for the next five years.

Frankie hugs the shirt against her and walks over to the white built-in wardrobes that fit the entire wall in front of the bed, running her hand along the smooth matte doors. She's always wanted built-in wardrobes. With the size of her bedroom, she'd have to choose between a bed or built-ins. Besides, she's never seen the point of decorating a rental beyond the soft furnishings. It feels too temporary, too transient. If she invested in decorating it, she'd get stuck there. She's been telling herself that for over a decade.

Frankie opens the far left door of the wardrobe and jumps back as a stack of random clothes drops from the top shelf and lands in a heap at her feet. Her side looks like a TK Maxx sale. Wide-eyed, she rummages through the clothing clutter, wondering why she's like this in this life. She's neat now. Not Toby level, just normal human level. As she pulls out items at random, she's pleased to see that her style doesn't seem to have strayed too far in this married life. She'd wear any of it today. She finds a pair of pale skinny jeans with subtle rips at the knees and quickly puts them on in case Toby returns. Then, she reaches both arms into the wardrobe and starts to remove all the clothing in bulk, piling it onto the bed behind her.

"Hey!" she whispers with a smile, when she sees her boho belt lying on the bottom of the cupboard. She bends down, picks it up, runs it through her fingers and wraps it around her hips, pushing the poppers in at the front and patting it when she's finished. She pushes open the cupboard, looks at herself in the mirror and sighs. It doesn't look as good as she remembers. Maybe just as bad as the butterfly clips in her hair. She rips it off and throws it on the bed.

With the rails and shelves empty, Frankie closes the left door and walks over to the right. Toby's side is just as she expected, his clothes arranged neatly by color and into item types. He was always so organized. The kind of person who'd decant different pasta into labeled Tupperware containers, even at uni. Frankie used to tease him about being old before his time. Little did she know it would lead to their demise.

Her eyes run over his pristine stacks, until they land on a pile that makes her skin prickle. His folded T-shirts. She squeezes her eyes tight in anger and petulantly ruffles the top one before shutting the door quickly and spinning around. Something on the floor by the bed catches her eye, and the prickles turn into giant spikes. The fucking Dustbuster. Or, "Trusty Dusty" as Toby would shout over the agonizing whirr as he did his daily morning vacuum on all fours, while making loud comments on how much of her hair was stuck in the carpet threads. It drove her mad, as it would anyone. At the time, she just accepted it as one of his quirks. She'd tell herself that there are far worse things than being cleaning-obsessed. She could have been with someone who had no sense of home hygiene at all, like Justin, who would scarf down Pot Noodles in bed after a night out and leave the container on the floor for days afterward. One

Christmas, Alice woke up to find him peeing into an empty Quality Street tub because he was too lazy to go to the loo. They broke up for a day, as a result.

The sound of deep laughter outside startles Frankie. She inches toward the window, and slowly peers out onto the street below. Her stomach lurches when she sees Toby in a white dressing gown holding grocery bags and talking to a Tesco delivery driver by the gate. They must be in the UK. Her heart deflates a little.

Frankie's so used to seeing Toby on social media that spotting him now in real life is like seeing a celebrity. He looks even more handsome in person. And even more handsome than he was at twenty-three, with silver flecks scattered at his temples and a dark stubble that makes his chiseled jawline more defined. When he turns around, she jumps back from the window, hoping he hasn't seen her.

Frankie hears a front door slam shut, and the grocery packets rustle as they're put down on the floor.

"Frankie?" Toby shouts.

"Fuck!" she whispers.

Then she hears steps coming up the stairs.

"Fuck!" she whispers again, panicking as she darts left and then right, before making a bolt for the en suite bathroom on the other side of the bed and slamming the door shut just as the bedroom door handle starts to turn. Her chest heaves up and down with heavy breaths as she leans her back against the door. The soft carpet hides the sound of footsteps. He could be anywhere.

"Happy birthday, Franks!" Toby bellows through the door. "What the hell happened to your wardrobe?"

Frankie gasps and lunges for the shower, switching it on in the hope the water noise will drown out her panting.

"Hi!" she shouts back. "Just in the shower!"

"No rush! Take as long as you like!" he replies.

"Um . . . OK?" Frankie responds, as if she wouldn't take as long as she likes on any day.

"I got some new shower mold wipes, they're under the sink," Toby shouts again. "Want me to fold your clothes up and put them away?"

"That's OK, I'll do it later!" Frankie responds, rolling her eyes, as she approaches the sink and stops abruptly at the sight of her reflection. She looks exactly the same, she's relieved to see, stroking her raised eyebrow. Her hair feels heavy on her neck. She scoops the waves up and twists them around, gathering them into a pile on top of her head. In search of a hair tie, she yanks open the top drawer of a bathroom cabinet next to the sink and spots an unopened box with a prescription on the cover. An address! Frankie grabs the packet and reads *Kingston* in type.

"Of course we're in Kingston," she whispers, as she flips the box to the front.

Her mouth drops open when she sees the label. Nafarelin. The IVF drug.

Eighteen

Frankie's fingers shake as she lifts up her T-shirt and looks at her stomach, her heart palpitating at the prospect of having a living human hijacking her insides. Dropping her shirt, she lowers the toilet lid, sits down and counts for ten seconds as she breathes in. How is married Frankie meant to feel about it? The Frankie she knows would be freaking out. The Frankie she knows *is* freaking out.

On the one hand, a baby might be a welcome change in a decade-long marriage. At thirty-six, she'll have been with Toby half her life. But you have to *want* kids. *Really* want them, as Alice once explained to Frankie over a glass of wine in her bomb site kitchen, six months into motherhood. Seconds later, Alice unexpectedly broke down into violent sobs about how exhausted and bored she was. How having Ellie was harder than she ever expected, relentless and thankless. How dirty and ugly she felt every day, having no time to properly shower

153

and pamper herself. How she was sick to death of having greasy hair and wearing snotty spew-stained leggings, but they were the only thing she felt comfortable in. How she was desperate to have just one morning when she woke up feeling ready to conquer the world instead of cave under the weight of it, but the sleepless nights made it an impossibility. How guilt-ridden she felt for feeling these things.

"I mean, of course I completely adore her, Franks." Alice sniffed. "When Ellie smiles, my heart melts into a puddle of warm, sticky goo. But when she wakes up my heart sinks into a pit of despair. Because I know that teeny-tiny window of time I had is over and it'll be hours before I can be alone and do something productive again. And when she is asleep, I don't want to be productive. I want to lie prostrate on the carpet and watch something that isn't cartoons. The house looks like shit. I look like shit. Am I a bad mum for not using those fifteen minutes to make organic chickpea and spinach muffins? Am I a bad mum for spending my day counting down the minutes until she naps again? Am I a bad mum for not talking to her constantly to help her reach her milestones?"

"No, you're a *great* mum for worrying about these things, Alice," Frankie said. "I'm pretty sure your mum didn't worry as much as you do. I know my mum didn't. My mum probably plonked me in a laundry basket in front of the washing machine while she went outside for a fag. You have nothing to feel guilty about. I blame the Internet. There's too much information floating about. Don't read so much."

Alice lifted her head up, took her wineglass and was milliseconds away from a sip when Ellie started whining through the monitor.

"Want me to go up?" Frankie asked, squeezing Alice's shoulder. Alice nodded gratefully.

A rhythmic bang on the bathroom door startles Frankie from her daydream. She doesn't answer. Toby knows that she's in the shower, why is he knocking again?

"I have a surprise for you when you're out!" he shouts.

"OK!" Frankie responds, standing up from the toilet and removing her T-shirt entirely, rotating her body back and forth to examine her naked self in the mirror for any changes. Nothing's changed here either except . . . Frankie spins around again. She has a star tattoo on her left shoulder blade. A tattoo! She always talked about getting one, but she never had the guts to commit to it. As she twists her neck to see it close up, a smirk spreads across her face. She likes this Frankie. Perhaps being married has brought out the rebel in her. Or maybe she's turning into her mum. Her face freezes in the mirror at the thought.

In the shower, Frankie makes a pledge to herself. To fully embrace married, possibly pregnant, life. After all, acting the part is the whole point of being here. To experience and understand what being married to Toby is like, so she can make her big choice. She has to be all in, or all out. She steps out of the shower, dries herself off quickly, coils a towel around her wet hair and puts on the white dressing gown hanging on the back of the door. It's inscribed *Mrs. McKenzie Martinez*. She smiles. The name has a nice ring to it. She takes a few confident steps toward the bathroom door, feels her stomach twist with anticipation, grabs the handle before she hesitates further and flings it open dramatically, the steam bellowing out behind her like the dry ice reveal on *Stars in Their Eyes*.

*

Toby is lying on top of the bed surrounded by red rose petals, which he has scattered across the covers. In the middle of the bed is a wooden tray table with filter coffee, croissants, orange juice, a vase of Frankie's favorite white roses and a small black velvet box. Despite her despairing at romantic gestures and shunning the spotlight, Toby's thoughtfulness always made her feel spoiled and special, and she's pleased to see he hasn't lost this side of him, even after this long. He always treated her like a queen, even when she didn't always return it. Or deserve it. The only time she's come close again to being treated like this was with Callum. He would also do grand—supposedly romantic—gestures, but they were more about him showing off than showering her.

"Wow!" Frankie exhales and forces a big grin to mask her butterflies.

She feels instantly shaky at the sight of him lying just a few feet away from her, and is worried that if she says anything more he'll hear the tremble in her voice. For a second, being here together feels forbidden, like an illicit affair. Like he's somehow cheating on Freya, his wife in the real world. But of course, this is the real world. And the Toby in front of her now, pouring her a coffee, hasn't even met Freya. Has he? As she climbs onto the bed next to him, she breathes him in. It's comforting. He feels familiar. He feels like home. He feels right. Remembering how it used to make him laugh, Frankie shuffles her head under the covers and nestles into his shoulder. Then she starts to rub her feet together and chirp like a cricket. She hears him chuckle.

"Whoa, whoa!" he says after a few seconds.

She pokes her head out from under the covers.

"I'm going to spill your coffee!" he says, holding the mug in the air.

"Wait, can I have this?" Frankie asks, sitting up. She takes the coffee and stares at it, the Nafarelin box flashing through her mind. It was unopened. Maybe she hasn't started the course.

"You're allowed two hundred milligrams of caffeine a day while we're doing IVF." Toby smiles and takes a sip of his.

So not pregnant. Yet.

Of course Toby would know this. He's always been a reliable swat. He would have read all the IVF books. She leans forward and kisses him on the cheek. He turns his cheek and kisses her lips, resting his hand on the back of her head and pushing her softly into him. She breathes in his Issey Miyake aftershave, flooding her mind with memories of the happiest times in their relationship. Nights out, days in, cozy weekends and just sitting quietly together soaking up each other's company. When they come up for air, Toby looks back and forth between her eyes, plants another kiss on her cheek and then nods toward a black velvet box on the breakfast tray.

"Want to open your present?" Toby whispers, making her skin tingle.

All Frankie wants to do is stare at his face from two inches away, while counting her lucky stars that she's been given this second chance to be with him again.

"Yes, please." She smiles as she leans back and reaches for the box.

"Wait, card first!" he says, reaching for the card and handing it to her.

Frankie carefully opens the envelope and smiles when she sees the front. It's a photo from their first date. A selfie they took in the laundry, with their beers raised and the dank concrete walls behind them. Toby has a silly grin on his face and Frankie is hiding a giant smile behind her bottle. It was always her favorite photo of them.

Inside, Toby's written an essay, as usual. His birthday cards always made Frankie feel terrible. He had a talent for writing touching messages that sounded like something out of *The Notebook*. Frankie—the actual writer—never knew what to write. Her messages were always brief, generic and a bit forced. By nature, she isn't as emotionally open. Toby wears his heart on his sleeve, she wears hers hidden under her jumper, with her arms tightly folded so no one can catch a glimpse.

Happy birthday Franks, aka Noodle, aka Frankie Hankie Pankie.

You're my love, my luck and my life. You're thirty-six years old! A spring chick, but even cuter. Thank you

*for sharing the last eighteen of them with me. We've hit
a few rough patches recently, but I feel like we've never
been stronger. I've never loved you more than I do this
morning.*

   *Here are 36 reasons why. 1. Your smile 2. The hand
you use to hide your smile. 3. Your snoring.*

The list goes on, but Frankie can't help but focus on one
part. *We've hit a few rough patches recently.* What does *that*
mean?

"Thank you," Frankie says, putting the card upright on the
bedside table.

She takes the box and lifts the lid slowly. Inside, lying on
black silk is a single silver key. She removes it, holds it up and
looks at him quizzically.

"Come on, you," Toby says, jumping out of bed. "Get your
slippers on."

Outside the bedroom is a small landing. There are framed
black-and-white photos hanging in two neat lines across the
walls, which Frankie stares at as she walks slowly past. The
only photo she vaguely recognizes is a selfie of the Awesome
Foursome in Ibiza. She stops and leans in. It's the moment that
never was. The moment that Frankie and Toby returned from
Torre des Savinar newly engaged. They're covered in streamer
confetti, holding champagne glasses and huge smiles. Frankie,
who was the same person back then, must have been having
the same thoughts. Fear, doubt and despair at the decision to
get engaged so young. But she's covered it up well here.

"Are you coming?" Toby shouts from somewhere down-stairs.

"Coming!" she shouts back.

Toby leads her through a dream kitchen with navy cup-boards and rose brass light fixtures hanging over a wooden is-land with a butler sink. It's all so grown-up, and Frankie can't quite believe it's hers. On one side of the kitchen is a living area with a sofa, footstool and huge flat-screen TV. On the other side is a wall of bifold doors. Toby opens one side and holds out his arm for her to take his hand. She steps through the doors and onto a decking area just outside, walking past a dark wooden table and chairs for six. The fresh air hits her instantly, cooling her hot cheeks. Taking her hand, he leads her across a small but perfectly manicured lawn, flanked by two rows of white roses. And at the end of the lawn is a small shed, with glass doors for a wall. Frankie glances at Toby, who turns to beam at her as they walk, the cold damp dew soaking into her slippers. When they reach the door, he steps aside and gestures for Frankie to open it up. She starts laughing as she does, embarrassed by the attention.

When she steps inside, Toby's close behind her. He hugs her from behind, reaches over to the wall and switches on the light. She gasps.

"What!" she says, turning around and looking at him.

"A castle fit for a queen," he replies, kissing her on the cheek.

Frankie steps forward into the toasty warm room and spins around a few times. The home office looks like it's been plucked from one of her Pinterest boards and magically brought to real life. At one end is a huge glass desk, with a comfy-looking white leather chair facing a large computer monitor. On the desk are photo frames, stationery holders, a proper mouse mat and coasters for coffee mugs. Behind the desk is a bookcase, with books arranged by color. And at the other end of the room is a small kitchenette with a fridge, kettle and mug tree. A huge armchair covered in neatly arranged blankets is behind them, next to a side table, oil heater and a fluffy white rug.

"Toby!" Frankie says, softly.

"Do you like it?"

"I don't like it, I love it!"

"This is why I've been staying up so late," he says. "I really wanted to tell you, especially after the other night, but I also really wanted it to be a surprise."

Frankie stares at him, wondering what he's talking about.

"This is . . . incredible. The nicest thing anyone's ever done for me," she says, in the hope that Toby hasn't done anything even bigger before.

He walks up to her, wraps her in his arms, lifts her up and kisses her. When he pulls back, he looks in her eyes and smiles.

"Stay here. Make yourself at home, and I'll fetch you your last caffeine fix for the day. You could even . . ." He pauses.

"What is it?"

"Well, I know it's your birthday, but that couples' counseling homework has to be in by tonight. You could take a look at it?"

Frankie feels her jaw drop. Couples' counseling? What possible reason do they have to be in couples' counseling?

Toby starts shaking his head vigorously. "Don't, actually. Sorry. It's your birthday. I shouldn't have brought it up."

"It's fine," Frankie says, feeling winded by the news. "If it has to be done by tonight, I'll do it. No problem."

He smiles at her and nods in thanks, before making his way across the lawn.

Frankie wanders over to the computer, takes a seat and wriggles herself into a comfortable position. Her heart flutters as she looks around, and it takes all her willpower not to emit a squeal of excitement. Why would she ever say no to this life? Toby is gorgeous, kind and thoughtful. She has a huge wardrobe and a home office that's almost the same size as her apartment.

She wiggles the mouse and inputs her trusty old password.

The screen comes to life and Frankie hits the email tab. The first email is from someone called Ed Slater. The subject is "Interview: today, 2 p.m." Frankie opens it, a wave of panic running through her that she should be doing—or have done something—by this afternoon.

McKenzie,

Interview confirmed with Jasper Dixon at Great Oaks Care Home at two. I know that interviewing another centenarian is hardly Pulitzer material, but the local punters love this shit.

We'll get you that national headline story soon.

Ed

P.S. Happy birthday!

P.P.S. Possible headline wordplay on Dixon—Dix Cent?
Decent? I'll shut up now.
Editor in Chief, *The Kingston Gazette*

Frankie opens up her browser and types in "Great Oaks Care Home." It's an old age home, about a five-minute drive from the house. She sighs and sits back. She likes talking to the elderly. Wise souls like Mr. Graham. She smiles, remembering how his sweet face lights up when she drops his Turkish Delight and Fanta off at the end of each day.

Then she turns back to the screen and sees a forward from Toby.

Just a quick reminder x

She scrolls down the email to find another email from a Dr. Zofia Zielinski.

Dear Frankie and Toby,
I'm feeling pleased with the progress we made today. Attached is the homework for this week. As always, do it separately and don't confer until our counseling session next Thursday.
Regards,
Dr Zofia

In her real life, Frankie would dream of being by Toby's side, like Freya. Wishing she hadn't said no, imagining how comfortable she'd be. It's not like Toby has completely changed. His obsession with tidiness might be grating, but he's so generous and caring. The girls used to joke that he was the unofficial campus counselor. And he still loves her so much, eighteen years later. He has a big heart. All the qualities that made Frankie fall in love with him years ago are still here, along with the honey-colored skin and big brown eyes that melt her insides.

It's not Toby who's the problem here. It's her. It always is. Frankie the Self-Saboteur feels furious with herself that she'd put this all at risk for a life adventure she didn't end up going on anyway.

Frankie opens the attachment, reads the first question and shoves her chair away from her desk, in shock.

List the reasons you want a divorce.

Nineteen

When Frankie enters the kitchen, Toby is pouring cake batter into a pan at the kitchen island.

"Is that a carrot cake?" Frankie asks.

"Of course! You have to have your favorite cake on your birthday, don't you? I mean, it's basically the law." He grins at her, wiping his hands on his apron and throwing a tea towel over his shoulder.

Frankie rushes up to him and throws her arms around his waist, burying her head into his chest and breathing in the smell of cake batter, mint soap and woody aftershave. The hug is a thank you for being so perfect, an apology for any hurt she's caused him, and it's a cling on for dear life, hoping desperately that she hasn't destroyed their relationship permanently.

"I love you," Frankie mumbles into his chest. It feels weird to say it out loud after so long, but in this moment she truly does. She wants to hold him like this forever and never let him go.

Toby leans down and kisses the top of her head.

"I love you too, Noodle," he whispers, wrapping his arms around her and squeezing her tightly.

"I'm so sorry," she says.

"It's OK. Everything is going to be OK. We just need to make a few changes. Like Dr Zofia said, relationships are about compromise. No one and nothing is perfect. I'm not. You're not. We just have to learn to live—maybe even love—the imperfections."

"You're perfect to me," Frankie whispers back. "We don't need therapy, do we?"

"Whoa," Toby replies, removing her from their clutch gently. "Don't say that."

"Why? There's nothing wrong with us, we're fine!" Frankie says, looking up at him as she pats his chest. Things evidently aren't *that* fine, but Frankie would rather not know. She doesn't want anything risking what she has right now, and in therapy all sorts of things could be dragged up.

"Frankie, that's what made us go to counseling in the first place. Last week you said you wanted to leave. You can't have changed your mind that quickly. We'll be fine, we just need to work through it. You were bothered by my behavior and bottling things up. Now it's time to get everything out in the open. Leave nothing unsaid."

"OK," she grumbles, although it's exactly what she doesn't want to do.

"And, you know, I think it'll be good for me to get a few things off my chest. Because, Franks, there are a few things that have been bothering me too."

Frankie sits down on the kitchen stool and picks a grape from the bunch in the bowl in front of her, biting half off.

"Like what?" she asks.

"Let's save it for our next session," Toby replies. "It's definitely not a discussion for your birthday."

Frankie falls silent, as she chews on the other grape half slowly, wondering what it could be.

"Just one thing," she says. "Name one thing I do that bothers you, and I'll stop doing it immediately."

"Fine," Toby says, sighing as he opens the kitchen drawer. When he turns around, he's holding the grape scissors. The ones he's had forever.

"You aren't using the grape scissors."

Frankie looks at her half-chewed grape and starts laughing. But stops when he doesn't respond in kind.

"I totally forgot, sorry."

"I've asked you a million times before, and you're still doing it."

"I'm sorry, I just don't understand what the big deal is!" Frankie exclaims, popping the rest of the grape in her mouth and shrugging.

"I know you think it's petty, but it's just a pet hate of mine. It leaves us with a depressing-looking bowl of stalks and I hate seeing it when I walk into this kitchen. You know how much it bothers me, and you know that I'm happiest when things are neat, but you carry on doing it."

Frankie takes the scissors from him and trims the stalk.

"I'll remember next time, promise," she says.

167

Toby sets the timer, leans across the island and pecks her on the temple.

"Thank you," he whispers. "That would mean a lot."

Then he walks over to the fridge and examines a to-do list that's placed on the door. He removes the magnetic wipe next to it, erases an activity from the top and carefully places the wipe back, spending a second to align it perfectly.

Toby has always been tidy, but this is more extreme than ever. The kind of obsessive behavior of someone who's deeply unhappy. Maybe it's not just about the grapes. Maybe it's about their entire existence.

Frankie looks around the room. When she first walked in here, she was bowled over by its beauty. Now all she feels is suffocated by its order. The cooking books are arranged by cuisine, and look like they've never been opened. The fake pot plants are arranged in height order. The candles look like they've never been lit and are perfectly level. The sofas look like they've never been sat on, the cushions placed symmetrically one across the other at exact angles, and perfectly plumped. This isn't a home. It's a show home. This is a show life. How would Toby cope with a toddler scribbling on the walls? Or would a toddler help him stop sweating the small stuff?

She presses her thumb and index finger together.

"Also." Toby turns around. "I know it's your birthday, but are you definitely going to put away those clothes upstairs? I wanted to show Justin the new bathroom, but it's a bit embarrassing up there now. I really am happy to do it for you, if you'd like?"

"Well, I know how much you *love* folding clothes, but I'll do it. I said I would. Promise," she says, squeezing her thumb and index finger together even harder.

"You know me!" Toby says with a smile.

"Hey, have you seen my phone?" Frankie asks Toby, changing the subject.

"In its normal place," Toby says, nonchalantly.

"Do you mind getting it for me?" Frankie asks. "I'm just going to make another coffee."

"*Decaf* coffee," Toby replies, dusting his hands on his apron and spinning around. He reaches up to open a cupboard behind him, and takes two phones from a shelf that Frankie can't reach. "I mean, technically we shouldn't because it's only eight forty-five, but I guess it's your birthday. I'm sure fifteen minutes won't do us any harm. I won't tell Dr Zofia if you don't!"

Frankie watches him hand her phone over, feeling the familiar panic of losing control rise inside her. Toby had often complained about how much time she spent on Facebook. Had this been one of his marital complaints?

"I just need to check if I have any birthday messages," she says, over the hiss of the coffee machine.

"Sure," he says curtly, as he hands her phone over.

Frankie glances at the screen to see ten new messages, and two missed phone calls from her mum and dad. When she places the phone beside her mug, Toby reaches over and turns the screen face down.

She stares at him.

"We're meant to be practicing being present with each other,

169

Franks. Besides, I really think the bedtime phone amnesty has helped, don't you? I feel like we're more connected. I'm definitely sleeping better. I don't know why we didn't do it before. It's not like we're missing out on anything between 10 p.m. and 9 a.m."

"Until we wake up one morning to find out that my dad has had a heart attack and is in hospital, or something," she replies.

"It's only for a month. If you want to go back to staring at a bright blue screen for hours before you fall asleep, it's your choice. I can't control that."

"Despite your best efforts," Frankie mutters.

"Look, I just think we should give it a fair shot. But let's change the subject. What are you thinking of for food tonight? Birthday girl's choice! I'll make anything you like. Alice said she'd bring dessert, so that's covered."

"Hmmm, something simple?" she says. "I don't want you to be stuck by the stove while everyone's here. What about a big charcuterie thingy? Meats, cheese, pickles, et cetera."

"Done!" he says. "Although, maybe we could level up with some steak and chips?"

"So . . . steak and chips?" she says, smiling.

"Yeah." He laughs.

This isn't a battle she can be bothered to pick.

"Did you use a decaf pod?" Toby asks, watching her take a sip of her coffee.

"Yep," Frankie replies tightly.

"Lucky I'm here to keep tabs!" Toby laughs.

"Shouldn't you be at work?" Frankie asks, wishing he was.

"I took the day off, remember?" Toby answers. "I didn't want to leave you to celebrate your birthday alone! The last time I did that, you went and got a tattoo without telling me!" He laughs, but Frankie isn't convinced Toby found it that funny.

"Well, I've got an interview at an old age home at 2 p.m. so I won't be here all day," Frankie replies, ignoring the barbed comment.

✳

After breakfast, Frankie takes her tea to the garden office to read through her phone messages alone, after finally accepting Toby's offer to pack away her wardrobe. While the idea of him folding her clothes in that painstaking way makes every inch of her body clench, she has limited time in this world and she doesn't want to waste a minute.

> **Alice:** Happy birthday hot stuff!
> Looking forward to later.
> Ellie's experimenting with a new
> shade of lippie.
> It's called Kinder Surprise.

Alice's message is accompanied by a picture of Ellie with chocolate smeared across her face.

> **Frankie:** It's a vibe!
> What time are you getting here?

Alice: Toby said 7

Frankie: Perfect

Frankie scrolls through her other messages. A few of them are from people she's never heard of. She replies with a blanket "Thank you! x" to all.

On Facebook, she's been tagged in photos with strangers in places she's never seen before. Clues that help her piece together the last few years. To her relief, none of the photos raise too many questions. As she had predicted at Torre des Savinar, her existence seems to have revolved entirely around the safety net of Surrey. Scrolling through the photos of bars, restaurants and walks, she seems happy. Maybe she didn't need to be so afraid of this. But that's social media for you, isn't it? Smiling on the outside, screaming on the inside. Her phone pings again.

Priya: Happy birthday, babe! I'm so sorry but I can't make it tonight. Deadline bollocks. Looks like it's going to be a late one.

Frankie: No problem, love, totally get it.

Priya: Boozy catch-up in Londers next week? Just the two of us?

> **Frankie:** A THOUSAND TIMES YES

> **Priya:** Cool
> Have you told him yet?

Frankie pauses. Told who what?

> **Frankie:** No . . .

> **Priya:** Frankie . . .
> Have you changed your mind?
> It's OK to change your mind

> **Frankie:** I'm not sure

And of course, she hasn't a clue. What could she have changed her mind about? Counseling? Frankie logs on to her computer. If she wants to discover the truth about what she is or isn't changing her mind about, her browser history should reveal everything. She clicks on Show All, her eyes expanding when her recent searches are revealed. There are pages upon pages of low-cost divorce lawyers, journalist jobs on LinkedIn and an article on "Can a baby save a marriage?"

> **Priya:** Well the flat's yours from
> November, if you still want it. x

A knock on the door startles her, and she presses the escape button quickly.

"Everything OK?" Toby asks, frowning.

"Yeah, fine, you just gave me a fright. I was . . . deep in thought." Frankie smiles back.

"Sounds promising! Hey, all good for Sunday roast at Gran's?" Tom asks, his phone in his hand, with Agnes presumably on the other end.

"Sounds wonderful," Frankie replies, even though she can think of nothing worse. At least she won't be here by then.

Twenty-two hours left.

Twenty

Frankie hasn't driven a car since she was twenty-one years old. She never needed one in London. That's the beauty of city living, you're only ever a stone's throw away from a train, Tube or bus stop to take you wherever you want to go. Or, in Frankie's case, a wave away from the comfort of a cab.

Sitting bolt upright with her nose an inch from the steering wheel, she drives down Kingston High Street like a learner. Every second, her eyes dart toward the sat-nav that's directing her to Great Oaks Care Home. Frankie glances in the rear-view mirror to see a long trail of cars behind her, and her fingers tighten their grip as her heart beats faster.

Why does Frankie feel so out of place in this world? She grew up in Surrey, this should feel familiar. And who wouldn't want to live in a world with a handsome and supportive husband who keeps their home immaculate, brings her breakfast in bed and builds her sheds? Who wouldn't want to live in this leafy, safe neighborhood with close friends around the corner?

And who wouldn't want a job that brings joy to the community? To add a bit of spice to an otherwise bland day for the elderly? It's a lot more meaningful than mocking celebrities for their manicure choices.

Perhaps she could learn to fit in here. Maybe she needs time to get used to it. Memories of her single city life are still fresh and it's only natural that she needs time to adjust. If she chooses this life, all that pressure she's under to reach those life milestones could disappear. Well, until other pressures start to emerge. Like kids. Or no kids. The weight of feeling like *this is it* for the rest of her life.

Frankie's brain hurts.

As she turns into the driveway of Great Oaks, the cars behind her rush past. She pulls into an empty parking space at the front of the care home, switches the engine off and drops her head onto the steering wheel, accidentally releasing a loud honk. She bounces back upright, and sees two old women in wheelchairs glaring at her through the window.

"Sorry!" she whispers, as if they can hear her.

Frankie likes the elderly, but she can't bear the thought of her body seizing up. In her heart, she's still sixteen and she can't imagine ever feeling differently.

She grabs her notepad and throws open her car door.

At the front door, she presses the buzzer and waits, listening to slow footsteps getting louder on the gravel behind her. She turns to see an elderly couple, one arm linked and the other clutching walking sticks, shuffle toward the front lawn.

They're whispering and giggling. The sight soothes her. Could that be her and Toby in fifty years' time?

Fifty years.

Frankie feels her forehead break into a sweat.

"Great Oaks, how can I help you?" a gentle voice sounds from the intercom.

But Frankie doesn't answer. Instead, she takes a few slow steps back.

"Hello?" the voice sounds again.

Frankie turns, runs down the steps and jumps back into the car. She grips the steering wheel tight and presses the back of her head hard against the leather headrest. She feels bad. Terrible, in fact. She's never missed a deadline, let alone an entire assignment. And poor Jasper Dixon is probably looking forward to this. She imagines him sitting alone in his room, waiting for company. She sighs, sits up, and goes to reopen the door. But pauses again.

Mabel did advise her to use her time here wisely. And it's not like she really exists in this world, is it? If she decides to come back here, she'll commit and give Jasper the best interview of his life. She'll bring flowers and chocolates, to celebrate.

Ignoring the inner voice that's tutting at her for being so selfish, she starts the car, and glances at the clock.

It's 2.05 p.m.

She's got five hours until her friends arrive. And eighteen hours left to figure out if this is the life she wants. Frankie turns up the radio, and speeds out of the driveway.

Twenty-One

Frankie has lived in her beloved Victorian mansion block on Clapham Common South Side for over twelve years. As she sits on the cool steps huddled up in a chunky gray cardigan she found on the back seat of the car, she sips a flat white from her favorite little indie coffee shop on The Pavement opposite Cock Pond.

She places a hand on the concrete beside her, remembering how much these steps have seen.

That night in her first week when she couldn't find her keys after the office Christmas party and emptied the entire contents of her handbag all over the porch.

That was how she met Tom.

"Um, hi there, hot mess! Need some help?" Tom giggled, standing in the front door wearing a navy flannel dressing gown and holding a glass of red.

"I'm so sorry!" Frankie panted, her hair falling in front of her face as she scrambled to gather her strewn makeup, pens, hairbrushes, heels, a squashed packet of Marlboro Lights and an array of broken lighters from city breaks around Europe. "I can't find my keys, I'm new here. I'm Frankie."

"Hi." He smiled and waved. "Tom. And . . . I think these might belong to you?"

He pointed to the keyhole, where Frankie's keys were dangling from the lock.

"Oh my god." Frankie's arms dropped to her sides, a half-eaten packet of Monster Munch falling from her bag and floating down the steps. "Sorry." She grimaced. "I was on the phone. Must have totally forgotten I was already halfway in. I've been at a Christmas party, so . . . ."

"You're shitfaced. No explanation needed. Been there, done that, will do it again," he said with a laugh. "It's about time we got a PIN pad, it's 2010 for god's sake. Anyway, fancy a nightcap in exchange for a cig?"

The next morning, Frankie woke up under a flannel dressing gown blanket on Tom's blue velvet sofa to the smell of bacon and the sound of him singing along to Katy Perry's "Firework" in a falsetto voice.

Almost thirteen years later and it feels like the first time she's here again. She cranes her neck up to her flat window on the fourth floor, noticing that it's ajar and wondering what life is being lived there now and whether they're sitting at the windowsill staring across at the common like she used to do on Saturday afternoons.

When she first arrived that December all those years ago, she was freshly single and full of hope. She had her mum's battered old suitcase at her feet and Potato the kangaroo in her pocket for company. Her heart was bursting with excitement about what stories would unfold here. About where these steps would take her, and who they'd welcome back. The following summer, to the delight of her neighbors, Frankie placed a few flowerpots by the front door to brighten the entrance. They aren't here now.

Behind her, the front door bursts open and a young woman dashes down the steps beside her and runs across the car park. The woman glances back in Frankie's direction without stopping, her carry cup in one hand while she types something on her phone in the other. Frankie smiles at the scene, wondering what adventure the woman is in such a hurry to embark on.

Maybe it's a first date, or even better, a second date. It feels like she's not had one for a long time, but second dates are so much easier, with the awkward small talk out of the way.

As the woman rushes across the South Side, darting between the traffic, Frankie feels a surge of envy at her freedom. She's going where she wants to, when she wants to and she has no one but herself to be responsible for. She'll get back home whenever she feels like it. Maybe she won't return until the morning. These steps are hers to come and go as she pleases. Frankie wishes they were hers.

Her phone pings.

> **Toby:** How is the interview going? What time are you going to be back?

180

Frankie stands up, brushing imaginary dirt off her lap. With sluggish and reluctant feet, she wanders away from her block, down the steps and across the road to the bench at Long Pond to visit the ducks.

These ducks were well fed by Frankie in her former life. It was payment for keeping her secret—and her company through some of her tougher times. When she felt like a loser because Callum had gone silent. When she felt lonely because her friends didn't have time to see her. When she felt lost because everything and everyone was changing around her, and she was just the same Frankie as she had been when she first arrived. She was just like the mansion block. While Clapham Common transformed over the years, with new shops opening every week, the building remained unchanged throughout. But maybe that's because it didn't need to change. Maybe it was perfectly fine just the way it was. If it's not broken, don't fix it. And if it is broken . . . well, it's easier to ignore it.

Frankie doesn't want to drive for an hour back to Kingston. She wants to bang on Tom's door, drag him to The Windmill and drink wine for five hours straight. She wants to inhale a bowl of potato wedges and sour cream, squished together on their favorite leather sofa. She wants to totter back to the mansion block afterward arm in arm, singing Katy Perry songs.

Then tomorrow morning, she wants to wake up on her own and when she likes, before wandering across the grass to Joseph's, where she'll pick up a flat white and two cinnamon swirl—one for her and one for Tom—taking the long route home around the common circumference, watching the same runners rush by. A few might even recognize her from her weekend morning routine, flashing her a quick smile as they pant past.

Toby's message should make her feel warm and fuzzy inside. In her old life, this is what she wanted. Or, at least, thought she wanted. Someone to come home to instead of Potato, someone to share a meal with, someone to cook a birthday cake for her. But now that she has it—now that she knows the freedom she'll have to sacrifice for it—she just wants to go back to the way things were. She presses reply to Toby.

> **Frankie:** Home by 6. Put the sparkling water on ice! :/

Why isn't she looking forward to this birthday dinner? She loves Alice more than anything.

> **Toby:** Aw. Don't worry, I'll make you a mocktail that'll knock your socks off!

Frankie smiles at his last message. Toby's trying so hard and here she is, barely trying at all. She's always believed that love can't be forced. But with this counseling and with enough time, could she love Toby like she used to?

A familiar giggle behind her breaks her thought, causing her to spin around on the bench.

It's Tom. He's walking her way fast, while chatting to someone on his mobile and waving a box from St. Joseph's in the air as he recounts what Frankie assumes is a tale from a late night.

"Spin? Are you mad? Of course I didn't go, I'm still spinning from those flaming sambucas. Nah, Joel was a good boy and stayed in. When are you back? OK. Cinema later? Yes, yes, I'll sign for your bloody parcel, stop panicking. See you later, turnip head."

I'll sign for your bloody parcel.

He must be on the phone to a neighbor. A neighbor that should be her.

When Tom catches her eye, she quickly turns back the other way, her heart beating loudly as she hears him approach. The bench sinks a little as he takes a seat on the other side. Frankie shuffles further away, her head fixed straight ahead and her eyes laser-focused on the ducks at the edge.

"Shit, sorry!" he says, as she glances quickly at him. "It's not me, it's these pastries, this box is at least five kilograms!"

Frankie smiles softly and pretends to sip her flat white, which she finished ten minutes ago. Tom looks exactly the same, with his big blue eyes and plump rosy cheeks, sitting under a head of frizzy yellow hair that led to the nickname SpongeTom Swear-Pants, which she coined a few weeks after their first meeting. With their hair, people would often assume they were siblings.

"Isn't Joseph's the BEST?" Tom says, pointing at her coffee cup. "Have you tried these cinnamon swirls? You'll never want to leave the common again they're so fucking good."

A lump forms in Frankie's throat, and she turns her head in the opposite direction so Tom doesn't see the tears in her eyes.

"Hey, are you OK?" Tom says, moving closer. "Who's done this to you?"

Frankie wipes the dripping tears away, and darts her eyes back to him with a strained smile.

"Sorry," she says, taking a deep breath in. "No one, I'm fine. I'm just going through a few things. I'll leave you in peace to enjoy that . . . cinnamon swirl."

"Wait," Tom says, his big eyes wide with worry. "Take this. It'll make you feel better, guaranteed."

He takes one cinnamon swirl, closes the box and hands it to her.

"My husband doesn't appreciate them anyway." Tom smiles. "And thus does not deserve the deliciousness."

It takes all Frankie's strength not to hug him, as she stands up and drops her coffee cup in the recycling bin.

"I'm fine," she says. "Really. Thanks though."

"Be kind to yourself, babe," Tom says, nodding at her. She feels his eyes on her back as she walks away, toward the last place she wants to visit before she returns to Kingston.

✳

Frankie isn't exactly proud of her emotional attachment to Kebab Palace, but the place smells like home to her. She'd stop in at least once a week, only ever late at night, feeling warmed and comforted by the sweet sticky air inside. Tom would tease her endlessly about it. But he was hardly one to talk. Tom had a secret attachment to tinned hot dog sausages, and kept a stash of them hidden in the cupboard under the sink.

"Hello and good afternoon!" Emir sings over the doorbell as she enters.

"Hi." She smiles, looking up at the menu, which she knows by heart.

"What can I get for you?" he asks.

"Um . . ." she murmurs quietly.

"I know what you want." He smiles. "It's my magic trick. I can read minds."

"Oh yeah?" She laughs.

He stares at her and strokes his smooth chin theatrically.

"Chicken shish with extra chili sauce." He points at her, his eyebrows raised.

"Hey presto!" Frankie giggles.

"New customers get a free drink, what would you like?" Emir says as he starts to assemble the kebab at his normal breakneck speed.

"Well, I'm not actually a new customer, so I think I'd be cheating," Frankie replies.

Emir pauses and looks up. "Really? I don't remember seeing you. I remember everybody. OK, so as an apology you'll get a free Diet Coke. You like Diet Coke, yes?"

"Thanks, Emir." Frankie smiles.

"You even know my name! I'm so sorry, I'm embarrassed," he says, shaking his head. "What's your name? I'll remember for next time."

"Frankie," she says.

"OK, OK, Frankie, Frankie, Frankie. I'll never forget it, Frankie!" he shouts, as he wraps the shish tightly in foil and hands it across the counter, sliding a Diet Coke from the display across to her.

Frankie pays for the kebab and walks toward the door, staring at the step and wincing as she remembers the last time she was here.

"Hey, Frankie!" Emir shouts.

She turns around.

"Mind your step there." He smiles.

Twenty-Two

At 6.55 p.m., Frankie swings open the front door and sees Alice in front of her.

"Justin's just gone to the garage to get a six-pack," she says, beaming. "Happy birthday!"

Overcome with emotion at seeing her safe face, Frankie lunges at Alice and grabs her in both arms, clasping her as tight as she possibly can. The familiar scent of Chanel Allure escapes from behind her ear. Alice giggles and pretends to choke. When Frankie comes up for breath, Alice sees the tears in her eyes, drops the flowers and takes her in her arms for a second hug.

"Everything is going to be OK, Frankles, I promise," Alice whispers in Frankie's ear.

"You don't know that," Frankie murmurs back.

"Of course I do. I know everything, don't you remember?" Alice replies.

Frankie wishes Alice knew everything. There aren't any secrets Frankie's kept from her, and it feels like torture to keep this one. Although, if Frankie did tell her what was happening, Alice would probably have her sent for psychiatric tests.

"Allie!" Toby shouts, his bare feet thudding confidently on the hallway hardwood floor. He leans down to kiss her on both cheeks. Alice, to Frankie's surprise, looks stiff as he does it. But only Frankie would notice the microscopic shift in the body language of her oldest friend.

"Tobes," she replies, handing him the flowers. "Been busy in the kitchen, I see?"

"You know me." He smiles. "You know the drill. Shoes at the door!" he says, pointing to the empty shoe rack in the hall, which Frankie assumes is for guests.

Alice sticks out her tongue at him as he walks back to the kitchen with the gifts, catching Frankie's eye just afterward as she removes her denim jacket and bag and places them on the brass coat stand. They share a mischievous giggle.

"Priya can't make it," Frankie comments as they walk into the kitchen, and Alice takes a seat on an island stool.

"Oooh shocker! When was the last time she could make it?" Alice scoffs.

"At some point, you two will have to accept that she will never trek all the way out here," Toby says, popping open a bottle of Prosecco and pouring a sensible-sized glass for Alice.

"And me?" Frankie asks.

"You can't drink!" Toby laughs.

"Oh yeah. Yay," Frankie mutters.

"Priya could've made the effort, you know," Alice says. "We live in suburbia, not Siberia!"

"I know, but it's an hour and a half from North London," Toby replies. "It would be like us going out for supper in . . . Brighton. I don't blame her."

"Why didn't we book somewhere in town as a compromise?" Frankie asks.

Alice and Toby turn to her, as if she's said something outrageous.

"You two will soon realize how hard it is with kids," Alice replies. "I always feel like I'm watching the clock with a babysitter, and it adds a hundred quid to a night out. Priya doesn't have that problem."

"Yeah, but she shouldn't have to pay for our choice, either," Frankie responds, feeling personally affronted by Alice's attitude.

In the real world, Frankie is Priya. And it drives her mad when Alice always suggests she come down to Kingston. When Frankie comments about how far it is, Alice proposes she stay the night. But Frankie doesn't want to spend the night in a toddler's bed, waking at the crack of dawn with a five-year-old standing next to her asking to play. Why doesn't Alice understand that? She chose to have her life dictated by her kids, but why the hell should Frankie and Priya live under the dictatorship too?

"I thought she was moving, anyway? Didn't you say she was going to rent out her flat in Finchley and buy somewhere in Bracknell?" Toby asks.

"Something like that," Frankie replies guiltily, remembering their earlier texts.

*

"IT'S GREEN!" shouts Justin, slamming his beer bottle on the table. He's already sunk three, and Toby's only just served his surprise starter of stuffed avocados. Frankie has tried to love avocados. At least, Toby tried for years to make her love them until she got bored of the same argument every Saturday morning and eventually pretended she did to save the charade. There's something about the texture that reminds her of rot. And there's something about Toby trying to force them on her that puts her off too.

"It's black, I'm telling you," Harry says, laughing.

A few minutes after Justin arrived with the six-pack, there was another ring at the door. When Frankie opened it, she was greeted like family by a shriek and a bellow from a couple who she's never set eyes on. Harry and Grace, as she learned their names later, are close friends of theirs from down the road. Apparently. And their kids go to the local school with Ellie and Matthew.

"Sorry, I'm with Toby on this one. It's definitely black," Alice adds to the argument.

All five of them turn to Frankie, expecting an input.

"Hmmm . . ." she murmurs, squishing her spoon into the tomato salsa center of the avocado. She spies a bit of brown flesh and wants to be sick. "I'm going to say . . . green."

"Of course you'd say that." Toby rolls his eyes.

Frankie puts the avocado chunk in her mouth and feels it

squash between her teeth, trying hard not to grimace. She looks at him and shrugs.

"Whatever I think, you always want to think the opposite!" Toby explains.

"Hashtag married life, amiright?" Harry says.

"Isn't there an easy way of settling this?" Frankie says. "By . . . just looking outside?"

"I'll bet you ten pounds it's black," Toby shouts.

"Deal!" Justin replies, stroking his untamed red beard, removing the avocado smear that's been lodged there for the last five minutes. Frankie watches his stocky bare legs, muscular from years of rugby, stride toward the front door. He glances outside and fist punches the air. "I knew it!"

"I could have sworn it was rubbish day tomorrow," Alice cries. "Can I still use the baby brain excuse when the kids are eleven and eight?"

Frankie scoops the remaining avocado onto her spoon, shoves it quickly into her mouth and swallows it whole, washing it down with a gulp of alcohol-free beer that tastes like soap.

"Come on, guys," Grace says, glancing at Frankie. "Betting on what bin day it is tomorrow isn't exactly riveting birthday conversation. Surely we can do better than this? We aren't that old and boring are we?"

"Hey, speak for yourself, sweetheart," Justin replies. "I just won a tenner. Our Happy Meals tomorrow just got a little happier."

Toby reaches into his pocket and hands over a ten pound

note. "Fair enough, I'm a big enough man to admit when I'm wrong."

The truth is, Toby hated to admit he was wrong about anything. Like avocados. *"I promise, you'll love them one day!"*

"That was delicious, thanks, Tobes," Frankie says, putting her spoon down on her plate.

"I knew you'd come around to avo." Toby smiles.

"How about another bet?" Justin says, smirking. "I bet I can scrape this whole avocado onto my spoon and into my mouth."

"Justin, stop. First we're debating bin day like we're eighty years old. Now, we're debating how much food you can stuff into your beardhole like we're eight years old."

"And this rug is only a month old, so don't make a mess—" Toby starts.

"I bet a tenner you can't," Frankie interrupts. This childish debate is far more entertaining than the previous one.

"Deal!" Justin shouts. He throws his elbow up dramatically and holds the avocado close to his nose, as he inches the flesh out slowly and carefully with his spoon. Everyone falls silent as he holds the spoon up and opens his mouth so wide that Frankie can see the backs of his teeth. The lump falls off a second later, landing on the crotch of his white shorts.

"Fuck!" he shouts, dropping the spoon onto the plate.

"My eight-year-old husband, everybody. And you wonder why we don't go to fancy restaurants in central London?" Alice smiles, shaking her head.

"I knew you couldn't do it," Frankie says, laughing. "Tom's

proved many times that it's actually impossible to put an entire avocado in your mouth."

A silence falls across the table.

"Tom who?" Toby asks.

Frankie looks at Alice and Justin, who are staring at her with creased brows.

Frankie freezes. Of course they don't know Tom. He doesn't exist in her life here.

Choosing this life means she'll never see Tom again.

She'll never have a 5 p.m. fashion show before a night out. She'll never dance on the coffee table to "Don't Stop Movin'" at two in the morning, slumping onto the sofa in hysterics as Tom does his signature floppy arm dance, spilling wine onto the rug without a care in the world. She'll never shovel shakshuka eggs into her mouth in appreciative silence and wear big sunglasses the next day. She'll never have him to lounge over as they mainline the *Real Housewives of Beverly Hills* until bedtime.

Instead, she'll be sitting here in her perfect kitchen-diner, with the same people she's been sitting with for fifteen years, eating food she hates, discussing bin days and rating Justin's mouth-cramming as top dinner table content.

"Duh!" Frankie says, gently slapping herself on the forehead. "He's from work. I thought I'd told you about him before. He's always doing stupid stuff like that."

"Better watch out for Mr. Tom Steal Yo Girl, Tobes." Harry chuckles.

"Yeah, he's gay," Frankie says. "So, no."

"Hey, I've been meaning to ask you lot something," says Toby, changing the subject.

They look up.

"What insurance provider are you with? Now that the house is spruced up, I feel like we need to change."

"Oh!" Grace cries. "We've actually just switched. Funny story . . ."

Funny story? Really, Grace?

Grace's voice fades into the background as Frankie pushes the avocado shell around her plate.

She misses Tom. She misses her crummy flat. She misses her real life.

DEATHLY BORED WIFE goes on ALL-NIGHT BENDER after KILLING everyone at her BIRTHDAY DINNER.

Everyone but Alice, of course.

*

An hour later, Frankie is rinsing the plates at the sink and slowly stacking the dishwasher, half listening to the conversation behind her about some new school policies. Despite Toby's protests about the Birthday Girl clearing up, she insisted on doing it. She needed a break from the table. From gossiping about people she's supposed to know but hasn't the foggiest about. From pretending to care about the politics behind Meat-Free Monday lunches at St. Joseph's. Alice and Grace think it's brilliant that the school is making kids aware of the health benefits and harm to the planet. Harry and

Justin think they have no place to impose these beliefs on kids their age. Frankie would like to impose this frying pan on both of their faces. Hard.

She flinches when she feels a pair of hands on her shoulders. Toby, who's also stayed silent for most of the conversation, kisses her on the back of her head. She can't deny it's comforting. Frankie might have spent the evening feeling alienated from the rest of the parent group, but at least they're both child-free in this child-full life together. At least she has her plus one.

She pauses, holding the upturned frying pan in the air and watching the drops of water dripping slowly into the sink. She wonders how long they've been trying for. Years, months? She wonders whether the pressure of trying—and failing—to fall pregnant has had some impact on the state of their marriage.

Toby was always desperate to be a father. Even in their early twenties he played the name game. Years later, she'd spy his comments under Ellie and Matthew's photos, saying how cute they looked in their little outfits.

Frankie wasn't desperate to have children. She was curious, but never felt that she'd miss that much without them in her life. If she had them, great. If she didn't, she'd get over it. What concerns her more is that they're trying for children in a broken marriage. It would be bonkers to have children to try and fix a marriage that's hanging on by a thread. Add the weight of a newborn baby to it, and the thread would surely snap.

The guests decline Toby's offer of more wine, despite it being 9 p.m. Alice has an 8 a.m. swimming class with Ellie before school. Justin promised to take Matthew skateboarding before school. Grace and Harry have a kids' birthday party tomorrow afternoon and they don't want to be hungover.

"Ooooh wait, Toby! I've been meaning to ask you about the new music teacher!" Grace exclaims, slipping on her brogues at the front door.

"Maggie wants to join the choir, and of course Grace is desperate for some insider info." Harry chuckles.

"To be honest, I don't know her that well," Toby replies. "Geography and music don't really mix that often. She seems nice enough."

"And she is an *absolute* belter," Harry mutters.

"Harry!" Grace throws her scarf at him.

"It wasn't me, it was the wine!" He chuckles.

"You've only had two glasses," Frankie comments.

"I'm a total lightweight these days," Harry replies. "Kids will do that to you!"

And a lot more.

"What's her name again?" Grace asks, standing up.

"Miss Thompkins," Toby replies. "Freya Thompkins."

Frankie's head spins toward him.

"What?" Toby asks her.

"Sorry, nothing," Frankie says, shaking her head. "I thought I left the tap running."

✳

Frankie's been wiping the counters for ten minutes, deep in thought, when Toby reappears in his dressing gown.

"Bedtime already?" Frankie asks, glancing at her phone before putting it on the kitchen shelf next to his, like he asked her to earlier.

Ten p.m.

Ten hours left.

"Not quite." He smiles, reaching toward her.

She takes his soft warm hand and follows him up the stairs.

"Now close your eyes," he says, stopping at the bedroom door.

"Really?" She smiles, her heart beating faster at the idea of what might happen in the next few minutes. Frankie can't remember the last time she was naked in front of someone and just the idea of it makes her feel deeply uncomfortable. But if anyone is going to see her like that, at least it's him. It's been fifteen years, but Toby's still so familiar. It's like they've never been apart.

She closes her eyes and feels him lead her through the bedroom, and around the corner into the bathroom.

"OK, you can open them now," Toby whispers.

When Frankie does, tears instantly spring in her eyes. And it isn't because of the warm steam infused with lavender from what looks like a hundred tea candles around the bubble bath. It's because this is the first time that Frankie can remember anyone doing anything like this for her. Since Toby, all those years ago. How many of his bubble baths has she missed out on in the last thirteen years?

197

"What's wrong?" Toby asks, looking worried.

"Nothing, I'm just . . . thank you for being so good to me," Frankie says. "I don't think I deserve you."

Despite Toby being a model human in most ways, Frankie can't help but feel like he brings out the worst in her. His kindness makes her feel mean. His maturity makes her act childish. His rigid rule following brings out the rebel in her. She can't explain why he makes her behave like this. But shouldn't she be with someone who makes her a better person?

"I don't care for you, Franks, I love you more than anything in the world."

Frankie wants to say it back. She wants to feel it back. But the weight of his kindness, his generosity, his attention and his love is too much to bear.

Perhaps she could learn to love him again, even harder. The counseling could work. The IVF could work. They could have two kids by the time they're forty, for all she knows.

Then she remembers what Toby said.

I don't want to be an old dad.

Thirty-six isn't old. But thirteen years is a long time for Toby to wait for happiness. The happiness he has in an alternate universe with Freya. Now that Frankie's wearing Freya's shoes, she wonders whether she should return them to their rightful owner, free herself from a future of guilt and do the kindest thing by him she's probably ever done.

Twenty-Three

"You're upset," Mabel comments, leaning forward to rest her chin on clasped hands. "Tell me why."

"I'm damned if I stay, damned if I don't." Frankie sighs, despondently, back in The Station.

"How so?" Mabel asks.

"If I stay, I'm potentially denying Toby the chance to be a young, happy father with Freya. I'd spend my life riddled with guilt. If I go, I miss out on the chance to enjoy that life myself. And, I think it's a life I could come to love. In time. It might take some getting used to. But I could have overcome the petty irritations and accepted his imperfections. I mean, no one is perfect, but as a husband, Toby is probably as close as you could get to it."

"Miss out on the chance to enjoy that life yourself? Didn't look like you were enjoying it from up here," Mabel says, with a confused face. "I also find it fascinating that you spent the precious time you had in your new life, returning to your old one."

"I got freaked out by the old people at Great Oaks," Frankie explains. "I imagined Toby and I were that couple. Fifty years of child chat, folding and phone rules flashed in my head and made me panic. I thought it would be sensible to see how I'd react to my old neighborhood."

"You know, Frankie," Mable says, interrupting her thoughts, "this is about choosing your *whole* life. Not just about who you're with. Your life doesn't have to revolve entirely around your relationship. Romantic relationships are just one sliver of the big life pie. You should taste all of the slices. Where you live, who your friends are, what your work is, and most of all . . . who *you* are. What did you think of the Frankie you saw in the bathroom mirror?"

Frankie remembers the shiver of excitement that ran through her when she spotted the star tattoo on her back. Scratch under the conventional surface, and *that* Frankie wasn't so conventional after all. That she'd got the tattoo behind Toby's back sparked a second shiver. It showed Frankie that she was still in charge of who she was. She hadn't allowed herself to become Toby's Franks. She was Frankie's Frankie and she could do whatever the hell she liked.

"I loved her," Frankie replies. "She's strong, defiant, in charge. Being controlled is my biggest fear, and it's what I worried about most with Toby. I was scared of losing myself, letting go of my life, canceling my plans. But getting that tattoo in secret, knowing how much Toby hates them, makes me feel really proud of myself. I've been thinking that Toby brings out the worst in me. But, maybe he actually brings out the best in me?"

Frankie feels silly. Getting a tattoo is hardly a big deal. But it's a symbol for her. It comforts her to know that she'll never be controlled. Just like her mum.

Frankie pauses, remembering how she'd beg her mum to ditch the blue wig and bowler hat for parents' evening. How she'd plead with her to stop coming to The Dog and Duck to watch Frankie waitress, while swaying in front of the live band on an imaginary dance floor. How Frankie sulked for three days because Astrid swore at her headmistress in the school parking lot for sending Frankie home for wearing a short skirt.

Frankie's mum was just trying to cling on to her identity too. Making sure that nothing or no one would change who she was and always had been. She was strong, defiant and in control. Frankie has spent twenty years feeling her mother taught her nothing, leaving her to her own devices to look after herself. Maybe the lessons were right in front of her all along. Maybe she's more like her mum than she thinks. Perhaps that's a good thing.

"Well, I'd say that loving yourself is pretty important, wouldn't you?" Mabel comments.

Frankie's behavior in the last few years would suggest she hates herself. She has a horrible habit of putting herself down constantly. Her inner voice calls her a loser, an idiot, a complete dickhead a lot of the time. For being single. For fucking up dates. For renting at her age. For writing her column. For her weekly Saturday hangover. For her failure to grow up.

"I want to love myself in my real life," Frankie responds quietly. "But how can I love myself when everything I do makes me feel like shit? If I really loved myself, I wouldn't do those things. I wouldn't stuff myself with greasy food knowing I'll feel awful the next day. I wouldn't sabotage a perfectly decent date. I wouldn't write a bitchy column that I can't bear to read myself because I sound like such an arsehole. I wouldn't waste my money on booze, taxis and gyms I don't use, knowing full well that I'll be living off French onion soup at the end of the month. If I loved myself, I would look after myself. I loved Kingston Frankie. Not Clapham Frankie."

"From what I can tell, you *are* that Frankie. You are strong, defiant and in control. You're strong because you're self-reliant. You're defiant because you haven't been sucked into the life that's expected of you with the marriage, mortgage and kids. You're in control because you alone have the power to make any life choices you want to. You've created your life and it's one you should feel proud of. And you've done it all on your own."

"Why are you suddenly being so nice to me?" Frankie says, squinting her eyes. "What happened to the Mabel who told me to go and play a small violin?"

"Hey, I can be nice," Mabel replies.

"Look, I think Clapham Frankie has romanticized being with Toby. You've spent years imagining that if you'd married him you'd have the house, the kids, the emotional security. Sure, you have the house. But you don't have kids and you don't have the emotional security."

"Didn't love the sound of my job, either," Frankie adds. "What was my next assignment going to be? Someone who found a crisp that looks like King Charles? A big exposé on corruption at the heart of the local Women's Institute? Interviewing someone who grew an oversized pumpkin?"

"Pumpkin BEETS competition to a PULP!" Mabel smiles, looking pleased with herself.

They titter together.

Frankie sighs. "I just want to do something meaningful. I want to own something. Run something. Make a name for myself in my industry," Frankie ponders. "Isn't your column called "To Be Frankie"'? Mabel asks.

"Yeah, but I'd rather not have my name attached to that," Frankie responds. "I want people to respect my work, not be repelled by it."

"Does being with Toby prevent you from doing that? You can always switch jobs," Mabel suggests.

Can she have it all? Marry the kind man. Have the kids. Own a kick-ass business. Spend the summers in Kingston and the winters in Cozumel.

"There's no rush to decide," Mabel comments, interrupting her daydream. "You've still got your other lives to live."

She clicks the screen.

The Fortune

"Oh god," Frankie moans, sinking into her seat and hiding behind her hand when she sees who's on-screen.

Callum's ice-blue eyes send a shiver down her spine. His stare was like a magnet when she first met him, drawing her in. And like a carving knife when she last met him, cutting her out.

"I think you'll be pleasantly surprised," Mabel comments.

"Really?"

"How do you feel about being famous?" Mabel asks.

"It depends what for," Frankie says.

"A sex tape," Mabel replies.

"What?!" Frankie cries.

"Kidding." Mabel chuckles. "Serial killing."

Frankie stares at her, deadpan.

"To answer your question, no, I think being famous would be quite shit," Frankie says, remembering all the photos she's published of celebrities running away from photographers.

"Oh," Mabel responds, grimacing. "Well, that might be a bit of a problem then."

PART FIVE

Grow up or GLOW UP: WAG spends FORTUNE to look HALF her age

Twenty-Four

When Frankie opens her eyes, her mouth instantly drops open at the glowing glass and gold chandelier above, which is softly swaying and chiming. She sits up on a white leather U-shaped sofa that's big enough for twenty people. In front of it is a glass coffee table, with a huge vase of white roses on top. The cool breeze blowing through the house is coming from the open floor-to-ceiling glass doors overlooking a balcony the size of a tennis court. Beyond that, uninterrupted views of a deep blue sea.

Frankie swings her legs to the floor, a heavy weight at her feet taking her by surprise and throwing her off balance.

She winces and stares down at her ankles. A pair of impossibly high red patent stilettos dangle off her bronzed feet. Why she's wearing shoes indoors is a mystery. An even bigger mystery is why she's wearing heels. She hasn't worn them in years. She tuts and kicks them off, listening to them clatter as

207

they scatter across the giant Carrara marble tiles. Impressive tan, she thinks, admiring her skin as she strokes her leg. Not only is her leg tanned, it's velvety smooth. Shaving her legs is usually like a game of Whac-A-Mole. The hairs pop back up seemingly in seconds, no matter how long and hard or frequently she scrapes at her skin with a razor.

Frankie clambers up, twists and wiggles out of a wedgie. She's wearing a pair of frayed denim short shorts, and half of them disappeared into her pants during what she assumes was a post-lunch nap. Pulling down her tight white vest, her eyes wander to a nude portrait that takes up the entire wall behind the sofa. The woman has straight blond cascading hair and is biting provocatively into a red apple, the pink juices running between her fingers and down her décolletage. Her bits are covered up by a leopard-print scarf which weaves between her crossed legs like a snake. Frankie's eyebrows lift up as she passes. She wishes she was that confident. Presenting guests with a giant nude is quite the statement.

This is all very *Selling Sunset*, Frankie thinks, as she wanders through the open doors and across the balcony, her hair blowing glamorously in the wind and her eyes squinting in the glare of the sunshine. She furtively peers over the edge of the balcony wall to see a second balcony underneath her with an infinity pool. The pool water gushes like a waterfall along the side of the house, and rocky steps below it descend steeply onto a small sandy beach with two loungers pointing toward the waves. Frankie's stomach cramps from sudden vertigo and she steps back.

Hot air. Bright sunshine. Blue skies. White beach. She has a feeling she's not in Clapham anymore. And from what she's seen so far, she's OK with it.

Frankie drifts back inside and looks around her.

"Hello?" she calls out, wondering if she's here alone.

There's no response. Her eyes wander to the flowers in front of her, and she spots a heart-shaped card poking out from between the leaves. She leans forward, reaches for the card and turns it over to see a short typed message.

Happy birthday Frankie
I'm sorry I couldn't be with you to celebrate
Hope the gift makes up for my absence
I love you
CM

Frankie rolls her eyes. Callum would always sign off his messages with "CM' even after months of dating. It made her feel like one of his employees.

Callum was the sole heir to a media publishing empire. When she met him, he'd recently taken the reins from his ancient father and acquired *The Leak*. Their eyes had met in the lift when he took a tour of the offices. He asked her what she did, then he smiled and left, turning around to give her a lingering look as the lift doors closed. A few days later an email arrived in her inbox asking her for a business meeting to discuss the future of the column. Frankie, thinking she was about to get fired, found herself necking back negronis with him at a swanky hotel bar in Belgravia five hours later. Callum didn't mention the column once during their "business meeting."

What followed was months of love bombing. He showered her with gift—lingerie, clothing, champagne, weekends away—some of which she went on alone when a last-minute meeting came up. He would message her day and night with selfies of him in different hotel rooms around the world, telling her he loved and missed her and he couldn't wait to be with her.

His base was New York, and he was only ever in London for a few days. He had a private jet for crying out loud. The environmentalist in Frankie wanted to hate it, but it was hard not to feel a shiver of excitement when he talked about whisking her away to his Caribbean villa.

He was exactly what Toby wasn't, and at the time that's what Frankie craved. He was polished, traveled, cultured, exciting, different. She found herself getting sucked into the glamour and spat out into the gutter quite regularly. She hated that she'd always go back for more, telling herself that she'd give him one more chance because the reward might be worth the risk. When he was present, he was incredible. Attentive, interesting, generous and charismatic. Powerful, of course. With his slow skewed smile, he'd undress her with a hard stare and it took all her willpower not to follow the silent order in the middle of the restaurant.

The Callum fairy tale came crashing to a humiliating end in the summer of 2012 in Paris. Frankie had gone deep into her overdraft on dawn Eurostar tickets, a ridiculously expensive haircut and color, spray tan, full body wax and a weekend wardrobe that channeled Audrey Hepburn in *Breakfast at Tiffany's*. With the supermodels he schmoozed around regularly, she had to make the effort to be perfectly preened.

She waited for him for two hours in the hotel lobby at The Ritz. The room was under his name and she couldn't check in until he arrived. Then a curt text came through that he wasn't coming. A big deal was on the brink of disaster and he was on his way to Oslo instead. He was so sorry. He'd make it up to her. She should check in anyway and send him the bill.

But Frankie barely had the means to pay for a coffee, let alone a suite at one of the most expensive hotels in Europe. She had to phone her dad for money to get an earlier train home. And if that wasn't embarrassing enough, she had to explain why she was crying.

Frankie didn't like crying in front of her dad. Tears made him very uncomfortable. She imagined him giving her a pat on the back and telling her, *"Chin up!"*

What made matters worse was that the only available train seat was late at night. Frankie had to spend the whole day sitting on her brand-new small Samsonite suitcase at Gare du Nord, staring at the passersby and keeping her phone switched off so the battery didn't die.

She wanted to blame Callum. But really she could only blame herself for getting swept up in his bullshit. He was never going to be with her in the way she wanted him to. She was too small for him. Not in stature, in life. He is a Maxted, his dad influences prime ministers. She is a McKenzie, her dad influences garden plot counselors. Not that there's anything wrong with that, obviously. But how much did they really have in common, aside from a similar sense of acerbic humor and an interest in pricey cocktails? She was a little-known gossip columnist in a one-bedroom flat in Clapham. He should be with a Playboy Bunny in a penthouse in California.

On the train back home, she blocked him and deleted his number. A few weeks later, after a few wines, she unblocked him, hoping he'd sent her some begging messages.

But there was nothing. He hadn't contacted her at all.

Her final contact with him came a whole year later, when he happened to be visiting the office. The sight of him made her want to be sick. Worst of all, Frankie's desk was facing the glass-fronted boardroom, where he happened to spend the whole day. Most of it staring at her with Daniel-Cleaver-come-hither eyes. That night, he sent her an email.

> Can we start again?
> Seeing you today makes me realize just how much I've
> missed you.
> You keep me grounded.
> I need you.
> CM

Frankie spent a sleepless night wondering if she should reply. But she couldn't forget the self-loathing his behavior had sparked in her. She'd never felt so worthless, so foolish. She'd always had a complex about being his inferior, at work and in life, and the "you keep me grounded' comment only fueled this insecurity. He was up there, she was down here. When she woke up, she deleted his email. The next time he was scheduled to be at the office, she took the day off.

As Frankie plays with the card in her hand, she wonders how she'll ever be able to forget those dark days of him blowing hot and cold. And when Callum does return here, how will she be able to accept him? To accept that he's changed. No one ever really changes, do they?

Frankie walks across the living room to another glass staircase leading down to the floor below. Halfway down the stairs, she's greeted by a gold-framed mirror and when she sees her reflection she screams, steps back and grabs on to the banister before she falls down the steps behind her.

Inching forward, she turns her cheeks left and right to examine the stranger staring back at her. A stranger with golden glowing skin, a different nose and a pair of lips that look like two chipolatas hugging. Her hair is dead straight, white blond and definitely not all hers. It hangs heavily over her bony shoulders like a silk rug. She looks like she belongs on the set of *The Real Housewives of Beverly Hills*. She inches forward again. Her judgmental eyebrow is gone.

Frankie strokes her hair like it's a cat on her shoulder, and presses her full lips together. They feel like smooth, tight, overfilled balloons. Then it dawns on her. The woman staring back at her now is the nude woman in the portrait. She *is* that confident. But this isn't her. This has never been her. How much time must it take to make her look this way every day? In the early days, she could barely afford the cost and time it took to get ready for their sporadic dates. Will this life require her to be picture perfect at all times? A sense of relief washes over her that she only has twenty-four hours here. Does she sleep in these hair extensions? What about all this contouring? She hasn't a clue.

She continues down the glass steps and into a vast white and copper kitchen, where she spies a tall pile of newspapers on the island. At last, some clues to where she is.

She lifts the paper on the top of the pile. The *Los Angeles Times*! She's made it to Los Angeles! Frankie longed for Callum to whisk her away to Hollywood with him, and grins with excitement as her wide eyes pour across the front page. Then they land on an article at the bottom, and her smile vanishes.

"What the fuck?" she whispers.

Frankie's on the front cover in a pinstriped power suit.

Twenty-Five

**Standing By Her Man: An Exclusive Interview
With Frankie McKenzie**
*Frankie McKenzie talks to Adam Shannon about
rumors, run-ins and rebrands*

Frankie lowers the paper and stares ahead. Exactly how famous is she? Are there paparazzi lurking outside the house right now?

She peers out of the kitchen window at the six-foot steel electric gates in the distance. Should she listen out for drones? Her eyes drift up to the blue sky. A phone would be helpful. She needs to google herself.

When she googles "Frankie McKenzie' back home, all she gets is her bio on *The Leak* site, some old columns, and a few Facebook posts from a man in Coventry called Chester Beal who loathes her. He reposts her column every week just to in-form his thirty-three followers that she's scum. One week she was vermin. The next she was a simple poo emoji. It's almost amusing these days.

She turns back to the interview, wondering what kind of reception this Frankie McKenzie is getting.

Thirty-five-year-old, British-born, LA local Frankie McKenzie is the long-term (long-suffering to some) partner of publishing bad-boy Callum Maxted. After years shunning the celebrity spotlight, she's finally stepping out of his shadow in custom-made Casadei Blades. Rumors are swirling in Tinseltown about book deals, talk shows and reality TV. In this exclusive interview, McKenzie reveals her style secrets, her relationship tips and why she's ignoring the rumors of infidelity that have plagued their partnership for almost a decade.

So, Frankie. First, your new look is fantastic. What are your secrets?
Thanks, Adam, but I don't have any secrets. I see Dr. Ellen down in Melrose for my face. I go to Andy LeCompte in West Hollywood for my hair. And Dr. Jennier Herrman has been my skin angel in Beverly Hills. Our personal chef, Nina, makes it easy for me to avoid garbage and get my insides glowing.

Insides glowing? Frankie scoffs. She doesn't need a personal chef to get an inside glow. She could get one from a £5 oily fry-up from the greasy spoon down on Northcote Road.

A refreshingly honest answer!
Those who know me know I see things as black or white. Callum has worked hard and enjoyed great success. It would be ridiculous of me to ignore what we have. It's much easier to look fantastic when you have time and money. I'm truly blessed.

Truly blessed? Frankie hates this version of her. She cringes when she thinks of her friends and family reading this back home. And Callum hasn't worked a hard day in his life. He's been hanging off his father's coattails since he was eighteen.

They say more money, more problems. Do you agree?
More money, different problems. I have a huge roof over my head, fancy food in my kitchen, an expensive cellar full of rare wines and a luxury villa in the Caribbean. There was a time when I lived in a one-bedroom flat, surviving on packets of French onion soup and downing two-dollar bottles of store-brand wine. Sure, wealthy people have their problems, but let's not pretend. Our lives aren't *that* hard. Yes, we lack privacy. I can't grab a coffee without getting snapped, I have to read rumors

about my relationship on a daily basis. But it's part of
the Maxted deal. I knew what I was getting into and I
chose to come along for the ride. It's been pretty wild so
far.

A stiff upper lip. Classic Brit.
These lips aren't exactly stiff, have you seen them
recently? More like spongey.

Ha! When in LA, I guess.
Exactly. My friends back home barely recognize me
anymore. They all think I've gone a bit far. But I'm just
living my life how I want to out here. I'm not hurting
anyone, so why shouldn't I do what I like if it makes me
happy?

Are you happy, Frankie?
Of course I am. Wait, have you been talking to
my therapist? Oh, she's toast. Just kidding, Adam.
But if you can recommend a therapist, I'm looking for
a new one.

**Do you think your sense of humor is what attracted
Callum to you in the first place?**
What are you trying to say, that *I'm the funny one?*

Not at all. Moving on swiftly.
Chop chop.

How did you and Callum meet?

At my old office job. I was working on a column there, and Maxted Inc. bought the paper. Callum came in for a meeting, we exchanged glances in a lift and the next day I had an email asking me to meet him.

A classic office fairy-tale romance, then.

I guess. We were on and off for a couple of years. Callum was so busy with the acquisitions they were making at the time. But, eventually, we found each other again. It was the right time for both of us. It didn't take long for him to invite me to LA. I resigned the next day, and a month later, I was here in Malibu with my own private beach.

Frankie McKenzie, a girl from a run-of-the-mill semi in Surrey, now lives on a private beach in Malibu, California. Frankie blinks her eyes in disbelief as she looks out onto the infinity pool balcony, the sea horizon just visible through the rocky crags.

Do you miss London?

I miss my friends and family. Sometimes so much it hurts. But we keep in touch and I can visit them any time I want. I take comfort in that.

Are you planning a trip to see them?

I've been busy with the book and the show. But I'll get there soon, I'm sure. My mum lives in Goa, India.

219

She has a silent yoga retreat. I haven't seen her in three years. My dad still lives in my hometown. We flew him over last year. He hated it here. He doesn't feel comfortable around fancy things. He spent the whole time trying to scope out the best place to grow vegetables in my garden. And my friends all have their own lives now, you know. Kids, schools, careers. I hope to see them here one day.

Frankie sighs. What's the point in having all this money and space when you can't share it with the people you love? Her friends and family should be flying here every holiday. If Tom, Priya and Alice came here they'd have the time of their lives. And she'd love her mum to visit. Her mum loves the ocean, and it's so serene out here. Although she'd probably take one look at the minimalist decor and start insisting Frankie change it immediately. *"Sure it's vast, but it's a creative vacuum, Frankie! Utterly devoid of any soul!"* Frankie smiles, imagining her mum's voice echoing around the rooms.

Do you believe the latest rumors?
Which rumors? There are so many. I read the other day that I'd paid for a woman to be my surrogate butt. Apparently I got doctors to suck the fat out of her butt and put it in my butt. Honestly. I mean, does such a procedure even exist? No, really, tell me. Give me their number, my ass looks like it's been cartoon steamrolled.

Ha! The latest rumors about Callum having a girlfriend in each Maxted office.
They're false.

So you think those women are just making it up?
Look, Callum's an easy target. We've dealt with rumors like these for years. I'm not saying they're making it up, but I'm not saying they're telling the truth either. Callum has always been a huge flirt, and it's landed him in hot water many times. People just don't understand him like I do. Besides, what's the saying—there's no such thing as bad publicity? Every time Callum hits the headlines, we sell more newspapers. So, I'm not complaining. I know what the truth is behind closed doors.

For someone so black and white, that's a pretty gray answer.
Well, it's your only answer. Change the color of the font when you print this, if you like.

This Frankie's feisty. But why would she be so gullible? Of course Callum's had affairs. It's who he is and always has been. She has to know this. She has to be turning a blind eye to his behavior. Why would she go along with it, though? Frankie's never been the type to chase a life of fame and fortune. But maybe this Frankie does.

What about the photos of him in New York?
Which photos?

Come on, Frankie. The kiss across the table?
You can Photoshop anything these days.

The lingerie model in Central Park?
She's just a friend. I've met her several times.

The waitress in the Texas alleyway?
His only crime was asking her for a cigarette. He told
me he'd quit. I was furious.

So, what's next for you?
I'm in talks to be on a reality show next year. It's called
Frankie Goes to Hollywood and it's basically a bunch
of cameras following me around as I live my LA life.
I'm hoping it'll prove to the world that I'm more than
just an accessory. I do a lot out here, you know. I don't
just float around my infinity pool, ordering house staff
around. I spend about two hours a day doing that.
I'm kidding! Did you know I'm writing a book? It's
a memoir about my journey from rags to riches. I'm
also flipping a couple of properties down on Venice
Beach, doing all the interiors myself. And I'm in talks
to produce a swimsuit label inspired by the island of
Cozumel in Mexico.

Why Cozumel?
Years ago, before I met Callum, I was going to teach
English there. I'd booked a one-way flight, but life
got in the way. I visited it last year, and the island
was everything I dreamed it would be. The colors, the
streets, the fabrics. It's incredible. It's my homage to a
life that never was, but a life I think I would have loved.
You might be surprised to discover that I like the simple
things in life, Adam.

I'd never have guessed.

**Thanks for your time and your honesty Frankie. Any
final messages for our readers?**
Don't believe everything you read.

Frankie puts the newspaper down and leans against the
counter. This life, this version of herself, is going to take a
lot of getting used to. And she isn't quite sure if she loves her
or hates her. In a way, at least she's honest. But the privilege
pouring from her mouth leaves this Frankie with a bad taste in
hers. At least she still has a sense of humor about it all. What
Frankie can't get her head around is why she's stayed all these
years, knowing that Callum was playing away. Has she grown
so accustomed to this high life that she happily ignores his low-
life behavior?

A doorbell chime goes, and Frankie takes a deep breath.

Time to face the music. Or is it the paparazzi? Another interview, maybe? She needs to channel that confident Frankie McKenzie from the interview. She walks up the stairs, smooths her hair in the mirror en route, and when she reaches the double oak doors she pauses for a few seconds, her shaking hands clutching the huge handle. Her heart is pounding.

A flickering screen to the left of her catches her eye.

"It can't be!" Frankie screams.

Twenty-Six

Frankie throws open the door and runs into Tom's arms, jumping up on him like a dog happy to see her owner home.

"What are you guys doing here?" Frankie shouts, as she grabs Alice and Priya into the cuddle pack.

"Um, more like what the fuck are *you* doing here?" Priya says, breaking free from the hug and striding into the hallway.

"Tom, you said it was amazing." Priya turns to him. "You didn't say it was *Selling Sunset*!"

"Oh, it's ridiculous, really," Frankie says, suddenly embarrassed about the opulence.

"It's gorgeous, Frankles," Alice says, peering into the living room. "Wow, that chandelier. I feel like I'm on a cruise ship!"

She's not wrong. But it feels like a bit of a backhanded compliment.

"Excuse me," Tom says, standing in front of the portrait. "But who the fuck is that and what has she done with Frankie McKenzie?"

225

"Oh, I know, I'm a bit embarrassed about it. Callum surprised me with it." Frankie makes up a quick excuse.

"Didn't you have to sit for it?" Alice asks, one eyebrow raised.

"No, it was from a photo he took of me," Frankie explains, rubbing her temple.

"It would be more accurate if you switched that apple for a chicken shish," Tom quips.

"It's so good to see you guys here!" Frankie screams, bringing them together for another group hug and burying herself into their chests.

She never wants to let them go.

*

Taking her friends on a tour of the mansion isn't easy. It's the first time Frankie's seen it herself. At one point she announced Tom's en suite bedroom for the weekend and threw open the door to a toilet. He wondered if the en suite came with a bed. Frankie blamed her confusion on renovations, explaining how they'd moved things all around. They didn't question it, at least in front of her. But she noticed Alice side-glancing at Tom in a hallway mirror, when Frankie couldn't remember the way back to the kitchen.

Flying her friends in for her birthday was just Callum's style. Grand gestures that required minimal effort from him. His assistant would have coordinated the dates and booked the flights. Callum would have just footed the bill. Still, Frankie's elated to have them here. Just having the idea to fly her friends in was of itself a kindness. Or was it a distraction? Frankie has no idea where he is or what he's up to. But in a way, she's pleased he isn't here. Callum and her friends aren't exactly four peas in a pod. Without him, she can be completely herself. Things between Callum and Alice were always frosty, ever since his first no-show a few weeks into their relationship. Every time Frankie moaned about him, which was weekly toward the end, Alice never held back on her opinion via text.

Slimy, lazy, trust-fund twat.

Lying, cheating, two-faced toolbag.

A sack of turds in a pair of Tod's loafers.

When Frankie forwarded Alice the make-or-break email, she responded with a photo of her sticking up her two middle fingers and a message saying she wished she had more middle fingers to pull. Then she sent her a photo of Ellie and Matt also sticking their middle fingers up, with a message asking Frankie never to tell Justin.

Frankie pours four champagne—from the ceiling-high champagne fridge, no les—and watches Alice wander onto the pool balcony with her arms tightly folded. Frankie wonders what Alice's reaction was when she got back together with Callum in this life. Did they fight about it? Has their friendship fully recovered from Frankie's decision? Alice has seemed distant from the second she set foot in the door, but without the history, it's impossible for Frankie to know.

Tom springs into the kitchen wearing a pair of tiny black Speedos, a gold chain and enormous black aviators. He's followed by Priya, who's in a shimmering gold kimono and matching bikini, her pixie-cut black hair hidden under a huge Chanel straw.

"Poolside-ready?" Frankie comments, placing their flutes in their hands.

"Born poolside-ready, babes," Tom replies, taking a long sip, sighing and spinning around to face the ocean view with his elbows leaning on the island behind him. He shakes his head. "God, Frankie, you've really landed with your fake bum in the bloody butter, haven't you? The fancy lobster butter kind. I can't believe I have a famous friend. And not even like Gemma Collins famous, like . . . Phil Collins famous."

"Hardly." Frankie rolls her eyes. "I'm still the same person. With the same butt, thank you."

She takes a sip of champagne and misses her new lips completely.

"Shit!" she says, wiping the dribble from her chin.

"Not being funny, Franks, but how the fuck can you miss those lips?" Tom giggles.

"Oi!" Frankie says.

Priya looks up from her phone and chuckles.

"Oh yeah, and what are you laughing about?" Frankie says, playfully.

"Um, have you looked in the mirror?" Priya puts her phone down on the island. "Have you looked *at* the mirror? That mirror alone must be worth a cool hundy K alone. Are those real diamonds? Actually I don't want to know, I'll be sick."

"Of course they aren't!" Frankie cries, glancing toward

the mirror and doing a double take. Holy hell, they actually could be.

"Frankie . . . you fancy," Tom adds, strolling over to the mirror and stroking his eyebrows.

"OK, fine, I might look a little fancier and have a few fancy things. But I'm still just Frankie. Frankie from the block."

"Frankie from the block, my arse." Tom laughs as the three of them move toward the balcony.

"You're Francy."

"Pack it in," Frankie replies. "Or I'll have my security team escort you out."

Before they reach the door, Frankie pulls them to one side.

"Is she OK?" she whispers, nodding toward Alice. "She's barely said a word to me since you got here."

Priya shrugs.

"Seems fine to me," Tom adds, removing his sunglasses and handing them to Frankie. He slides back the balcony door and sprints across the deck before dive-bombing into the pool like a five-year-old. Alice screams and spins around with water dripping from her dark brown fringe and into her wide-open mouth.

"Tom, my hair, you dickhead! Now I'm going to have to wash it!" Alice yells.

"Here, let me help you," Tom says, throwing his arm back and pelting her with water.

She screams again, then dives into the pool on top of him fully clothed.

Perhaps she isn't being so uptight after all. But Frankie can't ignore her gut feeling that something is off between them.

*

"Frankie, Bella Hadid is staring at you from the balcony door," Tom says quietly, his mouth almost submerged in the water.

Frankie's heart starts to race as she turns around slowly.

Time for her B in GCSE drama to deliver.

"Hiya!" Frankie waves at a woman who does look a lot like Bella Hadid lingering in the balcony doorway. Her long brown legs climb under a short white apron, which is tied tightly at a waist that looks about the same girth as Frankie's neck.

"Hey, Frankie," says the woman, with a slow and breathy Valley voice.

"Hi! How are you doing?" Frankie says, climbing out of the pool and wrapping a towel around her. As she walks over, she knocks over an empty champagne bottle by the foot of a lounger. She notices the woman glance at the bottle as it clinks and rolls across the deck.

"Whoops, sorry," Frankie says, scurrying to pick it up and feeling her cheeks turn pink. She isn't sure why she's embarrassed. This is her house. She can do what she likes. But something about the woman suggests her wildest nights are on kombucha and herbal tea, without the *h*.

"I'm doing great," the woman says with a smile that hints of fake.

"Good, good," Frankie repeats, hugging the towel around her as she approaches.

"I'm just wondering when you'll want dinner," the woman says.

Nina. This is the Nina she mentioned in the article.

"Thanks, Nina," Frankie says. "What's the time now?"

"It's 8 p.m.," Nina replies, quickly glancing at the others behind Frankie.

Frankie turns around to see they've swum up to the edge of the pool and are staring at the exchange like a pack of hungry seals waiting to be fed. "Got any kippers you can throw at them?" Frankie jokes.

"Kippers?" Nina asks.

"Fish," Frankie replies, smiling.

"Oh right," Nina says, a look of concern flashing across her perfectly smooth and tanned face. "Cal didn't mention kippers, I'm so sorry. But I've prepared oysters for your first course, sashimi for your second, and we have baked lobster on the menu too."

Cal? Since when does he call himself Cal?

"Bloody hell, like seafood much?" Tom mutters.

"Oh, I'm sorry," Nina says, glancing at Tom and back at Frankie. "Cal mentioned you were on a diet, I hope that's OK?"

"That sounds amazing, Nina, thank you. Is half an hour OK?" Frankie replies, embarrassed that her humor was lost on her and wondering what the hell kind of diet she's on, or perhaps *been* put on.

"Sure." Nina smiles, stepping back through the balcony doors and disappearing into the kitchen.

"Has she been here the whole time?" Tom asks.

231

"I don't know." Frankie turns around and shrugs.

"Don't you get a bit scared in this big empty house, having no idea who's here or not?" Alice asks, pointedly.

"Sometimes," Frankie responds. "But Callum's here, so not really."

"Is he? He's never here when we call," Alice replies. "Although, I guess that's not very often these days."

Frankie catches Tom's eye. There is most definitely a problem between them. And Frankie's determined to fix it. Alice is too precious to let any life choice get in the way of their friendship.

*

The four of them giggle as they sit down to a candlelit spread, which feels far too smart for the state they're in. Tom's wearing a pool robe. Alice's hair is wrapped in a towel. Priya's sun hat has bent out of shape and she's swaying in her seat like a filthy rich old divorcée who's had one too many Manhattans by the pool at The Beverly Hills Hotel.

Tom attempts to shuck the first oyster, and sends it flying across the table. It lands on the sashimi platter. They stare at it in silence, then start laughing uncontrollably. After a few minutes, Frankie starts to shush them, worried that Nina will think they're laughing at her food. She definitely doesn't want to piss off a personal chef.

"Stop!" Frankie hisses. "Nina will think we're taking the piss out of her!"

"Neens needs to chill the eff out," Tom slurs. "We're just holiday vibes!"

"Well, she'll be cooking us breakfast, so if you want eggs Benedict without spit in your hollandaise, I suggest you pack it in," Frankie replies, smiling.

"This is fucking ridiculous," Alice says, a hiccup swiftly following. "Do you eat like this every night?"

"Yeah, I mean, who *are* you, Frankie McKenzie!" Priya shouts. She's been attempting to pick up a piece of sashimi with her chopsticks since they sat down ten minutes ago.

"I told you, I'm still me!" Frankie cries. "I haven't changed."

"Come on," Priya says. "You have a bit."

"Yeah, fine, so I look different. I know. But when in LA," Frankie replies.

"Nah, I'm not talking about the rich girl glow," Priya adds. "I'm talking about *you*. As a person. I'm just worried about you, that's all. *We're* worried about you. I think I speak for all of us, don't I?" she says, darting her eyes in Tom and Alice's directions.

"What are you worried about?" Frankie asks, genuinely interested to know.

"Where do we start?" Alice sighs.

Frankie looks at her.

"I'll start," Priya says, giving up on the sashimi and throwing her chopsticks down onto her plate. "What are you actually doing with your life out here? I mean, don't get me wrong, this is incredible. But it's all on Callum, right? What about *your* career? You haven't worked since you left *The*

Leak, and that was over a decade ago. Have you made any money of your own? Your CV is going to have a huge blank on it, and I'm just not sure you've thought about the risks of relying entirely on someone else for food, money and shelter. Sorry to lay it down so thick, Frankie. It's only because I love you and I'm being protective."

"What are you talking about?" Tom replies. "She's Frankie fucking McKenzie. Haven't you seen the *LA Times* cover?" Tom reaches to the chair next to him, takes the *LA Times* he was reader earlier, and slides it over to Alice. She sits up, her eyes expanded, and flicks to the interview. "If Callum dumps her," Tom continues excitedly, "She'll make millions on a tell-all book. An Oprah interview. I'm a PR expert, and she's like a PR gold mine."

"Yeah, not if that weird relationship prenup she signed has a clause that says she can't profit off the back of their breakup!" Priya adds, her arms flailing toward Frankie.

They turn to Frankie.

"I don't know," Frankie says, her nerves starting to unravel, her thumb and index finger clamped so hard she's going to have a small bruise in the morning.

They collectively sigh.

"But," Frankie says, remembering the interview, "I've got a reality show on the cards, and I'm writing a book. And a couple of houses I'm flipping. So it's not like I do nothing, actually. I'm really quite busy. I'm making money, I'll be OK."

"See, she'll be fine!" Tom says. "My turn now."

"Your turn, what?" Frankie responds.

"Oh, sorry, I thought we were all going around telling you why we're worried about you."

The other two nod. Frankie looks at them, hurt.

"So, I'm just sad that we hardly ever hear from you anymore. I mean, we text on WhatsApp and stuff, but you never visit. You hardly ever call. It makes me feel like you're not that interested in our lives anymore. I don't know, maybe you think we're all a bit mediocre now or something."

"Tom! I would never in a million years think that!" Frankie cries. "Besides, none of you are mediocre, so how can you say that? You're like London's best PR director, Priya's smashing it at *The Leak* and Alice is the best child wrangler this side of Surrey."

Priya leans forward. "What did you say I do?"

Frankie freezes. Priya is still at *The Leak*. Isn't she? Her mind races. Maybe these different lives have made her confused. *No*, she thinks. Priya was definitely still at *The Leak* in her real life. They'd been for drinks to celebrate her being promoted to head of sales the week before the kebab incident.

"I said you're smashing it at *The Leak*," Frankie replies.

"Wow." Tom grimaces.

"Frankie, I fucking left *The Leak* six months after you did!" Priya cries, looking hurt. "How can you not remember that whole saga? It was your boyfriend who cut the department, and made me lose my job."

"Fuck, yes. Sorry!" Frankie shakes her head. "Of course I know you aren't at *The Leak*."

"But," Tom adds, "Priya, as you know, Frankie, *is* smashing it at *The Hour*."

"Obviously," Frankie says, throwing a grateful look at Tom, who winks at her.

"Can I say something?" Alice says, closing the *LA Times* and looking up.

"Please, I want everything out in the open," Frankie says.

"Frankie, we've been best friends since we were nine years old. I know everything there is to know about you. So well that I could finish your sentences, before you even knew what you were going to say. I could predict exactly what you'd choose for every school lunch. Although, it wasn't that hard because it was always a bloody baked potato, beans and cheese."

Frankie chuckles.

"Yes, you're living some kind of *Pretty Woman* fairy-tale life, but is it really you? I'm just worried that you're out here all alone, with no one from home near you, no one to remind you where you're from. Everyone here is just so different. Everyone here is so unlike the Frankie I know. It just feels like you've detached yourself from your past for some reason, and I don't think it's healthy. You're Frankie Baked Potato, not Frankie Foie Gras."

"But I really am still that person," Frankie pleads. "Even if it doesn't look like it on the surface."

"I'm not so sure." Alice shakes her head. "I can't help feeling like Callum has driven a wedge between you and us, between you and the UK. You used to tell me all the time how you didn't want anyone to control your life, yet here you are.

Callum pressured you to come to LA. Callum's keeping you here. Callum's even controlling your own birthday party."

"That's hardly fair, it was meant to be a surprise," Frankie cuts in.

"I'm not talking about us flying over," Alice says. "I'm talking about this dinner. If it were up to you, we wouldn't be eating sashimi. You hate sashimi."

"Well, everyone eats it here. I guess I've got used to it," Frankie mutters, pouring herself another glass of wine, which is a bad idea.

"And what about this interview?" Alice continues. "You hate attention and now you're on the front page, talking about a camera crew following you around with a spotlight on your face. Maybe you haven't changed. But that makes me even more worried that you're getting sucked into situations that you're really uncomfortable with. Then one day, you're going to wake up and have a massive panic attack about what you put out there, and you won't be able to undo it."

Frankie silently sips her wine.

"I'm sorry if we sound harsh, Frankie," Alice says. "Like Priya said, it's only because we love you and we're worried about you."

"I feel like this is an intervention!" Frankie chuckles, and quickly stops when they don't respond in kind.

"I promise, I'm fine," Frankie reassures them. "But, you're all right. Priya, maybe I do need to start thinking of getting a proper career of my own that doesn't rely on empty fame or Callum. And, Tom, I promise I will visit more, and I'm ashamed that I haven't. The only excuse I have is that I'm a lazy cow. And, Alice, I see what you mean. Maybe I have let myself get swept up in a life that isn't really true to who I am. I'll have a chat with Callum when he's back from . . ."

Shit, she has no idea where he is.

". . . London, and see if we can make some changes."

There goes that look among the three of them again.

"Callum's not in London," Tom says. "He's in New York."

"Why don't you know where he is?" Priya asks.

"I'm just drunk! I knew he was in New York!" Frankie backtracks, but they look unconvinced. "It's hard to keep track, he's forever on a flight somewhere. What's the point of keeping tabs on him? By the time we touch base, he's already on his way to another city."

"Leaving you to rattle around here on your own, in your custom Casadei Blades," Tom quips.

When Nina walks into the dining room, they fall silent.

"And here's your green tea, ginseng and fennel surprises for dessert," Nina says, her lithe arms placing tiny bowls of quivering brown jelly in front of them.

"What's the surprise part?" Tom asks.

"They have an algae center." Nina smiles. Frankie's sure the smile has a dash of villain to it.

When she leaves the dining room, the four of them look at the pudding and groan.

"What do you think she'd do if I asked her to deep-fry a Mars bar?" Tom asks.

Twenty-Seven

It's 5 a.m. and Frankie is being tormented by blurry flashbacks from the conversation last night.

When she eventually located her bedroom at 1 a.m. she found her phone charging on her bedside table, with a few early birthday messages on it. She replied to her parents. The rest of the well-wishers can wait. Forever, for all she cares right now.

This Frankie needs to pay more attention to the most important people in her life. She needs to find her way back to the real Frankie, who seems to have got lost somewhere along the way.

Frankie isn't the kind of person to quit her career to become a kept woman. Or neglect her friends, her family and herself for a man. Let alone a man like Callum, who's flakier than a sausage roll from Greggs. Frankie's stomach rumbles. If she asked Nina for a sausage roll and ketchup, she'd probably get a lentil patty wrapped in spinach leaves with a side of tomato jus.

Her phone pings.

> **Callum:** Hi Spanks
> Hope you had a good night
> with the gang.
> CM

> **Frankie:** It was amazing.
> Thank you.

> **Callum:** I'm glad you're happy.

At least someone's confident she is.

> **Frankie:** What are you up to today?

Frankie stares at her screen for five minutes, then tosses it across the bed. She refuses to return to her old habits. Waiting for him to reply, lunging at every vibration, placing it screen down and tilting it up every few minutes to see if there's a message. Not today. Not ever again. She throws over the sprawling duvet cover and shuffles toward the end of the giant bed, pausing to catch her breath at one point. No wonder celebs are so buff. They get a full body workout before they've even got up.

She slips on a black silk robe hanging on the bedpost and opens what she presumes is a bathroom door. Her mouth slowly drops as she steps into a room that's even bigger than the bedroom. Running across the length of the wall in front of her is a mirrored glass dressing table framed by vanity lights. Rows upon rows of beauty products are arranged and stacked in neat clear boxes. A row of hair tools hang by hooks on the side. Built into the window on her right is a bath for at least four people, overlooking the ocean. The sun is just starting to peek over the horizon, and the sky's alight with orange and pink streaks that blend into a dusky blue.

In her short life, not much has taken Frankie's breath away.

The view of Kilchurn Castle on that disastrous family camping trip when she was twelve.

The sight of Ellie when she was one day old, which made all negative thoughts of losing Alice to mum life vanish.

Last year's Christmas card from her mum, which was her and ten yoga friends running into the sea wearing nothing but Santa hats.

Just as she turns to walk out of the bathroom, she spots a pod of dolphins jumping in the waves and gasps.

"Tom! Priya! Alice!" she shouts, running out of the bedroom and down the marble corridor. Her dressing gown flies out behind her, making her feel like she's having a movie star moment.

"Oi! Shush, you!" says someone downstairs.

Frankie peers over the mezzanine to find Tom staring up at her, with a coffee filter jug.

"People are sleeping, you muppet!" he says, smiling. "Don't think you can do what you like, just 'cause it's your birthday!"

"Dolphins!" she shout-whispers, pointing toward the sea.

Tom walks over to the balcony doors, slides them open and

steps outside. When Frankie eventually joins him, the dolphins have disappeared.

"Oh, Frankie, what is your life, eh?" Tom chuckles, then takes her under one arm. "I hope we weren't too brutal last night. And happy birthday."

"No," Frankie says, cuddling in. "I needed to hear it. Anyway, why are you up so early?"

"Well, for starters, jet lag's a slag. Then I couldn't stop worrying that you were feeling super low, so I came down to make you a birthday tea like the good old days and I spent half an hour looking for a bloody kettle. This isn't it, is it?"

"That looks like a coffeepot thing that Americans use," Frankie comments, taking the jug off him.

"Don't you know what it is?" Tom asks.

"Yeah, it's that," Frankie says, backtracking. "I don't know, I've never used it."

"Ohhh, I see. You send Nina in, do you?" Tom teases.

"I do not!" Frankie cries.

"OK, so show me where your kettle is. Let's make a cuppa and drink it on the beach."

But Frankie can't show Tom where the kettle is, because she doesn't know either. She blames Nina for moving things around, and they end up boiling their water in the microwave because Tom said that's how Americans make tea, much to Frankie's horror and much to Tom's confusion that she hasn't seen it for herself.

"None of my friends drink proper tea," she explains, wondering who her friends here are, as they tread carefully down the rocky steps toward the beach.

A cool breeze gives her goose bumps as they lie down on the loungers next to each other, take a first sip and grimace.

"Ugh," Tom says, sticking his tongue out at the taste of the tea. "How can you say you're happy here, when you have to put up with this piss?"

"I'm . . . not sure," Frankie replies honestly.

"I'm glad you're up, Frankles," Tom says. "I wanted to get you alone. Nothing confrontational like last night, don't worry."

"OK," Frankie mutters, sitting up.

"I'm not worried because you haven't been in contact much. I'm worried about your behavior here. It feels like you don't really . . . I don't know how to explain it. It feels like you're really confused. About everything. Here and at home. You don't know where half the rooms in the house are. You can't find your own kettle. You've forgotten huge details of your friends' lives. How come you didn't remember that Priya left *The Leak*? That was a massive thing between you two, given who your boyfriend is. Speaking of which, it concerns me that you don't seem to know where Callum is or what he's doing. Maybe you don't care, and if that's the case, fine. But I can't believe it would be the case. I know how much his behavior hurt you in the past. I have one simple question for you. Are you drinking too much?"

"What?" Frankie half laughs.

"I'm just wondering if you're drinking a lot. If that's what's causing the memory loss, the nonchalance toward Callum, the lack of communication. I've been racking my brain for what could have changed with you and that's the only logical solution I've thought of. I don't think LA would change you. You're not the type. Look, I love a drink, as you know, but I just wonder if the loneliness has got to you here. And if you're using booze to numb the pain of it. I promise I'm not being judgmental."

"Tom, I *promise* you I'm not confused because I'm drinking," Frankie says, her mind a hurricane of possible excuses for all those problems. "Like I said, the house layout is different. And yesterday I think I was so distracted by your arrival, my head was all over the place. The whole Callum cheating thing, I've got that under control. I'm going to speak to him when he gets back and get to the bottom of those rumors. And, if I think there's one grain of truth in them . . ." She pauses.

There's an entire sackful of truth in them.

". . . I'll end things. I don't know where Callum is because he never tells me."

"Why aren't you angrier about that?" Tom scoffs.

"I am! I'm fucking fuming, but I'm not going to let Callum ruin this precious time we have together!" Frankie's voice breaks. "He's done that too many times to us!"

Toward the end of their first "relationship," if you could call it that, Frankie couldn't go on a night out without bursting into tears five drinks in.

"OK," Tom says, jumping across to her lounger and taking her in his arms. "I'm sorry if I'm upsetting you. But, you know, you've really upset me too. So, let's call it even."

"I'm sorry I haven't been in touch, I'm a bloody awful friend." She sniffs.

"You're the absolute worst."

Frankie giggles.

"But in all seriousness, you've missed some pretty major things in my life, you little dirtbag. I can't believe you didn't fly back for my wedding. I was going to force you to do a special rap in front of everyone and everything. And you weren't there when we adopted Roger."

Frankie's eyes expand over Tom's shoulder.

"You were totally going to be his godmother as well," Tom adds.

Tom and Joel have a fucking *kid* now?

"Babysitting him once a month so we could take a romantic break from being cat parents, which is an exhausting job, I'll have you know."

Phew.

"I'm sorry. I really miss you, you know. Even if it doesn't feel like I do." Frankie rests her head on his shoulder.

"I miss you too. Now come on, dirtbag, let's go wash all that filth off in the sea," he says, grabbing her hand and pulling her off the lounger.

"It's going to be freezing!" Frankie whines, inching toward the water and flinching when the wash froths at her toes.

245

"Cold water is good for you!" Tom says, striding in and quickly shrieking. "Come on! It releases endorphins! And I think we could all do with that today."

Frankie lets out a long groan and throws her robe behind her. She walks into the water in giant steps, her arms crossed at her chest, which is tensing with each step as the water rises. When it reaches her chest, she submerges herself and feels an icy wave rinse over her, pulling her hair back from her face. Her hair extensions are so heavy with water, she struggles to stand up. When she does, she feels instantly better. Then she screams in delight. She swims over to Tom, who's bobbing in the waves a few feet in front of her.

"I want today to be about us, Tom," she shouts breathlessly as she treads the water. "The four of us. Can we please make today a No Callum Day? Anyone who says his name has to do a shot or something."

"Babes," Tom says, swimming up to her. "I'm afraid that's going to be tricky."

"Why?" she says, before diving under a wave.

When she comes back up, Tom's eyes are darting toward the house.

Frankie spins around in the water to see Callum standing on the balcony.

Twenty-Eight

The last time Frankie saw Callum in the flesh was through that boardroom wall ten years ago.

When Frankie walked into the office that morning, she was feeling perkier than she had done in months. It took her six months to get over Paris. And another six to let go of her distrust of all men and get back into dating. She'd even met someone with potential the night before. It was more sparklers than fireworks, but she wouldn't say no to a second date and that was progress. Progress too was straightening her hair for work every day, instead of scrunching it up into a messy bun on top of her head. It wasn't even a messy bun, it was an angry bun. But not that morning. That morning, she'd actually made an effort and was wearing a new jumper dress and knee-high boots that she'd found for a steal at the fancy Oxfam off the King's Road. She bounced into the lift, and looked herself up and down as she twisted in the mirror and felt on top of the world.

But then the smell hit her nostrils and she came tumbling down.

Wherever Callum went, he left behind a thick cloud of bergamot. When the doors closed and the lift began to rise, Frankie started to panic. No one had warned her he would be in. There was usually an all-staff email saying the owners would be visiting, and for everyone to get shit off their desks. Why hadn't someone told her? She scrambled for her phone in her handbag, her heart pounding, and when she saw Priya's message she felt like fainting.

> **Priya:** Don't panic Callum's here Don't go to your desk I'm in the kitchen

Frankie, head down, barged through the office doors and turned immediately right. She didn't want to bring attention to herself by running. She didn't want to risk bumping into him by dragging her heels either. As she got to the kitchen, she peered at her desk at the other end of the office. There was a large bunch of flowers on it with a card.

Fuck.

"Stop staring!" Priya hissed from the kitchen counter.

"Oh my god, Priya, I think he bought me flowers, what does that mean?" Frankie said, panting.

"Oh, Franks." Priya sighed, putting her hand on Frankie's heaving shoulder. "No, he didn't. Sorry. I bought some from downstairs and put them on your desk to make him think that you've got a boyfriend. You know, to show that piece of pig shit that you've moved on."

Frankie couldn't help but feel slightly disappointed. But Priya's gesture made her want to kiss her all over.

"You're the actual best, do you know that?" Frankie said, pouring herself a double-shot coffee with three sugars that wouldn't help with her trembling.

Callum was in the boardroom all day. Frankie had toyed with the idea of taking her laptop into a meeting room, but what she didn't want to do was make it obvious that his presence bothered her. So she strategized with Priya to completely ignore him. The position of her desk made it impossible to avoid him, but under no circumstances (Priya's orders) was she to look up and over. So, Frankie stared straight ahead at her screen all day, feeling his laser-like stare burning a hole in her left temple. The stomach cramps were agonizing. At one point, she saw him turn around to face the other way and glanced over, but caught Priya giving her a death stare from across the desks and quickly returned to whatever she wasn't working on because she was too distracted to do anything.

As soon as she sees Callum leaning on the balcony wall here in Malibu, the stomach cramps return. And this time, with a vengeance. It feels like something is violently chewing her insides.

"Oh fuck," Frankie mumbles through frozen lips, waving up at him.

"Well, that's a really healthy response to seeing your boyfriend," Tom comments.

She turns to him. "Did you know he was coming back this morning?" Frankie hisse accusingly.

"Had no fucking idea," Tom says, joining her in the feeble wave. "What I *do* know is that Alice and Priya are going to be piiiiisssssed!"

*

Clutching her towel with both hands to hide her shakes, Frankie finally reaches the top step onto the balcony and comes face-to-face with her tormentor.

In ten years, he hasn't changed. His jet-black hair is still unsalted. And apart from his subtle designer stubble, his pale skin is still impossibly smooth. It's the glowing result of a fastidious skin routine that took up two hours of his day, morning and night. How he afforded that time, what with his time being so precious, she never understood. When he droned on about how hard he'd been working, she mocked him with a "on your exfoliation technique?" or "on your teeth bleach routine?" It amused him. He wasn't used to women teasing him, he said. He liked how different she was to his normal dates. He loved how easy she was to be with. How cool she was around him. How not like other girls she was. Old Frankie would lap it up. This Frankie wants to slap Old Frankie across the face. And remind her that *other women are great.*

Callum stretches his arms out, swallows her in a clutch and rocks her from side to side as he kisses the top of her head.

"Agh, get off me!" Callum cries in his velvety-smooth public school voice. "I'm all wet now!"

"That's what she said," Tom jokes.

"You're the one who hugged me," Frankie mutters, as Callum gently pushes her away, spanks her bottom and picks up a freshly laundered towel from the basket next to him.

"Happy birthday, Spanks." He smiles, looking at her hair. "You went under? With your hair?"

"So?" she asks, smoothing it down.

"Nothing, just hope it doesn't frizz up too badly for you," he comments.

For you, more like.

He always preferred her hair to be poker straight.

He reaches out to shake Tom's hand, the trusty old Rolex glinting in the sun. He told her he would buy her a Rolex after their first date. He didn't.

"Tommy, my boy! It's been a while. Still a joker, I see," Callum says, his white teeth sparkling. The kind of teeth that would still smell minty after an all-you-can-eat Indian buffet on Brick Lane. Not that Callum would ever do that.

Callum was passionate about small plate food. The tinier the serving, the tastier it is was his theory. The expensive restaurants he chose—and he chose every time—would leave Frankie with a dinner-sized hole in her stomach. She remembers laughing at one plate they were served at a restaurant near Green Park. The plate belonged in a doll's house, and on it lay a single sun-dried tomato. Frankie asked if it was an umbilical cord stump. Callum, unamused, grimaced and "educated' her about the cherry tomato being sun-dried on the roof of an Italian monastery by Sicilian monks and preserved in E-La-Won Luxury Edition olive oil from Greece. Just ten small jars a year were produced.

"Well, I guess the Catholic Church doesn't need the money, do they?" she joked.

"The jars are one thousand three hundred dollars each," Callum responded, not laughing.

Callum wasn't always serious. He could make her cry with laughter impersonating the leadership team at *The Leak*. And he always had a sense of fun. It was never just dinner. It was dinner, drinks, dancing and after-parties until the small hours at a friend's penthouse in Mayfair.

When he was in a good mood, dates with Callum felt like a huge adventure was just around the corner. She would end up in a swanky hotel that she could never afford, or find herself talking to Hollywood stars at a celebrity party, or wake up in an entirely different city altogether. He made her feel like she lit up the room. He'd introduce her to his friends as "*the* Frankie McKenzie," or "London's next big thing" or "this generation's Caitlin Moran." Someone as charismatic as Callum could have anyone, but he chose her. That made her feel special.

When he was in a bad mood, he'd pull her and the whole world down with him. They'd end up watching *Formula 1* in silence, sipping whiskys on opposite sides of the sofa, his blue eyes dark and stormy, staring over the rim of his crystal glass at the screen.

Callum has only met Frankie's friends a couple of times. Each time he was bursting with charm. Generous, quick to laugh, silly or sensitive when he detected the need. He has an amazing ability to identify personality types within seconds, and he uses it to steer his conversation accordingly. He leans in, asks questions, and avoids small talk. He goes deep fast, and makes you feel like he wants to share your pain, your problems, your joy. When he talks to you, it feels like you're the only person in the universe that matters to him.

"Tom, I remember something about you," Callum says, with a finger stroking his dented chin. "You love cinnamon swirls, right?"

Tom laughs. "More than my husband, just between us."

"Right, that's settled. I'll go fetch us a batch from this incredible bakery in Malibu. But I have to warn you, these bad boys will ruin it for you. No other cinnamon swirl will ever compare."

"I'll just have to move here," Tom says.

"If that's all it takes for Frankie to have her bestie here, I'll buy the goddamn bakery!" Callum shouts.

At least he's in a good mood.

Talking of moods.

Alice appears in the balcony door behind Callum, wearing a white dressing gown and slippers, blowing on a mug of something hot. The steam is blowing up into her eyes, which is lucky because from the glimpse Frankie caught, they were steely.

"Hi, Callum," Alice says, forcing a smile so fake that Frankie wants to burst out laughing. Frankie's always had a problem composing herself in tense atmospheres.

"Hello, Alice, how are you?" Callum says, using his soft voice. "You're looking really well. How's Ellie and Matt? They must be . . . eleven and eight now? Wow. And how's Justin?"

"He's fine. More than fine. He's doing really well, actually."

"Great! How's that business of his going?"

Alice looks confused.

"The IT management start-up thingy." Callum waves his hand dismissively in the air. "I still feel awful that I never gave him feedback on that business plan of his. Time is a luxury for me."

"I'd never have guessed with the Rolex," Tom comments.

"Water under the bridge. I'd actually totally forgotten that he asked you," Alice says, shrugging.

Bingo.

Frankie stares at Alice from behind Callum's back. When Callum promised to look over Justin's business plan for an IT management start-up, he never followed through. And after Paris, Alice fixated on it for months, telling Frankie that if he didn't care about her friends, he didn't care about her. She was right, of course. Callum would always over-promise and under-deliver. Or like Evri, never deliver at all.

"Well, I'm sure it's flying," Callum says.

"Yeah, it is," Alice responds.

"Great, great." Callum nods, putting his hand in his navy chino shorts, the *C* of his belt glinting in the morning sun. Frankie notices he still wears Chanel belts. He has a collection.

She always regretted not stealing one when he wasn't looking. She doubted he would even notice.

Alice's pocket pings. She pulls out her phone and giggles.

"That's hysterical. Frankie, come look at this photo of Ellie," she says, waving at Frankie to come closer.

Frankie squints at Alice's screen.

> **Priya:** It might be her birthday, but I'm not coming down until he fucks off.

Twenty-Nine

"The coast is clear!" Frankie calls toward the second floor.

Priya's head pokes round a corner a few seconds later. "I only came because I didn't think he'd be here!" she screams at the three of them.

"I didn't know he was coming back early!" Frankie shouts. "Come and get a coffee."

Priya descends the stairs sulkily, her feet thumping on each step. When she comes around the corner, she gives Frankie a weak hug and mumbles a birthday greeting. Silently, she walks into the kitchen and pours herself a black coffee before turning around and sighing.

"To give the man credit, he's been lovely so far," Tom says, shrugging. "Maybe he's changed."

"He might have changed." Priya puts her coffee mug down. "Doesn't mean the past has. It's going to be so fucking awkward, you guys! The last thing I said to him was "You're a short-sighted wanker and you're running your daddy's business into the dirt." Sorry, Frankie. I'd had a few."

Frankie shrugs. "Look," she starts. "I'm really sorry you've been put in this position, I know it's not ideal. Callum and Nina are going to be back from the bakery with our breakfast in an hour. You have two options. One, you can leave right now and take a cab to LAX. He never has to know you were here. Or two, you can stay and just see how it goes. Tom's right, he has changed. Of course I'd love you to stay. But I'm not going to force you to."

Priya lifts both eyebrows to let her sunglasses slide down onto her face. She takes a long sip of her coffee, plonks it down onto the counter and wanders down the kitchen steps and across to the open balcony door. The air is already warm, and the sky-blue pool looks particularly inviting as it shimmers in the sunlight, the mist from the infinity waterfall floating through the air.

Tom, Alice and Frankie glance at each other.

"Fine," Priya replies eventually. "I'll stay. I'm sorry, Franks. I hate being mean about him in front of you. It's just that being fired was fucking tough and seeing him again is a big trigger. But, maybe he has . . . matured. It was years ago. I'm sure I did dickish things back then too."

Same, Frankie thinks.

"Hon, you did dickish things ten minutes ago," Tom comments, giving her a hug from behind. "Let's just use this opportunity to open our hearts, soothe our minds, and embrace past trauma as a learning—"

"Shut the fuck up, Tom," Priya interrupts.

Tom gasps dramatically. "I was making an emotional connection!"

Priya rolls her eyes and walks upstairs, presumably to get
dressed.

"Aren't you chilly?" Tom shouts after her. "With that stone-
cold heart of yours?"

Priya flashes him a middle finger and disappears behind the
corridor wall.

Frankie glances at Alice sheepishly. Frankie loathes drama,
and this is one drama she couldn't have predicted and can't fix,
in the next few hours anyway. She glances at her clock. It's 9
a.m. and she has five hours left to unravel what's really going
on here. Why did she stick with Callum after he sacked one
of her best friends? Why did Callum stick with *her* all these
years, when being faithful is so alien to him? These questions
are going to require an adult conversation. Her heart sinks at
the prospect of trying to talk honestly and openly with him.
She tried a few times in the past, but Callum made heart-to-
hearts impossible. Most times, he used diversion tactics, like
switching the subject, ordering another drink, or striking up a
conversation with the table next door. If those weren't options,
he'd use placation tactics. He would agree with her issue, tell
her what she wanted to hear, or reassure her that things would
change. He'd make promises he wouldn't keep, then shed croc-
odile tears when he broke them. What was infuriating, in ret-
rospect, was that Frankie ended up feeling sorry for him. She'd
even apologize for upsetting him, for god's sake.

But not today. Frankie isn't the Frankie he thinks she is.

She's going to get to the bottom of what's been going on here for the last ten years. There's a chance he has changed. Slim, of course. And seemingly unlikely given the *LA Times* article. But she owes it to herself to find out whether this life is her best choice for her long-term happiness. She often wondered what Callum was doing, and what she'd be doing if she'd replied to his email. She always said she would be in exactly the same position, just a year down the track. Little did she know she'd be five thousand miles away.

When Frankie comes downstairs after changing, she sees Alice and Tom lying on the pool loungers. She's wearing a floaty pink Zimmerman beach dress that made her instantly salivate as soon as she saw it hanging in her color-organized walk-in wardrobe and feels like a million bucks.

"Hey, Mabel," she whispers, twirling in the mirror. "Can I keep the clothes?"

Frankie approaches the balcony door, which is partly open, and overhears Alice and Tom talking in hushed voices. She pauses, with her hand on the glass.

"Al, there's no point in feeling guilty about it," Tom mutters. "It was her choice in the end. You didn't force her. I don't think *anyone* could ever force Priya to do anything."

"Didn't I? I laid a massive guilt trip on her. Told her I thought Frankie needed us." Alice moans. "Of course, her response was, "and where was Frankie when I needed her?""

"That was ten years ago, she should be over it by now. Besides, I know for a fact that Frankie tried everything in her power to persuade Callum to consider other options. It wasn't personal, it was business. Priya was the one making it personal. I wouldn't put it past her to do the same if she was in that position. She's a shark too. I don't think Frankie deserved to bear the brunt of it. What was she supposed to do, dump Callum? It probably wasn't even his decision."

"That's true. I think he does fuck all at that company," Alice responds.

"I think he fucks all at that company," Tom adds, scoffing.

"Shhh!" Alice hisses, giggling.

"I'm sorry, that was harsh. I just wish Frankie could see what we see. It's like she's been blinded by the lights of this place. I mean, that chandelier in the hall is probably visible from space."

Unexpectedly, Frankie feels her hackles rising in defense of Callum. Her friends clearly have a problem with him, but they don't seem to have a problem with all the perks he comes with. The private jet, the infinity pool, the open bar, the personal chef. While they lie there sunning themselves and gossiping about him, he's out there getting them breakfast. Tom's favorite too. And if they have a low opinion of Callum, their opinion of Frankie must be right down there with it. She feels like an idiot.

"Credit where credit's due though," Tom continues, just as Frankie starts to slide open the door.

"What?" Alice says.

"He did remember my favorite pastry. And went to fetch it. That was nice. Although Christ, it's taking him enough time, isn't it, I'm starving!"

"So nice. Thoughtful of him to put Frankie on a diet too," Alice mutters.

"LA traffic," Frankie interrupts them, ignoring Alice. "It's notoriously terrible."

She only knows that because another writer at *The Leak* pitched an idea for a column called "Caught in Traffic" that showed celebs behind the wheel. It didn't go anywhere, when they realized it could be dangerous having paparazzi snapping at the wheel.

Alice and Tom spin their necks around.

"Hiya, where have you been?" Tom says.

"Cute dress!" Alice cries.

Compensating, are we?

"Just been on the phone," Frankie says.

"To your agent?" Tom asks.

"No." Frankie smiles.

"Kris Jenner?"

"No," Frankie repeats.

"Lisa Vanderpump?"

"Yes! She's heading over right now with the dogs," Frankie replies.

"Don't toy with my heart like that." Tom sighs.

"I need to pee," Alice says, standing up. "Ugh, the joy of peeing without being pestered by my kids. I love LA!"

Callum's been gone for over an hour. It does seem like a big effort for a bakery. Frankie prays he delivers the goods when he comes back. She'd love him to prove them wrong. Maybe a part of her wants him to prove her wrong too.

Frankie hears the front door slam, and peers through the balcony glass. Callum and Nina are back, and they're carrying towers of pastry boxes and juice trays. A wave of gratitude washes over her. Callum might have been stingy with his time, but he was never stingy when it came to hosting guests. As she watches him and Nina start to lay out the pastries on the dining room table, she can't help but wonder if something really has changed in him. Perhaps it isn't wonder, perhaps it's just hope.

"Frankie's birthday breakfast is served, ladies and gents!" Callum shouts from the dining room.

"Hi." Frankie smiles at him. "This looks incredible."

"No," Callum says, looking her up and down, making her heart flutter. "You look incredible. I love that dress on you."

"Thanks." Frankie grins, walking toward him and planting a long kiss on his lips.

"Cal," Nina says, cutting the kiss short.

He breaks off the kiss, removes his arms from around Frankie's waist and turns to her.

"Would you like your supplements now?" she asks.

"Yes, please," he says. "Thanks for reminding me. What would we do without you, Nina?"

Nina smiles coyly as she turns around and retreats into the kitchen.

"Wow, this looks ah-mazing," Tom says, taking a seat. "Cheers, mate."

"My absolute pleasure, T-dawg, help yourself!" Callum replies.

262

"Thanks, I'm starving," Tom replies, lunging for a cinnamon swirl and tearing a huge chunk from the side. With his mouth full, he pauses, looks up at Callum and blurts out, "Holy fuck!"

Callum nods vigorously and cries, "I know, right? What did I tell you? I think it's the nutmeg. Or maybe the chili."

When Alice reappears from behind Callum, she gives Frankie a weird look that she can't decipher. Then she slowly takes a plate and a pastry. "Thanks for this," she says frostily.

God, give him a break, won't you?

"I hope you like them," Callum replies eagerly. "Hey, where's Priya? She did come, didn't she?"

The three of them glance at each other over their juice cups.

"She's just getting dressed," Tom quickly replies.

"Phew. For a moment I thought she didn't make it. You know, because of what happened. I really want to clear the air with her. I still feel awful about it. So does Frankie. It took Frankie a long time to forgive me, I tell you. But, you know, the decision was largely out of my hands."

"Hi, Callum," Priya says coolly, at the bottom of the stairs.

"Priya!" Callum cries. "You look so well, how have you been?"

"Yeah, fine," Priya replies.

You could cut the tension with a bendy spoon.

"I was just telling the others how terrible I feel about what happened at *The Leak*. I want to be open with you and tell you exactly what I told Frankie at the time. It wasn't personal, and it wasn't even my decision. It was the board's. To keep *The*

263

Leak going, we had to cut a quarter of the highest paid staff. In a seriously fucked-up way, it was testament to how well you'd done there."

"So I got punished for being good at my job?" Priya laughs.

"Yeah, like I said. It's fucked up. I didn't want to fire you, Priya. My family might own *The Leak*, but it doesn't mean we run it. I remember saying to Frankie that, in a way, I didn't feel too bad about you losing your job."

"Excuse me?" Priya says, crossing her arms.

"Because you're so bloody talented! I knew that you would be fine. More than fine. I knew that you'd walk away from *The Leak* and get snapped up instantly, probably with a step up as well."

God, he's good.

Priya's face softens.

"Did you?" Callum asks.

"I did actually," Priya responds.

"Fantastic, where did you end up?" Callum asks.

"*The Hour*," Priya says, her eyes darting between the table and him. "I'm global head of sales. The youngest they've had."

"Jesus, that must be intense," Callum replies, sipping his coffee. "But if anyone can handle it, I guess it's you. So, it's all worked out OK? More than OK by the sounds of it."

The four of them stare at Priya, collectively wishing she would relax so they could.

"Yeah, it's all good, Callum," she says, smiling. "Honestly, it's fine. It's in the past. We can move on."

"*The Hour* is killing it at the moment," Callum mutters,

sipping his coffee. "Maybe we should buy it. How attached are you to your job, Priya?"

Priya puts her hands on her hips and tilts her head at him.

"Kidding!" Callum laughs.

Priya starts laughing too, giving everyone else the green light to laugh.

This could just be OK, Frankie thinks, feeling a warmth toward Callum that she hasn't felt in a long time.

*

After breakfast, Callum offers some ideas for how to spend their day. But all everyone wants to do is lie on the beach. Frankie's pleased. She doesn't have long left here. As she fumbles through a drawer full of bikinis, her phone pings.

> **Alice:** Can you come to my room?
> It's urgent.

Thirty

Alice is pacing frantically by the window of her bedroom when Frankie walks in.

"Shut the door!" Alice whispers agitatedly, unraveling a strand of brown hair that she's wrapped around her finger.

Frankie follows the order, and leans against the door behind her.

"Are you OK? What's happened? Are the kids OK? Has something happened at home?" Frankie asks, her eyes wide as she watches Alice continue to patrol the room, wringing her hands.

Alice stops, turns to Frankie and exhales, her shoulders sinking as she does. The routine reminds Frankie of the time Alice discovered that Justin had taken out a huge lump of their savings for start-up capital. She was so furious about it that she took the next train up to London to see Frankie, so she could vent before confronting him. She wanted to make sure the conversation wasn't a fight, so she used Frankie for practice.

"You're scaring me," Frankie says.

"Home is fine. *Here* is the problem," Alice says through gritted teeth.

"Deep breaths," Frankie says calmly, wandering over to the bed and sitting down.

Callum has been nothing but charming from the moment he arrived. It can't be something he's said or done. Is Frankie the problem? Is Alice finally going to reveal what's been heavy on her mind for the past twenty-four hours?

"Look, if I've done something wrong—" Frankie begins.

"It's not *you*, Frankie! It really upsets me how you always think everything's your fault," Alice cries quietly. "For once, I wish you could see what others see in you. You aren't the problem. It's Callum."

"Okaaay," Frankie says, sighing. She's only been here for a day and she's already exhausted from defending him. "What's he done this time?"

"He's shagging Nina," Alice blurts out.

"What?" Frankie laughs.

"I saw them, Frankie. I was in the loo when they came home from the bakery. It's right next to the front door. I heard giggling, and when I cracked the door open, he was whispering things to her. I don't know what he was saying, but they were making her laugh. It felt a bit too familiar."

Frankie rises slowly and slides her hands deep into her dress pockets as she wanders over to the window. She starts laughing, and turns back around to Alice.

"What the hell is so funny?" Alice asks, her face looking more outraged by the second.

"Because of *course* Callum is shagging Nina," she says bitterly. "She has a pulse, doesn't she?" Frankie can't help but laugh.

A smirk spreads across Alice's face. "I'm not so sure about that. I have a strong suspicion she's an android."

"I wonder if he's programmed her to tell him how big his dick is," Frankie jokes.

"You. Have. A. Large. Penis. Insert. Penis. Now," Alice says robotically.

The two of them snort.

"Orgasm. Activated," Frankie adds, her shoulders jerking.

Once they've recovered from their giggling fit, Alice walks over to Frankie and gives her a hug.

"You're an idiot and I love you," Alice whispers in her ear.

When she leans back, she takes Frankie's hand.

"Why aren't you upset about this? I mean, I'm relieved. I expected you to deflate and collapse onto the floor like a stabbed balloon. You know, like you did when he dicked you around before."

Frankie can't tell her the truth, that none of this is real and it's all one big act.

"I think I'm anaesthetized to it. He's scarred me so many times that the whole area has gone numb." Frankie shrugs.

"So, why are you still here?" Alice asks, sounding exasperated.

"Honestly, I have no idea," Frankie replies truthfully.

Frankie starts throwing a few theories about her misplaced loyalty around in her head.

Her first theory is that she stays because she's become accustomed, or maybe addicted, to this lifestyle. But that doesn't make sense. Frankie's never been *that* interested in being Ms Moneybags. She's always wanted to have enough so that she isn't pleasantly surprised that her card goes through at the end of the month. But she's certainly not the type to sacrifice her happiness and dignity for it.

Her second theory is that Callum has some kind of hold over her. Is there a sex tape that he can blackmail her with? Or has she done something illegal that only he knows about? Frankie shakes her head. That's ridiculous. But so is her wardrobe.

Her third theory is the most plausible. She's too ashamed to admit she was a fool for getting back together with him. Too proud to return to London with her tail between her legs and listen to people say without saying, *Told you so!* Too stubborn to tell them they were right all along. That sounds more like the Frankie she knows.

"I have a question," Frankie says, slumping back onto the bed to stare up at the ceiling.

"Go on," Alice says, examining her C-section scar in the mirror.

"Why is he still with me? What's the point of having me

around, when he could have a different woman here every night? And probably does, when I'm asleep. I'm just an ordinary girl from Surrey, who eats baked beans and watches *Eggheads*. I'm hardly exciting or glamorous, am I?"

"Get up," Alice says sternly.

"What?" Frankie lifts her head.

"UP!" Alice yells, pulling on Frankie's arms and dragging her over to the mirror. "What do you see?" she asks, pointing at Frankie's reflection.

"I see a thirty-six-year-old blond woman who vaguely resembles me," Frankie murmurs.

"You know what I see? I see beautiful, smart and funny as hell. I see generous, loyal and kind. I see powerful, capable and strong. Frankie, of course he wants to be with you. Everyone knows you're worlds better than he will ever be. He should count his lucky stars that you're still here. When I walked in and saw that portrait in the hall, I was shocked. And it wasn't because it's basically a nude greeting, it was because the woman in the portrait is so confident. I was pleased for a while. I thought, Finally! Frankie loves herself. Every time you have a confidence wobble, I want you to channel Portrait Frankie. Confident, fierce, will-rip-your-face-off-with-my-bare-teeth-like-this-apple Frankie."

"Rar," Frankie says quietly.

"Louder," Alice says.

"Rar," Frankie repeats a bit louder, starting to giggle.

"Louder for the twat downstairs!" Alice shouts.

"RAAAAAR!" Frankie yells, adding a raised claw for effect.

"Ooooh sexy!" Alice laughs. "OK, so for my next trick. You know that pedestal that you've put Callum on?" She lifts her hand horizontally above them. "I want you to flick him off."

Frankie gives her a side-eye in the mirror.

"Go on!" Alice says.

Frankie slowly lifts her hand up and flicks the air above Alice's palm.

"Weeeeee pew!" Alice makes a bomb sound. "Now, I want you to put yourself up there instead."

Frankie frowns.

"Haven't got all day!" Alice shouts.

Frankie, confused, stands on her tiptoes and stretches her neck to rest her chin on Alice's palm.

"Like this?"

"Well, I was thinking that you'd mime it. Like, take a little imaginary Frankie off your shoulder and place it on here."

"Can I take my chin off your palm now?" Frankie says through clamped teeth.

"Yes, please do. You're being super awkward." Alice giggles, lowering her hand. "But you catch my drift, right? From the day you met Callum, you've placed him on this crazy high pedestal. Maybe he blinded you with his power, or his Rolex or his—"

"Eyes," Frankie comments.

"Whatever. What you see when you look at Callum is suave. Do you know what I see? Slimy. Cocky. Two-faced. Sorry, Frankie, it's a brutal truth. You see funny, I see fake. You see banging, I see bang average. You see successful, I see—"

"Dead people?" Callum's velvet voice interrupts.

Frankie's eyes explode in the mirror as her blood runs cold. She turns her head to see Callum leaning against the doorframe, carrying two coffees.

"Just thought I'd bring these up to you," he says, placing them on the side table by the door.

Was he listening?

"Who are you girls gossiping about then? Anyone I know?" Callum smiles.

"Channing Tatum," Alice comments.

"You think Channing Tatum is bang average?" Callum laughs. "Wow, Alice, I didn't realize you were so picky when it comes to men."

"I'm not. I just know a good man when I see one, that's all," Alice says coolly, picking at her mascara in the mirror.

"Can I talk to you in private?" Callum turns his eyes to Frankie.

"Is everything OK?" Frankie asks, in an everything's-peachy high-pitched voice.

"Hunky-dory," Callum replies. "I just haven't seen you alone since I got back. And I want the birthday girl to myself for a bit."

"Is ten years not enough for you, then?" Alice whispers, as Frankie closes the door behind her.

Thirty-One

Frankie follows Callum into their bedroom, and spots the *LA Times* on their bed. She wanders over to the paper, lifts it up and smiles at him.

"I can't believe I'm in the *LA Times*! It's so cool," she says, grinning at the article.

"Neither can I," Callum replies, staring out of the window.

"Are you proud of me?" She smiles, taking a seat on the bed.

"What the fuck were you thinking, Frankie?" Callum turns, his eyes glaring at her.

"What? Are you angry?" She scoffs. The old Frankie would have whimpered, but this Frankie doesn't give a shit.

"Were you ever going to tell me about this reality show you're planning? I'm sorry, but if you're inviting camera crews to follow you around like some desperate, bored housewife with nothing better to do, then I have a right to know about it. It's my life too, you know."

"You're never here anyway, Callum," Frankie says, staring

deadpan at him as he walks back and forth, stroking his hair back every few seconds.

"What about this book? First time I've heard of it. What are you going to put in there? Stuff about me? You have no right to do that, it's not fair. I've given you everything, Frankie. Everything! The house, the cars, the luxury holidays. Is that still not enough for you? Am *I* still not enough for you?"

Ah, the guilt tactic again. Callum would always find a way to twist the situation so that Frankie looked like she was a spoiled brat, hell-bent on hurting his feelings. *Well, it's not going to work this time, buddy.*

"If you knew me at all, Callum, you'd know I don't care about all that stuff. I'm baked beans, not foie gras. You'd know that time is more important to me than money. And you don't seem to have enough for me at all," Frankie says, glaring back at him.

"Look, I'm not angry, I'm just upset. You know how important privacy is to me, and here you are telling the whole town about what we get up to behind closed doors."

"I barely mention you in this piece!" Frankie cries.

"Exactly!" he retorts. "I'm supposed to be the one in the spotlight, not you!"

"I s that what this is about? You're . . . jealous of the attention on me?" she says quietly.

"For someone who claims to hate the spotlight, you're sure enjoying basking in it now, aren't you? And I'm not jealous, I'm confused. You hate attention. What's changed? Or maybe the question should be . . . who's changed you?"

The deflection tactic is a new one on her. Frankie feels her blood begin to boil. She crosses her arms tightly across her chest, for fear that at any minute her hands could spring from their lock and wrap themselves around his neck.

"Are you serious?" she asks, in disbelief of his audacity. And in disbelief that she ever dated him in the first place. Her eyesight might be a bit blurrier than it was at thirty, but she can see him for who he really is now with laser sharp focus.

"Is it them?" he asks, nodding toward the door. "Have your friends been in your ear about me? The way Alice looked at me just then, you'd think I was covered in stinking shit. I don't know why, I've been nothing but nice to her."

"Maybe it's because you're shagging Nina?" Frankie replies, shrugging.

Callum stops in his tracks, turns to her and puts his hands in his pockets. Then he lifts the corner of his mouth, in the way she used to find irresistible.

"What?" he splutters, blinking fast.

"Oh, for crying out loud, Callum, just admit it!" Frankie cries, throwing her hands on her head. "Alice saw you and Nina whispering and giggling when you came back from the bakery."

Frankie has never seen this side of Callum. He was always so cool and collected. She'd joke that he should be called Calm Maxted. But this Callum is a far cry from the one that she knows. He looks shaken. Perhaps it's because he feels the shift in power between them.

Frankie always let his behavior slide in the past. He was the cat, she was the mouse. But this mouse has got her tiny paw on assault rifles, hand grenades and an army tank, and she's on the warpath. She watches him stew on her outburst, silently strategizing. Conjuring up excuses, justifications, appropriate responses. How is he going to come back from this one?

"Alice is either blind, drunk, or lying, because she didn't see anything," he says finally. "Nina and I have been friends for ages. You whisper and giggle with Tom the whole time, you don't see me accusing you of shagging him."

"Well, Tom's gay. And we both know Alice isn't blind or drunk. And she certainly isn't a liar," Frankie replies.

"So, you're saying that I am?" Callum says.

"Yes!"

"So you trust Alice more than me?"

"Yes!"

"You have changed. Something's happened to you since I've been away, and the only thing I can think of is that Alice has set you against me, or maybe there's something else. Is there someone else, Frankie?"

"What the fuck, Callum? Stop trying to deflect the attention away from you! Answer the question, are you shagging Nina?"

"No, I'm not shagging Nina, OK?"

"Why would Alice lie about what she saw? What in the world does she gain from lying?"

"You! Frankie! She gains you! She's jealous of me and thinks I stole you away from her. She wants you back. That's what this is about. It makes total sense. She thinks I tore you two apart, and she's here to get you back. The more love you have for me, the less love you have for her. And she knows that this town ain't big enough for both of us."

"Bollocks," Frankie says.

"I find it very funny that after one day of Alice being here, you're back to old Frankie." He scoffs.

"What's that supposed to mean?"

"Have you looked in the mirror lately?"

Frankie takes a step to the side to look in the long mirror beside the cupboard. Her wild waves are back. She rolls her eyes and turns back to him.

"Do you honestly expect me to buy that theory? That Alice flew out here on some kind of revenge quest to make up a story about you and Nina? I used to respect you, Callum. Now I just feel sorry for you. You're pathetic, do you know that?"

"Don't . . . call me . . . that," Callum says, turning to her and straightening his spine.

Frankie frowns at him.

"You know my dad has called me pathetic my whole life. How can you be so cruel?" He frowns at her.

But this doesn't move her. And when she doesn't respond, he becomes even more belligerent.

"God, Frankie, what's happened to you? When I left last week you were a kind, warm, soft girl and suddenly you're this angry, cold, bitter woman in a power suit on the front page. How could you have changed so much in just a week?"

"Stop making this about me." Frankie sighs. "Look, we're going around in circles. How about we lay all our cards on the table and have an open and honest discussion about what we want. I'll start first, if you like?"

He shrugs.

"I want you to stop cheating on me with other women."

He starts to protest but she puts her finger up to her lips. "I want a career of my own. And I want to see my family and friends more. I want them to come here, and I want to go there several times a year. I want you to fire Nina, because her food is rank and her attitude stinks. And I want you to take back what you just said about Alice. Because if you don't, I'll never forgive you."

Callum takes a deep breath in, raises his eyebrows and says, "Consider it done."

It's not quite the confession she hoped for. But it's probably the best she's ever going to get from him in the time she has left.

"Do you know what I want?" Callum says. "I want to start again. Clean slate time. When your friends have gone, I want us to fly to the villa on St James, and spend a couple of weeks there just getting to know each other again. Learning to love each other again. I know I've been away a lot, and there's been too much distance. I love you so much, Frankie. I don't want to lose you. To anything."

Like a career, to her family, to her friends. This is never going to work.

"Why do you love me, Callum?" Frankie asks.

"What's not to love about you, Frankie? You're gorgeous, funny and kind. And you do this thing with the corner of your mouth. It's like a secret smile. It drives me wild whenever I think about it."

He walks slowly over to her, takes her hand and starts kissing her fingers. His signature pre-sex move hasn't changed. If anyone else did it, she'd gag, but Callum has a way of doing it that makes her want to remove her top immediately. His lips move up from her hand to the inside of her wrist, soft kisses along her goose bumps all the way up her arm. He leans forward and starts kissing the side of her neck. Soft kisses, no tongue. Just the way she likes it. She leans her neck back and thinks of how long it's been since anyone has touched her like this.

The thought sparks a wave of grief inside her, and she sits up abruptly.

"What's wrong?" he says, his face full of worry.

"I . . . need the bathroom," she says, getting up quickly.

An invite to St James, Callum's Caribbean villa, was all Frankie ever wanted when they were together. Well, not all, of course. A timely reply to a text message, a toothbrush at his London apartment, or an invite to meet his friends would have been nice too. Although, Callum didn't have that many friends. Acquaintances, yes. But they were generally business associates or employees. He didn't have an Alice, who knew him better than he knew himself. Or a Priya, who'd defend him to the death. Or a Tom, who'd make him double up with laughter when he felt his lowest. When Frankie asked him about his friends, he'd say they were scattered all over the world. A large but shallow pool. He'd blame his parents for moving him around the world more than a dozen times, among London,

New York and Geneva. He never stayed in one school for more than a couple of years, and back then there was no social media to stay in touch.

Callum had shown her photos of his holidays on St James, and she pretended to be fascinated, in as much as you can when viewing other people's holiday photos. Several times she threw the line out with an "I'd love to go!" but he never took the bait.

But now's her chance. The idea of a break on a Caribbean island sounds like just the tonic she needs. If only the company wasn't so toxic.

In the bathroom doorframe, she turns to him. He's lying on the bed, with his arms folded behind his head, and his slanted smile. Then something catches her attention on the bed frame. It's a clock. The time is 1.59.

Frankie smiles at him, closes the door, shuts her eyes and feels the whoosh of the lift returning her to safety.

Thirty-Two

"Well, that was dramatic!" Mabel cries, leaning forward and resting her chin on her hand at her office desk.

"You can say that again," Frankie replies, exhaling hard and leaning back in her chair.

"Did it change your mind about wanting a celebrity life?" Mabel smiles.

"It one hundred percent confirmed that I do not want a celebrity life," Frankie says. "It does make me hate my job even more though. I feed the beast at *The Leak*, don't I? At least mine was an interview, and I controlled the narrative. Imagine waking up and finding your picture plastered across every news outlet for absolutely nothing. Last year, I ran a picture of Jenny Jackson taking her bedsheets to be dry-cleaned. The headline was *Jenny Jackson airs her DIRTY LAUNDRY in PUBLIC* and the story gave readers a multiple choice quiz, asking them to guess who'd made them dirty the night before."

"Yeah, that was a low blow," Mabel comments. "But, hey, acknowledging it is the first step!"

Frankie nods in agreement.

"So, I want to hear everything. Your answer to "What if I'd got back together with Callum?" led to you living in a Malibu mansion, on the brink of stardom . . ."

". . . with an absent and unfaithful boyfriend, hanging on to my friendships by my fingernails, and feeling like a stranger in my own body and mind," Frankie finishes Mabel's sentence.

"I guess you have to consider if the pros outweigh the cons," Mabel says.

"I can't pretend not to be wowed by the lifestyle," Frankie says. "I think my bathtub in LA was bigger than my flat in London. Oh my god, and the walk-in wardrobe. Could I plonk the Malibu mansion on the Mexican beach? Swap Callum for Raphael, and then move all of my friends to Cozumel? Is that an option? I feel like anything's possible here."

"Sadly," Mabel says slowly, "no. None of your crossroads lead you to that life, I'm afraid. But we still have a couple more lives to live."

"The thing is, I know money doesn't buy you happiness and blah blah blah, but it does buy you peace of mind in many ways. I'd like to know that I'm not going to end up living in a cardboard box and dining off crumbs when I'm sixty."

Mabel stares at her.

"Does that happen to me in one of these lives?" Frankie cries.

"No." Mabel smiles. "But money can be made and lost,

Frankie. Nothing in this life—or any of these live—is ever guaranteed."

"Helpful, thank you," Frankie says.

"What have I told you before? Stop thinking so far ahead, stop trying to plan the future," Mabel replies.

"I feel like an idiot." Frankie sighs. "I can't believe I lasted that long with him. Ten years of being a kept woman, lied to and cheated on. It makes me question who I became. Whoever it was, I don't recognize her. The me I know would have abandoned that luxury ship years ago. I just can't understand what kept me there. My only guess is that I didn't want to admit to making a mistake getting back together with him. I was so broken when our relationship ended, and my friends made such an effort to pick up the pieces. Alice came to stay with me. Tom did my grocery shopping and cooked me dinner for a week. Priya took time off work—which she never doe—and whisked me away to a spa. For me to get back together with him, only to break it off months later, would have felt like I was taking the piss."

"They sound like the kind of friends who would rather pick up the pieces again than know you were unhappy," Mabel comments.

"They definitely are," Frankie replies. "But patience can run out."

"True," Mabel replies.

"Callum aside, the kept-woman status should have bothered me more. I might hate my job at *The Leak*, but I want to do something with my life. What do I do here every day? Get up when I want, have breakfast cooked for me, stroll along a private beach, lie by the pool, read books . . . hold on . . ."

Frankie pauses, when she realizes she's describing heaven.

"I mean, I've heard of worse . . ." Mabel adds.

"Fine, it sounds pretty fucking fantastic. But imagine doing that every single day, for the rest of eternity? Wouldn't it feel like *Groundhog Day*? I know myself, and I'd be bored to death. No wonder I was thinking of doing a reality show. I hate attention, but at least I'd be doing something. At least I'd have a camera crew to keep me company."

"I think you're forgetting that you do have friends in LA, Frankie," Mabel comments.

"Do I?" Frankie replies

"Yes, they messaged you on your birthday. You just didn't read them," Mabel adds as she starts to type something into her computer.

"OK, I'm not supposed to do this," Mabel continues. "But you play doubles once a week with three women from the neighborhood."

Frankie starts giggling. "Me? I play tennis in this life?"

"Yes," Mabel says, shifting her glasses up her nose.

"Seriously, Mabel," Frankie says. "The only time I've ever used a tennis racket was to swat flies on a camping trip in Cornwall six years ago."

Mabel looks back at her computer screen and starts laughing.

"You're also part of a scrapbooking club. You meet every Thursday afternoon," Mabel says, squinting at the screen.

"OK, wow, how bored am I?" Frankie replies, her cheeks puffing out as she exhales.

"Oh no," Mabel says, squinting at the screen and turning to Frankie.

"What?"

Mabel pivots her computer to show Frankie what's on the screen. It's a scrapbook full of photos of her friends, family, the Clapham mansion block, a Pret bacon bap and The Windmill beer garden.

"That's my scrapbook?" Frankie asks, her voice raised.

Mabel nods. "It might be the saddest thing I've ever seen," she whispers.

There were many times when Frankie felt lonely in London. When it was too late and too far for Priya to come in. When Tom and Joel were having a couple's night or romantic weekend away. When Alice was taking a kid to a playdate, looking after a sick kid at home, or trying to do both at the same time. Frankie tried to be understanding of the fact they weren't as free as she was. Maybe they even envied her availability to make impromptu plans for a night out, a day session or a spontaneous trip to the countryside. But it was hard not to feel isolated. Frankie never imagined that she'd end up lonely with Callum. When she daydreamed this *what-if* scenario she imagined fabulous dinners with him a few times a week, rock-star parties every Saturday, and romantic spa weekends away. Just the two of them, not his whole entourage. Her imagination got carried away at times. But never in a million years did she expect to pine so hard for her old life.

The scrapbook is sad, but it's proof that here she longs for her old life. That her old life had more going for it than she appreciated at the time.

"Shall we move on?" Mabel says.

"Aren't we done yet?" Frankie groans. "I feel like we've covered every crossroad I can remember. The one-way flight. The marriage proposal. The fortune. What else is there?"

"The fame," Mabel says.

"Fame?" Frankie repeats, confused.

"Does *In Deep* ring any bells?"

Frankie lowers her head into her hands.

PART SIX

From GOSS to GIRL BOSS:
Celebrity columnist chooses CAREER over KIDS

Thirty-Three

The day Callum eyeballed Frankie from the boardroom for six solid hours was the day she definitively decided to leave *The Leak*. The yearlong radio silence after Paris broke her heart. The laser-like stare through the glass burned a hole in her head. The threat of bumping into him regularly was too much to bear. She thought she had moved on, but the instant panic his visit produced in her made evident her post-relationship trauma hadn't healed. Nor would it, if she continued to come face-to-face with her trigger. Callum was not a case for exposure therapy, he was a case for a swift exit.

In another world, Frankie would have fumed about feeling forced out of her job by a man. But it wasn't like she loved it anyway. Her predicament gave her the push she needed to try something new. To rediscover her passion for writing stories with substance, and redirect her career away from the gossip column trap she'd unwittingly and unwillingly fallen into. He was a curse, but he was also a blessing in disguise. Callum the catalyst.

A fortnight after Callum sent his email, Frankie polished up her CV, penned her own glowing LinkedIn review for Priya to post, and went job hunting. She chopped her hair into a long bob, got a Brazilian blowout, bought a navy trouser suit, and made Tom practice interviewing her in exchange for a takeout pizza and a bottle of Tesco Finest plonk. Without fail, the interviews always ended up with a game of "would you rather." Tom would lower his face and stare at her over his glasses, and say seriously, "Would you rather have a toe for a nose, or a nose for a toe?" or "Would you rather smell like blue cheese or bad eggs?" They'd erupt into giggles, give up and toss a coin to see who had to go to the corner store for the second bottle and a pack of French Fancies.

The interview was for a reporter at *In Deep*, an exciting new magazine start-up with a mission to make people fall in love with long format features again. As its name made clear, it required in-depth research into meaty topics like space exploration, climate change, gender equality and social justice. Subjects she aspired to write about when she was at university, but that couldn't be a further stretch from the latest piece in her portfolio, "Star Quiz: Guess the Celebrity Ankles and Win a Toe Ring," which was hardly going to win her respect.

"I'd really rather not relive this," Frankie says, sighing.

"Why's that?" Mabel asks.

"I should never have gone in the first place. I don't know why I thought they'd be interested in someone like me."

As Frankie waited with twitching legs for the call into the interview room at *In Deep*, an older woman came and sat on the seat next to her. Frankie's eyes darted toward the folder on the woman's lap, which was bulging with clippings from *The Sunday Times*, *National Geographic*, and *The Spectator*. Frankie held her own folder closer to her chest to hide any evidence of *The Leak*.

"There was a woman sitting next to me. When I saw her portfolio, I realized I had a zero percent chance of getting the job, but a one hundred percent chance of making a complete fool of myself in front of a panel of proper journalists."

After a few minutes, Frankie stood up, turned to the woman next to her and mouthed, "Good luck," before making a beeline for the revolving glass door. On the Soho street outside, she closed her eyes and inhaled a big gulp of fresh air to cool off and calm down. Then she took her phone out, sent a text and scurried toward the pub on the corner, dropping her pitiful portfolio into a recycling bin she passed on the way.

"What happened?" Mabel asks.

"I left before they called me in," Frankie says. "I couldn't face the humiliation. I went and met Priya for a drink instead. And she told me that she'd heard rumors that senior management was being restructured and that Callum was relocating to LA to look after the US titles. So there was a good chance I'd never see him again."

"Did you carry on job hunting?"

"No," Frankie says. "That was my one and only interview."

291

"Maybe they saw something in you that you couldn't see yourself at the time," Mabel suggests.

"I bet they brought me in for the banter," Frankie says. "I know how brutal journalists can be."

"Frankie." Mabel sighs, switches the screen off and swivels around to face her. "You talk a lot about the fear of losing control over your life. But have you ever considered that the fear itself is controlling you? Your low self-esteem is letting big opportunities pass you by. This interview was a chance to break away from a job you loathed, but you gave up before you even bothered trying. If you'd gone to that interview, who knows what might have happened. Instead, you went back to living the same life that you were longing to change."

"Enough!" Frankie cries. "Please, just . . . stop. If you must know, I do regret bunking out on that interview. I feel terrible about it. Why are you even bringing this up? I thought the whole point of being here was to answer the *what-ifs*? You're just making me ask more of them. And what's worse is that every life choice in front of me seems worse than the next. Live a broke life in Mexico. Live a boring life with Toby. Or live a lonely life in LA. Oooh, spoilt for choice!" Frankie gives a sarcastic thumbs-up.

"Rude. Nothing wrong with a Bounty," Mabel mutters.

"Look, I want out." Frankie sighs, pushing her chair back and standing up. "I don't want to do this anymore."

"Why has this interview hit such a raw nerve with you?" Mabel asks. "You have no idea what happens next."

"I know exactly what happens next. I'll go for the job interview, be laughed out of the room, get reported to my editor at *The Leak* because journalists are like the Mafia, be fired, end up living in my dad's garage with Jet and writing the odd article for *Sewage Monthly*."

"Could be worse." Mabel shrugs.

"How?"

"You could write for . . . *Sewage Weekly*."

Frankie deadpans her.

"You could have a column called "To Be Stankie"?" Mabel suggests.

"Hilarious," Frankie states, pushing her chair in.

"It could be a big shit—sorry, I mean hit." Mabel smirks.

Frankie marches to the office door and grabs the handle.

"Oh, Frankie, sit down," Mabel implores her.

"If leaving now sends me forward instead of backward, I'm actually fine with it. I've made peace. I can't decide between those three options so far, and I doubt I'll be able to decide on the next two. So, let's just call it. Let me go."

"What about your friends and family?" Mabel asks.

"They'll be fine. They're busy people, living their own lives. It's not like there's a lot of them. My death will impact a very small pool of people. Of course they'll be upset, but people lose people every day. I'm not special. Hell, some people might even be secretly pleased. I can name at least ten celebrities who'll be relieved to see the end of 'To Be Frankie.' "

"Oh, Frankie," Mabel tuts and shakes her head. "You know what your problem is? You think you don't matter."

Frankie shrugs. "Do I matter?"

"OK, I'm not supposed to do this," Mabel says, standing up. "But follow me."

Frankie follows Mabel through the office door, and closely behind her as they weave their way through the panicked crowds toward the lift Frankie arrived in.

Thirty-Four

THURSDAY, AUGUST 31, 2023, 8 A.M.

When Frankie steps into the wooden hallway with wheat-painted walls, the smell of the patchouli reed diffuser surrounds her. She replaces it monthly for the residents of the fourth floor. As she has done for over twelve years.

She's home.

"Is this it? Are you letting me go?" Frankie turns to Mabel, beaming.

"Funny how this is the happiest you've looked since we started," Mabel comments, twisting the diffuser jar on the windowsill and placing her hands in her pockets.

A door opens behind them and they turn around.

"What's happening?" Frankie whispers, when she sees herself emerge from her flat door.

She's wearing the same outfit as her last day. The white chiffon top is stainless, her curls are fuzz free and she's wearing the new boot—blissfully unaware of the chaos they'll cause.

Real Frankie walks straight past them without as much as a glance.

"Come." Mabel nods her head, as they join her in the lift.

Frankie stares hard at the back of her own head. It isn't often she gets to see herself from this angle. She leans forward. She's comforted by the scent of her Kerastase shampoo, one of the little luxuries she treats herself to every month.

Mabel pulls her back as the lift doors slide open on the ground floor. They follow Real Frankie across the hallway, and watch her stop outside the front door. She picks up a copy of *The Times*, and returns to Mr. Graham's door, gently dropping it on the welcome mat. Then she walks out of the block door, taking a bottle of water out of her handbag. She spends the next thirty seconds tending to the flowerpots on the front steps.

"Happy birthday, Frankie!" a voice cries from behind them, followed by the slam of a door.

It's Mr. Graham. He waves at her from his flat.

"Thanks, Mr. Graham!" Real Frankie smiles.

"Beautiful day, isn't it?" Mr. Graham calls.

"Gorgeous," Frankie replies. "Need anything later? I'm sure I'll pick up a few things from the shops on my way home."

"If you wouldn't mind picking me up my usual?"

"A Turkish Delight and a can of Fanta?" Real Frankie smiles. "I'll leave them on your doorstep when I get home. I might be a bit late, though, I have a date!"

"Oh, a date! What a lucky man," Mr. Graham replies. "I hope he's worth your time."

"Me too." Frankie smiles half-heartedly.

She recognizes that expression on her face. It's hopeless.

When Real Frankie finishes spraying the flowerpots on the steps outside the block, they follow her down Clapham South Side toward the Tube station. Outside, she stops at the coffee van run by a young Polish woman called Maria who Frankie recently discovered was an aspiring stand-up comedian. They've had the same routine for months, since the van first parked there. Frankie noticed the name was "Wheely Good Coffee' and commented, "Where have you *bean* all my life?" with her first order, which made Maria giggle. Since then, they've always greeted each other with coffee puns. This morning, it was Maria's turn.

"Frankie! Why are you so latte this morning?" Maria smiles.

Frankie laughs and replies, "Better latte than never!" as she hands her carry cup across the counter and peers behind the corner of the van.

The trumpet busker is back again.

"I'll take two this morning, Maria, thanks," Frankie says.

As Frankie walks into the Tube at Clapham Common, she places the second coffee next to the trumpeter, who pauses mid-song to blow a fanfare as she passes, as is their usual exchange. She chuckles as she descends into the Underground, with Mabel and Frankie hot on her heels.

*

During the jam-packed rush hour ride on the Misery Line up to Old Street, Frankie starts considering her life choices again.

This journey is a stark reminder of what day-to-day living was like in London. Sure, she enjoyed her exchanges with Maria and Trumpet Boy, but is this what she really wants to do every day for the rest of her working life? As she cranes her neck away from a dank sleeve next to her, she tries to calculate the hours she will spend on this journey from now until she's sixty-five. She gives up after five seconds of fringe maths in her head.

When Real Frankie walks into the office, she removes her hand from her pocket and waves at Jolly Janine, whose face lights up as she waves back enthusiastically. The Frankie following behind her notices for the first time that everyone else walks straight past the reception desk without so much as a nod in Janine's direction. Perhaps Jolly Janine isn't so jolly after all. It must be lonely down here with no one to talk to all day.

At her desk, Frankie slumps onto the chair and removes her denim jacket, hanging it loosely behind her.

"Tea, Frankie?" says Art, the intern.

"I think it's my round, isn't it?" Frankie says, swiveling around. It's deadline day, but she can spare a few minutes. She's fond of Art.

"I'm happy to," Art says. "It's your birthday!"

"Yeah, but it's also deadline day, so I'm going to need your help with some headlines," Frankie replies.

"Really!" he exclaims, his eyes expanding.

Art has a first-class degree in English from Oxford. He's clever and keen, but super green, so no one trusts him with their precious pieces. But how is he supposed to learn if he doesn't get a chance? Unfortunately for Art, her research involves scrolling the social media accounts of D-list celebrities. She feels guilty every time she asks. Like she's leading him into the same trap she fell into when she first got here.

"Can you have a read of the first draft for this week's column and come up with some headline suggestions?" she asks. "Remember the style checklist too. Find the hook. Make it urgent. Keep it under ten words."

"Thanks, Frankie!" Art beams. "I'll do my best."

"I know you will," Frankie says. "Now let me get you a mug of writer's fuel."

Frankie and Mabel follow Real Frankie as she walks to the kitchen, smiling at her coworkers as she passes. Art stares at her with peachy-pink cheeks as she does, looking as pleased as punch with his proper assignment.

"And you think you have no impact on the people around you?" Mabel remarks. "Frankie, you might not think you're important to them, but they know that you are."

Frankie scans her work family, and sees them—and herself—in a whole new light.

"Frankie McKenzie!" bellows Paul du Toit, one of the founding editors. He's in the kitchen stirring a black coffee, wearing his signature tweed blazer and magenta cravat. "What's new in starland?"

"Same old." Frankie smiles, reaching for two mugs from the cupboard next to him. "Nightclub stumbles, Starbucks runs and Twitter spats. I'm the next best thing to Emily Maitlis, Paul."

"Do I sense sarcasm?" Paul says, clinking the spoon against his cup. "Your column is a consistent top performer, you know. It might not be *Newsnight*, but it's a light relief for lots of people."

"Not sure the celebs would agree."

"Oh, please." He waves his hand. "You're keeping them relevant."

"Thanks, Paul." Frankie smiles.

"Great piece this week, Frankie!" Marian Grange comments as she rushes past for the weekly ad sales meeting. "Using red nail polish as the hook? Genius. We're running an Essie advertorial underneath."

"Look at that," Mabel whispers. "Another Frankie fan."

Frankie knows her mindless column is a top performer. The fact might give her job security, but it does nothing for her personal pride. But maybe her biggest problem is her own intellectual snobbery. Thousands of readers click on her column every month. Does she think they're all mindless? She's giving *The Leak* readers what they want. An escape from the political scandals, world crises, economic doom and gloom. She just hates that her column has to be so harsh the whole time. She tried to re-angle it a few years ago to celebrate celebrity wins and moments of joy. But the clicks dropped fast.

"People want to read about heartache and pain, Frankie," Paul had said.

"Why, though? Can't I just run positive stories for a couple of weeks and see the impact on the clicks?" Frankie had begged.

"Because it distracts them from their own heartache and

pain! People want to know they aren't alone in their suffering. That celebrities have embarrassing moments, relationship problems, wardrobe malfunctions, weight issues, just like they do."

"Stars, they're just like us." Frankie sighed.

"Precisely. Now, go and find a story on Lorraine having piles or something," Paul concluded, pointing his finger at his office door, in good humor. "Actually not Lorraine," he called out. "She's a national treasure. Dig out some *more* dirt on Matt Hancock."

*

"Oh no, anywhere but here," Frankie says, as they stand outside Date Night watching the real Frankie walk in. She's already limping, having worn those damn boots all day.

"Come on," Mabel says, taking Frankie's arm.

"I really don't want to, I feel terrible about it," Frankie says, pulling her arm in the other direction.

"Just five minutes," Mabel says. "I want you to see what you're like on a date. And it's really important, Frankie. Because you think you're awful. You think they don't want to be there, and that you're wasting their time and yours."

"Well, I usually am!" Frankie cries, as she drags her heels behind Mabel through the doors.

"Maybe you should spend less time worried about what they think of you, and more time finding out if you actually like them." Mabel shakes her head.

Oli Sarpong is cuter than she recalls. A kind face with deep dimples, and soft eyes that stare into hers as she's talking. Frankie doesn't remember him looking at her like that. Then she glances over at herself to see that she's looking anywhere but at him. She's actively avoiding his gaze, her eyes darting all over the room. At her empty pint glass, which she twists in her hand. At the infatuated couple behind them. At the piano player beside them. If she'd just taken a moment to look into his eyes like he's looking into hers, perhaps she would have felt more confident about this date. But she'd given up on Oli before they'd even met. History had taught her that successful dating leads to boyfriends, who lead to heartbreak and humiliation. Perhaps it wasn't history. Perhaps it was just Callum.

Oli is telling her a story across the table, and from the look on her face Frankie can tell she isn't listening. She's staring at the couple behind him.

"So I've started teaching my niece and her friends to code. I know a lot of people think it's better for kids to be outdoors, but I think it's good to have a balance. I teach them the basics. But kids are like sponges, you know, they pick things up so quickly. Remi's already coded a game. You know what it's called? Chicken and Egg! They have to race each other. She's so smart." He laughs.

"Reeeeally?" Frankie replies, reaching for the cashews.

"God, I'm such a dick," Frankie says, squeezing her eyes shut. She can't bear to see herself like this. "If you wanted me to feel better about myself, this isn't working."

"Yes, this is one of your more dickish moments," Mabel

302

says. "But the fact still remains that the reason you weren't listening is because you have such a low opinion of yourself that you thought listening was pointless because this wasn't going anywhere."

"Still pretty selfish," Frankie says. "Oli's a good person. I am not."

"Yeah, you are. Good people admit when they're in the wrong. Bad people don't," Mabel comments.

Moments later, out of the corner of her eye, Frankie sees herself rushing toward the main door. She turns back to Oli, who starts applauding the piano player.

"Can we get out of here?" Frankie begs Mabel.

✳

"So, here we are," Mabel says, the bright lights around the Kebab Palace sign painting her face neon blue.

Frankie sees herself inside with her phone to her ear, giggling at Tom on the other end. She erupts into laughter, throws her head back and freezes.

Frankie turns to Mabel, frowning.

"We can carry on if you want to," Mabel says. "You can see the aftermath of your accident. But I wouldn't advise it. It's very difficult to watch."

Frankie looks at herself again through the glass, her eyes filling with tears. In that precise second, she looks so happy. Sure, she had her issues weighing her down. Another dud date. Another night on her own in bed, with friends' feeds for

303

company. But she also had her whole life ahead of her. Opportunities to change what was making her unhappy. She had no idea that she was about to lose it all.

"Let's go back," Frankie says, her voice cracking. "I want to visit my next crossroads."

"Great," Mabel says. "Let's see what would have happened had you done that interview."

Thirty-Five

When Frankie opens her eyes, she's in a large glass office with exposed brickwork and a wall of framed black-and-white photography. On the other side of the glass is an office full of desk workers. Some are wearing headphones and staring with purpose at their screens. Some are chatting animatedly together in huddles. And some are rushing through desk aisles, reminding Frankie of herself on deadline day. It's the type of glamorous office she'd pictured working at one day. Like the set of *The Bold Type*. Maybe she's in New York? She walks across the parquet floor, past the glass wall and toward the big window, admiring her white high-top trainers and the swing of her baggy blue boyfriend suit in the reflection. Frankie in this life looks pretty bloody cool. For the last few years, she's felt lost in fashion. An older Millennial, reluctant to surrender her skinny jeans and ballet flats, she's been stuck in a late-2000s time warp. And she finds some of the pieces at Zara so confus-

305

ing that she's too scared to try them on in case she gets her leg stuck in a sleeve.

Peering out of the window, she spots Spitalfields Market in the distance. The sight of a red bus whirring past comforts her. New York would have been exciting, but she needs calm after the emotional chaos of LA. Frankie swivels on her trainers and takes in the wall of photographs opposite her, squinting her eyes to make out the pictures.

"Oh my god," Frankie whispers.

In one of the photos, she's shaking hands with Arianna Huffington.

She takes a few steps forward, squinting harder.

"Oh my GOD," Frankie says, louder this time.

In another photo, she's in the middle of a hug sandwich with Zadie Smith and Marian Keyes.

She rushes toward the wall, losing all her cool in an instant.

"OH MY GOD!" she yells, at a photo of herself sitting next to Cher at an elaborate dinner table.

A knock on the glass door disrupts her whirling thoughts, and she turns to see a small twenty-something staring at her with a concerned look in his eye.

"Everything OK, boss? he asks before slapping himself on the forehead. "I mean Frankie. Sorry, I know you told me not to call you boss."

"That's OK . . ." Frankie replies after a few seconds spent processing the information, "How can I help?"

"Hey, Benji! Hey, Frankie!" a woman passing behind him shouts into the office.

"Hey, Niamh," Benji replies.

"Hey!" Frankie quickly adds with a weak wave.

"It's 9 a.m. and I just want to go through your diary for the day," Benji says, his head lowered as he taps on the tablet he's holding. He steps through the door and lets it close behind him.

"Of course, shoot," Frankie replies, walking calmly back to her desk and taking a seat on the green velvet chair.

"So first things first." He lifts his head and smiles sweetly, hugging the tablet close to his chest. "I'm not in tomorrow, so here's a little something. Don't worry, I haven't told anyone!"

He pulls out a box of French Fancies from behind him, and places them on her desk. "I know they're your guilty pleasure."

"That's very sweet of you, thank you," she says, taking the box of French Fancies and opening one side. "How did you know?"

"The empty boxes in your bin kind of gives it away." He giggles.

"Well, that would do it," Frankie says, blushing as she starts opening the side.

"Oh, are you going to eat one now?" he asks.

"Is that not OK?" she responds, her hand stuck in the box.

"Well, it's just that you have a meeting with a reporter from *The Big Five* in twenty minutes."

"Ah, right. Good catch." Frankie nods, extracting her hand, closing the box and placing it back on her desk next to a black mug with BADASS BOSS BITCH on the side, which makes her scowl.

"Then at ten, you have a meeting with MediaMob. At

eleven, you have an editorial scrum on Christmas features. At twelve, you have lunch with LoxyLix to talk about next month's TikTok collab. Super-excited about that by the way, did you see her reel last night? Girl's a genius. At two, you need to be at The Dorchester for the WWWomen Awards, then from there you head straight to Nobu in Knightsbridge for dinner at seven with Emily."

"Emily?" Frankie asks.

"Maitlis?" Benji says.

Frankie drops the French Fancies on her desk and grabs the arms of her chair, her mouth dropping open.

"Emily frickin' Maitlis?" Frankie cries.

"You have dinner with her every month, why are you so surprised?" the man asks.

Frankie quickly switches her expression to one that's sane and mutters, "I'm not, I just . . . thought it was next week, that's all."

He stares at her.

"Well, it sounds like a pretty full day, Benji. Think I need a kick! Would you mind getting me a coffee?" she asks him.

"I thought you were off caffeine?" he says.

"Good god, why on earth would I be off caffeine?" She laughs.

"Because of . . . last week?" he replies. "Is everything OK, b—Frankie? You seem a bit distracted?"

"I'm fine, I'm just . . . pumped. Big day ahead. Oat milk latte, please."

The man lifts his eyebrows, sighs, and shrugs. "Sure, no problem."

As soon as her office door closes behind him, she logs on to her screen and opens her emails to hunt for a clue in her signature.

Frankie McKenzie. I run The Show.

She clicks on The Show link and her eyes widen.

The site looks like a brighter, poppier version of the Huff-Post. She scrolls down through a sea of articles with a common female thread about women politicians, entrepreneurs, gamers, sports icons and influencers. She clicks on the About section.

The Show
Shining a spotlight on strong women.
The Show is a platform for women to share their struggles, stories and secrets to success in their field. By bringing the female experience to the fore, The Show aims to inspire women from every walk of life to learn, lead and lean in.

Frankie McKenzie, Founder
It was during her journalism degree at Sheffield University that Frankie first had the idea for The Show. It was the mid-noughties and male content dominated the Internet. Frankie wanted to plug the gap and reclaim the online space with women-centric stories. But it would take her

a few years of real-world media experience to gain the knowledge to start. She spent six years running her beloved pop column, "To Be Frankie," at *The Leak,* before moving to *In Deep,* where she spent two years profiling powerful people, before landing a regular interview feature "World-Changing Women." #WCW gave her the opportunity to connect with female figureheads internationally, many of whom would help Frankie with the advice, funding and inspiration she needed to start The Show.

A sudden aggressive throat clear from behind Frankie's screen makes her gasp. She pokes her head around the corner to see a familiar face a few feet away.

"What are you doing here?" Frankie says excitedly. If she smiled any wider, her jaw might lock.

"What the fuck do you mean, what am I doing here, you complete numpty?" Priya says, leaning her neck back and emptying a Smint into her mouth. The mint crackles in her mouth as she chews. She stares at Frankie, almost accusingly. Then she swallows. "It's nine fifteen. I'm always here."

"I know, I know," Frankie replies. "I'm kidding with you. You know, like, 'Oh, fancy seeing you here!' vibes."

"You're weird," Priya replies.

"Yeah, I know." Frankie has to agree.

"So," Priya says, folding her arms tightly across her chest. "Are we going to talk about last night?"

Frankie sighs.

What now, for fuck's sake.

Thirty-Six

"Two hours, Frankie!" Priya shouts.

"Shhh," Frankie says, glancing at some turning heads outside the office.

"We were on the phone for two hours at one in the morning. What the hell were you still doing here? You swore you would stop these insanely late nights. You are one all-nighter away from self-destructing, and I really don't want to pick up the pieces. I mean, I will, because I love you, but please don't make me. Not now, anyway. I've got way too much on my plate myself. Ad sales has three new starters this week and no one has any time to on-board them. Can you just put a pause on your imminent meltdown for like a month?"

"What do you mean? I'm fine!" Frankie cries. "I'm more than fine, I'm great. Can you believe all of this?" she says, looking around the office.

Priya follows Frankie's line of vision, then turns slowly back to her with one eyebrow raised.

"Are you drunk?"

"I'm not drunk, I just have a new appreciation of what we're doing here. It's bloody brilliant, isn't it? I mean, wow. Did you know I've got an interview with *The Big Five* this morning? *The Big Five*, Priya!"

"Yeeeah," Priya says slowly. "Frankie, they've interviewed you like three times already. It's cool, and I'm proud of you, but also . . . What's new? Also, who are you this morning? Last night you were a hot, blubbering mess and this morning you're all big dick energy."

"I think you mean big boobs energy," Frankie replies.

"Can we just be serious for a second," Priya says, shifting her seat closer to the desk and lowering her voice. "I'm really worried about you, Frankie. I don't want to get another call like that, you really fucking scared me. You told me that you were one click away from booking a one-way flight to Mexico. And I get it. You've built something bigger than you ever imagined and you're under a shit-ton of stress. But we're all in this together, Frankie. The Show isn't all on your shoulders. Sure, you started it, but take a look around you. Look at all the support you have. In here, out there. You built it, and they came. Now *use* them. Stop getting sucked into the details of the operation. You're so worried about how little time you have to see friends, meet guys, visit your mum. But you can make time if you learn to let go. I know you hate feeling like you aren't in control, but we've got this. Let us look after things here. Even if it's just for a week. Go and do a gong bath with your mum in Goa. Or plant some peas with your dad in Surrey. You need to recharge, because right now you're running on five percent. And I'm worried that your battery is about to go totally flat. Don't let us down. Go away, get your shit together, and come back with your head sorted."

"How am I meant to do that when I have back-to-back meetings?" Frankie replies.

"You're the boss. Benji will clear your diary," Priya says. "And I bet that all those meetings could be handled by someone else."

"How can someone else do an interview with *The Big Five*?" Frankie lifts her eyebrows.

"Get Benji to put on a wig." Priya smiles, standing and walking behind Frankie's desk. She leans down, takes the mouse and opens Frankie's calendar.

"Fine, do the interview," Priya mutters. "But Sally can do the MediaMob meeting. The overly keen editor in chief you literally just hired to run the editorial team can do the Christmas features, you shouldn't even have that in your diary. LoxyLix collab . . . who the fuck is LoxyLix?"

"A TikToker," Frankie replies, like she knows.

"Partnerships can do that," Priya comments, scrolling down.

"WWWoman Awards . . . Emily . . . dinner . . ." Priya stops scrolling and stands up. "OK, fine, one more day in the office, but cancel the rest of the week. I don't want to see your face here tomorrow morning."

"You're being a bit bossy for someone who isn't the boss," Frankie comments quietly, feeling her feathers ruffled by Priya's pushiness.

"And you aren't being bossy enough," Priya replies. "Look, you're the master of your show. If you want it to be a tragedy, I can't stop you. But I can't just sit here and do nothing, either. Not after last night. Do you even remember half of our conversation? I mean, I know you aren't drinking because of your panic attack last week, but you sounded a bit out of it."

Panic attack? That's a first. And that's why she's off the caffeine, and booze apparently.

"Vaguely. Fill me in, though. I was feeling wiped out," Frankie replies, fishing for more information.

"Weren't we all? Do these ring any bells? You said you'd written an all-staffer announcing your resignation. You were booking a one-way flight to Mexico, because, and I quote, it's something you should have done years ago. You were going to message Toby to see if he wanted to go with you, because you've decided that he's the one that got away."

"What? I don't think Toby is the one that got away!" Frankie laughs, although maybe this life has made her think that.

"That's not the worst part," Priya says, perching her bum on Frankie's desk.

"You told me you were setting up a meeting with Callum to see if Maxted Inc. wants to buy The Show."

"Oh my god! Over my dead body!" Frankie exclaims.

"Yes, over your dead body!" Priya cries. "Because I will kill you before that can ever happen."

"It would be The Shit Show," Frankie replies in a whisper.

"That's the exact joke you made last night," Priya says. "You need to sleep, my friend."

314

"No, she doesn't!" Benji chirps, knocking on the glass with his tablet. "She needs to knock back a Berocca and crack her best smile. For half an hour, anyway. Bonnie from *The Big Five* is going to be online and ready to go in ten minutes."

"I guess The Show must . . ." Frankie starts.

"Don't . . ." Priya says.

". . . go on." Frankie smiles.

"You did. You're such a nerd." Priya chuckles, shaking her head and walking toward the door. "Think about what I said, Frankie. For your sake and for our sakes."

✱

The Big Five is a podcast that interviews five people a week asking five provocative and personal questions in five minutes. It started off as a basic e-newsletter, quickly gained cult status, and it must have at least a million downloads a month. A profile in *The Big Five* means you're a big player. Frankie's been hooked since the first episode aired five years ago, featuring Whitney Wolfe Herd.

How Frankie has ended up on a podcast with Bonnie Brown, the founder, is beyond her. The same way she ended up in that photo on the wall doing karaoke with Gillian Anderson. Her heart pounds as she waits for Bonnie to let her into the call. She leans forward, noticing her dark eye bags in this light. She taps her fingers along them in a last-ditch attempt to calm them down.

"Hello?" Frankie says, leaning back and grabbing one earphone, as she sees Bonnie's face pop up in front of her, her hair scraped back under her trademark floral headband.

Frankie glances up at Benji, who's giving her a questioning thumbs-up from behind the glass wall. Frankie nods and returns the gesture.

"Frankie! How have you been, mate? Great to have you back on the show!" Bonnie says in her familiar Burnley accent.

It makes Frankie instantly panic. She can't do this. Frankie's never been interviewed in her life, and she has nothing interesting to say. What if Bonnie asks her about the business? She's only been here for an hour. She pushes her nails against the desk until they hurt.

"Frankie, are you still there?" Bonnie asks, looking into the camera.

"Great to be here, Bonnie!" Frankie replies, immediately wishing she hadn't responded with such a cliché. "Sorry, there was a bit of a lag. All fixed now."

"Wonderful," Bonnie says. "We haven't actually started the official recording yet. But don't worry if there are any technical hiccups along the way, we can sort them out in post. Nothing to freak out about. But you know that already, don't you? How many times have we had you on the show? I think this is the fourth, isn't it?"

"That's right!" Frankie says, without a clue.

"Oh no, wait, this is the third, my producer has just told me," Bonnie corrects them both. "I guess you're so busy they all blend into one, don't they? On that note, I really appreciate your time with me today."

"The pleasure's all mine, Bonnie," Frankie responds with another cringeworthy cookie-cutter response.

"Well, as you know, we aren't taking up much of your time as it's only five minutes long! And I don't want to steal any more of it, so I guess let's get cracking with the first question. I'll just do a quick intro and then we'll get started. Ready?"

"Born ready!"

Die.

Oh, wait, she already did.

Frankie's cheeks are burning, and she's pleased this is a podcast and not a video interview.

"The podcast and video will go live next month, just so you know," Bonnie comments.

"Video?" Frankie replies.

"Yeah, we've started uploading these videos to the site as people were asking for more video content. Is that OK?"

"Of course!" Frankie responds, brushing a flyaway hair from her forehead.

"Don't worry, you look fab, like always." Bonnie smiles.

Then she quickly turns to her mic and begins talking at speed.

"Welcome back to *The Big Five*, everyone, we've got a really exciting show for you today. Our first guest is a familiar face, and the founder of the hugely successful news site The Show, where women share struggles, stories and secrets to success in their field. Starting out as a scrappy site that she circulated among former city coworkers, The Show now has over twenty million unique visitors a month across the world and offices in London, LA, New York, Sydney and, recently, Tokyo. It's Frankie McKenzie, hello, Frankie! How have you been?"

Twenty million unique visitors. What the actual hell.

All of a sudden, Frankie's mouth feels like it's filled with cotton wool. A cough attack is coming. Right now. She grabs the water bottle in front of her and takes a big sip, but it goes down the wrong way and she starts to splutter. She tries to swallow, but it only makes it worse and soon the cough takes hold of her entire body. Frankie slams her finger down on the mute button and swivels away from the screen to hide her exploding face, her shoulders shaking, her eyes filling with tears and her lungs gasping for relief.

"Oh dear, Frankie? Are you OK?" Bonnie says.

"Sor—" Frankie tries to apologize, but her lungs won't let her, and she remembers she's on mute so all Bonnie can see is the back of her head and her flailing arms.

Frankie was not ready for this. Nor was she born ready. She should have listened to Priya and got Benji to do it. This is humiliating. If she can't even get past an introduction, how is she going to answer any actual questions? Is she going to faint at the first one? After what feels like an hour, she turns around, dabs under her eyes with a tissue from her desk and unmutes.

"Oh god, I'm so sorry, Bonnie!" she cries, her voice croaking. "My water went down the wrong way. I just need a minute."

"Of course, take your time."

"I'm OK, I'm fine," Frankie replies, taking another sip of water, cautiously this time.

"Great, so let me just lead into that one again. It's Frankie McKenzie, hello, Frankie! How have you been?"

"I've been brilliant, thanks, Bonnie," Frankie says, her voice back to normal. "We've been working on some brilliant Christmas features for the next edition . . ."

You said brilliant *twice.*

"And we're really excited about them. They're going to be brilliant."

For fuck's sake.

"Well, that's *brilliant* to hear!" Bonnie giggles. "So, let's get cracking, Frankie. Everyone knows you're an outspoken feminist and The Show has done a lot to push for women's rights. But before The Show, you had a column at *The Leak* called 'To Be Frankie', which, at the time, attracted fair criticism for its treatment of female celebrities. My question is this. Do you regret it?"

Frankie takes a deep breath. In recent times, managing the comments section of "To Be Frankie' has become a full-time job for their community manager. The response was always the same. They'd thank them for their feedback and tell them it would be factored into the next editorial meeting. Of course it never was. If the clicks were there, they didn't care.

"I never intended for 'To Be Frankie' to become a Burn Book for female celebrities, Bonnie. When I started, the aim was to share candid views on what celebrities of every gender were getting up to. But in this digital age, our work is constantly monitored and measured. *The Leak* had an entire team dedicated to measuring click rates in real time, doing social listening, testing headlines to see which performed better. Getting eyeballs to engage has never been so competitive. So, when the team saw which articles were performing better—which was invariably female celebrities and their fashion choice—then I was briefed to do more of what worked. It's what *The Leak* readers wanted. Toward the end, the column didn't look anything like the original pitch I made to the editor in chief. I was embarrassed to have my name attached to it. But do I regret it? No, I don't think I do. I think writing 'To Be Frankie' almost incentivized me to make a go of it with The Show. The rage I felt at having to write it at times gave me the angry energy I needed to start all this. Who knows if I'd have had the motivation without that experience? It was also my first job in the media. I was surrounded by brilliant people who gave me an incredible opportunity and some invaluable, lifelong lessons. And I want to do the same with the amazing young team I have here."

"Firstly, can I just say, fantastic *Mean Girls* ref there, Frankie." Bonnie laughs. "Such an interesting response, I can see what you . . ."

Frankie feels her shoulders lower and her breathing slow. That was a good response, if she does say so herself. She doesn't need to panic. She can do this. She's Frankie Fucking McKenzie. She runs this fucking show.

But Priya's suggestion of spending a week at home didn't fall on deaf ears. She does want to see her dad. But she only has twenty-two hours left to spare.

Thirty-Seven

Frankie stands in front of 4 Hastings Close, the semi between Surbiton and New Malden that her dad moved into after the divorce. She scans his pristine front garden for anything that's changed. But it's the same as it always has been, and she takes comfort in this. The brick path leading up to the front door is still framed by the low pruned hedge, and behind it sits his pride and joy—a stone birdbath water fountain with a cherub on top. At Christmas, he'd place an elf hat on the cherub and chuckle softly with delight at the silliness.

"Morning, Betty, morning, Bob," she whispers to the garden gnomes flanking the front doorstep, as she presses the doorbell and hears the familiar *Friends* theme tune ring out, followed by a cacophony of squeaky snarls and barks coming from Lesley's pack of prickly Chihuahuas.

"Les! The dogs!" she hears her dad's voice cry, as loudly as he can.

"Phoebe! Rachel! Chandler! Come on, into the conservatory!" Lesley's voice rings in the background.

When the door opens and she sees her dad's rosy face, she throws herself into his arms and buries her face in his chest. The outburst comes as a surprise to her, and she's sure it comes as a shock to him too. Usually, they'd greet with a quick peck on the cheek and a side hug.

"Hello, love!" her dad says, gently patting her on the back. "What's all this about, then?"

"Oh, nothing," Frankie says, quickly pulling herself together and then pulling away. "I just feel like I haven't seen you in ages."

"You're working hard, love, it's OK, we're very proud of you," he replies, giving her shoulder a quick squeeze as he helps her remove her handbag.

Frankie slips her shoes off at the same time, and places her bag down on the floor, staring at the huge framed photograph of the dogs in front of her. Each dog is wearing a different wig; one blond, one dark, and one sandy with distinctive layers at the front. It doesn't take a genius to guess which is which. "F.U.R.I.E.N.D.S" is spelt out on top, in the *Friends* logo.

"Well, this is a lovely surprise!" Lesley calls from down the hallway. "Do you love it?" she asks, when she sees Frankie studying the photo. "Your father bought me a photo shoot for Christmas. My babies look like little stars, don't they?"

"I thought we'd be in it too," her dad comments. "Sometimes, I think Lesley wishes I had fur and four legs."

"A woman can only dream, dear." Lesley giggles, rubbing

his arm. "Now, you couldn't have come at a better time. How do you fancy a slice of cake for lunch?" she says, taking Frankie by the hand and guiding her down the hallway.

In the kitchen, there's a carrot cake on the island.

"Quick, get the candles out, dear!" Lesley chirps.

"You really don't have to." Frankie smiles, feeling a sudden wave of guilt about keeping Lesley at arm's length all her life.

"Nonsense! It's your birthday!"

"Tomorrow," Frankie adds.

"Well, yes, but you've probably got big party plans with all your friends for tomorrow!" Lesley replies.

The split might have been amicable, but being close to Lesley when she came on the scene a few years later still felt like a betrayal. Especially considering how different she was from Frankie's mum. Lesley likes things spick-and-span. She covers their cream three-piece sofa suite in clear plastic in case of spills. Lesley doesn't like change. She wears the same ballet flats from Marks & Spencer in three different neutral colors: dark tan, medium tan and light tan. Lesley, a retired nurse, sticks to a rigid routine that's mapped out on the kitchen calendar, even though it's had the same weekly entries for years. Her life is aerobics at David Lloyd, coffee at Costa, shopping at Costco, and dog training in the park at the end of their cul-de-sac. Having Jet festering in the garage with his "art' must infuriate her, but kudos to her that she's never complained about it. At least, not to Frankie's knowledge.

"Is Jet here?" Frankie asks, opening the birthday card and jumping back when it blasts out the "Happy Birthday" song.

"Sorry, love, he's at Jade's. They're working on some new project," her dad replies.

"They're literally glued at the hip," Lesley mutters.

"Literally?" Frankie asks.

"Last week, they used up all your father's superglue to stick their naked hips together. Then they took a bunch of photo—nude ones!—to use for Jade's final submission for art school. I mean, who the bloody hell do they think they are, John Lennon and Yoko Ono?"

Her dad titters.

"Anyway, they had a nightmare removing the glue and I had to get in there with some nail polish remover to help. I'm scarred for life!"

"Oh my god." Frankie laughs.

"Kids." Her dad shakes his head.

"They're not kids, though, Eric, they're in their thirties now! They need a swift strike to the head with a reality stick, if you ask me. But, it's not for me to say anything. Your father's got to deal with it. I think he's an enabler."

"OK, Les, let's drop it and cut the cake. Frankie, can you believe I made this myself! With my own carrots!" her dad says, beaming, as he hands her the knife.

"Wow, Dad, I didn't know you could bake!" Frankie replies.

"I've just started," he said. "I'm getting into all sorts of baked vegetable loaves. The allotment has really delivered this year and there's only so many roasted carrots and courgettes we can eat."

"Tell me about it," Lesley chimes in.

"Did you know that you can make a cake with courgette? Incredible," her dad says, ignoring the comment.

"I think your father has found his calling." Lesley smiles, patting him on the back. "I keep telling him he should set up a stall at the Saturday market, but he refuses."

Frankie doesn't blame him. Setting up her mum's art stall on Saturdays at dawn must have put him off markets for life.

"I'd love to see the allotment, Dad," Frankie comments, taking a bite of carrot cake and humming with pleasure as she chews.

Her dad's face lights up. "Really?"

"Yes! Why wouldn't I?"

"Well, you've never shown an interest before," he comments. "I'd be delighted to. Let's get some tea in a flask and have a wander."

*

The allotment is a five-minute stroll from the house, and Frankie's sure it's the main reason they moved here in the first place. Her dad's plot is a rose between thorns, and looks like the only plot properly cared for.

"Have you made any friends here, Dad?" Frankie asks, taking a seat on a camping chair he's unfurled for her from a small shed on the side.

"Loads!"

"Really?" Frankie says, surprised.

"My plants are my friends. I talk to them all the time, and you know what, they're really good listeners."

Frankie chuckles. No wonder she loves watering the flowerpots in Clapham. She got it from her dada.

A quiet but comfortable moment passes between them as she sips her tea and watches her dad crouch down to remove a few dead leaves from the patch.

"Dad, can I ask you a question?"

"Shoot!" He smiles, pointing at a plant in front of him and looking pleased with himself.

"Are you happy?"

"Of course! Why are you asking me that?" he replies, brushing his hands on his trousers. "Don't I seem happy?"

"No, you seem very happy. I was just wondering. Maybe my birthday has got me thinking about big life questions."

"I have everything I've ever wanted. Great kids. Kind wife. Roof over my head." He smiles.

"So you're pleased with the choices you've made?" Frankie asks.

"I think I've made the right ones along the way, yes." He nods.

"What about mum, though? Do you think you made a bad choice in being with her? Do you ever wish you could turn back time and do it differently?"

"Never! If I didn't marry your mum, I wouldn't have you." He laughs. "Marrying your mum was probably one of the best choices I ever made."

"I guess the split wasn't that tough either," Frankie comments.

"Well, it had its moments. It wasn't all sunshine and rainbows, love."

"Really?"

"We made it seem that way to you, because the last thing we wanted was for you to feel like your whole world was collapsing. So we put on a united front and said we were still best friends. We both agreed that the relationship had run its course, but there were painful moments. Your mum was and still is so bright and full of life that when she left everything felt . . . dark. And a bit empty. It was an easy choice but a hard goodbye. But, eventually, the light came in again and it led me here. And, you know, being a doctor always helped me gain perspective on things when I was going through tough times. Nothing brings you back down to earth like very sick people. When I had too many thoughts running through my head, I'd think of them. They made me appreciate how fortunate I am to have what I have."

Frankie's never heard her father talk so openly about anything. He was always quietly amused in the corner, watching Frankie's mum enjoy the spotlight she so loved.

"Frankie, are you OK? You don't seem like yourself today. You seem distracted. Do you have a lot of work on your mind?"

My entire life is on my mind.

"Yeah, things are pretty busy at the moment," she replies, taking a sip of her tea.

"I do worry about you," he comments. "I'm so proud of what you've built. But I have to admit that I'm concerned about the weight of it too. Your friend Priya called me yesterday."

"Priya called you? How did she get your number?" Frankie asks.

Priya must be seriously worried about Frankie if she'd go to that effort. Priya barely knows her family.

"From the panic attack. Don't you remember? You called me from her phone because you'd broken yours," her dad replies, frowning. "Priya told me you'd deliberately flushed yours down the toilet."

Frankie bursts out laughing.

"Well, I'm always happy to see you smiling, but I really think you need to take this a little more seriously. She said you were very upset. Frankie, your professional life should never cost you your personal happiness. Sometimes, success means saying goodbye. If you did decide to take a break from it all, I'd still be proud of you. Maybe even prouder—if that's possible—because I'd know you were looking after yourself and putting yourself first. And I think that's really important."

"I promise I will take better care of myself," she replies, pursing her lips.

But it's hard to take it all seriously, when she hasn't really lived through it.

"Are you having boy trouble, Frankie?"

"What? No, Dad, I'm not," she says quickly. "Why would I be?"

"I don't know, I was just checking up, I guess. I'm glad to

hear it. Obviously, it would be lovely to meet someone nice, but I just wanted to make sure that the pressure of finding a boyfriend wasn't adding to your load. Do you know, when you broke up with Toby I was actually relieved."

"Really? But you were always going on about what a great guy he was," Frankie replies.

"He was a great guy, can't fault him. Well, I can, actually. His clothes were too neat. They looked like they needed to be hung in a museum or something. Aside from that, he was a decent bloke. But it was far too young for you to be committing to forever. Forever is a long time. Where's the fun in rushing into it?"

"And here I thought you were all for conformity, Dad," Frankie says.

"I know I come across as conventional now," he replies. "But let's not forget I was daring enough to marry your mother. I haven't always been this boring."

"Ah, Dad, you're not boring," Frankie says unconvincingly.

"I'm a total bore! Proud of it, too." He chuckles. "But I think you're the best mix of your mother and me. A sensible head with an appetite for adventure."

"What does Jet have?"

"An appetite for my Cadbury Fingers." Her dad rolls his eyes. "I'm just kidding. He'll find his place in the world when the time is right. Some people just need a little longer to figure things out."

*

Sitting at the kitchen table after another slice of cake, followed by a picnic lunch, half of which went to the dogs, Frankie glances at the time. It's 4 p.m.

Seventeen hours left.

"Dad, mind if I pop out for a bit?" Frankie asks.

"Of course, love! We don't have plans, do we, Les?"

Lesley pauses her raspberry blowing and peers out from behind Rachel's belly to shake her head.

"Need a lift?" her dad asks.

"No thanks. Fancy some fresh air. It's only a fifteen-minute walk, anyway. See you later," Frankie says, standing up and making her way to the door. She pauses in the hallway, then rushes back to give her dad a long hug.

"Love you, Francesca," he says, patting her head.

"Love you too, Dad." She smiles, with one final squeeze.

Thirty-Eight

When Alice and Justin first bought their terraced house on the outskirts of Kingston, she thought it was weirdly grown-up. She begged them to stay in the city, sent them links to flats just a bit further away. But they wanted space, and they sure got more here than in Zone 2. A movement by her feet startles her, and she jumps to the side of the road. It's a ridiculously cute poodle panting at a tightly stretched lead, looking up at her with its tongue hanging out and a pink bow balanced on the curls between her ears. She feels like she's seen this poodle somewhere before.

"Hello, you," she says, bending down to scratch the poodle behind the neck.

"Sorry!" a voice cries from down the street, followed by rushing steps.

Frankie stands up. And comes face-to-face with Oli Sarpong.

"Oh! Hey!" Frankie says, remembering too late that he hasn't a clue who she is. "Cute dog!"

His eyes linger on hers for a second longer than they should and her heart starts pounding.

Why is he acting like he recognizes her?

"Thanks," he eventually says. "Chicken hasn't mastered the art of personal space yet." He smiles, bending down to pick her up and pecking her on the cheek. Chicken starts licking his nose madly, and the adorableness of the kissing frenzy makes Frankie want to join in. Oli's much sexier than she remembers, and with his white-framed glasses and slim-fit black turtleneck he looks like a cool Scandinavian tech guru who's just delivered a viral TED Talk.

"Ah, that's OK. She's welcome to invade my personal space any day," she replies, meaning it.

"Yeeeah," Oli replies. "You say that now. Let's see what you say when you have an audience every time you go to the toilet."

Frankie laughs.

"Lovely day, isn't it?" Oli says, looking up.

"It is," Frankie says, smiling. "But I am excited about autumn. Nothing beats a walk on a crisp and sunny day."

Oli grins at her and replies, "I feel exactly the same way!"

"Well, I'm going this way." Frankie nods toward the road to the left, after a minute-long lull. "Enjoy your walkies, Chicken!" she says, booping her on the nose. When she does, Chicken sticks her tongue out, making her laugh even more. "Bye," she says softly, smiling at Oli as she turns the corner.

"Have a good one." Oli smiles back, watching her leave, with Chicken curled up cozily on his broad chest.

After a few minutes, Frankie glances over her shoulder and

sees he's still walking behind her. They share an awkward nod. Then a horrible realization hits her. He's friends with Justin.

Is he also on his way to Alice's house?

When Frankie eventually reaches the front door, she rocks back and forth in her trainers, not daring to look back.

"I thought this might happen," Oli says from behind her.

Frankie turns around and pretends to be surprised to see him.

"You're Frankie, right?" he asks, with a pointed finger.

"How do you know my—" Frankie starts to reply, but she's interrupted by the front door swinging wide open.

"Shit, Frankie!" Toby says with wide eyes and a mouth full of food.

"Toby!" Frankie cries, the sight of him a few inches from her sending a punch to her gut. "What are you doing here?"

"The rest of us are just out back. I was just . . . getting a napkin from the kitchen. We're having a barbecue. Bit of an impromptu post-work Wednesday thing, last of the decent weather and all that. Did Alice and Justin not tell you?"

"No, no, they didn't," Frankie says, looking at her feet and wishing the ground would swallow her whole.

"Righto," Toby says. "Well, it's . . . really great to see you. You're looking well."

"Really great or really awkward?" Frankie laughs.

Toby's face squirms a bit. "Bit awkward, I guess." He chuckles.

Oli shuffles behind her.

"Sorry, mate," Toby says, craning his neck behind Frankie. "You must be Oli?"

"Hiya," Oli replies casually with a quick wave.

"Oh, wait, did you two come together?" Toby asks, looking confused as his eyes dart between the two of them.

"Not like that," Frankie says quickly.

"Frankie?" Alice cries, appearing behind Toby with a puzzled look on her face. "What are you doing here? I thought you said you couldn't make it?"

Frankie, feeling relieved to hear she'd been invited, stares at her, bewildered. Alice stares back at her with the same expression.

"Oh, hey, Oli!" Alice finally says. "Glad you managed to get out of work early too. Come in, come in. Just is in the garden and has a beer with your name on it. Frankie, um, I need to show you something upstairs."

Frankie squeezes past Toby, quietly inhaling his Issey Miyake to see if it stirs something in her. It doesn't. Perhaps being married to him for twenty-four hours has finally settled the *what-if.*

*

Alice closes her bedroom door behind her and leans back on it.

"I only invited Toby because you said you couldn't make it!" Alice whispers rapidly. "Why did you just show up? He's here with *her!*"

"Who?" Frankie asks.

"What do you mean, who? His wife! Freya!"

"Oh shit," Frankie says, feeling sick. "Well, I can just slip out."

"You can't slip out now, it'll look really weird. And because we've been up here, it'll look like I've told you to go and I'll look like the bad guy."

"Well," Frankie says, "I'll just have to deal with it. I only popped around to say hi because I'm staying at my dad's."

"What's happened?" Alice says, sitting on the bed looking worried. "Why are you at your dad's? Is this because of the panic attack? Priya told me everything. And she told me about the phone call too. I was going to call for a long chat tomorrow, after things had calmed down."

"I'm fine," Frankie replies. "Honestly. Think I just need to step back and breathe for a bit."

"I'm really happy to hear that. I can't remember when you last had a break. And I'm really glad you're here, I just wish I'd known so I could have somehow stopped Toby and Freya from coming."

Frankie starts shaking her head. "No, I wouldn't want you to do that. Toby is my past. It's high time I left him there. I'll be fine, promise. I just need a large glass of wine."

"Should you be drinking?" Alice asks.

"Why does everyone keep asking me that?" Frankie cries.

"Because you had a panic attack last week," Alice replies matter-of-factly.

"Yeah, OK, but I'm fine now. Jeez," Frankie says.

At the bottom of the stairs, Frankie pauses and turns back to Alice. "Hey, that guy who came in after me. Oli, right?" Frankie whispers.

"You *know* that's Oli, Frankie. I've tried to set you up a million times," Alice whispers back, rolling her eyes.

"How does he know my name?" Frankie asks.

"Justin told him. He's been asking about you since I uploaded the photos from my birthday last year." Alice smiles, and does an over-the-top wink, nudging Frankie in the ribs.

As Frankie approaches the group, already half a glass of wine down for Dutch courage, Chicken bounds up to her and starts licking her ankles. She could kiss Chicken for making her feel so loved in front of what could be a tough crowd.

"Frankie Pants! Happy birthday eve!" Justin shouts, holding up his hands to greet her with a pair of barbecue tongs in one and a beer in the other. "Alice said you couldn't make it!"

"Ah, well, I managed to take five from the media circus," Frankie explains, glancing around the circle and spotting Freya instantly. She turns her eyes to the flames of Justin's makeshift barbecue barrel. "Where are the kids, Just?"

"Oh, they're upstairs with their real parents," he comments before clarifying. "iPads."

"Ah," Frankie replies, taking a sip of wine.

"Frankie runs The Show," Justin explains to a few faces she doesn't recognize. "You know, that website for women?"

Like a Mexican wave, they all lift their eyebrows and spin their heads back at her.

"I thought I recognized you!" a pregnant woman in a denim jumpsuit says, her mouth wide open. "I *love* The Show! That recent piece you did on older mothers was so inspiring. Made me feel a lot better about being branded a geriatric mum in my medical notes."

"You? A geriatric? You don't look a day over sixty," Justin quips.

"Don't, Justin, I probably *will* look sixty in six months' time!" the pregnant woman groans.

"Ah, you really won't," Freya chimes in with a voice like treacle, all sweet and gooey. "You'll be full of love. That baby will keep you young!"

"Hmmm, not so sure about that," the pregnant woman replies. "Have you seen those before-and-after-kids pics doing the rounds at the moment? Horrifying."

Freya turns to Frankie with big, innocent blue eyes, framed by a long brunette bob.

"Do you have kids, Frankie?" she asks.

Obviously not. Wouldn't they have come up by now?

"I don't, no," Frankie replies, having a large gulp of wine.

"You don't know?! Boozy birthday lunch, was it, Franks?" Justin cracks another tedious gag.

"And with gags like these, I guess you've been on the beers since breakfast?" Oli chimes in.

Why must people ask the kid question? As a parent, the topic of kids is bound to come up at some point, given children are a 24/7 job. If someone has kids, you'll find out soon enough. Frankie has a thought for the merchandise section of the site. A T-shirt that says, "Don't ask me if I have kids." Or perhaps just "No, I don't have kids."

Frankie's desperate not to look directly at her, but she can't leave Freya hanging like that. Toby will think she's being odd, and that's the last thing she wants him to think.

"You two have two, is that right?" Frankie asks, glancing between them both.

"Oh, well, I'm glad I haven't totally ballooned yet," Freya chirps. "Not that there's anything wrong with that, of course. I'm six months along with number three." She beams, stroking her tummy.

Frankie glances down and sees a hint of a bump.

"Ah, that's amazing! Congratulations," Frankie says, turning to Toby, who looks sheepish when he really shouldn't. "I'm really happy for you, Tobes."

"Thanks, Franks," he says, taking a sip of beer and looking at his feet. "We're super-excited. It's a little boy this time!"

"Ah, a tiny Toby!" Frankie laughs. "Let me guess what you're going to call him. Frankie?"

The crowd titters and Toby blushes.

Frankie is happy for him. Three kids. He's talked about having kids since their first conversation at uni. Who knows, it could have been with her if the IVF had continued. It could still be her if she returns to that life.

Toby turns to Freya, and kisses her on the cheek before asking her if he can get her a chair. She nods and kisses him back, watching him walk away to find one.

"He's a good guy," Frankie comments.

"He really is," Freya coos with a smile. It hints at pity, which Frankie doesn't appreciate. "We're very happy. I mean, our life is nowhere near as exciting as yours, but we both like the simple things, I guess. You probably think it's all a bit boring out here!"

"I actually don't," Frankie replies. "There's a lot to be said for a quiet life. Besides, three kids? I'm sure your life is a lot more adventurous than mine!"

Is it, though?

Frankie can think of a few more adventures to compete. Like living in Mexico or having dinner with Cher. But you can't say that, of course.

"Didn't I see you having lunch with the prime minister of Finland last week?" the pregnant woman who's been listening in interjects.

Did she?

"Yep," Frankie replies.

"I mean, if I had the choice between dinner with the prime minister of Finland or a baby who pukes up every few minutes, I know what I'm choosing." The pregnant woman laughs.

"Well then, I recommend you *don't* have dinner with Justin Bieber," Frankie jokes, as if that's something she's actually done. Maybe it is?

A chuckle beside her makes her turn. It's Oli. He's holding a bottle of wine and offers to fill her glass, which she gratefully accepts.

They exchange a look and smile at each other.

"So," Oli says to her, turning into her as the rest of the

group start a debate on whether the charcoal is ready for the meat. "I've been known to click on The Show from time to time," he says, pushing up his glasses. "I feel a bit starstruck, to be honest. That's how I knew who you were earlier." He clears his throat. The telltale sign of a little white lie.

"Oh, it's not because you asked Justin who I was from a Facebook photo?" Frankie teases him, surprising herself with her chutzpah.

Oli throws his neck back and laughs with abandon, before hiding his face in his hand.

"Well, that's embarrassing," he finally says. "Yeah, OK. I forget, you're a journalist. You're right, I did ask him who you were. What can I say, I've got a thing for curls. Not that I was . . . objectifying you . . . or just judging you on your . . ."

"I didn't think that," Frankie saves him.

"Phew," Oli says, suddenly looking around.

"Chicken's ready to go on!" Justin yells, making them both jump. "Alice! Can you bring out the chicken!"

"Hold on, where's my Chicken?" Oli says, spinning on his heels to scan.

"Chicken?" he shouts.

"Chicken!" Justin shouts too.

"Yes, OK!" Alice screams from the sliding doors. "Jesus, I heard you the first time!"

Oli looks genuinely worried. "Chicken?" he says, quieter this time.

Frankie puts her wine down on the table and places her hand on his arm. "I'll help you look for her."

"Thanks," he says, flustered. "She's so small I'm always paranoid that she'll dart through the tiniest fence or hole."

"You go that side; I'll go this side," Frankie says.

As they walk on opposite sides of the garden, calling for Chicken one after the other, Frankie looks across at him and has a flashback to their first date, when she persuaded herself that he was just another first-date flake who wouldn't be interested in her. But today is different. Oli didn't know Frankie was going to be here. His sweetness isn't an act. This is who he is. Now, the only thing she's convinced of is that she was too quick to assume he wouldn't like her. It also helped that he asked about her first. Perhaps that's why she was so comfortable teasing him. The chutzpah was because of him.

Behind an oak tree at the end of the garden is a small wooden shed. As Frankie approaches, she hears little sniffs coming from under the door. She crouches down and sees Chicken's miniature nose poking out. Smiling, she boops it and out sticks her tiny tongue. Frankie smiles, gently pulls open the door and steps inside, switching on the soft lights, picking Chicken up and letting her lick her neck with little flicks.

"Good girl!" Frankie sings, her heart melting. Maybe the solution to all her stress is this.

"There you are!" Oli grins, stooping down to step into the shed.

"Go to Daddy," Frankie says, handing his precious cargo over.

"Thank you," Oli says, putting his nose against Chicken's

before putting her down and letting her bounce back into the garden.

When he stands up, Frankie finds his face two inches from hers, his smooth lips glowing in the golden lights.

"I guess we should get back to the others," she says, staring at him, her stomach cartwheeling.

"Yeah," he says, turning toward the door.

But then he turns back. "I know this is going to sound odd, but I swear we've met before," he says.

"We have," she replies.

"Have we?" he asks.

But Frankie can't answer him truthfully. She can't answer him at all. So she follows the urge swelling inside her and takes his fingers in hers. Sure, they've spent a little under an hour together in this life, but what has she got to lose? She'll be gone in the morning. Why the hell not.

Oli squeezes her fingers back softly. Frankie leans into him and plants a soft kiss on his lips.

Who is *she in this life?*

Oli brings his hands up and gently holds her neck, kissing her a little harder.

"Frankie?" Alice shouts from somewhere close by.

They both fling their eyes open, their lips still pressed together. Frankie pulls away, disappointed it didn't last longer.

"We better get back out there," Frankie says, squeezing his hand. Oli keeps hold of hers as he opens the shed door behind him and steps out into the light with Frankie following close behind.

*

It's midnight when Frankie leaves the barbecue. As she approaches the road corner, she hears Oli call her name and feels her stomach twist with delight. When she turns around, she wants to burst out laughing at the sight of him and Chicken running after her in unison. Chicken's ears are flapping with each stride and Oli's glasses are bouncing up and down.

"Wait up!" Oli says, panting, leaning over and resting his hands on his knees.

"You OK there?" Frankie says, crouching down to give Chicken a rub behind the ears.

"Hmm hmm," he says unconvincingly. "I've been going a bit too hard at the gym this week, I think it's catching up with me."

"Oh, really?" Frankie says, looking up at him and tilting her head to one side with a smirk.

"Yeah, I didn't think I could pull that off." He laughs. "I think the last time I went to the gym, everyone still wore fluoro shell suits."

Perhaps Oli isn't too perfect after all. Maybe he eats kebabs on a school night too.

"Where are you headed?" he asks.

"Just around the corner, actually. Well, fifteen-minute walk. I'm staying at my dad's tonight in Surbiton."

"Can I walk with you? I'll get a train from Surbiton anyway." Frankie nods, pleased for their company.

As they walk, Frankie decides to use the opportunity to

learn a little more about Oli. All the things she could have learned if she'd given him a chance on their first date. And this time, she properly listens. When he talks about his niece's interest in tech, Frankie suggests that she should visit The Show at half-term and spend some time with the team. His eyes light up at the suggestion.

"This is me," Frankie says, as they approach the iron gates. Chicken starts growling.

"Someone's devastated." Frankie laughs.

"Well, why wouldn't she be?" Oli smiles.

The growl suddenly morphs into surprisingly loud yaps for someone so small. Oli bends down and swoops her up into his arms, whispering hushes in her ears. It doesn't work. Chicken has gone into full-on berserk mode, jumps out of his arms and sprints toward the front door, the lead dragging behind her.

"Shit, sorry!" Oli says, rushing after her.

The hall lights flicker on and a chorus of equally shrill yaps sound from the other side.

"Oh, shush, you three!" Lesley shrieks from the other side.

"Frankie?" her dad calls.

"Yes, it's just me, Dad!" Frankie calls back, approaching the front step. "And . . ." She looks at Oli. "My friend Oli. And his dog, Chicken."

The door swings open and the four of them stare at each other, while a whirlwind of fluffiness spirals out of control at their feet. Her dad and Lesley are in matching red velvet dressing gowns.

"Oh, hello, who's this?" Her dad beams, embarrassingly broadly.

"Hi, I'm Oli," he says, reaching his hand out. "And this is Chicken. I'm sorry it's so late, I was just walking Frankie home."

"Well, that's very chivalrous of you, Oli," Lesley replies, looking intensely at Frankie with the same level of subtlety as Chandler, who's just mounted Chicken at her feet.

"Oh my god, get off her!" Frankie murmurs, gently shoving him off with her foot.

"Fancy a nightcap, Oli?" Lesley asks, stepping back and gesturing toward the kitchen. "We were just about to make some hot chocolate. Or coffee, if you'd prefer?"

Oli glances at Frankie for approval. Old Frankie would be dying with embarrassment. But New Frankie, who has just under nine hours left here, thinks she might as well make the most of them.

She gives a subtle nod.

"Coffee would be great, thank you." Oli smiles, picking Chicken up and straightening the lopsided bow on her head.

When Frankie enters the kitchen, she sees Jet leaning on the island.

"Jet!" she shrieks.

"Sister," he replies nonchalantly with a quick nod. "Stranger." He nods at Oli.

"Still playing it cool?" Frankie smiles.

"Still playing it straight?" Jet asks.

"Oli, Jet, Jet, Oli," Frankie says.

Jet salutes Oli with the paintbrush he has in his hand, andthen proceeds to dip the paintbrush in his hot chocolate and start dabbing at the blank piece of paper in front of him.

"What are you painting?" Oli asks. Frankie appreciates him behaving like this is totally normal.

"A sign for the protest I'm attending tomorrow," Jet says.

"What are you protesting about?" Oli asks.

"Food waste," Jet replies.

"But aren't you just wasting food by doing that?" Oli laughs, glancing at the others in the room for reassurance that he isn't the mad one.

"Don't bother, Oli," Lesley says, putting a cup of coffee on the island in front of him.

"I guess it's meant to be . . . ironic?" Oli asks.

Jet's head flies up. "Thank you! Finally, someone gets it!"

"Wouldn't you make more of an impact if you . . ."

Frankie puts her hand gently on Oli's arm and shakes her head. He stops talking.

*

"So, that's the one half of my crazy family." Frankie laughs awkwardly at the gate.

"Maybe I'll get to meet the other half one day." Oli smiles, taking her hand in his and squeezing it.

"You'd have to fly to Goa." Frankie squeezes back.

"Well, I've always wanted to Goa to India . . ." he responds and then winces. "That was awful, wasn't it?"

"It's late, you're forgiven," she whispers, leaning toward him and kissing him. When they come up for air, they look down at the street and see Chicken staring at them.

"So, Chicken wants to know if she can have your number. She says she wants to see Chandler again." Oli smiles.

Thirty-Nine

Mabel has a twinkle in her eye and a sly smirk on her face as she taps her pen against the desk, waiting for Frankie to compose herself from last night's kissing. Meeting Oli in that life was entirely unexpected, but it shouldn't have been. Oli and Justin are friends, it makes sense for him to have been there. It felt completely different too. With other people around, the pressure was off. The spotlight on them was gone. The conversations around the barbecue silenced the running commentary in her head. And there were zero expectations for the end of the night, which meant Frankie could relax. She could be herself.

"So," Mabel says. "How did boss life feel?"

"Confusing," Frankie replies. "Like all the others. Promising at the start, problems in the middle, potential at the end. Why can't everything just be . . . fine. No trouble, no big drama. Why can't I be a boss without collapsing under the pressure and having panic attacks? All I want is a calm life. I feel like none of these lives have a happy ending."

"OK, Frankie." Mabel sighs. "You aren't getting it, so I'm going to get a bit serious with you now."

"OK," Frankie replies, full of anticipation.

"We don't write your life story up here. You write the chapters with the choices you make and you're in charge of your happy ending. Life will throw you curveballs, but you just have to catch them and carry on. You have the power to control how you react to the problems, the trouble, the drama. You've got to stop fixating on what others are doing, and start fixating on what you're doing. Work out your priorities. What's most important to you? What makes you happiest? Love? Family? Friends? Travel? Professional accomplishments? In my experience, when you focus on your main priority, the rest all falls into place afterward."

"How?" Frankie cries. "I still don't know what makes me happiest. Even after all this, I can't figure it out. This whole process has made it even harder because I now have too many options! You said at the beginning that I shouldappreciate what an amazing opportunity this is, but all it's done is made me more confused. If I can't make a choice, what happens then? Should I just go forward to The Final Destination? Because right now, it feels like that's the easiest option."

"Relax," Mabel says. "I will help you, I promise. I know these lives have probably thrown up more questions than answers, but we don't have to make the decision yet."

"And what's with the weird life crossover with Oli? I wasn't prepared for that," Frankie mutters.

"That's the kind of curveball I'm talking about. From the looks of it, you made a pretty good catch," Mabel replies.

"Does it mean we're together if I choose that life?" Frankie asks.

"No idea."

"On our date, I thought he was a boring nerd who I'd never see again. But I snogged the face off that boring nerd five minutes after meeting him and then was happy to introduce him to most of my family. I've never made the first move. With anyone, ever. Where did this confidence come from?" Frankie wonders.

"Maybe all these lives have made you more confident," Mabel suggests.

"Or maybe I just knew it would end soon, so I had nothing to lose," Frankie says with a shrug.

"Perhaps you should ask yourself what you have to lose in your real life too. But first, it's time we visited your final crossroads. Up you get," Mabel says, pushing her chair back and waving Frankie toward the lift.

Frankie runs through her crossroads in her head. The one-way flight. The marriage proposal. The fortune. The fame. Flashing back to the last few years of her life, nothing in particular stands out for her.

After the interview, she settled back into ordinary life. Every day was the same. *The Leak*, the flat, Friday nights in with Tom, Saturdays with herself, Sundays with a mountain of laundry and a marathon on Netflix. There was one time when she almost booked a trip to climb Kilimanjaro, but shut the page down when she realized the gear would cost her two months' rent. And she almost joined a paddleboarding club, but when she arrived at the set-off point she just kept on walking. It was five degrees and the other members were all high-fiving with shivering blue hands. Were those important crossroads? Was she going to end up being a mountain explorer or falling for a paddle-boarder? Neither scenario is plausible. Then again, did she think she'd end up on a reality show in LA? Or having weekly dinners with Emily Maitlis? No.

"In you go," Mabel says, ushering her into the lift.

"Where am I going?" Frankie asks as the lift doors close.

"To the loo!" Mabel calls out.

"What?" Frankie yells, her stomach rising as the lift descends below into black.

When the lift doors open, Frankie's staring back at herself in a mirror. Something catches her eye in the corner. It's a small piece of graffiti written with eyeliner:

I am not what happened to me, I am what I choose to become—Jung

PART SEVEN

What's WRONG with her? Woman DITCHED on BIRTHDAY DATE

Forty

Frankie hears the muffled sound of the pianist as she squeezes the edge of the sink and sucks in a long deep breath. It sounds like he's singing "All of Me' by John Legend, and to be fair, it's good. Old Frankie would have rolled her eyes at saccharine lyrics and accused them of pressuring people to surrender themselves. But New Frankie has a fresh perspective. The song isn't asking people to surrender their identities, it's asking people to celebrate the joy of loving openly, fiercely and fearlessly. And that's what Frankie must learn to do. Not necessarily with Oli, or with any potential partner. She could sing it to herself and it would still make sense. She stares at herself and sings quietly along to the lyrics.

Suddenly, the door swings open and Frankie shuts up. The young woman from the table in the window walks past her, her trainers making tiny squeaks on the stone floor.

355

"Y'alright?" She smiles as she places her bag on the bathroom sink and rummages in it.

"Yeah, all good, thanks," Frankie replies, pretending to fix her hair.

The young woman applies some lip gloss, throws it back in her bag and wiggles her bra into place.

"I have a confession." Frankie turns to her.

"You what?" The woman freezes, her eyes wide.

"I caught a moment between you and your boyfriend earlier, where you were staring into each other's eyes and it was just so incredibly lovely that I wish I'd taken a photo for you."

"Oh gawd, that's embarrassing." The woman giggles, looking down into her bag.

"How long have you been together?" Frankie asks.

"We're not together." The woman glances up and shakes her head. "This is our second date."

"You're joking!" Frankie cries. "You look like you've just got engaged or something."

"Nah," the woman says. "I don't even know his second name."

"Wow," Frankie comments. "Think there'll be a third?"

"Not sure. Maybe? I'm happy right here right now. That's all I care about. Who knows how I'll feel next week! Worrying about *will we* or *won't we* has never got me anywhere."

"Sound advice," Frankie comments.

"How's *your* night going?" the woman asks, sliding her bag onto her shoulder.

"Yeah, OK, I think," Frankie responds. "He hasn't left yet so that's a good sign."

The woman laughs. "All you can be is yourself, right? If it's not good enough, it's not your problem."

"Thanks," Frankie responds. "I actually really needed to hear that."

"Good luck!" She smiles, and walks out of the door.

Frankie looks into the mirror and feels excited about what's about to unfold. She thinks back to the feel of his soft lips on hers, his big fingers clutching hers tightly. His eyes staring so closely into hers that she could see delicate flecks of olive and tan. She picks up her jacket and bag, swings open the bathroom door and feels her blister burn at her heel, which is a painful reminder to calm down.

When Frankie turns the corner, their table is empty. Frowning, she scans the room to see if she's got the wrong one. Nope, this is definitely their table. She sits back down, drapes her jacket over the back of the chair, puts her bag on the floor and waits. He must have gone to the bathroom. Frankie taps her foot against the floor and starts biting her lip. Something's wrong. She can feel it. She looks under the table. His bag is gone. She bites her lip harder.

"Love?" she hears someone call quietly close by. Frankie looks up and sees the piano player, who's on a break, looking at her with pity etched on his face. "I'm really sorry," he says leaning forward. "I hate to break this to you, but that bloke you were with? He ran out about five minutes ago. Took his bag, and everything."

Frankie's heart starts pounding with the humiliation of being ditched mid-date. But she can't talk. She did the exact same thing to him before. Perhaps the lesson in all of this is to be more considerate of other people's feelings. Because this really fucking hurts. She glances over to the woman from the bathroom, who gives her a nod and raises her glass for a cheer from afar.

"You OK?" the pianist says kindly. "Don't think the twat paid for his share of the bill either, by the way. So, on the bright side, it looks like you dodged a bullet."

Frankie nods and purses her lips. She's going to start crying, and she needs to leave now. She can't face the humiliation of sitting abandoned in a restaurant called Date Night, surrounded by other couples as she sobs into the dregs of her wine. She leans back in her chair and waves to the waitress, who saunters over.

"What can I get you?" she asks.

"The bill, please," she says, avoiding eye contact so the waitress can't see her tears.

"Oh!" she says, surprised. "One sec, then."

"Make it quick, mate," the pianist comments and out of the corner of Frankie's eye she sees them exchange a look.

"I'll be right back," the waitress says.

As Frankie pays the bill, the pianist starts playing again. This time, it's an acoustic version of "No Scrubs" by TLC, and she could kiss him for being so kind. Keeping her head down, she lifts it in his direction for a second to mouth a quick thanks, feeling ashamed by the mean thoughts she had about him before.

When Frankie's feet land on the pavement outside, she pauses for a minute to let the cool air soothe her red-hot cheeks. Then, she slips her right heel out of her boot, presses down on the leather and starts limping down the road. Is it déjà vu if she knows she's lived this twice and remembers both times vividly?

Frankie: You owe me a spa weekend

Alice: What happened??

Frankie doesn't have the energy to go into the details. She scrolls her phone to find someone to pep her up.

"He ditched me," Frankie says when she hears Tom answer the phone.

"Um . . . what?" Tom says slowly.

"He did a runner while I was in the loo. Left me with the bill too." She laughs, because if she doesn't she'll cry.

"What the fuck? Why did Alice set you up with such a monster? I'm so angry!" Tom shouts down the phone.

Frankie remembers their final phone call. The one where Tom told her she wasn't a horrible person for deserting Oli. If only she'd known that he'd done it to her first. She wouldn't have felt so bad. She would have saved face.

"Yeah, same." Frankie scoffs. "Well, more embarrassed than angry. I guess I can't be angry if someone doesn't like me, can I?"

"I guess not. He could have had the decency to say bye or

359

leave his half, what a bloody cheapskate," Tom replies. "Where are you now, want to come over?"

"Nah, I'm OK. I'm limping down Clapham High Street feeling sorry for myself. So sorry for myself that I'm going to get a kebab. Want anything?"

"Why are you limping?" Tom asks.

"Blister," Frankie explains.

"Oh dear. Joel just cooked ramen. There's enough for three if you prefer?"

"All good. I need something greasy," Frankie comments.

"Fair enough, Frankles. Text me when you get home. And call me tomorrow for fun plans. We want to visit that new exhibition at the Hayward Gallery, if you're in?"

"I'm in," Frankie replies, unsure where she'll be tomorrow. "Chat tomorrow, Teabag."

"Looove you," he coos.

The truth is, Frankie wants to return to the start. She wants to retrace her steps to figure out if she could have seen it coming. What's troubling her is that this was supposed to be a big life crossroads. She took the other path. She went back to the table, yet she ended up in exactly the same position, just fifteen minutes later. When she reaches Kebab Palace, she sees Emir stooped outside the front step.

"You OK, Emir?" she asks, peering over his shoulder.

He looks up at her and shakes his head. "Some idiot dropped his kebab out here and didn't bother to pick it up. It's dangerous, you know. Anyone could slip and really hurt themselves."

"Or die from a subdural hematoma," she comments.

Emir stares at her, puzzled, before eventually asking, "Chicken shish with extra chili sauce?"

"That's the one." Frankie smiles.

＊

With her kebab still warm in her hand, and her head still intact, Frankie kicks off her boots in the hallway and breathes a sigh of relief. She bends down, picks them up, and makes her way slowly up the stairs, counting each step in her head as she always does. At her front door, she pulls out her keys, pushes them in, jangles them about and feels the lock release.

Then her phone pings.

She drops her boots and pulls her phone out from her pocket.

Frankie shoves the front door open with her foot as the wiggling three dots show that he's typing, her hands still full of phone and kebab. When she looks up, she's back in Mabel's office. No phone. No kebab. No answers.

PART EIGHT

FLIGHTY woman FINALLY commits to LIFE DECISION

Forty-One

Mabel's office looks like a scene from a detective show, where the DI is about to crack the case. Around the room's perimeter are five whiteboards plastered in photographs, sticky notes and scribbles. Frankie wanders past each, examining the evidence from her alternative lives. The fifth whiteboard is notably bare.

"Why did you bring me back so early?" Frankie turns to Mabel, who's standing by the first whiteboard. "I had twenty-four hours in all the others."

"I didn't bring you back early," Mabel explains. "You arrived at the present."

"But in all the other lives I stuck around longer—the whole next day!"

"Yes, because you didn't slip on a kebab in those versions."

"But I didn't here, either!" Frankie exclaims, feeling frustrated.

"True, but it is the same life. I don't make the rules, Frankie, but I have to work to them," Mabel tells her.

365

"Do you at least know what Oli was going to say?" Frankie asks.

"I'm afraid I don't," Mabel replies.

"I'm guessing it was going to be an apology." Frankie sighs. "Which is more than I did for him."

"The only way to find out is to choose that life," Mabel says. "But we're getting ahead of ourselves."

Frankie sits on the office chair and swivels it to face her first board.

What if she'd taken that one-way flight to Mexico?

Her life in Cozumel couldn't have been further from Kingston. Life in Kingston was sticking to plans; life in Cozumel was sticking a finger up at plans. In Mexico, she felt like she had the power to do exactly as she pleased.

She closes her eyes and rewinds to the smell of warm air and dusty streets, the hot concrete under her bare feet as she walked along the promenade and stared out into an ocean paradise.

Sure, she had financial stresses, but they could be fixed. Yes, she had some fears around the uncertainty of her future, but isn't that what's to love about this life? And although she felt out of control, she felt more in control in Mexico than in her marriage.

One of the best things about being in Cozumel was reconnecting with her mum after so many years of feeling distant and detached. Not just physically, but emotionally too. It was the relationship she's always wanted so desperately.

Could she have the same kind of relationship if she chose

a different life? She can't imagine it in Kingston. She can't imagine it in California. Or London. But in Mexico, she was more like her mum than ever. And she felt invigorated by it. In Mexico, Frankie felt like she could go in any direction. She was only responsible for her own happiness. She was free. Free from an office, free from a relationship, free from . . . the rest of her family and friends.

And then it hits her. A life on the move means a life without them. Without her career too. She wouldn't be qualified to teach at home. And with a week at *The Leak* in her job experiences, she'd have to start from scratch.

"Mexico, eh? It's a hard one," Mabel says, staring at the board.

Frankie nods.

"I think my problem is that I want to have it all. I want to travel, but I want my friends near. I want to be with someone, but I don't want to feel tied down. My life dreams are basically impossible to reach. I will have to make sacrifices. I will have to figure out what makes me happiest and choose that, even if it means letting go of the rest. And once I've made that choice, I have to commit to it. I can't look back."

That's what Frankie's been doing all her life. Living in the past. Clinging on to things she should let go of because she doesn't want to close any chapters. Closing chapters means saying goodbye, and she's too scared to make a forever choice and mess up her chance to live the life she was meant to.

"So where does this leave you with Mexico?" Mabel asks.

"I need more time. Do I have time?"

"A bit. Let's move on," Mabel replies. "What if you'd said yes to marrying Tidy Toby?"

The married life. Living in a show home in Kingston with an easy, if not inspiring, job at a local paper. Of course, there was the glaring issue of counseling and her plans to leave. Would she see these plans through if she returned? Or would the counseling work? Frankie flashes back to the conversation with her dad on the allotment. She remembers how satisfied he seemed with his life choices. Happy, calm, content. The only drama in his life was *The Archers*.

"Why wouldn't I want that life? His obsession with order pisses me off, but nobody's perfect. Toby's kind, considerate, handsome . . ."

"A control freak . . ." Mabel adds.

"Yeah, OK. That's a bigger issue, I suppose."

"I think you're forgetting the biggest issue," Mabel says, tapping her pen to her chin.

"I don't love him," Frankie says quietly.

"Bingo was his name-o."

"I love him as a *friend*. And maybe that's what some marriages are. Friendship. Like my parents."

"They split up and they're much happier now."

"I mean, I care about Toby," Frankie continues. "I want him to be happy. I'm just not sure I want to be responsible for his happiness. Freya can do that."

"You've got your own happiness to be responsible for," Mabel replies. "How did you feel meeting her in the flesh after stalking her for so long?" she asks.

"I didn't stalk her!"

"Pffff." Mabel's eyes roll.

"OK, fine, maybe I did a bit. I don't know, strangely at peace. It felt like closure after years of wondering what if I was her," Frankie replies.

"Shall we move on?" Mabel asks, taking a picture of LA Frankie's nude apple portrait off the wall. "What do we think of . . . what did Tom call you? Francy? How was it being her?"

"Hands down, the strangest experience of my life. Or . . . lives," Frankie replies.

"Did any part of it appeal?" Mabel asks.

"The money, of course. Who wouldn't want to have no money problems?" Frankie scoffs.

"And the star status?"

"For what, though? For being with Callum? For being rich? That's hardly something to be proud of, is it? The idea of being on the other side of my 'Being Frankie' column makes me cringe. I want to be able to go and get a kebab in peace, without it being a tabloid headline."

"Frankie pours CURVES into tights and CHILI SAUCE onto kebab!" Mabel comments.

"You're getting good at that." Frankie nods.

"Thank you. You weren't doing nothing in Malibu, though. What about the memoir?" Mabel says.

Frankie laughs. "What was I going to fill a memoir with? I'm not sure I'd done anything in my life worth reading about. There was no suffering, no learning, no worthy achievement. Who was I kidding?"

"The reality show?" Mabel asks.

"Callum was right about that. For someone who hates the spotlight, that was going to be a very strange career move. I guess I really did have nothing else going on."

"You're forgetting what I've said before, Frankie," Mabel comments. "You can choose a life and make changes. You could go back to LA and return to journalism. Or do something worthy if you want. You could even break up with Callum. The only thing that's stopping you . . . is you."

"I suppose." Frankie contemplates it. "But why hadn't I done that already?"

"I can't answer that." Mabel shrugs.

"Like I said, I was probably too proud to admit my mistake," Frankie replies. "Or maybe it's just me up to my old tricks, being too lazy to change."

Perhaps returning to LA would give her a head start. With a fortune and a familiar name, she already has a platform. She could fill her life with real purpose.

"Hey," Mabel says, sternly. "If you're so lazy, how do you explain The Show?"

Mabel stands in front of the whiteboard and slams her hand against the surface.

"I can't," Frankie says.

"I have a theory," Mabel says. "You were in your comfort zone at *The Leak*. Landing the job at *In Deep* flung you far out of it. But it made you realize that you are far more capable than you give yourself credit for. Going for that job interview was the first step you needed to start believing in yourself. You aren't lazy, Frankie. You've just lost your confidence by sticking to the safety of what you know. By not challenging yourself."

"What about the panic attacks, the stress? Why was I searching for one-way flights to Mexico, when I had this fabulously successful life? It clearly wasn't making me happy. Will I try and book a flight every time I face a challenge?" Frankie cries. "I mean, maybe that's a sign that Mexico is my answer? Is that the life I should choose, if that's the life I keep on longing for?"

"It's normal to feel like running away in times of stress," Mabel replies. "And, like I said before, no one can stop you. If you choose this life, and discover you're unhappy, you can go ahead and finally get on that one-way flight."

"Wait," Frankie says, her eyes wide.

Mabel tilts her head.

"I've suddenly thought of a way I could choose all of these lives," Frankie says, her eyes widening further. "I could . . . go back to LA. Then use my celebrity to launch The Show. Then fly to Mexico and run the site from there! Then . . . fly my family and friends over and force them to live there. Wait, that won't work."

"And Oli?" Mabel asks. "Does he get a look in? He seemed to really like you."

"He bailed on me on our first date!"

"But not at the barbecue," Mabel replies.

"Was that because it was The Show version of me?" Frankie replies. "I don't want to be with someone who's just enamored by my professional success. I want a plus one, whatever my status."

"Let's talk about that first date," Mabel says, stepping forward.

"I think you mean the worst date," Frankie corrects her.

"Was it really the worst?" Mabel asks. "You're exaggerating."

"I'm not," Frankie replies.

"So you think that first date was worse than that time you were stood up in Paris, unable to get home?" Mabel asks.

"Thank you for that reminder," Frankie says. "But yes, it was worse. I should have seen it coming from Callum. But I didn't expect it from Oli. It's better to be ditched by a nob than a nice guy. The only positive is that I don't have to feel bad anymore about ditching him. Because he wasn't even there to *be* ditched."

"OK, so less about Oli, let's look at the rest of this life. If you choose this life, you're choosing to go back to exactly what you know. How does that make you feel?"

"At least I know what I'm doing in this life. No surprises. No big adjustments," Frankie comments.

"But no change, either," Mabel says.

Frankie shrugs.

"Unless you make it happen," Mabel adds, raising her eyebrows and folding her arms as she marches back to behind her desk.

Frankie swivels in her chair as she does. "What do you think Oli was going to say?" Frankie asks contemplatively.

"There's only one way to find out," Mabel replies.

"By choosing that life," Frankie answers.

"That's right," Mabel concludes.

"I'm not going to choose a life just to find out what a text message was going to say." Frankie scoffs. "It was just a first date."

"That would be crazy," Mabel replies.

"So what happens now?" Frankie asks.

"Now, you choose which life you want to go back to," Mabel says, standing up.

"What, right now? I need more time!" Frankie cries, her hands clutching at the chair arms.

"Of course, there is another option," Mabel says ominously. "You can forget about these lives and move forward. You could avoid having to choose altogether and head straight to The Final Destination."

Forty-Two

Comfort.

Freedom.

Fortune.

Fame.

Or more of the same. With the added mystery of the message from Oli Sarpong. But Mabel's right, it would be crazy to base the rest of her life on a text that says "Hey."

Nor should she determine her destiny with one first date. If she chooses to go back to her same life, that first date could turn out like all the others. Oli was probably going to say, "Sorry to sprint off, but there's just no spark." Although, if that was the case, why did they have such a connection at the barbecue?

But even if he did blow her off, Frankie feels like she might be fine with it. Sure, she liked him more than the others. She had romantic relationships in three of these lives, and none of them made her heart full. And none of them made her heart feel as full as the relationship she had with her mum in Mexico. Or the relationship she has with Tom in Clapham.

Toby was kind, but she wanted to bolt. Raphael was sweet, but she wanted to flick him away. And Callum was a complete scumbag, who she wanted to kick to the kerb. Oli? She barely knows him. All she's got to go on is a gut feeling that he's a good one. And if he isn't, then she hasn't lost anything. She's gained, in fact. She dodged a bullet, like the piano man said.

Relationships are just one slice of the big life pie.

If Frankie does return to the same life, things won't be the same at all. Because with the answers to the *what-ifs*, she has the know-how to be happier than before. She knows she has to reconnect with her mum. She knows she has to be grateful for her friendships. She knows she has to appreciate everything she has in this life that she's made all for herself.

Frankie strolls around The Station foyer, taking a ten-minute break before returning to Mabel's office with her decision. She said she needed the space, but this was the worst place to come. As it was at the start, the foyer is filled with frantic people rushing around the floor trying to find their office. Trying to figure out what the hell is going on. Frankie's tempted to tell passersby, "It'll be OK," but she stays quiet. She remembers her frame of mind when she first arrived, and she wouldn't have believed her, either.

When Frankie passes the coffee shop, she hears a tap on the window. She turns around and sees a familiar shock of curly white hair bouncing behind the glass with each wave. Frankie smiles and walks in.

"You're still here!" Winnie exclaims with a wide smile.

"So are you!" Frankie laughs.

"But you're young and fit, I thought you'd be racing back down there to one of those lives they offered you!"

"I can't decide which life is right for me," Frankie says, taking a seat and staring out of the glass at a woman her age who's frozen to the spot in the chaos, with her eyes squeezed shut and her fists clenched at her hips.

"Isn't that a good thing?" Winnie says. "If it's such a hard choice to make, that must mean that all those lives can offer you something. So, whatever life you choose you're winning. Right?"

Frankie hadn't looked at it that way. She nods pensively.

"Besides, just because you have to choose one of these lives, it doesn't mean you're stuck in that one life forever."

"I'll be stuck with memories and mistakes, though, won't I? You can't change the past."

"No. And you shouldn't want to, either. Your past is what brought you here in the first place. All those so-called mistakes you made have given you this miracle chance to find happiness. I don't know what lives are on your table, but my advice would be to choose the simplest one. Humans don't need much. My Buddhist teacher told me that humans only need nine basic things to feel happy."

"What are they?" Frankie says, sitting up. Finally, some practical help to make her choice.

"Now, let's see. My memory is so fuzzy these days. Attention, which means being part of a community. Goals, even simple ones like daily tasks. A healthy body helps a healthy mind . . . how much have I done?"

"Three," Frankie says, glancing at the clock above the café counter. She has to be back in the office in eight minutes. "Wait a minute, I need to write this down," Frankie says, beckoning the waiter. He obliges when she asks him if she can borrow his notepad and pen.

"Right, hold on," Winnie whispers.

Frankie holds the pen to the paper.

"Attention, goals, health . . ." Frankie repeats, scribbling them down.

"Ah, four, a higher purpose," Winnie says. "Doing something good for the world. Five . . . creative stimulation. Six . . ."

"You're doing well, Winnie," Frankie says.

"Six, security. Seven, status, so having your skills recognized. Eight is intimacy, be it friends or a partner. And the last one is . . . control."

"So, attention, goals, health, purpose, stimulation, security, status, intimacy, control."

"Of course, the last one doesn't mean control over situations or people. It means controlling what you can. The only thing we can really control in our lives is ourselves."

Frankie could kiss her.

"I can't tell you how helpful that is, Winnie, thank you." Frankie smiles. "I hate making decisions on my own."

"That's what friends are for, love," Winnie replies. "See

what life ticks those boxes, and you're on to a winner. And even if it doesn't tick all of them yet, it doesn't mean you can't start ticking them off when you get there."

"I really can't thank you enough," Frankie says, scraping her chair back.

"Glad I could help," Winnie says.

"I wish I could return the favor," Frankie says.

"There is one thing you could do," Winnie says quietly.

"What's that?"

"You could visit Alfred Warne at St. Vincent's Hospice for the Terminally Ill in Bromley. And tell him that Winnie is sorry she didn't say goodbye."

Frankie's gasps, her eyes filling with tears.

"Winnie," Frankie croaks, leaning across the table and placing her hand on top of hers. "I'm so sorry."

"It's OK. I've got all the time in the world now," Winnie replies. "I was on my way to see him when it happened. He'll be wondering where the bloody hell I am with hisJaffa Cakes."

"Why don't you go back?" Frankie asks.

"Because he doesn't have long. So, I figure I'll just wait here to see if he joins me," Winnie explains. "We've always done everything together."

"How long were you married?" Frankie asks.

"Married? Oh no, love, I've never been married. Too much of a free spirit. Alfred's my twin brother."

"I don't know what to say. I'm tempted to say I hope you aren't waiting long, but that seems like a very insensitive remark."

"Don't worry. The Alfred I knew left us a long time ago," Winnie explains. "Besides, we shouldn't fear death. I think it's something we should talk about more. We're all facing it. It's one of the few certainties in life. Learning to accept death as our fate makes us appreciate every single day we have. I sure as hell made sure that my days counted down there." She laughs.

Frankie walks around the table and hugs Winnie, whispering a thank-you in her ear.

A few minutes later, she enters Mabel's office.

"I've made my choice," she announces.

Forty-Three

There are only two train platforms at The Station. One is marked Forward. One is marked Backward.

Frankie and Mabel are standing in between them, a breeze blowing through their hair as both trains roll silently into the station at the same time. With white coaches and mirrored windows, there's a calmness to them that comforts Frankie. A scattering of guides and clients gather on the platform around them. With a loud whoosh, the doors of both trains open simultaneously, and Frankie watches with fascination at the others making their choice.

"Do most people choose to go back?" Frankie asks Mabel, as she stares at a young woman wave from the door of the Backward train.

"They do," Mabel says. "I've only had a few Forward clients. Most people realize they have so much to return to, even if they arrive feeling they don't. And then there are those who are simply curious to find out what happens at The Final Destination. They arrive scared and leave excited."

"I'm excited," Frankie comments.

"Good." Mabel glances at her. "Glad I could do my job."

"I think you've done more than your job," Frankie replies. "You've changed my life."

"You've changed your life, Frankie. Now, remember what I told you."

"Don't tell a soul. Or The Big Dog will bite."

"Exactly," Mabel replies.

"What does that even mean?"

"Let's just say the headline would read, IDIOT *whistle-blower gets MAJOR BOLLOCKING.*"

"IDIOT swears life of SECRECY," Frankie responds.

"Better," Mabel replies.

"IDIOT says, "THANKS FOR EVERYTHING, I'LL REALLY MISS YOU"."

"Now you really are an idiot. I've got a reputation to hold here," Mabel says, glancing around.

Frankie takes a deep breath and takes Mabel in her arms.

"Good luck, Frankie," Mabel whispers in her ear.

Frankie pulls away and walks toward her train. She fills her lungs, steps into the carriage and turns to give Mabel one final wave.

Mabel is gesturing frantically at her.

IDIOT gets on WRONG TRAIN, ends up in HELL! Mabel shouts.

Frankie shrieks and jumps off. Then she sees Mabel laughing.

"It's so easy with you!"

"YOU'RE THE IDIOT," Frankie yells back, jumping on the train again.

"Bye," Mabel mouths at her as the engine fires up.

Frankie picks a seat near the door, next to a young woman in doctor's scrubs. They exchange a glance, but stay silent, as the train starts to pull quietly away. The windows show nothing of what's outside. In the mirror reflection, she sees the doctor's head poke around.

"Are you excited?" she says softly.

Frankie turns her head and flashes a soft smile.

"I really am," she says, looking back at the window.

"I'm still not sure if I believe this is happening." The woman chuckles. "Surely this is a coma?"

"Could be," Frankie replies. "Still, it's been . . . an eye-opener."

"Good luck," she hears the doctor whisper.

"You too," Frankie answers, squeezing her hands together as she feels the train speed up.

It doesn't take long. Five minutes, maybe. Frankie's body lurches forward as the train slows quickly and comes to a complete stop and the lights flick on. She blinks a few times to adjust, and turns to the doctor. She's gone.

A Tannoy sounds from a speaker next to her seat.

Frankie McKenzie, you have arrived. Please exit the train immediately. Frankie McKenzie, you have arrived. Please exit the train immediately. Frankie McKenzie, you have arrived. Please exit the train immediately.

Frankie stands up and squeezes through the aisle, gripping on to the chair tops as she braces for what she's about to step into. In the vestibule, she sees a glowing green light. She reaches forward, presses it, and feels a gust of wind blow her hair as the door slides open.

Forty-Four

Frankie is standing outside her apartment. She reaches for the keys in her pocket and slots them into her door. With her kebab and her phone in one hand, she pushes the door wide open, steps into her hallway and looks around at the familiar scene.

On bad days, she hates this flat. But tonight, she sees it with fresh eyes.

Yes, it's small. But it's the perfect size for her right now. Yes, it's cluttered. But everything in here is a piece of her life story—so far. It all reminds her of what she's done, where she's been, and who she loves. The quilt her mother crocheted for her when she first moved in. The photo montage on the hall wall, with pictures of the people who make her happy. Alice in Ibiza. Priya at the Christmas party last year. Tom on a podium at Heaven from a few summers ago. Frankie glances toward the bedroom area. OK, so she needs to do something about the black mold in the ceiling corner, which she's sure is killing her. She should text her landlord.

Frankie turns her phone screen around and sees a message from Oli.

Oli: Hey

Oli: . . .

Continuing to stare at her screen, she places her kebab on the hall dresser and waits.

Oli: I'm so sorry, I'm such an idiot.
I went to the Boots down the road to
get you a blister plaster for your feet.
But they were out, so I had to go to
the chemist further away.
I didn't realize how long I took!
#numbskull
Then when I came back the piano guy
said you'd paid the bill and gone.
Where are you now?
Could I call?
Could we begin again?
xxx

For some reason, Frankie does something she's never done before. She presses the call button.

On the phone, they chat for over an hour. A chat that should have happened across a table, but a chat nonetheless. In a way, not seeing him makes it easier to be open. The conversation moves quickly from small talk to deep and meaningfuls, and Frankie finds herself spilling her heart about work, her family and her friends without fearing he'll run a mile. Oli confides in her about his past relationships, and admits he's been wanting to meet her since seeing a photo of her on Justin's Facebook last year. When they say good night, Frankie's cheeks hurt from her smiling. Not just because it's the best date she's had in years. Not because she thinks it's the beginning of a fairy-tale romance. Not because they've already lined up a second date for this Wednesday. Frankie's beaming because tomorrow is a brand-new day and she has big plans.

Forty-Five

"Morning, sexy," the soft voice whispers in her ear.

Frankie murmurs. She's slept for eight straight hours and could easily sleep for another eight if she didn't have work. She slowly opens her eyes, rolls over and screams at the sight of a pair of blue eyes two inches from hers, scrambling up onto her pillow and holding Potato the kangaroo to her heart.

"Happy birthday to you, happy birthday to you!" Tom sings, far too loudly for seven o'clock in the morning.

"Agh, please!" Frankie shouts back, covering her ears. "Besides, my birthday was yesterday!"

"Oh, come on, Frankles." Tom laughs, jumping under the covers next to her and pulling the duvet up to his chin. "As if I wasn't going to do something for your birthday week. This is your fault for not waking up earlier."

"It's the morning after my birthday, and I'll lie if I want to," Frankie mutters, rubbing her eyes.

387

"But I've got a big surprise for you in the kitchen," he says. "And I have to be at work in an hour, so stop taking your sweet time."

"OK, OK," Frankie says, swinging her legs over the side and standing up.

Frankie wraps her dressing gown around her and drags her feet to the kitchen area, poking her head around the corner first. When she sees what's on the island, she throws her head in her hands.

"OK, everyone, one, two, three . . . happy birthday to you, happy birthday to you, happy birthday, dear Frankie . . ." they all sing.

Joel's in the kitchen. Alice, Justin and the kids are crowded around the camera on Frankie's iPad. Priya's on Tom's phone. Her mum is on his laptop, with a crowd of strangers wearing flower garlands and sarongs behind her. And her dad, Lesley and Jet are on her laptop.

When the song finishes, and the choir clicks off, it's just Tom, Joel and Frankie, with a round of Buck's Fizz and a bucket of cinnamon swirls.

"Sorry it's a day late, but as it's just so impossible to get everyone together these days, this was the next best thing," Tom explains, tearing into a swirl with his teeth, and rolling his eyes in ecstasy.

"Big plans for your birthday weekend, Frankie?" Joel asks, pushing his glasses up his nose and taking a cautious sip of Buck's Fizz. Frankie's surprised he's having a drink. Tom always jokes that he's Joel's mistress on the side of his marriage to work.

"Actually, yes," Frankie says.

"Hey! What are you doing? I thought we'd have one of our normal Friday nights. I even bought mini candles for the French Fancies!" Tom cries, with his mouth full.

✳

Jeremy, Frankie's editor, has always been good to her. The guilt swells inside of her as she knocks quietly on his door, poking her head around the frame to see him wave her in enthusiastically. When she walks in, he gestures at her to sit down.

"Frankie!" Jeremy says with a big grin. "It's been a while since we've had a one to one. Someone tells me . . . was your birthday yesterday? Happy belated birthday!"

His sweetness is going to make this conversation extra bitter.

"Thanks," Frankie says, squirming a little on the seat in front of him.

"So, is everything OK? Have something to pitch? Want to take off early today to celebrate? Deadline's over, so I'm sure it'll be OK."

"No, I'm OK, thank you, though," Frankie starts.

Jeremy nods expectantly.

"Jez, I've been here for over twelve years," Frankie begins.

"Ah," Jeremy says, his smile down-turning as he sits up in his seat.

389

"Twelve years is a long time to stay in one place, isn't it?" Frankie explains. "And I love it here, but I'm going through some personal changes, and I need to take some time off. Like, a long time off."

"How long are we talking?" Jeremy asks, looking curious.

"Well, indefinitely. I'm handing in my notice, I'm so sorry," Frankie says, grimacing.

"Wow," Jeremy replies, puffing his cheeks as he exhales. "Is there anything I can do to change your mind? Is it the money?"

"It's not the money, it's the work," Frankie says "I just feel like 'To Be Franki' has run its course for me. I need a break from that Frankie. I need to explore some different paths."

"Would you consider doing some freelance work for us? It doesn't have to be the column, of course," Jeremy asks.

Frankie thinks for a second. Earning some extra cash on the side isn't the worst idea.

"Sure," Frankie says. "I'd be happy to do some proper features. I could pitch a few things to you?"

"I'd love to hear them!" Jeremy cries excitedly.

At her desk, ten minutes later, Frankie completes a purchase of theshow.co.uk.

A knock on her desk startles her, and she shuts down the page. Janine is hovering over her desk with a large courier package in her hand.

"This came for you." Janine smiles, placing it on her desk.

"Thanks," Frankie says, smiling at her.

Frankie rips open the cardboard and frowns. Inside is a pile of random toiletries. Stain remover. Red nail polish. Mints. Blister plasters. A tiny shampoo and conditioner. Smiling, she opens the card.

> *Happy (belated) birthday!*
> *Truth is, I didn't just get you blister plasters.*
> *I got you a birthday present too. Thirty-six of them*
> *to be precise. And that's why I took so long.*
> *Hope you have a great birthday weekend, and look*
> *forward to catching up next week for the second date. x*
> *PS. Don't judge me! Boots is hardly Selfridges. But*
> *who doesn't need flight socks?*
> *xxx*

The final line is certainly fitting for what Frankie's about to do next.

*

"Darling!" her mum screams with her face an inch from the screen.

"Hi, Mum." Frankie beams.

"Did you love your post-birthday breakfast? The gang was so excited to take part. I talk about you all the time, I think they feel like you're their daughter too!"

"What happened to it being a silent yoga retreat?" Frankie laughs.

"Well, turns out the silent part wasn't quite the right fit for

391

me. I've moved down a beach to a place where we practice laughing yoga. Much better."

"Well, that's good," Frankie says, "because I've just booked a ticket to come and see you!"

Astrid's mouth drops open.

"Brian! Brian!" she screeches across whatever room she's in. "Frankie's coming to see us!"

She hears a distant cheer and starts giggling. Her mum looks back into the phone as she walks fast, palm trees towering above her.

"Oh, Frankie, just look," she says, turning the phone around to show her a view of the ocean at a forty-five-degree angle. "This is what you can look forward to! And this!" she yells, spinning back and showing her face. "Me, of course! When are you coming?"

"I'll be there in a month." Frankie laughs.

"And how long are you coming for? Come for a month. Come for three months!" her mum cries.

"Maybe," Frankie says. "I'm a little more flexible with my time these days."

"I've died, Frankie! I've died and I've gone to heaven," her mum shrieks.

"Same, Mum," Frankie replies.

*

It's 6 p.m. and Frankie's waiting in the office hallway, staring at the pink and peach sunset falling over London.

Her phone pings.

> **Alice:** Fancy a drink on Wednesday?

> **Frankie:** Ha, very funny.

> **Alice:** Why didn't you tell me you were going out with Oli again???

> **Frankie:** We only planned it last night!

> **Alice:** So?! I expect updates every second.

> **Frankie:** Yeah, I think I'm probably going to take it a little slower than that.

> **Alice:** Whatevs. What are you doing tonight?

> **Frankie:** Just a standard French Friday.

> **Alice:** French wine and French Fancies? My Friday is going to be wild. Food fights and falling asleep with a foot in my face.

> **Frankie:** When is Justin going to grow up?

> **Alice:** Ha!

The glass door to the floor swings open and Priya marches through, pulling her handbag over her shoulder as she does.

"Ready?" Priya says.

Frankie nods, putting her phone in her pocket as they step into the lift at the same time and spin around to face the doors in unison.

"Ugh, I'm so bummed that Summer Fridays are ending soon."

"When I'm in charge, Summer Fridays will be all year round," Frankie says, staring at her.

"When you're in charge?"

"Yep."

"Wait, why are you being weird?" Priya looks at her, her eyes narrowing. "You have ten seconds to tell me. When we hit the ground floor I have to sprint or I'll miss the train."

"Oh, nothing. I just resigned today," Frankie announces, shrugging like it's no big deal.

"What the actual fuck?" Priya turns to her and grabs her arm.

"Yup," Frankie says. "How would you like to work at London's most exciting start-up media platform? All-year-long Summer Fridays?"

Priya stares at her.

"Fuck it, I'll get the next train," she says. "But you're walking me to the station and telling me everything on the way. I knew there was something going on with you. You aren't you today."

"I'm not going to Waterloo, I'm going to Victoria." Frankie laughs.

"Victoria? Why?" Priya asks.

"I'm swinging by Bromley," Frankie replies.

"Swinging by Bromley? Bromley's miles away! What's in Bromley? Who's in Bromley?"

"Just a . . . friend from another life," Frankie replies, as a gust of wind rushes down Roupell Street. She shivers and places her hands in her jacket pockets. In the right pocket, she wraps her hand protectively around the packet of Jaffa Cakes. In the left, she squeezes the piece of paper with the address for St. Vincent's Hospice.

"Bloody hell, when did it get so cold?" Priya comments gruffly, hugging her jacket close to her chest.

"How would you feel about escaping the cold for a bit?" Frankie asks.

"Where would we go?" Priya asks, darting between the other commuters.

"Goa," Frankie responds. "I'm going to see my mum. I was thinking of resurrecting that failed Manchester trip. Seeing if Tom and Alice want to come too."

"Sounds ideal," Priya says. "But can you just promise me one thing? This isn't just a pipe dream. We're actually going to get our arses into gear and organize this properly."

"One hundred percent," Frankie replies. "I'll send you the details this weekend."

"I like Today Frankie." Priya smiles, grabbing Frankie by the shoulders.

"Me too," Frankie replies.

"Today's Frankie is doing things, going places and kicking some life ass."

"I really am." Frankie laughs.

"Now, I want to know everything. How did Jeremy take it? And what's this about starting something up? Is this that idea you've had for ages? The one I've been badgering you about? Are you seriously finally doing it? Because I've had some thoughts about how it could work . . ."

As Priya rattles on excitedly, Frankie lowers her head and watches her trusty old trainers as they quickly squelch across the cobbled London streets. Her feet might not be sinking into the velvety smooth sand of a Mexican beach. They might not be popping out of the bubbles of a candlelit bath drawn just for her. They might not be strapped into a pair of thousand-dollar heels, marching across Carrara marble. Or striding across a stage to pick up an award.

But Frankie's feet are finally out of the quicksand. She's finally making the big life decisions that she's delayed for so long. Frankie is finally taking charge of her precious finite time in this world. And she is bursting with excitement to begin again.

Acknowledgments

They say it takes a village to raise a child and the same goes for this book. Without the support and encouragement of my village, *Begin Again* wouldn't be here today.

The first villagers I'd like to thank are Hayley Steed and Elinor Davies, my literary agents at Madeleine Milburn. Hayley started all this by taking on my debut, *The Shelf*, and making Helly Acton books an actual thing. I can't believe I've had two boy babies, thus ruining the chance of a glorious Hayley Acton mash-up name.

The next villagers I'd like to thank are Sarah Bauer, Hannah Bond, and Katie Meegan, my editorial team. Their creativity, knowledge, and humor make my edits a joy, not a chore. Thank you for all the above and for being so patient with my first draft. At times, you must have wondered if I was typing it out one key at a time with my big left toe.

Finally, thank you to the villagers helping me to raise my human children so that I can write. To my husband, Chris, for always sharing the parental load. To my parents, Mary and Colin, and my parents-in-law, Alex and Tony, for the childcare. We're so lucky and grateful for your help.

Author Note

Dearest Reader,

Thank you for choosing to read *Begin Again*, my third book.

The idea for this book was born from a habit I have of perpetually wondering "What if?" and imagining how my life would have unfolded had I made different decisions along the way. I don't do this in a negative or despondent way. It's pure curiosity.

I feel like my life story has been split into several distinct chapters. These chapters all start with a *Begin Again* moment for me. A crossroads moment, where things might have turned out very differently had I made other choices.

Like, what if I'd chosen to stay in law instead of getting into advertising? Would I ever have written my debut novel, *The Shelf*? Or what if I'd chosen to stay in London instead of moving to Australia when I was twenty-six? Would I have ever met my husband, Chris, and had my two boys?

What if I'd chosen to stay with my first husband, instead of leaving our marriage after six miserable months? Would I be stuck in Australia, forever far away from my previous family in England? This one doesn't bear thinking about. The morning I decided to pack my things was probably my biggest ever *Begin Again* moment. I'm so grateful for the inner strength I found to make the decision and take the plunge. It wasn't just inner strength, of course. The support of my family and friends gave me the courage I needed to believe I could leave as well.

My other big *Begin Again* moment came four years later, when I decided to leave Sydney after six years. It was a tough call. I'd be leaving the friends, lifestyle, and climate I loved. The years I'd spent aching for my family back home came to head at a Christmas lunch I'd been kindly invited to—surrounded by a few friends, but none of them close ones. As I sat spooning some potatoes onto my plate, I paused, with an epiphany. Suddenly, I really didn't want to be there anymore. I left lunch early, booked a one-way ticket that night, resigned from work that week, and put all my worldly possessions up for sale that month. Six weeks later, I was staring at Sydney's stunning harbor from above on the plane. Sad to say goodbye but excited to soon be in London, thirty-two, single, with one suitcase to my name, and ready to start afresh.

Sometimes, when I look back, I don't recognize the person I used to be. They say that people don't change, but I'm not so sure about that. If you'd told me a decade ago that I'd end up living a quiet rural life in a quaint English village, I'd have laughed at you and loudly ordered another round of tequilas at my favorite Bondi Beach bar. My experiences and the people I've met in my life story—the good, the bad, and the ugly—have had a big influence on the choices I've made. These choices have made me evolve into the person I am now.

Almost forty and far from perfect, but feeling confident that my past choices were the right ones for me.

What are some of your *Begin Again* moments in life? What if you'd made different choices along the way?

If you'd like to get involved in a wider conversation about my books, please do review *Begin Again* on Amazon, on Goodreads, on any other e-store, on your own blog and social media accounts, or talk about it with friends, family, or reading groups! Sharing your thoughts helps other readers, and I always enjoy hearing about what people experience from my writing.

All the best,
Helly
xxx